HORSE-HORSE
TIGER-TIGER

馬馬虎虎

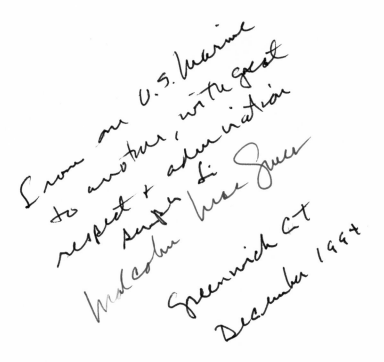

From one U.S. Marine
to another, with great
respect + admiration

Semper Fi

Malcolm McConnell

Greenwich CT
December 1994

HORSE-HORSE TIGER-TIGER

A World War II Fiftieth Anniversary Chronicle of
A Passage of Arms and a Rite of Passage

馬馬虎虎

MALCOLM S. MacGRUER

HORSE-HORSE TIGER-TIGER is fiction, and all the characters are products of the author's imagination or are fictionalized. The various major military events are based on historical fact. The words and acts of historical personages are based on accounts of their words and deeds as developed through research or as witnessed by the author.

Chinese words in the text appear in modified Wade-Giles transliteration, in use prior to the Communist takeover of the mainland, rather than in the current, and confusing, Pin-Yin transliteration.

The border of the endpaper map was designed using trigrams from *I Ching (The Book of Changes)* traced back to the 12th century B.C. The eight sets of parallel lines are composed of two basic elements— a straight line and a broken line—and symbolize yang (positive) and yin (negative) to represent, among other things, the elements and cardinal directions.

Copyright ©1994 by Malcolm S. MacGruer
Published in a limited edition by Mereside House, PO Box 1069, Madison CT 06443.
All rights reserved. No part of the contents of this book may be reproduced by any means without written permission from the publisher.

Designed and composed by Martha Poole Merwin of Merwin & Co. in Dorset, Vermont.
Printed, using acid-free paper, and bound by Cushing-Malloy Inc. of Ann Arbor, Michigan.

Library of Congress Catalog Card Number 94-77797
ISBN 0-9642624-0-1

for Amanda, Duncan and Pegret
and the members of Platoon Fifty,
Eighth Recruit Battalion, USMCR
Parris Island, South Carolina
January 1943

Acknowledgments

THE AUTHOR IS GRATEFUL for the motivation and encouragement received from many quarters, particularly from readers who offered suggestions and corrected errors, and especially for the inspiration and counsel of the following:

C. Peter Austin, former sergeant, Tenth Mountain Division, who earned two Bronze Stars in the mountains of Italy.

General Robert H. Barrow, USMC (Ret.), former Commandant of the Marine Corps and member of the Joint Chiefs of Staff, friend and comrade-in-arms, who served with the author in China and whose long friendship contributed to the author's effort.

Ms. Clara Chen, manager of the East Asia Collection in the Sterling Library at Yale University, for her help in researching and transliteration.

Stephen C. Hirschman, editor, writer and instructor, who taught the author more than was in his lectures.

Martha Poole Merwin, unflappable designer, editor, reviser and polisher, who possesses the unique qualities of creativity and patience without which the book would not have seen the light of day.

C. Gorham Phillips, author, mentor, pundit, erudite exemplar, motivator and friend of fifty years, who showed the author how it could be done.

Major General Andrew L. Watson (Ret.), CB, Colonel, The Black Watch (Forty-second Highland Regiment), and former Chief of Staff Allied Forces Northern Europe (NATO), who was born in India and guided the author in the India section of the book.

Bernard L. Yudain, writer and former editor at *Time* magazine for his enthusiastic encouragement.

And Pegret MacGruer, the author's beloved wife, for her patience, support, suggestions and reading and re-reading the manuscript—and for putting up with him when he was in China both without her in 1944-45 and with her in 1987.

M.S.M.
Madison, Connecticut
February 1994

Table of Contents

Preface

MORE THAN FIFTY YEARS HAVE PASSED since the boot camp of 1943, and nearly fifty years have fled since the victorious end of World War II, and because memories have dimmed and history may not have taught, it is prudent perhaps to recall the conditions of the times that this story covers....

In the spring of 1944 the unmistakable signs of Allied superiority over the warring Axis powers were becoming more and more evident as the momentum of battle swung to the side of the Allied forces. In Europe the RAF and the U.S. Eighth and Tenth Air Forces were pounding coastal landing zones, destroying the factories of the Ruhr and harassing the German retreat on the Italian front as the Allies approached the Eternal City, Rome. The Royal Navy and the U.S. Navy had mastered the convoy system and their effective antisubmarine warfare was assuring an almost uninterrupted supply of men, munitions and materiel to the island fortress of England from which General Dwight D. Eisenhower would launch the greatest and most successful seaborne invasion of all times, Operation Overlord.

In Russia the Wermacht had been brought to a humiliating halt at Stalingrad on the Volga by the Russian host and was being defeated along a thousand-mile front in the cruel Russian snow. Field Marshall Friedrich von Paulus and his Sixth German Army were captives of Marshalls Mikhail Shumilov, Nikolai Nikolaevich Voronov and Greorgi Zhukov. Nazi forces between the Volga and the Don were following the example of Napoleon in retreat.

General Douglas MacArthur, in command of U.S. forces in the Southwest Pacific, was island hopping, isolating Japanese forces and occupying strategic points at New Guinea and in the Admiralty Islands in preparation for an all-out effort to retake the Philippines. Admiral Chester Nimitz's forces had subdued Tarawa in the Central Pacific and were attacking the

Marianas, Palau and the Carolines. As Overlord was about to be launched in Europe, Japan's strength was being buffeted by Allied arms pushing through Japan's Pacific perimeter, cutting off hundreds of thousands of troops beyond hope of rescue.

Only in the China-Burma-India theater were the fortunes of war favoring the Japanese, who had pushed across the India-Burma border and were threatening Imphal and Kohima in the Indian province of Assam. While the Allies were achieving arduous successes in other parts of the world, on mainland China the Nipponese, under General Shunroku Hata, began the largest land offensive of the Asian war, which would knock out almost every base of the U.S. Fourteenth Air Force, capture provinces in which over one hundred million people lived, kill more than half a million Chinese soldiers in battles taking the critical Hankow-Canton rail line, further isolating the occupied coastal cities and caging Chungking and the Nationalist government in its shrinking domain in western China. The Japanese called the offensive *Ichigo*.

And in the United States idealistic innocent young men were being made acquainted with the arts of war and wondering what their brush strokes would portray in the panoply of war painted on the great canvas of history.

This chronicle is about Ichigo and some of those young American men who, as famed historian Samuel Eliot Morison wrote, did some unusual and remarkable things.

Prologue

HUNAN 1945

THE FLAKES WERE BIGGER NOW. The snow had been fine and wind-driven when he wrapped up in his blanket and now was sifting through the empty chink in the logs by his feet. Squinting, he could see the big flakes drifting past the slit. Warm air aloft? Less wind? His breath misted and hovered before it became rime on his beard, his blanket, on the shallow timber ceiling. He was stiff. And hungry. And lost.

He had climbed most of the previous day, mapless but aware that uphill was generally west. And while it meant struggling into the wind, his route should be bringing him closer to the downslope that tumbled to the river far below. The last few gray hours before dark had been the worst. Stinging sleet as the altitude increased. Bad footing and poor visibility. His chest burned and his ears sang, but he could still hear pursuit. The occasional shout or piercing whinny. Sometimes a shot.

Then the sleet turned to snow and Ian Wallace damned his footprints. He stopped to listen, but he could hear only the rush of the wind and his own heavy breathing. He turned his head and opened his mouth and strained to hear. His ears popped. He waited…. nothing.

When he had passed the tree line the ridge above was lost in gray mist and snow, and the wind was a weight against him. Back in the shelter of the trees he had literally stumbled on the charcoal burner's fallen hut and pushed limbs and snow aside and crawled in, spent. He had lain for a time until his body cadence slowed, and then he checked his assets.

Number one: he was ahead of them; it was snowing harder; it was dark.

Number two: he still had his weapon, the Model 70 with the Lyman scope. The sling was like a board (it was leather... could he eat it if he had to?). The bolt was stiff but working. He had a half-unit of fire... about thirty rounds.

Number three: he still had some biscuits, some dried fruit and two rice balls. The water in his canteen was a block of ice, but he could eat snow. And he didn't have to relieve himself. At this altitude he lost moisture through his body, not his bladder. His shirt was soaked. He had no frostbite.

Then he had stuffed his rifle under his belt between his parka and his shirt, wrapped his blanket around his feet and his poncho around his body and shoulders, pulled his hood over his head and face and hoped he wouldn't go to sleep forever. If the Japanese don't get you, old hypothermia will.

Now he lay unmoving—watching and listening. The thump of heavy snow from a bough quickened him, but he heard nothing else. No birds, beasts or bad guys up here, he thought. Just Ian Wallace, half a world from home: hungry, cold, separated from his unit and with an urgency to rid his bowels of the bacilli that kept him in almost perpetual cramps. It wasn't so bad before he lost his paregoric. The tincture of opium had eased the pain of his bloody evacuations and given him some Dutch courage to boot.

But he'd lost the medicine with his musette bag that held it *and* dry socks, compass, map, field dressings and a 1911 blued Colt .45 that he should have been wearing on his hip. That musette bag with his own India-inked rendering of the Corps' eagle, globe and anchor on it should give them something to wonder about.

Thought we were all in the islands, did you? Not quite. Some of us are playing spook right here behind your lines dressed like slopehead civilians except for boots, dogtags and the USMC device on the cloth cap. Yessir, I'm your basic blond, blue-eyed, six-four, two-hundred-twenty-pound Chinese, a colonel in the *Kuomintang* armed forces, accruing a lieutenant's extra-hazardous duty pay with the paymaster in Arlington, Virginia. I hope I get to spend it.

But he'd lost his bag in the fire-fight by the railroad cut they had tried to reconnoiter. There had been eight of them: seven Chinese guerrillas, one of whom was his interpreter, and himself. But they discovered to their cost that the Hankow-Canton railroad was no longer patrolled by Japanese recruits—fifteen-year-olds in new-ish uniforms carrying old Danzig '98 rifles with dust covers and five rounds of ammunition apiece.

Instead they ran into seasoned troops from the Indochina peninsula, browned and booted, with Arisaka rifles and Nambu light machine-guns and plenty of ammunition. They shot low like combat veterans. Not high and hurried. And they wiped the unit out. Almost. Despite his orders his Chinese, trained by him and equipped with M1 carbines, had moved in late, like Chinese, in growing daylight and almost without concealment. He was watching carefully to locate and note guard-posts when the firing started, and as he dove for cover he saw his people go down. The earth around him became a beaten zone as the machine-guns searched the ground in short bursts. His bag was yards away where it had fallen. With his toes and elbows he moved himself from cover to cover and had reached the hillside bamboo trees when they found his gear. He was about three *li*, a mile, up the mountain when he saw some of them on little Chinese horses following his trail.

Well, he now thought, I shouldn't be surprised about the seasoned opposition. The U.S. Navy was effectively blocking the sea lanes to the islands and to the Indochina peninsula, so this rail line has assumed an even greater importance to a determined enemy. He realized how important it was for him to get this information back to his main group some hundreds of li across the mountains and rivers of occupied territory. And this new intelligence would require a change in plan for the train raid they expected to make later in the spring.

He had learned of the train through his Annamite house-boy, Nien. Nien's cousin had worked for the Japanese general in charge of allied prisoners on Hainan island off the south coast of the mainland. He had fled to Nanning in Kwangsi and told Nien of the movement of prisoners north by rail from Haikou camp in March. The word was that they would be ferried across Hainan Straight and loaded in boxcars for the trip north.

"Your house-boy's cousin!" his commanding officer had said. "What the hell kind of hard intelligence do you call that?"

But Ian had prevailed and had been given sixty Chinese guerrillas to plan and execute an operation to rescue prisoners from a special train that would be carrying American pilots.

For the Japanese these men would make particularly good hostages for bargaining as the war ground down further and peace talks might have to begin. But first they had to be transported to Japan, overland as much of the way as possible.

Through the *Tai Li* organization, the Chinese equivalent of the German *Gestapo* Ian was convinced, communication was established with agents on Hainan to get information on the movement of the Americans. How reliable that would be was anyone's guess, but it was all they had to go on.

The Chinese-American Composite Wing (CACW) of the Fourteenth Air Force might agree to try to coordinate a rail-line bombing to block passage of the train so his guerrilla group could ambush the guards and get the Americans off the train and up into the mountains, hopefully without pursuit or casualty.

Ian himself was to lead a small reconnaissance force to scout the rail cut that was to be blocked. Additionally he was to mesh all the disparate parts of this operation despite communication problems, inter-Allied and inter-service rivalries, a notorious Chinese inability to be on schedule and lukewarm support from his own commander.

Well, here he was, alone on a mountain wondering how the hell he ever got his ass in such a bind.

One redeeming feature of his condition, he mused, was that at least he hadn't been born Chinese. What history of migrations, of Viking forays, of Celtic copulations, of Scottish clearances and German unifications, of other fortunate couplings—what genetic bouillabaisse had foreordained that he would be born in Massachusetts? Good God, he might have been born in a hovel in Hunan and lived as these people did facing nothing but toil, starvation and disease, without roads, without electricity, without sanitation, damned near without the wheel, binding feet, throwing girls on the dung heap if they couldn't be sold, blind from trachoma, tormented by scabies and sentenced to a life of honey-buckets and dysentery. How could anyone live like that? *But he was.*

The direction in which education starts a man determines his future life.

— Plato
The Republic

MASSACHUSETTS 1942

HE LEFT THE INFIRMARY IN THE MORNING feeling quite tired but much improved in spirits, a little light-headed and weak but out of the delirium and the boredom. He had feared the flu would keep him in the infirmary so long that he would miss the Marine recruiting officer, who was only on the campus for today. His collar could not keep out the edge of the wind and he hunched his shoulders against the gray mist. The hill was not steep but tiring; he caught his breath in a doorway, then pushed on.

He had dreamed confused, colored dreams in the past week—the color impressed him and made it difficult to remember when reality began. He was quite sure that the young nurse had rubbed him with alcohol and was quite sure she had not slept with him despite his vivid recollection of it. He could get no clues from her eyes nor a lingering hand. One morning he believed he had enlisted already and the realness of the feeling astonished him.

Though his mother wanted him to be a minister, as a boy he had played Marine, not soldier nor padre. He was influenced, he supposed, by the books of Capt. John W. Thomason, USMC. Also by his family's quiet pride in ancestral patriotism. Books by Kenneth Roberts instilled in him a feeling for his country that he found hard to articulate. He could recite Oliver Wendell Holmes's "Old Ironsides"... "Ay, tear her tattered ensign down! Long has it

waved on high. And many an eye has danced to see that banner in the sky."
He knew about Peebles and Hull and Stephen Decatur. He thought Benedict
Arnold was an outstanding leader who did a dumb thing.

He'd read Arthur Guy Empey and Erich Maria Remarque. He always
stood silently for two minutes at 11 A.M. on November 11. And the Marine
Hymn raised his goose flesh.

Near the crest of the hill the stained, dark-green Victorian building smelling of floor oil had a poster tacked to one pillar announcing that the Marine
recruiting party was doing business inside until this afternoon.

He went in and was the only student there. An officer and a sailor with a
red cross on his arm handed him forms that he filled out except for the birth-
place of his father (who had died when Ian was an infant), which he could
not recall, and without mention that his studies were pre-divinity school
courses. The bulky doctor who examined him remarked that his skin was
very moist and took his blood pressure twice. And there was some embarrassment when he made water in a small bottle while the sailor with the red
cross, the recruiting officer and the doctor watched. The sailor's and the officer's eyes met. Is that why he's not leading troops, Wallace wondered.

The officer, with whom he talked, was disappointing, with polished nails
and a faint scent—nor did he appear to care that Wallace had wanted to be a
Marine rather than a soldier or a sailor ever since he could remember. The
officer had not heard of nor read John Thomason's efforts nor could he recall
Thomason's fine swirling line sketches of battle. The short talk reached a
routine plane quickly, and the officer ended it by saying Wallace would hear
in a month and shook hands without looking up.

In the next six weeks he received a number of tan kraft envelopes inviting
him to participate in correspondence courses and he dutifully took one on,
hoping it would help him in the special recruit program in which he was trying to enlist: finish college and then go to boot camp at Parris Island, South
Carolina, with other college graduates in their own special platoon. Is that
good or bad? And if you make it through boot camp then you go to Officer
Candidates Class at Quantico, Virginia. If he didn't cut it at OCC he'd be sent
to a rifle platoon at Camp LeJeune, North Carolina. If he made it he'd be
commissioned a second lieutenant and stay on at Reserve Officers Class
(ROC) for accelerated, intensive training as a Marine officer.

He wondered if his boyhood and teen experiences on the farm, where he, his brother, Peter, and his widowed and withdrawn mother lived with his grandfather, and his experiences in the forests would help him. He was certainly a good shot. He kept himself in spending money by ridding the farm of red squirrel pests. He would shoot them with his Remington pump-action .22, cut off their tails and turn them in to his grandfather for a quarter apiece. He got about a dollar a week. But he didn't get paid for doing chores, for keeping woodboxes full, for lugging milk cans, for hand turning the DeLaval separator, for dumping, burning and burying the trash or for minding six hundred chickens. To make a little more money he ran a trap line in the winter. Skunks mostly—he could get thirty-five cents for a good black pelt at the Supply Store, though this endeavor never made him very popular on the bus to school. But it taught him how to move in the woods at night. He knew how to deal with fright. He wasn't sure about fear. And he was no longer squeamish at the sight of blood. Skinning and curing hides had cured him of that, as had calving and beheading the weekly chicken for Sunday dinner.

Wallace was informed that he had been accepted as a recruit and should go to Boston to First Naval District Headquarters and be sworn in during the first week in April. His call to active duty would occur in due course. He would have to go to Boston on the first Saturday of the month because on that day he could cut classes. He was an outstanding student in his Saturday courses but on the ragged edge in one course, analytical geometry, in which he was taking make-up Monday through Friday. He couldn't jeopardize his upcoming senior year scholarship, so Saturday it would have to be. That meant he would have to leave college at the crack of dawn, hitchhike to Boston (no bus fare), get sworn and hitchhike back in time for late afternoon rehearsal with the Smith College glee club before the joint concert that evening.

That Saturday was a long one. Wallace left before breakfast was served at the fraternity house and walked and hitched all the way to the Hub, arriving in late morning. He was examined once more (two blood pressure tests again... what, me excited?) and was back on the road walking and hitching by a little after noon. No time and no money for lunch, but he was lucky and in two rides was back in time for rehearsal. He felt quite proud. And hungry.

During the rehearsal with the men and girls he sang hard, and as the blood went from his head to his diaphragm he watched the blackness come slowly from the edges of his vision toward the center until through a tunnel he could see only the conductor's startled face, which too disappeared. He fell to the stage floor, out like a light.

Hot coffee and food in a stranger's room in the dormitory next to the hall brought him around, and Wallace sang with gusto at the concert and danced with Irene, his assigned Smith girl, with light heart and feet. He kissed her good-night with relish though politely. He was elated because today's decision and action were the first of any consequence that were entirely his own.

Wallace did well in the spring term even though he was frequently apprehensive about being called to active duty before he'd have a chance to earn his degree. He knew the Corps had "guaranteed" that would not happen. But the war was not going well for the Allies in the Pacific, and he fretted some. The college decided to accelerate the next semester, the start of his senior year, and begin in July rather than September. He was eager to have an outstanding record so he applied himself with great concentration. He honored in his toughest courses—straight "A"s in Comparative Religions VII and in his philosophy major—worried about his aspirations to be a minister and yet be a Marine, worked in the student bookstore and waited on table at the fraternity to defray his room and board expenses, sang in the interdenominational chapel choir seven days a week (a paying job), was college carillonneur twice a day seven days a week (a paying job) and managed to hold his position as center on the varsity lacrosse team. When he tried out for the lead in the Drama Club's production of Eugene O'Neill's "Marco Millions" the dean called him in and suggested he back off.

There were fewer and fewer classmates as one by one his friends left for the service. His roommate, Avery Cooper, left for the Naval Air Corps to go to basic school in St. Louis and learn to fly. Wallace wondered if he were letting down the side by not getting in sooner. Many returned to visit during their leaves after being commissioned and before going to their next stations. Ian was impressed and a little jealous. One of them was lost, a week after he had seen him, in the Coconut Grove fire in Boston. Not in action, but a first loss and it sobered him.

Wallace spent two weeks in June between his junior and senior classes at home on the farm, pitching forkfuls of hay over his head to the wagon being pulled by two patient shire horses. The dried hay seed filled his hair and made his sweaty back itch. When he blew his nose after shifting hay in the mow, sliced by shafts of dusty sunlight, his handkerchief was black. And he spent time assuring his mother he had done the right thing. She was worried. Ian's brother was already an Army officer serving in plain clothes in the

Counter Intelligence Corps, and she felt the double risk was too much to bear. His grandfather—a classical scholar who had eschewed Amherst's post-graduation offer of faculty membership for the satisfactions of the soil, who surrounded the family with books in Latin, Greek and English, who taught Latin (that was not taught in the little local high school) to Ian to meet the college entrance requirement, and who had been a surrogate parent since his father died years ago—was quietly proud and trounced him regularly in their nightly cribbage games. His tired mother would sit near them reading, occasionally watching them. She rarely spoke. On Sundays they attended the little Presbyterian church where Ian had gone to Sunday School and sung in the choir; after the college chapel the church seemed small and cramped.

The summer passed quickly. Many classes were held outdoors; Wallace reveled in the intellectual challenge posed by his comparative religions course and by the philosophy department chairman, who was his seminar professor and who had fertilized the religious seed planted by family, church and study. The Nazis had invaded Russia the previous summer, which made the semi-reds on the faculty feel much less sensitive and touchy about the Russo-German Pact of 1939, and there were again great arguments and debates in the political science courses. In August the Marines landed on Guadalcanal. Wallace followed the island battle avidly and devoured all that *Time* and the *New York Herald Tribune* had to say about it. He worried about whether enlisting had been the right thing to do. He slept badly.

The football season was enhanced by the addition of service teams that played against the bigger universities. Through a series of comparative score calculations Wallace determined that his team could have beaten Iowa Pre-Flight, the number one team in the country. And, despite the war, alumni returned for home football games, perhaps hanging on to one of the only realities they had left. After Saturday evening dinner at the fraternity Wallace would stand with his brothers, alumni and undergraduate, on the front portico of the wonderful Greek revival house and eighty voices would sing in harmony about ancestral brothers who had supported and defended each other in battle, real and mythical. One weekend Coop, now Ensign Avery Cooper, wearing his Naval aviator's greens and his gold pilot's wings, stood beside him as they sang. That night the traffic stopped to listen, and men from other fraternities gathered on the lawn to hear and applaud the last moment of an ending tradition.

It was a wet January morning as Ian and Peter Wallace walked across Thirty-fourth Street toward Pennsylvania Station, and the sounds of the taxi and bus horns seemed louder as they always do in the New York rain. Pedestrians hurried quietly with heads down, intent on getting where they were going quickly.

"Was it bad at home?" asked Peter. "How did the Aged Parent handle the leave-taking?"

"It was damp and not particularly easy but over in a hurry, thank God. Poor Mom. She's so quiet and worries so. She works too hard and never sees anyone except Grandfather and the hired couple. She said she'd hoped I'd go to divinity school, and now I'm off to war. She cried."

"She's been that way ever since Father died. I remember her when she was full of fun. It's sad," Peter said.

"Well, I'm awfully glad I got to stay with you and your amiable consort for at least one night," Ian said.

They entered the station and went down the steps to the main waiting room where a Marine sergeant was herding nervous recruits toward the gate. Ian checked in with him and then stood talking with his brother until the gate opened and the sergeant headed them toward the special car that would take them to Yemassee, South Carolina. As he went down the steps to the platform he looked up to see Peter grinning through the iron railings.

"Don't forget to wear your rubbers," his brother shouted.

A great hoot went up from the recruits.

"In the rain or in the sack?" Ian shouted back.

More hoots until the sergeant shouted, "Knock it off!" and herded them onto their car with its stale smells, straight prickly seats and dirty windows. The doors slammed. The car lurched and they left for war.

Wallace looked over the crowd as he edged his way toward a seat. Most of these volunteers were in baggy slacks, sweaters and leather or cloth jackets of some kind, carrying small cloth satchels or nothing. Many needed a shave, and more carried comic books than did not. They were noisy and shouting in their nervousness, bragging about what they would do in boot camp and in the Pacific. He'd heard plenty of tough language and barnyard talk before but never had he heard it used so frequently, so vehemently in every sentence. The smell of the packed car was subtly changing as the odors of the bodies overtook the lingering staleness of earlier smokers, the unpleasant antiseptic smell of the toilets not quite covering their odor of use, the coal smoke that inevitably found its way from the engine into the coaches. Why did this car still seem redolent of smoke, he wondered. They were on the electrified Pennsylvania Railroad line between New York and Washington. Maybe there were special cars for recruits. Old ones.

He found a seat next to a man who also wore a sport coat and tie and sat with his rain coat and small overnight bag in his lap.

"Mind if I join you?" Wallace asked.

The man looked up, and Wallace could see that quick inventory was being taken.

"You bet. Sit down."

The man shifted his haunches to make more room, and Wallace threw his coat and bag on the overhead rack and sat down on the hard seat.

He put out his hand and said: "Ian Wallace."

"I'm John Perry," said the man.

"What program are you in?" asked Wallace, quite sure that he and Perry were the only two men in the car who had been to college. They stood out like sore thumbs.

"I want to get to OCC in Quantico after boot camp," fenced Perry, not wanting to say anything about the college program for fear of offending, creating a caste system or, if overheard, starting a fight.

"Same here," said Wallace and they both smiled.

"Where you from?" asked Ian.

"Long Island, Patchogue mostly, and Princeton. How about you?"

"Cummington, that's Massachusetts, and Amherst."

"Amherst?" Perry squinted at him. "Lacrosse," he said. "You were captain and you played center on the first mid-field line and you whipped us."

"First time ever," said Wallace looking hard at Perry. "First defense, weren't you, and you clubbed me black and blue and should have been ejected!"

They smiled and shook hands again and said: "Damn!"

Wallace and Perry ran out of talk before they got to Philadelphia. Wallace dozed and dreamed. He woke up in Philadelphia when another car of recruits was connected to their coach with a clang. More uniformed Marines appeared in the car, one of them holding a recruit by the collar. He yelled for quiet.

"Any you people try to get off this train again, for booze or for anything, you get left behind and listed as a deserter. You got that? You got that? Some of you would look pretty good blindfolded and up against the wall! Just try me!"

South of Wilmington it was evident that there was plenty of booze on the car. Wallace never saw anybody take a swig, but he could smell it. Except for an occasional beer he didn't drink, nor did he smoke, and the combination of these smells was very apparent to him. He drowsily wondered if he would be less of a Marine if he didn't drink or smoke. Or chew. Or read comics. Or swear a lot. Barnyard talk he could handle, and he could tell and laugh at a good strong joke. But there was a lot of use of the Lord's name, in vain.

Well, he thought, as he remembered a night with the college chaplain and two other Episcopal fathers, men of the cloth can have a sense of humor and if I may eventually be one I don't want to lose my perspective. He and the fathers, one of them wearing a monk's cassock with a rope at the waist and a hair shirt underneath, had had a rollicking evening after a seminar on How To Apply to Union Theological Seminary and a parish house dance, sitting on the floor in the empty pantry drinking beer, roaring out lewd songs and laughing themselves silly. He remembered "The Abominable Table Manners of the Crowned Heads of Europe"—*Queen Wilhelmina has a trick, of eating oysters off a stick. Her gown's cut low and not too tight, and those that slip...*

"Washington," said Perry, and Wallace awoke with a start. They were in the switching yards just short of Union Depot and another car of recruits was being coupled to the train.

"More meat," said a man across the aisle. Wallace nodded... and hoped they would be fed something before too long.

South of D.C., on the tracks of the Richmond, Fredericksburg and Potomac Railroad, they passed the station for Marine Corps Schools, Quantico, Virginia.

"I sure as hell hope to get off a train here in about three months," said Perry.

"You'll never make it," said Wallace. "You've got to get through Parris Island first."

"You'll salute me someday. You want to bet?"

Wallace snorted and looked out the window. He'd like to read, but he didn't think that pulling out his *Soldier's Bible* or his *Bibliotheque Larousse* miniature of *Plato's Republic* was such a hot idea, and he gradually drowsed. His introduction to philosophy had been as much due to his grandfather's suggestion as it had been because the classes were not popular and hence small. If he was really interested in the ministry, his grandfather had said, study history and philosophy. And the small classes had allowed him much more opportunity to have dialogue with department members than normally would be the case. He was known and liked by his instructors and professors. His seminars were almost tutorial sessions. He argued about Kant, Hegel, Descartes and Hobbes. He wrote papers on Plato and Epictetus. *Cogito ergo sum* was a thrilling notion. He felt that his studies were helping to shape and form him.

Yet part of him was the result of his ancestry, he knew. How else was it that he could be frugal—*use it up, wear it out, make it do or do without*—hard working and conscience driven?

He guiltily conceded to himself that he'd love to be an indolent slob, one of the *lotophagi*, a lotus-eater. But he knew it would drive him crazy.

"You want some?" he heard. Perry was shaking him and pointing to the food that was being passed out. Dry, tough sandwiches and terrible boiling coffee in paper cups. He didn't know whether he was sipping coffee grounds or soot now that they were back on a coal burning line. It was awful.

"What the hell you call this?" shouted one of the recruits in the middle of the car. A chorus of foul grumbles became a chant about the food.

"At ease!" shouted the sergeant. The grumbling subsided. "Nobody drafted you people. You will eat what you get and consider yourself lucky. If I hear any more bitching there won't be a next meal 'til you're at Parris Island."

They dozed, ate again in the darkened car and dozed some more as the train swayed and bucked its way down the Atlantic Coast Line on the Southern's tracks. They passed Fayetteville and then Florence. South of Orangeburg they waited on a siding as a train of flatcars laden with trucks and tanks went slowly by. And shortly after dawn they crept onto a spur and jolted to a halt, in Yemassee, South Carolina.

Dear God, prayed Ian, *have I done the right thing?*

*Our life is at all times and before anything else
the consciousness of what we can do.*

— Jose Ortega y Gasset
The Revolt of the Masses

SOUTH CAROLINA 1943

THE EAST COAST MARINE CORPS RECRUIT DEPOT is located on 8,500 acres of desolate sand, scrub brush, live oaks, Spanish moss, pines and poison sumac. Called Parris Island, it is named after its original owner, who was also the first treasurer of the state of South Carolina. Located on Port Royal Sound, it is approximately eight hundred rail miles south of New York. Marines had been posted there since 1891, and the post had a reputation that inspired fear in recruits and pride in those who made it through. Its sister recruit depot in San Diego turned out candy-assed Marines according to the drill instructors who would make men out of the trainload of boots that arrived at Yemassee.

Parris Island, at thirty-one degrees ten minutes north latitude, is on roughly the same parallel as Tiajuana, Mexico; Tucson, Arizona; Rabat, Morocco; and Lahore, India. It is perishingly humid and hot in the summer and piercingly damp, windy and cold in the winter.

Ian Wallace and the other recruits stood shivering in the early wind by the siding while sergeants and corporals shouted orders and collected men into groups of about sixty. Olive-green trailer trucks with flat-bed trailers backed slowly toward each group. The trailers looked like topless green cattle cars, and as they stopped the rear gates were lowered and formed ladders for the recruits to climb aboard. Wallace and Perry were in the middle of their group as it pushed and shoved its way toward the front of the trailer. When they couldn't go any farther they stopped, with their grips between their feet.

"We still got nine men ain't aboard," roared a sergeant. "Make room!"

"Ain't no more room!"

"You, driver," shouted the sergeant. "Make room for more men!"

The driver put the tractor in low gear, revved the engine and let out the clutch. The truck shot forward ten feet and the driver hit the air brakes. The men on the trailer accordioned into each other toward the front, and the other nine men clambered on. The rear gate was pushed up, slammed home, and the truck started its journey through Beaufort and Port Royal, across the Horse Island bridge and causeway and through the main gate of the Marine recruit depot.

As the trucks ground down the avenue between the first palm trees Wallace had ever seen and sturdy trees hung with gray streamers and green leaves even in January, Ian saw groups of men in blue fatigues with large white "P"s stenciled on their backs. They were raking and shoveling and brushing the edge of the roadway and were guarded by Marines in khakis carrying rifles.

When the trucks went by the "P"s shouted in unison: "You'll be sor-reee!" The recruits could hear the recurring call as each truck passed on its way to a group of red-brick buildings at an intersection and plaza dominated by a bronze statue of a Marine in World War I uniform, a machine-gun over his right shoulder, a pistol held aloft in his left hand. The trucks stopped in a line, and the men were ordered off to stand in groups on the pavement.

A corporal came up to each group and shouted that he would read off platoon assignments. As each recruit yelled his name he was told what platoon number he was assigned to and where to assemble. The groups shifted and surged and by some magic were sorted out. Wallace was assigned to Platoon Fifty, Eighth Recruit Battalion, and most of the men in that group seemed to be dressed much like him and Perry, who was assigned to Platoon Forty-eight.

A platoon sergeant in greens with a leather belt, overseas cap, two rows of ribbons, four hash marks and shined high-cut shoes approached the group, stood directly in front of them and shook his head. Wallace noted that the color of his khaki shirt and tie differed from the rest of the noncommissioned officers he had seen. The sergeant put his hands on his hips and spoke:

"All right, you people, pay attention to what I've got to say 'cause I'm only going to say it once. I am Platoon Sergeant Rose, George Daniel Rose. I am your drill instructor.

"I've been in the Corps for seventeen years and a DI for long enough to know all the tricks. While you're here you'll do as I or the assistant DI says. You will speak to us only when spoken to or when you request a formal meeting. You will do as you are told or face the consequences. You saw some of the consequences sweeping the road on your way in.

"You will address all noncommissioned officers and officers as 'sir.' When any DI comes to your hut the first one to see him will shout 'ATTEN-TION!' and you will drop whatever you are doing and assume that position.

"We are now going to the quartermaster and draw your gear. So pick up your duffel and get yourselves into four lines facing to your left: tallest in front, shortest to the rear. When I say 'March' start off on your left foot and listen to my cadence."

The platoon shuffled and bumped and half-way aligned themselves. Rose hooted: "Forward... HARCH!" Platoon Fifty, sixty raggedy-ass out-of-step boots, started forward to the call of the DI's cadence: a lilting, semi-Southern, almost musical, all-Marine litany which they would hear for the rest of their Marine days. It thrilled Wallace.

"Awn hup areep hup y'layouf... hup areep hup y'layouf."

At the Eighth Recruit Battalion area Wallace and nine other men were as-signed to Quonset hut "A" at the head of a street of thirteen huts. Each hut held one squad: ten men. Twelve huts were occupied by two platoons of sixty men each: Platoon Fifty on both sides of the top of the street, Platoon Forty-eight in the other six huts. The thirteenth hut housed the DIs for the two pla-toons. The DIs' hut was directly across from hut A.

The Quonsets had space heaters in them in the middle of each building. The cots were arranged two to a side at each end, perpendicular to the wall, and one to each side in the middle, parallel to the wall. Ian staked out his gear at one of the single bunks in the middle near the stove.

They took the stapled tags off their newly issued clothing, stored their gear in what they presumed to be the prescribed manner according to the red *Fleet Marine Force Manual* they had been issued, changed into green her-ringbone twill fatigues, rough-side-out high-cut field shoes and overseas caps with each man's name on cardboard behind the hat's bronze Marine emblem, fell out and marched off to the battalion barbershop.

They walked back to the platoon area two or three at a time, astonished at what a change had been wrought. Despite differing heights, weights and distinguishing facial characteristics, in their uniforms and their baldness they were all starting to look alike.

They were lectured that evening by the DI on: military courtesy, the fact that they would double-time to the mess hall (and stroll back), the need to memorize their General Orders from the *FMF Manual*, when reveille would sound, how much time there would be to shave, dress, police the hut and its area and make the bunks and store their gear in a military manner before falling out for chow. And they learned about the "word."

"Some people never seem to get the word," Platoon Sergeant Rose said. "You know what the 'word' is O'Reilly?"

Francis Xavier O'Reilly, a hefty, red-haired, blue-eyed, freckled product of Georgetown University, replied that he wasn't quite sure what the DI meant, sir.

"The 'word' is the latest info. It's the latest scuttlebutt. It's the standing orders. It's the latest dope from the DI. You know when the 'word' got started? Lemme tell you.

"Back in 1775 there was a Navy guy named John Paul Jones, and he commanded a frigate named the *Bonne Homme Richard*. And he tells the Congress he better have some Marines to show the sailors how to shoot and to man the fighting tops with their muskets so's to pick off the British officers on the enemy's decks. Well he gets his Marines—good shots, too—and he gets in a sea fight with a Limey ship called *Serapis*. And they fight for hours blowing each other apart until the Limey captain shouts to Jones 'Will you strike?' an' Jones hollers back 'I have not yet begun to fight.' An' this one Marine in the fighting tops turns to his mate an' says 'They's always some dumb sonofabitch who don't get the word.' "

There were stifled guffaws from the platoon, but Rose continued...

"So this Marine drops a grenade right down the powder hatch of the *Serapis*, blows her bottom out, and that was that. You people make sure you got the word so I don't have to drop nothing down your hatch to blow your bottom out!"

Wallace knew the story was mostly apocryphal and knew it was in 1779 that Jones had fought at night in the North Sea, lashed to his adversary, the muzzles of the guns almost touching, rigging entangled, and that when the British struck, Jones transferred his flag to the *Serapis* because *Bonne*

Homme Richard was sinking. Well, thought Wallace, the Marine version was a pretty good yarn, a sea story, part of the Marine myth, the Corps lore. Certainly the literary license didn't do any harm. And he'd be damned sure he got the word.

"You people start thinking about Tenth Day inspection now 'cause I want this platoon to be number one in the battalion. You'll know how to do close-order drill, how to strip your rifles, the manual of arms, your General Orders, how to stow your gear and the history of the Corps. Is that clear?"

"YES, SIR!"

"And that's the word. You can bet on it! Dismissed!"

The wash racks, concrete tables with exposed pipes and faucets, with surfaces sloped toward the center for drainage and with wire clotheslines overhead, were located at the bottom of the platoon street across from hut L. Now they all understood the reason why they had been issued galvanized pails, wooden bristle brushes and yellow soap. They were expected to be in clean fatigues (dungarees) no matter what happened, and the time spent at the racks was beneficial in ways they hadn't thought of. You could always get the word at the racks. It was a social center. A place to shoot the breeze. You found out how friends in other squads were making out. Ian talked with Perry there, and they learned the tricks that would make dungarees fade quicker so you looked more salty and less like a boot.

"You ready for Tenth Day?" asked Perry.

"I haven't memorized so much since the multiplication tables," said Wallace.

"Or the Catechism," said Fix, short for Francis Xavier O'Reilly, scrubbing his dungaree jacket hard against the concrete surface.

And they were ready. Rose tried not to show it, but he had to be pleased at how well they'd done. So he chewed them out about being sloppy at close-order drill, and they fell out for what the DI called a little practice.

"Just 'cause you come off as honor platoon today don't mean fuck-all. We are now going to drill the 'Simon sez' way. No command will be executed unless preceded by 'Simon sez' do so-and-so. Is that clear?"

"YES, SIR!"

"Anybody fucks up he falls out, and we see who lasts longest. Simon sez... P'toon... forward... Hunh!"

Platoon Fifty stepped out smartly. Simon sez right flank... Hunh. Simon sez layouf flank… Hunh. Simon sez column right… Hunh. First command on the left foot, command of execution on the next left.

"Th'rear… Hunh!"

On the next left foot the men of the platoon pivoted one hundred eighty degrees and, with the same cadence, marched to the rear. Except Wallace, who kept marching straight ahead and collided with the man in front whose rifle flew from his grasp and clattered to the deck. The rest of Wallace's squad in a confusion of arms and legs ran into the man who had dropped his piece as Wallace, lacking any other command, continued to try to march ahead. The balance of the platoon continued to march smartly to the rear.

"Simon sez… P'toon… Halt!… Simon sez… Order… Harms!… You people stand fast. Wallace! Fall out! Over here on the double!"

At trail arms Wallace ran fifteen yards to the DI. He came to attention before him. Most of the platoon were standing rigidly in ranks, except for the five who had collided with Wallace and each other and were now facing various points of the compass. At rigid attention. The man without his rifle and hat was trembling.

"Wallace, I am damned glad there are no other platoons on this parade ground. You understand?"

In the cold and biting wind that hissed across the drill field Wallace felt sweat running under his shirt. He looked directly at the DI's face but focused on the middle distance, not Rose's eyes.

"Yes, sir!"

"Why am I glad, Wallace?"

"Sir, if I were you I wouldn't want anyone else to see what a bunch of screw-ups Platoon Fifty is, sir."

"Wallace, I never said this to any of you people before, but you're supposed to be a smart bunch. This is a special platoon. But we treat you like everyone else. Like the yahoos from Georgia and Alabama. Like the punks from New York. Like the rubes from Ohio. No special treatment. So why can't you college boys do at least as good as those other people?"

Wallace wasn't sure whether this was a rhetorical question or whether he was expected to answer. Rose waited.

"Sir," said Wallace, still focusing on the middle distance, "They think too much and don't listen enough. They anticipate the command because for four years they've been told to reason, to question, to understand. They're thinking, not listening."

"Do you know why we play 'Simon sez'?" Rose asked.

"Sir, we play 'Simon sez' to learn to listen carefully to orders and not go off half-cocked, sir."

"So how come you got it right and fifty-nine other boots screwed up?"

Wallace didn't answer.

Rose told the platoon to fall out and to "assemble on me." They stood at ease, wondered how badly Wallace had been reamed and cast smirking glances in his direction. He sidled away from the DI and stood at the edge of the group.

Rose paced back and forth in front of the platoon, hands clasped behind his back, stopping occasionally to glare at them. They began to shift uncomfortably. His eyes didn't miss a man.

"You people are a disaster. One man gets it right and fifty-nine of you fuck up!"

The platoon stiffened. Wallace was right?

"You people think too much! You don't listen! When I give commands I don't want you trying to figure out the next one. Normally the commands come in cadence. But we're gonna drill now, and I'm gonna delay the second command until I'm damn good and ready to give it. You people listen, listen, listen! Don't you do one goddam thing until you hear me holler. Is that clear?"

"YES, SIR!"

"Fall in!"

The platoon fell in, dressed right and stood at attention.

"Right... Fhace!"

"Right shoulder..." There was a long pause, and the man on Wallace's left twitched.

"Harms!" Palms smashed the fore-grips in unison. The tight slings slapped. Hands whacked rifle butts in cadence, and rifles were smashed to right shoulders.

"Forward..." The platoon leaned ahead.

"Belay that!" The platoon straightened.

"Forward... Harch! Awn hup areep hup y'layouf... hup a reep... hup y'layouf."

For an hour without stop they drilled, eyes riveted to the neck of the man in front. Forty inches back to breast, one hundred twenty paces to the minute. They concentrated on Rose.

They did not screw up. They beat him. And Rose won.

Wallace was awed.

The ball of twine they had been issued was a godsend. Lengths of it, called tie-ties, were cut and used to hang laundry (no clothes pins). Loops of it were used to hang their Ml rifles under the starboard steel bunk support rail. Wallace liked the language, too. Left and right: port and starboard. Floor: deck. Ceiling: overhead. Wall: bulkhead. Stairs: ladder. Toilet: head. Rifle: piece or rifle, never gun. Leave the post: go ashore. Saloon: slop chute. And the "Able, Baker, Charlie, Dog" phonetic alphabet. He liked the lingo and picked it up naturally. He presumed that the use of so many four-letter Anglo-Saxon expletives by Marines was the result of long tradition and the limited vocabulary of enlisted men. He tried to avoid the use of most of the words but was curious about them.

Sitting in the hut after the day's duty they talked about it. There was a lot of reference to fecal matter, they decided, and the word could be used as a verb or a noun in its four-letter form or as an adjective, as in "shitty detail." The explosive word for sexual intercourse was high on the list of words used most often. It, too, could be used as a noun, a verb, an expletive or an adjective, as in "bet your fucking life."

"I wonder," said Fix O'Reilly, "what part of speech it is in the phrase 'throw it the fuck overboard!'"

They roared and asked Fix to do his take-off of the DI. Fix looked out the window at the end of the hut, about-faced, placed his hands behind his back and slowly paced the length of the hut looking at each man. He pushed out his belly.

"You people gotta pay attention to what I say! When I say line up alphabetically by size I mean line up alphabetically by size. When I say jump you say how far. When I say what is an M1 you say it's a gas operated, clip fed, semiautomatic shoulder weapon. When I say what is a Marine you say it's a chow fed, fully automatic, gas operated person." Fix lifted his leg and noisily and copiously passed wind. Someone shouted "ATTENTION!" and they all laughed until they saw Rose standing in the doorway.... They all snapped to.

"O'Reilly, get your hat, your cartridge belt and rifle, and come with me. The rest of you carry on."

Fix followed the DI out the door, and the squad silently went back to reading the *FMF Manual*, learning about "rocks and shoals," Corps lingo for

Military Code of Justice.

Fix returned just before last call soaked with sweat and covered with mud, his rifle filthy.

"The son of a bitch ran me almost to the rifle range at high port and made me crawl under the wire at the obstacle course and run around the parade ground and…" he stopped, out of breath.

"Was he with you all the way?" asked Wallace.

"Yes, but why does he have to do all that. Why do they put us through all this crap anyway?"

"Don't bug yourself about it," said Wallace. "Do it, whatever they ask, and get it behind you. They're probably trying to find out who's going to break or question or disobey orders. For a buck-ass private in the rear rank there's no need to know 'why.' "

O'Reilly looked down at the deck. "A Rose is a rose is a son of a bitch. Shee-it."

"An expletive," said Wallace, as he took Fix's rifle to clean it, and O'Reilly and the rest of the squad doubled over.

Ian Wallace lay on his sack in the dark, reviewed the day and what he'd learned and thought about tomorrow and what he had to look forward to. He'd learned the practice from his grandfather before each nightly cribbage game at the farm. Don't bring in the hay when it's damp. Make the butter to-morrow. And in college. Was he prepared for the next day's hour test on Kant's *Critique of Pure Reason*?

Today he thought that he learned some lessons from Platoon Sergeant George Daniel Rose. Listen. Tell it straight. Don't ridicule your superiors. Don't ask the troops to do anything you wouldn't do yourself. He'd seen Rose outside the DI's hut when he smuggled Fix's rifle out to the head to run it under the steaming hot water of the showers. Rose was talking to the assistant DI, Corporal McHugh, and Rose's uniform was every bit as filthy as O'Reilly's.

Rose was sending a clear message. Wallace hoped the platoon was getting the word. They should be. Ian remembered that when they had been marched naked through the dispensary with numbers painted on their arms with iodine so a record could be made of their shots, Rose had watched all of them and had helped carry out the big guy from Maine who fainted at the first needle. And when he made them play tackle football in the sand with just their boondocker boots and dungaree trousers on, after the shots, he had been right with them, running, breathless and blowing his whistle. They thought they would die, their arms hurt so much and their chests heaved, and they lost their appetites, and they fevered and sweated and sacked out empty and early. But the next morning when half of the other platoons were reporting to sickbay Platoon Fifty double-timed to morning calisthenics, to the showers and to the mess hall where they put down enormous quantities of horsecock (sausage) and beans.

And grits. When you don't want grits you get grits, Wallace thought.

Lying there he wondered if he was changing. He still had the same objectives: come out at the top of his platoon, shoot "expert" (experts got more pay, too), make his family and the Corps proud of him. But he found it harder and harder to reconcile his previous considerations of the ministry with the combat training he was being given. Hell, somebody had to fight or there would be no world to minister to if the bad guys won. And the Bible was contradictory on the issue as well. "An eye for an eye, a tooth for a tooth.... turn the other cheek." He drifted off to sleep.

Not all the men in hut A were gung-ho. Fix was. Wallace was. And so were seven of the others. But one man, Grimes, was a mess. He didn't do his policing jobs so the squad policed up after him to avoid bad marks from Corporal McHugh, who regularly inspected the huts. In spite of the squads' efforts they got bad marks two weeks in a row. They had to settle it with Grimes.

"Fuck you," he said. "Is it going to make me fight any better or get me home quicker?"

They thought the DIs were onto Grimes but couldn't be sure.

The DIs had to know that Grimes was always last in formation, rifle always dirty, lousy blanket tension on his bunk—rather silently insolent. He never smiled and he looked like he had blocked too many kicks at Fordham, in the Bronx. He was a poor advertisement for his university. He ought to get transferred to the punishment platoon, although that was something most people didn't even want to think about.

At chow one evening Grimes didn't finish the food on his compartmented metal tray; as he walked toward the garbage can the mess sergeant stopped him and told him to finish what he'd taken. Grimes said, "You eat it," dropped the tray upside down on the deck and ducked out.

Next morning when the squad returned from morning chow, Grimes's mattress was rolled up. His blankets, sea bag, footlocker, rifle, everything—

gone. They hoped that Grimes was applying his Bachelor of Arts degree to the care and maintenance of the Parris Island entrance roads or breaking rock at the Portsmouth Naval Prison.

Before going to sleep that night Wallace thought about the day's lesson. Number one: the DIs had the word. And number two: Newton's Third Law of Motion applied not only to physics but also to the military—for every action there is an equal and opposite reaction. He also thought he was prepared for tomorrow's last inspection before moving to the rifle range.

Platoon Fifty was honor platoon again, and as they marched off the parade ground the post band piped up playing the Marine Hymn. They'd never marched to anything but Rose's or McHugh's cadence, and the lift the music gave them was tremendous. They almost strutted. Their arms swung a little higher, their backs were a little stiffer, heads held a little higher, and their pieces were perfectly aligned.

They fell out and went to their huts to stow their gear for movement to the wooden barracks at the rifle range. Wooden barracks! With heads inside the same building instead of one hundred twenty yards down the platoon street!

Trucks arrived for their footlockers and sea bags, but the platoon would hike the six miles to the range, down the macadam road, rifles at sling arms. Going to the range was like going to church and getting married, to your rifle. It was not entered into lightly, but reverently and with promises to honor and obey. They had been engaged to their rifles before, but now, after proper instruction by the high priests of riflery, the range instructors, they would fire for record. It was, as Fix put it, the first time they would put anything into their pieces and was the climax of this union between man and weapon.

Route march is a casual way of getting from one place to another and is usually used over rough terrain. But the road to the range was metaled, and after the first few miles the platoon was strung out with the guys with the short legs, the feather merchants, falling behind. Rose gave a five-minute break after the first hour, and the break lasted about ten minutes to wait for the rear ranks to arrive.

"You people keep closed up," said Rose before they fell in to get under way again. "You want to arrive at the range looking like a bunch of yahoos?"

They fell in and trudged off looking, Wallace thought, like Coxey's Army. When the range barracks were coming into view Ian, squad leader, first squad, noticed that they were pretty strung out again, and so he nudged the squad leader to his right and started to count cadence, the Marine way, quietly though not quite under his breath. The other two squad leaders in the first section picked it up quietly and fell into step. The next couple of ranks also fell into step and instead of following the cadence call they joined it, and then the whole first section of Platoon Fifty was marching in step, swinging along.

George Daniel Rose heard it happening behind him as the boots' shuffle turned into a measured tread and the trainees picked up the cadence, and the lilting "awn hup areep hup y'layouf" came from the throats of his men.

Rose turned and marched backwards and watched as the second section double-timed to catch up, fell into step and picked up the cadence call... "hup areep hup y'layouf." He turned about without saying a word, marching with them to B Barracks.

"P'toon... HALT!"

"Layouf... FHACE!"

"Order... HARMS!... Rest."

The senior range NCO, a gunnery sergeant covered with hash marks, was standing by the steps to B Barracks waiting for them. His khaki was the same shade as Rose's. Rose walked up to him.

"How, Gunny," said Rose.

"How, Dan," said the gunnery sergeant, "Got yourself a bunch of aces? Bunch of hot-shots? Not too many outfits swing in here making music. You got sumpin special goin'?"

Rose lowered his voice: "You bet your sweet ass I do."

"Got any money you want to put on it?"

"You bet your sweet ass I do," said Rose. The two sergeants turned and walked away from the platoon. Rose stopped and turned toward the men. "The smoking lamp is lit," he called and then he and the gunny huddled over their bet while the platoon shuffled and lit up.

What Fix O'Reilly had thought were little graveyards in remembrance of boots who hadn't made it turned out to be little white aiming crosses they would use for snapping in. Snapping in was "dry firing," learning the various positions they would use when firing for record, off hand (from the shoulder), kneeling, sitting, prone. Learning how to sight with both eyes open, to breathe in, exhale halfway, hold it and squeeze (not pull) the trigger while balancing the front sight blade in the center of the rear sight and on the target.

They learned how to adjust their slings and make the damned leathers help hold their rifles steady in the most awkward positions.

"I can't put my elbows on my ankles. I can't sit on my right foot. When the hell do they ever think we'll be in these dumb damned positions when were fighting!" Fix was fit to be tied.

"You're not supposed to wonder about that. You're just supposed to do it," said Ian. He personally had wondered the same thing as he had forced his breath out and contracted his belly and forced his elbows onto his ankles in the sitting position. The arrangement did give him stability and the use of the sling helped to steady the rifle. He remembered reading a smuggled copy of the *Kama Sutra* in comparative religion class and pondered the Hindu positions for love-making, grateful that a thoughtful Marine Corps had decreed that only four positions were necessary for firing one's weapon. He mentally paraphrased the old Corps adage—*This is my rifle, this is my gun... This position's for fighting, this position's for fun.*

They did physical drill under arms every morning... overhead swings—muzzles, butts, butts, muzzles... knee bends, rifles extended at full arm's length before them... leg lifts... sit-ups... push-ups... running in place at high port... jumping jacks with rifles. They double-timed back to the barracks to shower before chow. They spent endless hours snapping in until the breathing and the trigger squeeze were second nature.

On the range itself they learned procedure and how to man the butts where the targets were pulled, spotted and pasted. And they learned speed. "Spot number three and get the lead out of your ass! Pull those targets! Run 'em up! Run 'em up! Run 'em up!" It was work, and they had to police the butts when the firing was over and double-time back to the barracks for inspection... equipment on the bunk.

They were preparing for a visit from the Corps commandant, rumored to be coming just before the platoon would fire for record, and the range had to be perfect—paste pots clean, firing positions squared away, barracks policed, rifles spotless. The DI said there would be no formal inspection, that the commandant would just show up and watch a normal day's training and Platoon Fifty had better not fuck up. The platoon knew the day he arrived because they were given a breakfast the likes of which they had never seen, just in case the commandant dropped by. They double-timed everywhere they went.

They drew duty in the butts after an unbelievable noon meal, but the firing that had started out smartly after chow soon began to lag. And the targets were slow to be spotted and pasted. Guys were passing out, and the range instructors were shouting until there came the word "cease firing… secure the butts."

Fix and Wallace looked down the concrete step from which they had worked target thirty-two and saw that half the platoon was out cold on the deck or doubled over and retching and soiling themselves.

"What the hell!" said Wallace as he watched the sergeant in charge fall to the ground.

"Jesus!" said Fix and cranked up the EE8B phone to the firing line. "What's happening?" he shouted.

"Everybody's passed out or puking their guts out," said the boot on the other end of the wire. "Stay put until I get some word."

"What the hell do you think it is?" asked Wallace.

"Beats the shit out of me."

"Not funny," said Wallace and ran to the end of the butts to see what was happening on the firing line. The big red pennant, Baker, had been lowered to indicate that firing had ceased, and Ian heard sirens and saw ambulances, 6x6 trucks and weapons carriers converging on the line. He rushed back to tell Fix and found him unconscious on the deck, and looking around saw that he was the only man on his feet. He picked up the phone and shouted into it and got no reply. He called over and over and got no answer.

He ran to the end of the butts again and saw people being loaded into the vehicles and ran back to the phone and called again. No answer. They damned well better send some help to this end, Ian thought, and grabbed Maggie's Drawers, the red flag that is waved in front of a target that has been missed, and pushed the pole above the butts and waved it and waved it while holding the phone to his ear.

"Anybody on the wire?" came the call.

"Private Wallace, Platoon Fifty, sir. Everybody else is down and they need help."

"Hang on. We'll get some transportation down there right away."

When the trucks arrived some of the boots were able to get into them under their own steam, but most of them had to be lifted, including the NCO in charge. Many of them still had the dry heaves and cramps.

"You all right, son?" asked the Marine gunner (warrant officer) who seemed to be in command of the detail.

"Yes, sir. So far," said Wallace, not knowing what had afflicted all the others.

A Navy j.g. doctor appeared from one of the trucks and walked up to Wallace. He felt his forehead and took a quick pulse and said: "Well, if it hasn't hit you by now it probably won't," and turned and made a "start 'em up" signal. The truck engines burst into life and started to grind up toward the line. The warrant officer shouted to Ian as he swung onto the last vehicle: "You're in charge of these butts. Stay put until you're relieved."

"Aye, aye sir," said Wallace.

Wallace looked about him at the mess that had been left behind. Rifles that had been carefully stacked were now knocked over and strewn on the deck. The stench of puke and crap was pervasive. Some targets were half up or half down. Paste pots were overturned. Spotters and patches were everywhere. Shrugging, he began to collect the rifles and stack them in the prescribed manner. He lowered all targets and righted all paste pots. He found the high-pressure hose valve and flushed all the spilled paste, vomit and feces down the storm drain at the far end of the butts. He tried the phone again, but it was dead.

Wallace took his rifle from its stack, slung it over his shoulder and began to pace up and down the length of his "command." The shadows were getting deep long before he heard the distinctive sound of a jeep engine. He hoped it was coming to these butts. The engine stopped some distance off, then started again and slowly faded away.

Maybe I should wave "Maggie's Drawers" again, he thought. No. Somebody will come. They'd better.

He heard the jeep engine again, and this time it seemed to be coming closer, accompanied by another vehicle. As Wallace reached the end of the butts where the dirt road joined it, he saw a jeep and a weapons carrier slowing as they reached the end of the track. Wallace stood at attention not knowing what the word might be.

Squinting into the setting sunlight he saw Platoon Sergeant George Daniel Rose vault out of the weapons carrier and stride toward him. He stopped and looked at Wallace without saying a word. He strode past him and looked at the butts, the stacked rifles, the pots and the markers all stowed and shipshape, the decks hosed down. He turned back and said to Wallace: "All right. At ease, Wallace. Lend a hand and let's get these weapons into that three-quarter ton and get back to barracks."

Wallace, Rose and the Pfc jeep driver collected the pieces and carefully laid them in the vehicle. "Probably don't make much difference how we handle 'em," said the DI. "They'll have to be zeroed in all over again after getting whacked around like that. O.K., son, get in the wagon. You're riding in style this evening."

On the ride back toward B Barracks Ian noticed that fully two thirds of the range targets were at half mast or otherwise unsecured, and turned to Rose.

"Sir?"

"What is it?"

"What's happened?"

"Everybody's got the pukes or the shits. How come you don't?"

"Beats me, sir," said Wallace.

"They say some graduate asshole from cooks and bakers school put soap powder in the biscuit mix by mistake. It took the commandant by storm."

Ian almost choked. Rose looked at him.

"What's the matter? Think it's funny? Didn't you eat the biscuits? You too good for Marine Corps biscuits?" But Rose was grinning. "I didn't either," he said.

Long tents had been erected as temporary hospital shelters, and slit trenches had been dug as latrines in the field across the macadam road from the barracks. The prevailing wind was away from the barracks, thank God, thought Ian as he unloaded fifty-nine rifles from the weapons carrier and jeep. He leaned them up against wooden racks by the steam tables where they had stopped and where Rose had said to him that those pieces better be cleaned before last call. One by one Ian field-stripped the M1s, ran hot soapy patches and then dry patches through them and gave them a light coating of oil before reassembling them, one by one. He missed chow, but the day had robbed him of any appetite, and after he moved all the rifles to their respective slots in the rifle rack in B Barracks he showered and sat on his bunk.

Rose, in fresh khakis, walked into the squad bay. He and Wallace were alone in the building. Corporal McHugh was sharing the delights of food poisoning with the boots across the road.

"You play acey-deucy?" asked the DI.

"No, sir," said Wallace.

"Cribbage?"

"Yes, sir," said Wallace.

"Come on," said Rose and led the way into the DI's quarters. Wallace had never seen the inside of this spartan room. Two bunks, two footlockers, two standing metal lockers, a wooden table and two simple wooden chairs. McHugh's and Rose's campaign hats were on top of the standing lockers, the only decoration in the room.

"Don't look like much," said Rose, "but these is only temporary quarters for us when we're at the range. You keep your mouth shut about being in here, though."

Rose opened his standing locker and took a cribbage board and a dog-eared rubber-banded deck of cards from the top shelf. He saw Ian staring at the khakis hanging in the locker.

"What're you looking at?"

"Sir, I was wondering how come your khaki is a different color from the others I see. Same color as the senior range gunny."

Rose dragged a chair up to the unpainted wood table and got the pegs from the bottom of the cribbage board. He took the rubber-band from the cards and said, "Sit."

They sat down at opposite sides of the table, and Rose began to shuffle the cards slowly.

"That khaki you asked about is what we call China khaki. Made in China and issued to the Marines on China duty. Gunny and me served two cruises there, the Legation Guard in Peking and then in Shanghai with the Fifth Marines. He's good people, by the way, and I got a bet with him that you folks are going to shoot good. Anyway, the Chinese couldn't exactly match the GI color. And we got kind of uppity about it until Captain Thomason told us it set us apart as something special in the Corps."

"*Salt Winds and Gobi Dust,*" said Ian.

"What?"

"Thomason's *Salt Winds and Gobi Dust,*" said Ian and started to explain but was interrupted by Rose.

"You know that book?"

"Yes, sir, I've read it. Several times."

"I'll be goddamned," said Rose. "I never seen anyone ever heard of that book but some China Horse Marines and old hands like Gunny Ruditis and me. Cut the cards."

Rose dealt and cut the five of spades after discarding two of his cards to match Ian's discard in the crib. After they pegged (even) Ian laid down his hand. Double run of three for eight. He counted it out and looked at the hand Rose laid out. Two fives, jack of spades, king of diamonds.

"Fifteen two, fifteen four, fifteen six, eight, ten, twelve, fourteen and six is twenty," said the DI and moved his peg.

"And one for his nibs," said Ian pegging what Rose had missed.

"Son of a bitch!" said Rose.

Training was delayed for two days while the range complement recovered from what was referred to as the biscuit party. On pre-record day the platoon fired the record course for familiarization and Wallace fired "expert."

"It don't count 'til record day," said McHugh, recovered from his bout with the shits and full of it all over again. Nobody in the platoon failed to "qualify," and they could see that Rose was mentally rubbing his hands in anticipation of winning his bet with Ruditis.

At mail call McHugh called out the names of boots who had received letters. Wallace did not get much mail. An occasional letter from Peter at first, but now he presumed his brother had shipped out, for that mail had stopped. He heard from his mother, pedestrian things about the garden and the difficult winter and best wishes from his grandfather, who, strangely, never wrote. He had bought the gold engraved USMC stationary at the PX on a rarely allowed visit there and had written to many of his friends from college who were now in the service, but responses were slow in coming. The mail had to find people, and people were on the move. Today he had a letter from Coop, his old roommate, who indicated he was somewhere in the southwest Pacific, though the censor had cut out a considerable portion of the letter. Wallace understood that Coop was flying Navy F4F fighter planes as the censor had left in the phrase that Cooper said he felt like a real wildcat.

At chow Ian didn't feel very hungry and ate little. He felt light-headed on the way back to the barracks and hoped to hell he wasn't going to be sick. Record day was tomorrow.

He woke up in a white ward just as the sun was coming up. He was cold under the blankets and shivering uncontrollably. He turned his head on the pillow, looked down the long room and saw nothing but prone figures in blankets on cots. He tried to sit up and fell back. A Navy corpsman ambled down the aisle between the cots and saw that Ian was awake. Ian made an effort to sit up again but fell back covered with sweat.

"Lay back," said the corpsman, "and take it easy."

"Record day," said Wallace, "Gotta go."

"You ain't shootin' for no record today, boy."

"What's the matter with me?" asked Ian.

"Cat fever," said the corpsman. "Most everybody gets it one time or another. You just happen to got it now." He stuck a thermometer in Wallace's mouth and walked to the end of the ward. When he came back he read Ian's temperature.

"Hundred and three," he said. "Too sick to shoot but not too sick to swab. Take it easy."

A cart was pushed by with bowls of some thick steaming gray gruel that they were told to eat even if it made them throw up.

Wallace forced most of his down, not sure how long it would stay there. He slept for a time and was awakened by the medical party making its rounds. Wallace recognized the corpsman, and he thought the Navy j.g. doctor was the same man he had seen in the butts three days ago. They took his temperature again. Hundred and one.

At about 1100 he was given a gray terry-cloth robe and paper slippers and told to report to the Charge-of-Quarters at the end of the ward. He and three other patients were given pails and mops and assigned the duty of swabbing all the heads on their deck. The toilets were revolting; Ian thought he would add his gray gruel to the mess but was able to control himself and sloshed and swabbed and stood in his wet paper-clad feet wondering how this was helping him to overcome his affliction. He swabbed the ward decks in the afternoon and concluded that this was pretty motivational work... motivating him to get the hell out of sickbay.

The next morning his temperature was normal, and he was again assigned swabbing duty in the heads. In one of them he encountered the Navy doctor pulling up his pants. Well, what the hell, he thought.

"Sir?" he said.

The officer turned around. "You spoke to me?"

Go for it, he thought. "With respect, sir, if I'm able to do swab duty am I not able to get discharged? I missed firing for record and I want to catch my platoon."

The j.g. squinted at him. "The guy at the butts, right?"

"Yes, sir," said Wallace.

"Your platoon's already fired and gone back to the hut area. You'd have to get special permission from the battalion office to shoot for record with some other bunch, and they don't like to do that."

"I'd like to try, sir," said Wallace.

"You grunts are crazy," said the j.g. and walked out of the head.

Wallace was discharged about 0900, and in his dirty dungarees, sweating slightly, he walked two miles to the battalion area and found the office. A Pfc who behaved like a noncommissioned colonel gave him a hard time, but he finally got to see the first lieutenant. After a couple of phone calls the officer told him to go to the range and report to the NCO on line six. He'd have to walk or hitch. No transportation was available. He walked the first two miles and than got a ride in a kitchen van that stank of rancid food.

He found the NCO on line six and reported that he had been told he could fire for record with the platoon on the line. It was Ruditis. The gunny looked at him. "You was with Rose's platoon, right?"

"Yes, sir."

"Where's your rifle?"

"Probably taken back to the hut area, sir. I been in sickbay."

"Come on."

They went to the armorer's truck, and Ruditis told the buck sergeant armorer to hand him a slick, smooth piece as a temporary issue for this lad and to give him no shit. The armorer handed the gunny an M1 that had only four digits in the rifle number, the slide and receiver were made of old gray monel metal. A museum piece. "Don't drop it, boy," said the gunny.

They walked to position forty, five or six positions from the end of the group that was getting ready to fire.

"Hold fire!" shouted Ruditis.

Wallace adjusted the soft, supple sling. The stock fitted his cheek perfectly. He could smell the linseed oil on the wood, the light oil on the metal. He thought of the sweet smell of Hoppe's cleaning solvent he'd used on his guns at home. The range corporal walked up and handed the gunny clips of .30 caliber ammunition that he put on Wallace's poncho.

"Tell 'em to run up target forty and let this kid take some sighting shots," ordered the gunny.

Target forty came up and Ian, in the prone position though you don't shoot prone at two hundred yards but you do to zero in, looked at the gunny.

"Load and lock," said Ruditis.

Ian pushed the clip into the receiver, and the bolt slammed forward carrying the first round into the chamber. He put on the safety.

"Tell the butts we're zeroing in on target forty," the gunny said to the telephone talker.

"O.K., kid, take your time and squeeze off a couple."

Ian checked the rear sight for zero windage, two hundred yards elevation and pushed the stock to his cheek. He exhaled and held his breath, held the sights at six o'clock on the bull and squeezed off the first round. The target dropped and was run up again, spotted at three o'clock just outside the black.

"Take another," said the gunny. Wallace squeezed off the second round. Three o'clock just outside the black.

"Try one click left windage," said the gunny.

Wallace adjusted the sight, held his breath and squeezed it off. Middle of the black.

"O.K.," said the gunny to the line corporal, "Get on with it."

Wallace put them all in the black from two hundred yards.

At three hundred yards he was starting to draw a crowd. The line corporal, the gunny, the telephone talker and the armorer were gathered behind him. During rapid fire the gunny made sure that his second clip was ready at hand. In the sitting position Wallace rocked with the recoil and squeezed in rhythm as the sights came back to the bull. All in the black.

"Don't nobody say anything," said the gunny to the crowd. To Wallace he said: "Keep that piece pointed towards the butts, and let's get back to the five hundred line."

The gunnery sergeant had never seen anyone shoot "possible," every shot in the bull, but this kid was sure as hell taking a swing at it. And the poor fucker had walked out from sickbay and hadn't had any chow. And was using somebody else's rifle.

Wallace was light-headed walking back to the five hundred yard line. He wanted to do as well as he could, but he didn't want to wind up as a range instructor, wearing a gold bar, riding boots, jodhpurs and a campaign hat. And carrying one of those stupid little sticks.

He laid out his poncho and put his clips in easy reach. The targets seemed infinitesimal. The bull's eye like a fly speck. He remembered something from Thomason's *Fix Bayonets!* At Blanc Mont the Boche had learned new respect for rifle fire that killed at seven hundred yards. This was five hundred. Go for it.

His first clip was fired very slowly. He was getting pretty nervous. All in the black. He let out a long breath and, keeping the muzzle pointed at the butts, rolled over on his back and looked at the sky. The gunny sat down on the ground next to him, cross-legged.

"Take your time, kid. You already got expert made and only one clip to go."

Ian rolled over.

"Load and lock! Ready on the right? Ready on the left! All ready on the firing line! Unlock! Commence firing!"

The target wavered. The rifle wavered. His eyes watered. Shit. He took a deep breath.

The gunny, the corporal, the armorer, the platoon sergeant of the platoon firing for record, the telephone talker and the range major were all squatting behind position forty.

"Jesus, Jesus, Jesus," breathed the gunny.

Wallace squeezed off the round. The white spotter came up. In the black for five more. Three more rounds and three more in the black. Four to go. His stomach hurt and he was dripping. The sweat was running into his eyes. He rubbed his hand across his forehead. Everything was blurred. He waited. The firing on the rest of the line had ceased. Four to go.

He closed his eyes and prayed, "…if this cup not pass from me…," and squeezed off the last rounds. The target was slow coming up after his last shot. Then it was pulled up and immediately went back down again. No spotter.

"Ask them what the hell they're doing," shouted the major to the telephone talker. "All those others were in the black. Can't they find this one!"

The target came up hesitantly. A black spotter. He'd hit the four ring on his last shot.

"I don't believe it," said the gunny. "Ski," he said to the armorer, "get that weapons carrier fired up and we'll go and look. Tell those people in the butts to keep that target up 'til we get there."

They were all pounding Wallace on the back and shouting that those assholes in the butts didn't know what they were doing; Wallace slowly took off the sling, checked the chamber, left the bolt back and keeping the muzzle toward the butts handed the weapon to the armorer. "Thanks for the use of your piece, sir. It shoots great," he said, picking up his brass.

"You don't shoot so goddam bad yourself, kid," said the sergeant.

"Come on, you people, let's get to the butts. You too, Wallace."

They piled into the weapons carrier and sped past the other boots, who watched goggle-eyed as one of their number accompanied by more rank than they had ever seen in one place roared down to the targets.

"Lower forty," said the major when they had reached it. The target slowly came down and they pushed in between it and the concrete parapet. The man who was spotting showed them where the last round had hit. It was in the four ring but looked as if it almost touched the bull at about eight o'clock. If a hit even touches the black it's a five.

"That's a five," said the gunny.

"Damned close," said the major. "Whaddya think, Wallace?"

Wallace looked at the hole. He was exhausted. He looked at the men watching him. He looked at the hit again. Screw it.

"It's a four, sir," said Wallace.

"O.K., his call. It's a four. That's fine shooting, son, and it took more guts to call that last shot than to shoot all the others. Secure the butts!"

Gunnery Sergeant Ruditis took him back to Platoon Fifty in his jeep and stopped at the end of the platoon street in front of Quonset hut A.

"Hey Rose," he called. "I got one of your wandering boys!"

Rose came out of the hut. "Where did you find him?"

"Out on the range."

"How did he do?"

"The sonofabitch is too goddam good!"

"O.K.," said Rose. "Pay up."

Wallace slept rolled up in a borrowed blanket after shooting the breeze with the rest of the squad, who hadn't heard what had happened. The next morning when the battalion office opened Ian was ordered to report there and pick up his gear from battalion stores. He went into the guard room and stood at attention in front of the sergeant of the guard's desk. The sergeant didn't look up but said, "Whaddya want?"

"Sir, I was told to report here to pick up my gear from battalion stores."

"What's your name?"

"Private Wallace, sir, Platoon Fifty."

The sergeant looked up, scrutinized him, referred to a list on the desk and said, "Your gear is in the store room at the end of the passageway. But your rifle's at the armory, next door. What the hell did you shoot with yesterday, anyway?"

"Belonged to Sergeant Bojanowski, sir. It shoots pretty straight."

"Bet your ass Ski will never shoot it again. He'll have it bronzed and mounted and tell sea-stories about it. O.K., kid, go get your gear. I'll tell 'em you're coming."

Halfway down the passageway someone shouted "Gangway!" and Wallace stepped aside to let the officer pass. But the officer, the first lieutenant who had told Ian to walk to the range, stopped and looked at him.

"I hear you found line six."

"Yes, sir."

"Lotta talk about it, but don't let it go to your head."

"No, sir," said Wallace. The lieutenant said, "Carry on," and walked on down the passageway.

When Wallace got back to the hut the word was that they were to put on their greens, go to the post tailor in formation to have Pfc stripes sewn to the left sleeves of their blouses. That would distinguish them from the other boots during their last two days and would earn them Pfc pay when they reached Quantico.

While they were going through the slow process at the tailor's they heard a field music sound pay call on his bugle... *PAY DAY! PAY DAY! tum tum ta ta tum tum ta ta ta ta tum!*

"Gonna collect some cash," said Francis Xavier O'Reilly.

"Gonna collect some bets," said Corporal McHugh.

They marched to the hut where pay call was being held, lined up single file and marched in one at a time. The paymaster was sitting at a blanket-covered table with two MPs behind him, his cash box and his .45 automatic on the blanket and Rose sitting to starboard of him with the platoon roster. They stated their names and numbers and with one hand reached out and picked up the money that had been counted out, signed the receipt, about-faced and marched out straight to the PX.

They bought qualification badges, cigarettes and other small stores and boasted and strutted their way back to the huts. Ian bumped into John Perry of Platoon Forty-eight. He'd failed to qualify. "They'll find work for you," said Wallace. "Make you a field music or put you in a transportation company."

Perry didn't smile. After noon chow, just to bring them down a peg, Rose ordered "field day" for all hands. That meant back into dungarees, out with the buckets, swabs and brooms, line up the footlockers and make sure their contents were complete and in the right place, clean the already clean windows, hose out the heads, police the area, tighten the bunk blankets, sweep the sand off the duck boards and be ready for inspection by 1500 hours.

Fix was in his element, washing windows and muttering just loud enough to be heard by the others in the hut. " 'What's your first General Order, son?....' 'Sir, I will walk my post from flank to flank and salute all assholes above my rank....' 'Do you have instructions, sir?' 'Yes. Anybody's got one, draw one. Anybody ain't got one, turn one in....' 'Anything else, sir?' 'Yes. When I say police the area all I want to see is assholes and elbows!....' 'Son, you miss all them wimmin you had when you was a civilian?' 'No, sir.' 'Why not?' 'Sir, I am a charter member of the Meat-Beaters' Blue Book.' "

Rose made them all clean their rifles one more time and told them that they would clean them again after tomorrow's last inspection and parade, before they turned the weapons in at the armory. Wallace broke the handle off a toothbrush so that he could keep just the bristles in his pocket. He would use that little brush during formation before inspection to whisk the sand out of the butt plate of his rifle. He wanted to be as squared away as possible on this last inspection.

They sat around in the hut in the evening and told extravagant lies about the first time they had sex. Ian made his up out of the whole cloth and hoped, as a cherry, that he was knowledgeable enough to sound convincing: a farm girl, in the hay loft, hay seeds up the nose, scratchy hay in the tail, one of her shoes lost down in the pile. He said he was a jack rabbit. Laughter. The guy from Taunton, Massachusetts, told about doing it on the porch glider after a high school homecoming prom one November Saturday night. Pants around his ankles. Her legs over his shoulders. The glider squeaking. Colder than North Atlantic whale shit. She stopped him in school just before Christmas and whispered she had to see him. "Jesus, what a Christmas present!" he said. She came around in January, he said, but she would never look him in the eye again.

"How about some shakes and sandwiches?" some one asked.

"From whom? The tooth fairy?"

"How about from the main base PX. We draw straws, and the man who draws the short one gets the dough and the orders from us and cuts across the parade ground where it's dark. In and out of the soda counter in a flash! What the hell, we're Pfcs now!"

Wallace got the short straw (on purpose?), got into his greens, boondockers, shirt, wrinkled field scarf (tie) and his fore-and-aft hat. He pinned on his expert rifle and expert pistol medals. He collected their money and said he'd get them all the same order for the sake of speed and simplicity. The vote was eight to two for ham and cheese sandwiches and chocolate shakes.

He went out the back door of the hut and stayed out of the lights until he got to the street that separated the recruit battalion area from the parade ground. He brazened it out and marched across the road and onto the parade ground where he angled off so his course would bring him to the darkest part of the street by the PX. He went up the steps and into the smoky, noisy, hot interior of the fountain area and stood in a crowd at the counter. Everybody's shirts were starched, their shoes were shined and they had a good deal more hair showing under their caps than Ian did. He felt very uncomfortable.

The corporal running the fountain was the man who took Wallace's order. He looked at Ian's expert badges. He put the order in and came back, leaned over the counter and hissed at Wallace: "You're crazy. If they catch you it's your ass, you know. The minute I give you your sack you get the hell out of here, and if you're caught I ain't never seen you!"

Wallace gave him the money and without waiting for change angled out the door to the stares of a number of curious patrons. He walked slowly across the street but when he got to the darkness of the parade ground he bolted. Running relieved his anxiety, and he slowed down before he reached the hut to catch his breath. Only the road to cross and he'd make it. He waited in the shadows for a vehicle to pass and crossed immediately behind it, passing into the darkness of the hut area.

He paused at the rear door of hut A, squared away his hat and said to himself, what the hell... let's give them a little thrill. He knocked loudly on the door and in his most commanding voice shouted: "ATTEN-HUT!" and stepped inside.

The squad was standing at attention, and Wallace was staring directly into the eyes of Platoon Sergeant George Daniel Rose, DI, who, hands on hips, was in the opposite door. Wallace swallowed quickly and marched the length of the hut and came to attention directly in front of Rose and looked him in the eye.

"Sir, yours was the ham and cheese with the chocolate shake, I believe," and, reaching into the sack, gave one of each to the DI, who took them.

"Wallace," said Rose, "put that stuff down and come with me. The rest of you people carry on."

Wallace followed Rose across the platoon street and into the DI's quarters and stood at attention. McHugh was not there. Rose put down the refreshments and turned around and scowled at Wallace.

"Thought you'd scare 'em, did you?"

"Yes, sir."

"Well, I beat you to it and was just wondering where you were when you opened that back door and I nailed you, too." He paused. "O.K., take it easy. Sit down."

Ian did as he was told and didn't know what was coming next.

"Anybody except the squad know what you were up to?"

"The PX corporal said he'd swear he'd never seen me, and I got a couple of funny looks on the way out, but nobody blew a whistle."

"O.K.," said the DI, grinning. "We'll put it down to a little extra scouting and patrolling duty."

He got out a canteen cup and poured half the shake in it and gave Wallace the cardboard container with the other half. He unwrapped the sandwich, gave Ian half and took a bite.

"No matter what you get, it always tastes like cardboard."

"Not to me," said Wallace, chewing. "Forbidden fruit is always sweetest, regardless of the taste."

"You're lucky as hell. You want to play a hand?"

"Where's McHugh?"

"Don't worry about him spilling the beans. He's gone to Savannah (Rose pronounced it Savanaw) to the slop chutes, and he'll be lucky to be back for first call. Cut the cards."

They played, and Rose skunked him the first game. After the second game they were even. Rose put the cards down and his feet up.

"The Corps is family you know. I wouldn't know what to do out of it. You take care of it, it takes care of you. I've heard bugles and drums in China and Nicaragua and Haiti, and the Corps took care of its own no matter how rough it got. You keep your eyes peeled, don't be a smart ass, and you'll do good in this outfit. And the way this war is going, and if you're lucky, you may wind up going from some island to China or Japan. Don't knock them people, by the way. They's more people eat with sticks than with knives and forks, and the Chinese believe they're the center of the universe. Call themselves the Middle Kingdom, and there's more of them than anybody. They'd fight as good as the Japanese if they had the gear and some leadership. And the women are special, though it ain't true what they say about 'em. And the Nips are good fighters. Look what they done on the Canal. They can live on nothing, maybe a little rice and mud. They ain't never had nothing before they got in the army, anyway. Fighting's tied to religion for 'em so they don't mind dying. Tough monkeys. And you gotta be tougher.

"Listen to me, will you. I haven't strung that many words together since Christ was in boot camp." Rose stood up and stuck out his hand, which Wallace shook.

"You'll do good, Wallace. Just make your people want to be better than anybody, especially the slopeheads. Go hit the sack," said Rose.

Back in the hut they asked what the DI had done.

"Gave me some advice," said Wallace. The squad raised their eyebrows and looked at each other with knowing smiles.

Wallace lay in his bunk and thought over the past several days. The best defense is a good offense... as in the affair of the chocolate milk shakes and sandwiches. Don't kid about another guy's failures; you'll lose him as a friend. Count your blessings you didn't wind up like Grimes or any of the others who couldn't hack it. And that you didn't pass out from the cold on the pistol range like those other two guys. Instead you shot expert, and that wasn't easy. A .45 automatic weighs almost three pounds when loaded with a seven-round clip. Try holding that at arms length in a cold cross-wind.... "You gotta aim that thing, boy, and hit what you're looking at. That round ain't gonna knock anybody down any more than it knocked you down when you fired it (Newton's Third Law again?). So put that round where it'll stop a man. Makes a big hole so pick your spot." ...Final inspection and parade tomorrow. A band, they say. And reviewing officers. Rose wants to be honor platoon again. Going to Quantico (Kwan-ee-ko) the day after. Just as tough, a lot of bivouacs. But they don't yell at you as much, and you get liberty after Saturday noon on most weekends. And Pfc pay: $54 a month. I've never seen fifty-four dollars at one time. What do you do with it? He slept.

They polished and burnished and buffed and oiled and straightened and marched with eleven other platoons onto the parade ground to the music of the post band and lined up across the field from the reviewing officers. While the band played "Under the Double Eagle" and the "Washington Post March" over and over, the platoons took their turns marching in review. At the end the senior reviewing officer hooted that Platoon Fifty-three was honor platoon for the day. Platoon Fifty-three! Bunch of red necks from Georgia! Just because they did that fancy twirl with their rifles at port arms as they passed the brass. Bunch of mush-mouths you can't even understand!

Platoon Fifty marched back to the hut area and Rose halted them, took them to "order arms" and then "rest."

Corporal McHugh stood behind and to one side of Rose as the DI looked at them and started to pace back and forth. The platoon was used to the pacing, and it usually preceded an outburst. Well, hell, they'd tried, and just because they didn't do some fancy "twirl arms" crap was no reason to dump on them. And anyway they were going to Virginia tomorrow. Rose stopped and rocked back on his heels, rolled up on his toes and assumed "parade rest."

"I oughta be mad at you people for letting a bunch of yahoos from Georgia beat you out for honor platoon today. But I got thinking about it and I said to myself: 'Why, shit, all those punks can do is march. They can't think. They can't shoot. They only been honor platoon once, been saving it up for today. It don't mean anything.' "

Platoon Sergeant George Daniel Rose started to pace again.

"You people been honor platoon six weeks out of ten. No platoon ever done that before. You people shoot good... nineteen experts and one near-goddam-possible, and twenty-two sharpshooters. No platoon done that before, either. You looked sharp most of the time and took all the crap that McHugh and I could hand out without beating your gums. (Chuckles.) Couple of you may have even learned something."

He stopped in front of O'Reilly. "Some of you can't stick your belly out as far as you could when you was pretending to be me." (Laughter.) "And all of you are going to find out what being responsible for the other guy is like once you get to Quantico." He looked down at the deck and then back up. "I been proud to serve with you here and I'd be proud to serve with you again." (Cheers!)

"AT EASE! Belay that. Nobody told you to pipe up!"

He glowered and paced again.

"Corporal McHugh will take over now and get you to quartermaster stores, where you will turn in your weapons and the gear you're not taking with you. Corporal, dismiss the platoon and have 'em round up their stuff."

McHugh called the platoon to attention, admonished them to have their gear ready in fifteen minutes and dismissed them. As they ran to the huts Rose stopped Wallace and said: "Follow me."

What the hell? thought Wallace and followed Rose into the DI's hut and stood at attention. Rose went to his locker and rummaged in it and came out with a clean, folded, starched China khaki shirt and field scarf. He handed them to Ian and said: "These are for you. Wear 'em with care, and when some old salt says you're too young to have 'em and where did you get 'em, you tell him that they were given to you by Platoon Sergeant George Daniel Rose and Master Gunnery Sergeant Edward Ruditis."

Badness you can get easily, in quantity.
The road is smooth, and it lies close by.
But in front of excellence the immortal gods have put sweat,
and long and steep is the way to it, and rough at first.
But when you come to the top, then it is easy, even though it is hard.

— Hesiod
Works and Days

QUANTICO 1943

FIX, PERRY AND WALLACE COMMANDEERED two facing seats in the squalid day coach that took them from South Carolina to Quantico. Fix had a window seat facing forward and Wallace was on the aisle. Perry sat across from them, facing to the rear with Fix's and Ian's feet on either side of him. The train swayed and lurched when they were under way, regardless of the speed. And whenever another train passed on the southbound tracks, the windows of their car were almost blasted out. The first time Fix jumped a foot.

"Fight me for the window seat, will you?" said Wallace. "Serves you right."

"Hope you enjoy the elbows and butts in your face when these guys try to maneuver back and forth to the head," Fix said.

Fix was right. They dozed intermittently through the night, waking each time the train stopped, usually in the middle of nowhere it seemed, and Wallace was bumped and battered all night long. It did no good to complain, for the men could not help being thrown from side to side as the car threatened to leave the tracks. Conversation was impossible. They were served no chow. Wallace napped off and on and wondered what Quantico would be like. Would there be more opportunity to take advantage of his experience and education? He understood that there would be much more classroom work in addition to many more field exercises than had been the case at Parris Island. At boot camp they tried to beat the individuality out of you and beat Marine mythology into you. It seemed to work on most boots, though Wallace felt that a lot of the crap they had to take had been silly. He took it simply to prove he could and to finish as high up in the platoon as he could. He guessed he'd do the same at Quantico but wondered how eight years of French language study, ancient and modern history, Elizabethan drama, music, geology, comparative religion, Bible study, Psychology 101 and his philosophy major would help. Maybe he'd get to apply a little trigonometry. He was certainly going to get closer to the earth than he'd ever been in his geology courses.

The train pulled into Quantico at 6:30 A.M., and they off-loaded and marched to their new homes... brick barracks.

The Virginia scenery differed drastically from P.I. They could see the Potomac, and there were lawns and paved streets and hills and "normal" trees. And a lot of "school troops," who would oppose them during field problems, strutted around looking salty and tough. There was an NCO club directly across from C Barracks where O'Reilly, Perry and Wallace were assigned, but the club was off limits to them. And up the hill behind the rows of brick barracks was the Waller Building, an old stucco-covered, mansard-roofed Victorian structure that housed the Officers' Club and BOQ (bachelor officers' quarters). To the north end of the base was the Post Theater and the Post Exchange, and running down toward the river to the east was a street of civilian shops and small eateries. Sutlers' Row, Wallace called it, after the peddlers who sold goods and food to the troops in wars of the eighteenth and nineteenth centuries.

After drawing weapons and gear they went to C Barracks to stow their stuff. The M1s were wrapped in pinkish-brown paper (Fix called it butcher's paper... "Ugh," said Ian) and stiff with Cosmoline, a petroleum-based preservative that had to be cleaned off with rags or by such other method as they could devise. A couple of the candidates were obviously knowledgeable about this process, having been enlisted men previously, and made reasonable suggestions. Without solvents it was a filthy and time consuming job, but Ian guessed it must be teaching them something.

They had steel helmets now, and field transport packs and web equipment, bayonets, first aid pouches and real go-to-meeting shoes, low-quarter ones that were expected to shine... put your eye out when you looked at them. They heard about the legendary Marine Corps "spit shine." Old soft skivvy shirt and Kiwi polish, son; never touch 'em with a brush. Some of the smart money finished the shine with an application of Aqua Velva or Skin Bracer. Hardens the polish they said. No question but it made the feet smell better. Wallace, O'Reilly and Perry were the only candidates from Parris Island in their squad. The rest of the group came from San Diego and were clannish. One of them, a man named Lewis, kept talking about the "tolerances" on his M1's action, sliding the bolt back and forth. Ian didn't know what tolerances were unless possibly they were what he harbored for people with whom he did not agree. Their squad was First Squad, First Platoon, C Company. Ian was squad leader because of his height.

Their squad bay was on the second deck of C Barracks, first one to the right at the head of the ladder. The NCOs who ran the company, three corporals, had a room of their own. Each corporal was responsible for one of the three platoons in the company, and they rotated command when the day's activity involved the entire company. Unless it was a parade or parade ground inspection, and then First Lieutenant Hynes took over. Captain Davis was the senior officer at the barracks but usually was busy doing administrative work in his second deck office at the rear of the barracks, overlooking the company street.

The candidates wore greens at all times except for physical drill and field exercises. A step up in the world. Dressed in their greens they assembled after their first evening chow for some advice from Captain Davis. Standing at ease in formation on the company street they listened to him.

"You won't find this place like P.I. or Dago," he stated, "because we're going to put a lot more on your backs here than you ever thought was possible when you were in boot camp. Those of you who are mustangs (former NCOs) stand just as much of a chance of not finishing as any of these exboots. You don't make it here, you go to a rifle company at Camp LeJeune as a buck-ass private in the rear rank.

"We expect you to do as you are ordered. There will be no harassment. You are expected to behave the way an officer candidate should. But let me tell you that if you don't measure up you will pay for it. We expect you to put your head into the classroom work and your muscle into the field work. If you think it's tough here, wait 'til you get to the islands.

"If you need to speak to me or any of your officers you will respectfully request an audience through your platoon corporal.

"NCOs, take over!"

They were dismissed and went back in the barracks. Corporal Mark Ryan, First Platoon NCO came into the squad bay, and the squad stood awkwardly at attention.

More advice: "You people listen to what I say, because I won't say things twice. You call me 'Corporal,' not 'Sir,' and there's no need to spring to attention or shout it out when I come around because I'll be in and out of here all the time. You keep your gear stowed properly and the bay policed so I don't have to hand out any punishment or restrictions, and you'll get along all right. You'll find the training schedule on the bulletin board at the top of the ladder, along with post regulations and the word on uniform of the day. Don't believe all the dope you hear at the scuttlebutt (drinking fountain). Check the bulletin board every day. Reveille's at oh-five-twenty-five, and you will fall in on the company street at oh-five-thirty for roll call. Word on equipment is on the board."

He turned on his heel and went to the next squad bay to confound and please his listeners with a repeat of the same litany he had just recited. How many times, thought Wallace, has he done that and how many more times will he do it? Ian and Fix went to the bulletin board and saw that they were to fall out dressed in boondockers, dungaree trousers, skivvy shirts and rifles at 0530 not only tomorrow morning but every morning except Sundays.

The board further noted that they would receive weapons training on mortars, both 80mm and 61mm, machine-guns, M1917 cal .30 (heavy), M1919A4 cal .30 (light), the air-cooled M2 cal .50, the M3 37mm antitank gun, Browning automatic rifle M1918A2 caliber .30, 3.5-inch antitank rocket and the Mk II fragmentation hand grenade. Days devoted to the various weapons were noted as were days for inspections (at least weekly), classroom hours for study of "Tactics of the Squad In the Attack," map reading, topographical features, command theory and on and on. There were also two weeks toward the end of the schedule on which "Three Day War" and "Seven Day War" were listed.

"I guess that's when we fight the school troops," Fix said.

"Maybe," answered Ian, "but the scuttlebutt is that school troops can attack or infiltrate on any field exercise, so maybe we shouldn't take anything for granted."

"It sure as hell looks like a heavier schedule than we had at P.I.," Fix said.

"No tougher than Dago," boasted Dick Lewis, the tolerance man, who had been reading over their shoulders. "Easier. Look at that. Liberty every Saturday noon but one. Don't have to be back 'til last call Sunday. That's not so tough."

"O.K.," said Fix, "if it's so easy I'll appreciate all the help you can hand out."

"Well then, here's the word on going ashore," Lewis advised. "You got to present yourself to the corporal before liberty and show him a clean shirt and field scarf to wear on the next duty day, and you got to show him a pack of rubbers. They're to wear when you're on liberty."

"Condoms?" Wallace asked.

"What the hell you think I mean? Overshoes? For Christ's sake!" Lewis stormed away.

"It's obvious that Corporal Ryan doesn't trust Catholic abstinence or Protestant prudery," said Fix.

"And he doesn't approve of any of his charges coming down with a bad cold in the pants," said Ian. "So watch yourself."

"And best wishes to you, too," said O'Reilly.

Physical drill every morning was torture. It was twice as long as they were used to, and they ran a good deal farther than they were prepared for. Mostly uphill and at high port. They exercised at a parade ground on the hill behind the Waller Building, and Corporal Ryan was tough on them. Fix nicknamed him Torquemada.

"Who the hell is Torquemada," asked Perry, breathless.

"He was a Dominican monk, head of the inquisition in Spain," said Ian.

"You ain't Catholic," said Fix. "How the hell'd you know that?"

"Unlike so many of my Catholic friends," said Ian, "I can read."

The run downhill to the barracks was just as fatiguing as the run up. They were exhausted when they got back to the barracks. And the day had not yet really begun.

Trying to stay awake in class became a major challenge, and Ian forced himself to concentrate on what was being said. He took notes, unlike most of the other candidates, and as he re-read them they seemed to make sense from a practical point of view. Cover versus concealment. Topographical crest versus military crest. Enfilading fire. Hand signals. Field sanitation. Rates of fire. Maximum effective ranges. Effective radii of bursts. Troop intervals under fire. First aid. Platoon frontages in the attack and on defense. Supporting weapons. And of course the marvelous VD film in full color.

This sure was different from P.I. mused Ian. *Alors, autre temps, autre moeurs.*

"I was really studying to join the diplomatic corps, not the Marine Corps," said Fix as they sat on their bunks at the end of a long, long day. "Takes all I can do to be diplomatic with that damn Corporal Ryan, though. Wouldn't you think another Irishman would treat a kinsman with a little more care and concern?"

"He's no tougher on you than on anybody else," said Perry. "He's unreachable."

"Were you really planning a career in the State Department?" asked Ian.

"You bet," said Fix. "My old man is a career civil servant in the Commerce Department, and I certainly don't want to wind up like that in spite of the good pension he'll get. And State sounds great. I've got some friends who took the exams and say they're not too tough. A couple of the guys are already posted, and their letters are pretty enthusiastic. I guess I'm going to see the world through a rear sight, though. What were you going to be, Perry?"

"Dad's in the stock brokerage business. Commutes from Patchogue to New York. Went to Princeton. So did I. Not much imagination, I guess. Thought I'd follow him into his business. Hope I get to do it. What about you, Ian?" asked Perry.

"I've lived on a farm with my mother and grandfather, and while I enjoyed the country and being out of doors and in the woods, I've had a hankering to be a minister since serious study in college. A practical minister. Not some smooth-talking preacher who takes tea with the ladies, but somebody who could be of real help to people. Not a missionary overseas but maybe a missionary among the young. Help keep 'em from going off the deep end. Stuff a little of the Puritan ethic in 'em while I'm young enough to be listened to."

"How do you reconcile the Marine Corps with the ministry, for God's sake?" asked Perry.

"It's difficult," Ian replied, "but I feel compelled to help defend what's right. I couldn't and wouldn't ask for deferment as a junior in college hoping to go to theological seminary. So I wanted to be among the best, and here I am."

"What about 'thou shalt not kill?' " asked O'Reilly.

"I think about it a lot, and it bothers me. I thought about it on the range, but that was targets and doing as well as you could. Bayonet practice really gets me... all the yelling and grunting. Somehow close-range stuff seems worse than the impersonal long-range shelling or bombing. I don't know. I'm pretty simplistic about it, I guess.... 'Render therefore to Caesar the things that are Caesar's, and to God the things that are God's.' "

"I still don't see how you can reconcile the two," said Perry.

"I can't," said Wallace. "I live with what the psychologists call cognitive dissonance and do the best I know how."

Lying in his bunk that night after taps Ian wondered what he'd do when the time came for him to test himself, to squeeze the trigger, to pull the lanyard, to throw the grenade. He'd better do as well as he could in Candidates Class and ROC so his choice of duty would be most favorably looked upon. Most of the new second lieutenants would become platoon leaders in one of the new Marine divisions. And second lieutenants and tent pegs were expendable. If he was to serve his country, as well as his somewhat diluted conscience, he'd have to apply himself as hard as he ever had and call up all his competitive resources. They had served him well at school and at P.I.

Tomorrow the platoon was off on a three-day exercise. Better sleep.

They left after morning chow. Steel helmets, dungarees, boondockers, cartridge belts and rifles, combat packs, ponchos, shelter halves. They had dried rations and C-rations in their packs and a canteen of water to last them for the whole seventeen miles it would take them to get to their bivouac area. Water discipline was to be enforced.

The first few miles took them west on the paved entrance road until they reached Triangle, Virginia, on route U.S. 1. They fell out for five minutes on the west side of the road before heading off into the boondocks. The March weather was damp but cool, and at route step they moved pretty well for the first few hours, Corporal Ryan in the lead. After the third five-minute rest, Ryan told them they were only doing about two and a half miles an hour and at that rate wouldn't reach their objective before next week. He said they'd be stepping out some now, so keep closed up and watch your step. Lots of roots and rocks. And keep your eyes peeled for school troops. Don't want to be "ambushed." Two men were designated as point men and the platoon took off at a killing pace.

At each stop they put out perimeter guards and changed the point men. They did not stop to eat. Eat when we get there, Ryan said.

A slow misting rain started and dripped off the back of their helmets and down their necks. They reversed their rifles at sling arms, butts up, muzzles down to keep the bores dry. And their feet got wet and they started to blister. Several men dropped out and were left where they fell. Ryan told them to change their socks and catch up. The rain grew heavier and the sky darker as they trudged on. No sense stopping to sit in the wet, Ryan told them, so they pushed on without rest.

After five and a half hours the point men signaled stop, and Ryan sprinted up to them. The three peered over a rise, and Ryan turned back toward the platoon and signaled "down." The men sank to the mud and waited, glad for the rest even in the muck. Shortly Ryan returned.

"School troop patrol out there, reconnoitering our bivouac area. Gone now, so we'll go on in and set up camp. The smoking lamp is out until we find out just where those troops are," said Ryan. "Tobacco smoke smell carries in the rain. Come on."

They found as much concealment as they could, put up their shelter halves, ditched them to keep the running ground water out, dug slit trenches, posted perimeter guards and ate cold C-rations.

Wallace and O'Reilly put their shelter halves together and had just crawled in when Ryan appeared. "Wallace, you got guard duty from twenty- to twenty-four hundred. O'Reilly, you're on from midnight to oh-four-hundred."

Lousy assignments, but at least they'd each have the tiny tent alone for four hours.

Wallace put on his gear and his poncho, relieved the west guard and began to patrol his sector of the bivouac area. He thought that this was playing at cowboys and Indians, but he knew he'd feel silly if he screwed up. At one point Ryan scared the hell out of him by appearing silently and then telling him to keep more alert. He also told him he'd sent three men back to pick up the stragglers and guide them to the bivouac and to watch out for them. Then he vanished. He's good, thought Ian. Well, so am I. I've spent enough nights in the woods stalking game to know what I'm doing. So he trod more carefully, avoiding branches and keeping his poncho from snagging and his helmet from crashing into low limbs. Every few paces he stopped to listen.

Slight breeze from the northwest. Dripping rain. He moved again.

In the second hour, chilled to the bone, feet soaked, he stopped to listen and thought he heard an alien sound. He held his breath and strained to listen. Movement. More than one person. He heard muffled groans, curses. He slipped to where he would intercept them and stood behind a large oak. He heard Perry whisper to the men, and Ian stepped out, identifying himself in a hoarse voice. Perry jumped and said: "Jesus!"

"You got them all?" asked Wallace.

"Only three of them. That's all there were. They're in bad shape."

"Bivouac's that way," Ian said, pointing. "Keep those people quiet. I heard you way back."

"Lucky the school troops didn't hear us," said Perry.

"Did you see 'em?"

"Yeah, about a mile back we could smell wood smoke, and then we saw a fire. They were cooking something under a tent fly. Too hungry to hear us or come after us."

"Tell me about hungry!" said Wallace. "How many of them do you think there were?"

"About ten, I'd guess. And just as wet as we are."

"That doesn't mean much," said Wallace. "Keep your eyes peeled. You've only got about three hundred yards to go."

Perry led his men off, trying to be stealthy and doing badly. Well, thought Ian, Ryan will know they're coming anyhow. He continued his patrol, stopping to listen frequently. Something caused him to stand rooted to one spot, He couldn't hear anything different, but something was amiss. He lifted his head, turned it this way and that, checked out of the corners of his eyes for night movement. Then he knew what had made him stand so still. He smelled wood smoke. Not smoke, really, but clothes that had been in the smoke. He slipped off his helmet, slid out of his poncho and covered his rifle on the ground with it. On his hands and knees he silently followed the smell upwind. He paused.

Movement to his right. He saw what he thought was a smooth lump next to a small fir and watched it. It became a man, and it slithered forward on its belly. When the man was opposite Wallace, Ian landed on the man's back with both knees whooshing the breath out him, and grabbing him by the throat with one hand, pulling his head roughly back with the other.

"You make one sound and I'll break your neck."

Ian tore off the man's knitted cap and stuffed it in the man's mouth. Still kneeling on him he took off his victim's belt and strapped the man's arms behind him, tightly, above the elbows. He found cord that the man had been carrying and rigged a hobble at the man's ankles and made him stand. The man's trousers fell to his feet. Didn't need the hobble, thought Ian.

Wallace looked at his wrist watch. The radium dial showed him he had a half hour to go. He tied the man to a tree and waited.

He wondered if his prisoner had come alone or if there were more. He listened. Should be hearing Fix coming to relieve him pretty soon. He heard noise behind him and turned. He could dimly make out his catch straining at his cords. Wallace crept up to him and gave him just enough rifle butt in the belly to produce a startled grunt. Then he waved his index in front of the man's eyes. No, no.

At 0015 Wallace had not yet been relieved. He'd patrolled his sector carefully, checking his prisoner, tightening the ropes. The man's bare legs were shaking, and his trousers lay about his feet wicking up moisture from the ground and collecting what fell from the sky and from tree limbs. Every time Ian stopped to check, he waved his finger in front of the man's eyes. No, no. And made a threatening gesture with his rifle butt.

He had to relieve his bladder urgently and gave momentary consideration to pee-ing down the man's leg to prevent any noise. Would warm up the poor bastard, too. In more ways than one. He settled for a tree and hoped no more surprises would happen while he was busy, with his fly open. His stream was silent. It steamed.

At 0045 Ian was more and more concerned. Where the hell was Fix? Had the whole outfit pulled out? No. He'd have heard them. But you don't leave your post until relieved, so he carried on. Several times he thought he heard movement in the brush. Each time he stayed as silent as the grave, but nothing happened. After each such false alarm he checked his prisoner. Still there. Ian finally pulled up the man's pants and tied them around his waist with the last of the cord. The man was shaking violently.

I better get relieved pretty damned soon or I'll have a corpse on my hands, Ian thought.

At about 0115 Corporal Ryan materialized out of the dark and hissed at Wallace:

"What the hell you doing here?"

"Waiting to be relieved." said Wallace.

"What do you mean? Where's O'Reilly?"

"That's what I'd like to know," answered Ian.

"Well, for Christ's sake, he's not in his tent. Hasn't been for over an hour!"

"Maybe some school troops caught him. They've been around and I caught one."

"You're shittin' me!" said Ryan. "Where?"

"Right about here. I tied him to a tree."

"Show me."

When they got there Ryan inspected the man. "Don't recognize him. But we better get him into some blankets or the shit will hit the fan. You stay on your post, and I'll take him in and send you a relief. Oh, are those salty bastards going to be pissed off! They get gold stars for bringing in candidates, but they don't lose their own. Haven't while I've been here. Maybe we can engineer a trade for O'Reilly. Hot shit!"

Wallace was relieved by Dick Lewis about 0145. He hoped Lewis had tolerance for this kind of cold, wet work. Ian stole back to his shelter half and crawled in. It was a mare's nest. There'd obviously been a struggle. He crawled back out and found Ryan and the prisoner, who was wrapped in blankets, under a pine tree. It seemed they'd had a belt of something for their breath reeked. Ryan noticed Wallace sniffing and said, "Keep your mouth shut. I'm trying to keep him alive."

Wallace told the corporal about the signs of struggle and wondered aloud if there was an interior guard at the bivouac in addition to the perimeter guard.

"You'll have your chance to make constructive suggestions in the morning. Beat it. Hit the sack."

In the morning the weather was clear and the platoon moved to a demonstration area. There the school troops, who were about a thousand yards across open fields in the shelter of some woods, debouched and gave a demonstration of the platoon in the attack, leap-frogging from one position to another under covering fire. Their use of concealment was astonishing. Lieutenant Hynes, who had obviously spent the night in a nice warm sack, lectured them on what they were observing. He kept slapping his starched dungaree trousers with his swagger stick. Perry asked Ian if he thought Hynes had ever killed anybody with that toothpick.

Perry, Lewis and Wallace talked at the smoking break about what had happened to Fix. When Ryan had reported to Hynes that morning he had said the platoon was "all present or accounted for, sir." The three men wondered if the corporal knew something about O'Reilly's whereabouts that he had not shared with the men.

They had cold C-rations for chow at 1100, and then Ryan called them into a semi-circle. Seated on the ground, they answered questions from the corporal about what they had seen that morning. As soon as Hynes disappeared Ryan asked about the night before. What had the troops learned. There were lots of good comments, and Wallace again brought up the matter of interior guard. Ryan glared at him and asked if he had any other comments he'd like to offer. Not knowing enough to keep his mouth shut, Wallace suggested that maybe it would be a good idea to have passwords and also some signals for use in identifying troops in the dark.

"We'll get to that!" snorted Ryan and led them off to the afternoon's exercise.

"He's sore at you," said Perry as they slogged back to their bivouac site after a strenuous afternoon. "He had you doing all the grunt work on that exercise. Maybe you'd better be less quick with suggestions."

"Was I wrong?" asked Wallace.

"No, your ideas seemed pretty right, but it wasn't so right to make 'em in public. Ryan thinks you're trying to show him up."

That night they used a password and had an interior guard. Wallace drew that duty from midnight to 0400. He thought about what he'd learned on the exercise, and it all seemed militarily sound. He wasn't too sure what he'd learned about dealing with touchy noncoms.

When he got back to his shelter half, Fix was in it, asleep. Ian shook him. "Where did you come from?"

"Lewis and Perry snuck into the school troops area and found me about 0200. Brought me back, and my rifle, and reported the fact to Corporal Ryan. He tells us we're all on report. Me for being caught, and them for leaving the area without permission. I wouldn't be surprised if he doesn't have something in mind for you, too."

"Well, it's good you're back. Are you O.K.?"

"Just a bum ankle. But you better watch out. Ryan thinks you fouled up either by being in cahoots with Dick and John or by letting them get out without being seen or reported missing."

Wallace had trouble sleeping. He thought he'd done his best. Maybe he'd better roll with things a little.

In the morning Corporal Ryan told Ian he was on report with the others and would get no weekend liberty. In addition, since Fix, with his bad ankle, was going back to the barracks in the supply truck, Wallace would carry Fix's rifle as well as his own on the seventeen-mile hike back to Quantico. That's another 8.94 pounds, thought Ian. Why can't it go back in the truck with O'Reilly? But he was getting smarter and didn't ask.

Back in the company office Ryan lost no time in telling the officers that he had a school troop prisoner and that he had put four of his men on report. The captain, who had been around for a time and seen his share of noncoms, congratulated Ryan and told him to take the prisoner over to school troop barracks, get a receipt for him, watch his own back and on the way out send in the four men on report.

Lewis, Perry, O'Reilly and Wallace, three of them muddy, sweaty and soaked from the rain that followed them for the last six miles of their return hike, stood at dripping attention before the captain. Lieutenant Hynes stood behind the captain, who was seated at his desk.

"How come you got captured, O'Reilly?" asked the captain.

"Sir, first thing I knew two men had me gagged and blindfolded and my hands tied behind me, right in the tent."

"Who had been assigned to interior guard duty?" asked Hynes.

Silence. The men looked out of the corners of their eyes at each other.

"Well?"

Here I go again, thought Wallace. "Sir, there was no interior guard assignment. Maybe because of the rain it was figured no one would try to infiltrate. I was perimeter guard, though."

"So somebody got through, right?"

"Yes, sir," said Wallace. "But not all of them."

"I understand that. One of them was caught. Do you know who did that?"

"Wallace did, sir," said Fix.

The captain switched his glance back to Wallace. "How did you know it wasn't one of your own men? Didn't he have the password?"

Silence.

"Well?"

Perry spoke up: "We had no password, sir."

Lieutenant Hynes raised his eyebrows as the captain continued, addressing himself to Ian: "How did you know it wasn't one of your own men?"

"Sir," said Wallace, "I could smell him. His clothes were full of wood smoke. We'd had no fires, and Candidate Perry, sir, had told me after he came back from picking up our drop-outs that he'd seen school troops gathered around a cook fire under a tent fly. Told me that when he passed through my guard-post, sir."

"Ah," said the captain. "And you two decided to rescue your pal without permission, the next night?"

"Yes, sir," the men said together.

"Were interior guards posted that night?" asked Lieutenant Hynes.

"Sir," said Wallace, "I was interior guard from midnight to zero-four-hundred. When I was relieved O'Reilly was back in the tent. I didn't see anybody leave or return to the bivouac, sir."

"How come?"

"Sir, no excuses. I think I was more worried about people getting into the area than I was about people getting out. Being the only guard made it difficult to patrol the entire bivouac."

"That's an excuse, but we'll let it go," said Captain Davis. "Any more questions, Lieutenant?"

"Yes, sir," said Hynes. "Wallace, were you carrying two rifles when I saw the platoon in the company street just before you were dismissed?"

"Yes, sir."

"Who's was the second piece?"

"It was mine, sir," said O'Reilly.

"How come it wasn't in the truck with you?"

"Sir, I was ordered to leave it behind."

Lieutenant Hynes looked at Captain Davis and said: "That's all, sir."

"You men are dismissed. Go get cleaned up."

"Yes, sir," the four men said, about-faced and marched out.

"What do you think, Jim?" Davis asked his lieutenant.

"Sir, I think those four look like pretty good men. They showed initiative. They performed well under bad conditions in their first field exercise.

They seemed reluctant to point fingers at anybody. They were in a tough situation here, and I think they did well."

"I agree," said the captain. "Anything else?"

"Captain Davis, I think it is time I took Corporal Mark Ryan by the stacking swivel and had a chat with him."

"I agree. You'll make a good officer yet."

Following the Monday-through-Wednesday field problem the rest of the week was spent in physical drill, double-time, classroom work, policing the barracks and weapons study. The sun came out on Thursday, and by Friday when they were outdoors at the machine-gun range the earth was becoming dry and dusty again. Dragging the .30 caliber heavy MGs from one position to another raised a cloud of dust. It got in their eyes, their noses, their throats, their guns.

Nonetheless, they fired, made sure the cleats and jamming handles were secure and didn't rattle loose from the impact of firing. They cursed, spat, hollered and grunted and were surprised. John Perry, who didn't qualify on the rifle range at P.I., was a genius with the fully automatic guns. His touch was light on the triggers. He couldn't miss. When it was his turn to fire the last course of the day Perry finished up by firing *"down in the barn yard, bay rum"* with his last seven shots.

A range gunnery sergeant came strolling up. "Who's the smart-ass musician?" he demanded.

"I fired last," said Perry.

"You put time in a machine-gun company somewhere? Do I know you?"

"No, sergeant, I don't think so. I'm new here."

"Well, kid, you done good and anybody can play the trigger like that is what we're looking for."

Perry had visions of lugging over one hundred pounds of barrel, tripod, water can and a two-hundred-fifty-round belt of ammunition for the rest of his career in the Corps. He looked at the sergeant and said: "Thanks for the good word, but I'm hoping to qualify for flight school."

"Shit," said the gunnery sergeant. "Then break down that gun and get it back to the armory." He turned and marched down the line.

"When he asked if he didn't know you from somewhere," said Wallace as the two men struggled with the heavy weapon, "why didn't you say maybe it was at Princeton?"

Saturday morning was parade ground inspection. Uniform of the day: greens, shined low-cuts, fore-and-aft hats, cartridge belts, name tags. They stood at rest in the hot spring sun after marching a mile to the parade field. Each man was making sure his weapon was in perfect condition. Some of them had blackened their front sights. All of them had cleaned the bore and lightly oiled it, oiled and polished the stock, checked the action for smoothness and were worried about sand getting into the serrations on the butt plate. Ian was using his little toothbrush head to clean off the plate as he watched Lieutenant Hynes and Captain Davis at the head of the line waiting for Lieutenant Colonel Hume who, with a lieutenant from B Company, was finishing his inspection of that company's third platoon. Hume, thought Ian, and wondered if he was a descendant of David Hume, the eighteenth-century British philosopher. He remembered Hume's "The most lively thought is still inferior to the dullest sensation."

This Hume didn't look like a dull sensation by any stretch of the imagination. He was short and stocky and barrel-chested with a bulldog jaw into which he stuffed a short pipe after he returned Hynes's salute and stood talking with him. And rows of campaign ribbons.

Hume knocked out his pipe, jammed it in his left breast blouse pocket and nodded to Hynes to lead on. Hynes called the platoon, already at open ranks, to attention. Ian was caught short as he quickly tried to put away his toothbrush head in his own blouse pocket, and just managed to come to attention with the rest of the men.

Corporal Ryan joined Davis, Hynes and Hume, with his notebook and a glare in his eye that said "don't screw up!" Hynes brought the first squad to inspection arms and Wallace as squad leader was first to be checked. Lieutenant Colonel Hume stopped directly in front of Ian and with a lightening-like motion brought up his right arm. Ian left the rifle floating in mid-air just as Hume's big hand snatched it away. The inspecting officer twirled the rifle, checked the front sight, looked at the butt plate, put his thumb in the receiver to reflect light up the bore (God, keep that action open and the bolt from smashing Hume's thumb, prayed Ian) and squinted down the barrel. He twirled the rifle again and hurled it at Wallace who brought his hands up just in time to grasp the weapon by the balance and the small of the stock. Just like it says in the book. Wallace felt better. Hume stood in front of him and looked him up and down. His eyes stopped at Ian's breast. His nostrils dilated. He scowled. He looked at Ian's name tag.

"Wallace," he growled, "button that pocket!"

Holding the balance of the rifle firmly in his left hand, Ian released his grip on the small of the stock with his right hand and reached out and buttoned Lieutenant Colonel Hume's left breast pocket, where he had stuffed his pipe. Wallace saw Lieutenant Hynes's shoulders stiffen, Captain Davis shake his head and Corporal Ryan's eyes roll out of sight.

Without changing his expression Lieutenant Colonel Hume reached out with his right hand and buttoned Wallace's left breast pocket where he had jammed his toothbrush. He looked directly into Ian's eyes (was that a twinkle?) and sidestepped smartly to the next man. Ian saw Ryan writing furiously in his notebook. Before the inspection was over they heard a rifle clatter to the deck. Some poor slob had bad reaction time, back in the second section. He'd be spending his weekend at the barracks, too. And sleeping with his rifle.

When inspection of the platoon was completed and Lieutenant Colonel Hume and Captain Davis had moved to the next unit, Hynes and Ryan marched back to front and center of their men. Hynes spoke: "Some of you men behaved like you'd never been to boot camp." He looked at Wallace and at someone else in the second section. "You should have done better. Corporal, take these people back to barracks and read 'em the riot act!"

Hynes strode off.

Corporal Ryan shouted: "Close ranks... Harch!... Dress right... Dress!... Ready... Front! Layouf Face! Right shoulder... Harms! Forward... Harch! Awn hup areep hup y'layouf."

He marched them not along the macadam road to the barracks but across the parade ground to a dirt track that led away from where the men desperately wanted to be: by their lockers getting ready to go ashore. The dust started to rise immediately. It coated their shoes, shined for inspection and liberty. It collected on their greens, their sweaty skin and clung to the oil on and in their rifles. It filled their noses and throats.

After about half a mile the dirt track joined the paved road. Ryan, leading the platoon, only had dust on his shoes. The rest of him was still shipshape. He led the men to the company street behind the barracks, halted them, gave them "left face" and left them at attention, scowled at them, then ordered "rest."

As Ryan was pulling out his notebook Wallace cleared his dusty throat and spat the muck to one side. Immediately the second floor window in the company office flew open and Captain Davis leaned out, hands on the window sill, and shouted: "Corporal! Get me the name of that man who spat in ranks!"

"Sir!" said Ryan, and ordered the platoon to attention. Then he ordered "open ranks" and yelled: "That man what spat in ranks! One pace forward... Harch!"

The entire platoon took one step to the front. The office window slammed and Corporal Ryan started to rant: "Think you're so smart do you! I'll show you who's smart! All of you, not just those of you who are on report and restricted, will fall out and go to the second deck and be ready for inspection by the bunk in fifteen minutes! Clean clothes! Clean rifles! Shined shoes! No one goes ashore until they pass my personal inspection! Fall out!"

The men busted their way through the door and up the ladder, bitching and moaning about missing the train to D.C., being late for their dates, and what a prick Ryan was. And how do you get to be a son of a bitch like Davis? Go to Harvard.

Wallace stopped at the scuttlebutt, rinsed out his mouth and took a long swig of water. When he stood up Corporal Ryan was glaring at him. "You just spit in the scuttlebutt! I seen you! You spit in the scuttlebutt! You're on report again and you just lost next weekend, too! Get outa here and get ready for inspection!"

By 1300 all the candidates except the "Four Musketeers," as they now called themselves, and the man who had dropped his rifle, were on liberty. Lewis and Perry were swabbing decks, and Fix and Ian had been given the filthy job of shining the tin buckets that all the candidates used every day for cleaning the decks. The pails were crusted with grime, old wax, dried soap. If they had been cleaned in the last ten years Fix said he'd eat his hat with a salad fork. There were forty buckets to be worked on. Plenty of yellow soap and bales of steel wool. Wallace suggested that they'd need their bayonets to gouge off some of the accumulated crap on the pails, so they collected them, gathered up the work and moved into the shower room. There, sitting in their skivvy drawers and little else they began to work. Shined! The damned buckets were black!

It took over an hour to get a couple of buckets looking half way decent.

The damned things were dented and bent. The steel wool wouldn't get into the crevices and the bayonets could only scrape off just so much of the guck. Their knuckles were bleeding. They took a break for a minute, and just then Corporal Ryan stuck his head in the shower room and shouted: "Who told you people to stop? You keep going on them buckets until every one of 'em is done. You don't leave the barracks or do nothing except go to mess until you've finished!"

He walked on down the hallway to the company office and Fix said: "He's the kind of a shit who gives shit a bad name!" Grumbling, they went back to work. Fix wondered aloud what the guys on liberty would be doing about now. Making contacts. Scouting and patrolling. Visiting the slop chutes. "Marines don't pay for it, you know," he said.

"Pay for what?" asked Ian.

"Why, you dumb jerk, they don't pay for anything… if they're smart. First beer's on the house, then somebody picks up the tab for the next, and then, if you're smart, you move to the next saloon. And at night, if you've made the right contacts, you should come up with a free sack and somebody to share it with." He raised his eyebrows.

"Great!" said Ian. "But what about museums and galleries and the public buildings and monuments?"

"Jesus H. Christ, may God forgive me, but you are something else. How are you going to spend your time if you ever get any liberty?"

"There's a girl I used to know at Smith College who is working at the Navy Department, and I expect to see her. And see all the sights. And forget this sort of chicken-shit business for a few hours anyway. I suppose we'll go out some, but the slop chutes aren't where I think I'd take her."

"Well, I guess that makes sense. But don't get too much of a reputation as a Christer. Better hell around a bit with the guys," Fix recommended.

They heard the company office door close and looked up as Corporal Ryan poked his head in the shower room. "Fuck you," he said. "Fuck the both of you!" And he stomped off to the NCOs' quarters.

When Fix and Ian quit at about 1700 to clean up for chow, they had done a passable job on fifteen buckets. Their knuckles looked like hamburger. Their finger tips were raw. As they turned the corner toward the squad bay they saw Ryan backing out of the NCO room dragging his footlocker with his sea bag over his shoulder. He pretended not to see them as he hoisted his locker with both hands and struggled down the ladder to the first deck and out the barracks door.

"Holy shit," said Fix. "What's that all about?"

"Beats me," replied Ian. "Looks like he's going somewhere for good."

"You bet it's 'for good,' " said Fix. "If it hadn't been for that bum, you and I and Lewis and Perry would be sopping 'em up in D.C. right now."

"Newton's Third Law of Motion," said Wallace.

"You bet!" said O'Reilly. "He sure as hell is in motion now!"

Lewis and Perry called Ian and Fix "The Bucket Brigade." They called Perry and Lewis "Swab Jockeys." All four of them were finished mopping and polishing by late Sunday afternoon and sat talking about their preferred duty once they had been commissioned and completed Reserve Officers Class.

"I want to fly," said Perry. "That was no hokum I handed the machine-gun sergeant the other day. I figure if I can do well enough here to get my first choice of duty, that's what I'll put in for."

"The broads will flip over those gold wings," said Fix. "Keep 'em away from your joy stick!"

"Har, har," said Perry.

"*God,* Fix!" said Ian.

"A little levity never hurt anyone," said O'Reilly. "Me, I'm gonna put in for sea duty. Sea School at Norfolk Navy Yard. Assignment to a capital ship. Sleep on sheets every night. Three square meals a day! Going to get me on one of those big new Essex class carriers."

"You'll do nothing but throw swabbies in the brig and serve as court recorder in courts martial," said Lewis.

"Beats eating mud and ducking every time somebody farts," Fix retorted. "What're you going to put in for?"

Lewis thought for a moment. Then he said: "If you don't specify what your preference is they send you to LeJeune to a rifle company, most likely. With the new divisions forming they're probably going to send us all to rifle companies regardless of what we list as duty preferences. So I'll probably ask for a rifle company assignment, since I'm sure to be sent there anyway. Make some points that way."

They all looked at Wallace. "I don't know," he said. "This up-close killing bothers the hell out of me, even though I know it's no more reprehensible than long-distance killing. Somehow I'd feel detached from it if I could pull the lanyard on an artillery piece or fly a fighter plane. Or even serve on a battleship. I'll probably put in for flight training, then sea duty, and to prove I'm not chicken I'll put in for a rifle company. But you've got to score almost four-oh in everything to get your choice of duty. And us Four Musketeers are making a lousy start."

Ian and Fix were showering as some of the men started to return from liberty. A couple of candidates came into the showers and were boasting about their conquests. They looked pretty well dragged out, and Fix and Ian kidded them. A third man joined them in the showers but didn't enter the banter. He seemed to be more interested in careful inspection of his private parts.

Fix began to sing:

> *A night in June,*
> *A big red moon,*
> *A girl all dressed in yellow.*
> *Two ruby lips,*
> *Two snow-white tits,*
> *And oh, what a lucky fellow.*
> *But now, alas*
> *Ten days have passed.*
> *His joy has turned to sorrow.*
> *Two pimples pink*
> *Upon his dink*
> *And there'll be more tomorrow.*

The guy laughed, snapped a wet towel at Fix's crotch and sprinted down the hall.

In the sack Wallace wondered what was happening to him. He hoped he was absorbing something useful other than weaponry and tactics. What was he learning about himself, his peers and his superiors? Don't be too quick to judge a man... he was pretty sure about that. Be careful who you ridicule, if ridicule you must. Open your mouth to superiors only when you have to or when it is clearly to your advantage... this is not a debating society. And continue to do the best you can without being aloof or an ass-kisser. Joke around with the guys a little more. Do I really want flight training or sea school, or is it because I think my chances are better? When did I say my prayers last...?

The platoon fell out for roll call Monday morning, shivering in their skivvy shirts and wondering who would be the NCO in charge. They heard the other outfits going through their ritual, the count-off by each squad and the squad leader reports to the NCO in charge. What the hell was happening to First Platoon, C Company? Was somebody looking through the office window to see what they'd do without leadership? Testing them? They heard the other platoons double-time to physical drill and stood quietly at rest, craning their necks from time to time to see what might be happening.

In a couple of minutes the rear barracks door opened and out came a man in dungaree trousers and skivvy shirt, no rifle, but carrying a clipboard. He looked familiar to Ian. The man stopped, facing them with his feet set apart, hands behind his back, clipboard under his arm.

"Good morning. I am Corporal Thomas Shadwell and, as of this morning, your platoon NCO. I have spent most of the night going over your file jackets and feel I know something about each of you. The good and the bad. My suggestion is to do what I say, don't screw up and we'll get along."

They must teach all of them that speech at instructor's school, Wallace thought. Shadwell sure as hell looked familiar.

"We'll continue with the regular training schedule, and don't expect it to be any easier because I'm new to you. In fact it'll probably be tougher, because I am a real believer in physical fitness. If your body can't do what you ask of it then your mind starts telling you things it shouldn't. We're not going to let that happen. I'm confident that we'll get along because I have been with this platoon before and know some of you intimately." He looked directly at Ian.

Wallace squinted. My God! That's the guy I captured in the boondocks just last week! Oh baby, we're in for it now.

That was the morning they learned to do the duck-walk with their rifles extended over their heads.

As the spring weather warmed up the men sweated not only during physical drill under arms but in all the field exercises and in the classrooms as well. Most classes were held in Quonset huts that the sun turned into ovens. All written tests were done in pencil. Ink would run from the sweat on their hands. Fix said it was probably a good thing they weren't commissioned yet, because then they'd be gentlemen by act of congress, and gentlemen aren't supposed to sweat. Wallace always marveled at one particular instructor. He was a light colonel and he would pace back and forth while lecturing from the dais. It must have been hotter up there than down on the benches, but the man never showed a trace of perspiration. His field scarf never wilted. No dark stains showed at his armpits or down the back of his shirt. He didn't have to wipe his face with a handkerchief to keep the sweat from his eyes. He'd been wounded on the Canal, and Perry surmised that when the man had been given a transfusion it had been ice-water instead of blood. Wallace thought Perry was probably right. The man wore a perpetual scowl.

And Corporal Thomas Shadwell wasn't a bunch of smiles either. But he sweated. When he led physical drill he exercised along with the men. When they went in the field he was with them on the hikes, not riding to their destination in a jeep the way some instructors did. And he got them in good shape. Wallace thought he was in pretty good shape before he went to Parris Island but found out he was wrong. And here at Quantico, again, he learned that there's always room for improvement. O'Reilly's belly was now flat and hard and all of them had legs and lungs that would take them for miles.

They lugged mortar tubes, base plates, cloverleafs of mortar ammunition; they dug fox holes and trenches; they "attacked" uphill; they did night azimuth problems; they paraded; they carried reels of heavy communication wire; they fired every weapon used by a Marine rifle company; they were fired over by 75s and 105s so they could learn the peculiar sound of shells passing overhead; they hunkered down in holes while tanks drove directly over them. And then they went on weekend liberty and raised hell.

Wallace had made his connection with the girl from Smith. Her name was Irene Gregg, a tall blonde girl with green eyes who had been his date at glee club concerts. She and five other girls lived in a rented red-brick house on Mount Pleasant Street in the northwest part of Washington. The house was easy to get to—you took the Mount Pleasant trolley car and got off on the corner of the block. Wallace enjoyed the ride from downtown, especially after the train ride on the RF&P. The northbound train was crowded when they got on it, and then when it stopped at Fort Belvoir, Army engineers would shoehorn themselves aboard. By the time the short ride to D.C. was ended they were usually hot and rumpled and tired of standing. But the trolley ride was quiet. There must have been rubber liners on the wheels, and the suspension was soft and the acceleration quick and smooth. Wallace had only been on trolleys twice before... once on the cross-town Forty-second Street line in New York, where on one summer visit he rode in an open car that had wicker seats running fore and aft and facing outboard. Another time the family had gone to Pittsfield, and his grandfather had given him a ride on the Berkshire Street Railway, a noisy Toonerville Trolley kind of conveyance with an enormous cowcatcher on each end.

These Washington machines were modern marvels. And the fare was a lot better than taking a cab, if you could get one.

He'd prepared for his first liberty by phoning Irene to see if they could have a Saturday date. She'd said sure, and why didn't he spend the night instead of trying to get a hotel room or sleeping in some lobby. Ian didn't know what "spend the night" meant, but couldn't believe that something indecent was involved. Irene's background and upbringing were much the same as his, and he was sure the suggestion was innocent. But he didn't tell Fix or the guys about it. He simply said he had a date.

They joked and kidded about their plans for the weekend and boasted about the conquests they planned to make. They agreed that if they couldn't get together for drinks Saturday night at the Statler bar, they'd certainly get together for the train ride back to Quantico.

Wallace continued to be amazed at the casual way sex was regarded, or said to be regarded, by most of the men. At college Ian had only heard of perhaps two or three people who claimed to have really done it. Plenty of necking and some petting, but for Pete's sake you had to get the girls back to the dorm by ten P.M. But most of his friends at school, and the few girls he had met, had been reared and nurtured on the same traditional values. Nice girls didn't, and good men saved it for the wedding night.

But still he fretted. He asked Lewis whether, now that Shadwell was in charge, the regulation about passing a personal inspection with a clean shirt and field scarf and a condom was necessary before going ashore. Lewis assured him it was. Well, thought Ian, this will be a new experience and took himself off to the PX.

He stood by the cash register at the cigarette counter where they had told him the rubbers were sold and waited for a clerk. Shortly a Pfc appeared and said, "Whaddya want, kid?"

"I'm going ashore," said Ian, more than a little self-conscious.

"Good for you," said the Pfc. "What do you want?"

Pretty obviously this guy wasn't going to be any help so Ian blurted out, "I want some condoms."

The Pfc clerk looked at the blushing candidate and then scanned the PX for the clerk the farthest away.

"Hey! Podbielniak!" he shouted to a sergeant at the top of his lungs, effectively silencing all the other Marines at the counter who turned to stare. "Where do we keep the rubbers?"

"What does he need?" shouted Podbielniak. "Small, medium or large?"

"Whaddya say, kid?" asked the clerk.

Ian was nonplused. "Assorted," he said.

Wallace got so that he looked forward more and more each week to his visits to Mount Pleasant Street. The girls were all attractive and quick. They all worked for government departments. They all had boy friends on a fairly steady basis. Ian guessed he was Irene's regular guy. The other girls paid little attention to him except for a tall, freckled redhead named Diana Bliss, whom he would catch looking at him from time to time. Each Sunday evening he'd ask Irene, "Next weekend?" and she would smile yes. They made a sort of bunk for Ian on the third floor in the laundry room. There were two laundry tubs with wooden lids that were almost long enough to accommodate his frame when he stretched out, and Irene provided him with a blanket and a pillow. He had to share the toilet on the second floor with the girls, and that was dicey sometimes, but he soon got used to the flimsy things that hung over the shower rail and the mysterious jars, bottles and boxes that cluttered the room. He got an extra razor, toothbrush and comb at Peoples Drug Store on the corner and kept them on the shelf in the laundry room.

Occasionally he would bump into some other man on the first floor Sunday mornings who had slept on the sofa. He guessed that the girls kept the second floor for themselves, he had the third floor and the transients got what was left. The girls jokingly called their house "The Gayety" after the famed Minsky burlesque house in New York. It was anything but that.

Wallace and Irene did most of the sightseeing he'd hoped for. The Capitol, the White House (seen through the iron fence), the Monument, Lincoln Memorial, Smithsonian and the Washington Cathedral. They never ran into any of Ian's friends.

They usually cooked at the Gayety on Saturday nights, listened to good music and had an occasional drink. In the warm evening they would sit in the one chair on the little front porch, Irene in his lap. He was learning how to mix a drink that Irene liked to sip... equal parts of bourbon whiskey and dry sherry. It seemed awfully strong to Wallace, but it sure felt good going down, and when it made that little warm explosion in his belly he liked the feeling. He decided to name the drink after the egg-laying mash he had fed the Rhode Island Red hens on the farm: Lay-or-Bust. Irene thought that was wicked and loved it. Sometimes sitting on the porch Irene would put her arm around his neck and put her face against his. That frequently made him uncomfortable, and he'd squirm and hope she didn't notice.

Sunday they sometimes went to church, but always read the paper and tried to do the crossword puzzle. It was a relaxing escape from the pressure of training.

"What did you do this weekend?" Perry asked Ian.

"Played house," he answered.

"Jesus, not again! Don't you ever do anything?"

"The only wild thing he's ever done," said Lewis, "is to read *Captain Billy's Whiz Bang*!"

"Well, what did you do, Lewis?" asked Wallace.

"Perfect weekend. Had a steak. Got drunk. Got laid. And phoned my mother."

Wallace thought about that in bed and decided that he and Irene had better see some of the other guys next weekend. He hoped they wouldn't be with the girls they'd been talking about. Fix called his friend the "Saber Lady." Lewis was squiring some gal with the nickname of "Black Banana." Perry seemed to find someone new each Saturday.

He phoned Irene about a get-together with his friends and warned her about who might show up. She told him to stop being protective and that she thought it sounded like fun. Wallace lined up the guys and they all agreed to meet at Mount Pleasant Street at about 1600 on Saturday afternoon, with dates.

The week was a hot and difficult one. They were taken to loading areas and shown how to climb down rope netting into landing craft, Higgins boats. The Potomac was calm but the boats were unsteady. Two guys fell from the nets, one onto a Higgins, and one into the water between the Higgins and the bulkhead. He lost his rifle, his pack and his helmet. And a lot of points with his platoon leader. Fortunately he'd had his helmet and pack straps loose so he wasn't decapitated or dragged to the bottom. They made him dive for his gear and though the air was hot, the Potomac was icy and he damned near passed out. The man who fell into the boat suffered a concussion and was taken to the base hospital.

The next day they ran what Corporal Shadwell described as the "varsity obstacle course." In full gear and against a stop watch. There were rope climbs, wall scalings, stream crossings, pop-up targets, hidden machine-guns, simulated shelling (real explosions... TNT Ian supposed) with dirt and smoke, dugouts to be cleaned out, trip wires and mines. At the end they crawled on their bellies under barbed wire while live machine-gun fire cut the air over their heads. Wallace noticed wooden safety stops below which the gun muzzles could not be lowered. But then, all it would take is for some jerk to put his head up. Or his tail.

Shadwell said the platoon did well. Everybody finished in good time. And now we'll take a little hike out into the boondocks. After about ten miles they came to their bivouac area, and they had to dig in and post guards. They were to be part of a night exercise, between 1900 and 2200 hours. They went to the demonstration field as it was getting dark. The platoon sat on a sloping rise overlooking a field several hundred yards across. There were woods on the other side.

An officer explained to them that the first demonstration would be night noises and they were to identify them. He said the noises would be made about five hundred yards to their front. The men sat in silence. They heard an unmistakable liquid rushing sound. "Someone is taking a piss!" Right. They were told do it down a tree or your rifle or anything but not directly on the ground. Shadwell looked at Wallace with a frown.

They heard metal against metal. "Somebody's fixing bayonets!" Right. You gotta be careful doing that.

They heard a sliding click. "Rifle bolt closing." Right. Now watch.

They saw a small orange flame, then two indistinct blurs, the flame disappeared and they saw two remaining red glowing points. "Two guys lit cigarettes on one match!" Right. And you could see them at five hundred yards!

"Now watch." They heard a hissing pop and a magnesium flare burst over the middle of the field. "What do you see?"

"Dirt, shell holes, stumps, barbed wire entanglements."

"O.K. Watch again, but don't look at the flare; you'll lose what little night vision you've got left."

Another hissing pop and brilliant white light. Same tableau. The officer blew his whistle, and out of the field rose a full squad of school troops, plainly visible now that they were moving and with their faces unshielded from the flare. "Remember that. Head down and don't move."

"All right," said Shadwell, "it's our turn. On your bellies and crawl across that field. By squad, three minutes apart. I don't want to see any of you when the lights go on! I'll meet you at the edge of the woods. First squad! Get with it!'

It was slow, hot, dirty work. They felt naked every time a flare went off. Some men slid into water-filled shell holes and had to stay there when they heard the hiss-pop. But they all made it O.K. except for Wallace, who tore his leg on some wire, though that didn't hold him up.

They got back to bivouac, and Shadwell told Wallace he had perimeter guard duty from midnight to 0400. "You're good at that," he said.

Ian broke open his first aid kit, bandaged his leg and went on guard. Long day, Buster, he told himself, but don't you go to sleep. He should have focused all his attention on his sector, but he found himself thinking about Irene. Such a pretty girl. Blonde, green eyes, good figure, good family, smart, quick-witted. And she liked him. And she liked most of the things he liked. He thought she'd probably like him to be a little more forward, but he didn't feel it was right to get into the heavy stuff, because that could mean commitments and possible disappointments. And who knows where I'll be in three months, he thought.

He was startled by a small sound and slid behind a tree. A man was stealthily coming past him. As the man passed Ian stepped behind him and put the muzzle of his rifle in the middle of the man's back. "Halt!" he hissed. "Who goes there?"

"Shadwell. Corporal Thomas Shadwell."

"Turn around and be recognized."

Shadwell turned around.

"I'm still pretty good at it," said Ian.

Wednesday they hiked back to their barracks, arriving just before noon. Shadwell told them to fall out and get cleaned up for chow—clean dungarees and fore-and-aft hats—and be in the company street in five minutes. After chow they marched to the "gas chamber" for gas mask drill. They were instructed in how to wear their masks and the dangers of removing them while gas was still present and quizzed on the various identifying characteristics of the different gasses. Wallace doubted they'd encounter gas attacks in the field, though there had been some talk of use of gas by the Japanese in China. They learned that mustard gas smelled like garlic, horseradish or mustard. Phosgene like musty hay (how many city boys would that help?). Chlorpicrin like anise or fly paper and caused severe coughing, crying and vomiting. They were advised that it was poor form, and quite probably fatal, to puke in your mask. Chlorine was highly pungent and a big killer in the First War.

After they'd been lectured on no fewer than sixteen chemical agents, they were herded into a large, one-floor wooden building with rough wooden benches. A practical demonstration, they were told. You will be shut up in this building and you will put on your masks, by command. You will then be gassed. You will sit here until you are told to remove your masks. Is that clear?

The doors closed, and a loud speaker ordered them to don their masks. The masks were hot and difficult to breathe in. Ian could feel the sweat start immediately on his forehead under the mask. His eye-pieces started to fog. Am I getting a little bit panicky, he wondered. No, they're not going to kill us. But he noticed faces looking in at all the viewing ports. He heard no "gas" sounds but noticed that wherever he was perspiring he started to sting. Other guys were looking at each other and making hand gestures. One man started to stand up in panic, but Ian put his arm out and restrained him. After an eternity the loudspeaker came on and told them the doors would open. As soon as the doors were open they were to remove their masks and then leave the building. A bell sounded, the doors opened, the men removed their masks and gasped. They room was still full of gas!

They gasped, choked, wept, held their breath and knocked each other down to escape and fell coughing and retching on the ground outside.

The gas officer walked up and down in front of them. "There's always a great temptation to remove those goddam uncomfortable things, especially when you're advancing at double-time in the attack or doing other physical exertion. But don't you do it until you know the gas has dissipated or are shown it has. That stuff you just got dosed with was only tear gas. The effects are temporary and pretty harmless. Remember this little exercise the next time you want to be a smart ass and take off your mask. Is that clear?"

"Yes, sir!"

They marched back to the barracks and Shadwell told them "field day," police up the squad bays and be ready for inspection, junk on the bunk, wearing greens in fifteen minutes.

In the sack that night Wallace wondered how it could only be Wednesday evening. My God! Two and a half more days to go before liberty. That is if he didn't screw up. He'd learned some things, he knew he had. He'd learned he could do things he never thought he could have done. He'd learned he could do them about as well as anybody else. That did something to his pride. Was that a sin? He noticed that the whole platoon was tougher, prouder, and daring Shadwell to try something else.

Thursday they fell out after morning chow in dungarees, boondockers, cartridge belts with ponchos folded over the back, steel helmets and no rifles. They were marched to parade ground number two where they stood at ease in the warming sun for about ten minutes, when trucks started to arrive. Trucks! "The Marine Corps doesn't have any trucks! The Army's got the trucks! All the Corps has got is mules and they're for carryin' 75mm pack howitzers! Who's goin' to ride in those things?"

Corporal Shadwell had to show them how to clamber aboard by the numbers, and then they were off down dusty roads for over an hour. The men in the trucks at the tail of the column were caked and crusted with gray dirt when they arrived at a hillside clearing in the forest. Must be about twenty acres, Ian guessed. On the far side there were trees shattered by shell fire. There appeared to have been some burning, too. Between the platoon and the trees were a number of tank hulks, shell holes and blasted concertina wire.

They off-loaded and sat on the deck while an officer explained to them that they would now see the effects of the 3.5 bazooka rocket on tanks, of white phosphorus (Willy Peter) shells on troops and of machine-gun fire on wire.

They could hear the first WP shells coming in and watched in horrified fascination as the rounds burst in the trees and showered down sprays of white smoke filled with burning phosphorus that started fires immediately in the trees and on the ground. If the WP touches the skin there's no way to put it out. They watched soberly as the fires burned.

A sergeant of school troops and a loader set themselves up with a bazooka as the officer explained that the head of the rocket round was a "shaped charge," which concentrated the explosive force to such an extent that the steel armor plating of the tank melted and sent lethal needles of hot steel into the interior of the tank. "We'll put some meat in the tank so you can see what happens," said the officer.

A Pfc walked out to the tanks, dodging shell holes and wire, threw a couple of live chickens into each hulk and slammed the hatch covers. The rockets were basically noiseless when fired and sounded unique when they exploded. The first round hit a bogie on the right-hand tank and blew it off. The next round hit the pock-marked turret and left a new hole. The left-hand tank got the same treatment.

"You people," said Corporal Shadwell, "will go out and inspect those tanks and see what those rounds can do. Wallace, take the first squad."

Ian reached the right-hand tank first, climbed up and uncleated the hatch. He opened it and was assailed by the reek of explosive, hot metal and the remains of previous platoons of chickens. He looked down the hatch and saw guts, feathers, blood and one chicken still flopping. He hung down the hatch by his waist and grabbed the fowl, stood up, wrung what was left of its neck and threw it back in the tank. He turned around and said, "Next," and saw that the squad stood motionless, staring at him. "Come on," he said, "let's go!" and jumped to the ground. They clambered up the tank for a look while Ian wiped the blood from his hands on what grass he could find. He led them back to the edge of the clearing and Shadwell asked, "What were you doing leaning into the tank?"

"Gave one of the birds the coup de grâce," said Wallace.

"Why bother?" asked the corporal. "He'd have croaked soon enough."

"Might make some of the guys puke to see him flopping around in the mess and feathers. All that tank needs is a helping of vomit sitting there in the hot sun, and you'll have a different kind of demonstration on your hands."

O'Reilly looked at Perry and said, "Did you see what that guy did? He wrung that bloody chickens neck! Would you do that?"

"No, I'm not sure I could. And Wallace is the guy who talks about his distaste for close-in killing."

"Well," said Lewis, "he comes from a farm and maybe he's used to it."

Fix said, "I think he'd rather the bird was dead than have it wounded and mutilated and squawking. Still I couldn't have done it."

"Hey," announced Lewis, "we got us a new nickname for Wallace… how about 'Wringer'?"

They slapped knees and laughed and made puns about bell ringers, ringer athletes and wringers that grandma's tit got caught in, and pretty soon the whole platoon was roaring.

"Knock it off," shouted Shadwell, and they did. But the folklore was firmly planted and the name stuck. And when people asked about Wallace's nickname, the story seemed to generate new respect for him.

After the platoon had watched .30 caliber MG rounds chew up some concertina wire strung by school troops, they scrambled back on the trucks. Another dusty trip took them to an area where there had obviously been a lot of explosive activity. A clearing in the woods again, and they were led into a wide, deep trench. If they stood on the fire-step they could see over the parapet, and twenty to thirty yards away the ground was all chewed up. An officer stood at ground level behind the trench. He wore a First Division patch on his shoulder, a Guadalcanal veteran.

"I'm going to teach you about grenades," he said. "Hand grenades. They are lethal and dangerous and not to be fucked around with, so you pay strict attention to what I've got to say. This is the MK II fragmentation grenade." He held one up for them to see. He ran through the nomenclature of the weapon, the effective range and burst radius, how to pull the pin (not with your teeth) and release the handle. He recommended releasing the handle before throwing and counting for two seconds, then throwing. With this procedure there would be no time for an enemy to throw the grenade back.

"And that's what you have to do," he said, "if one lands near you. You can't run fast enough to get away. One of those fifty-two serrated iron parts will catch you in the sweetbreads and they'll send your mother a gold star for the window. Pick it up and throw it back. If you can't reach it, fall flat. Is that clear?"

"Yes, sir!"

With dummy grenades he demonstrated how to throw the thing. Not an overhand baseball throw. The grenade weighed one and a quarter pounds, and you could dislocate something if you didn't treat it right. They all practiced with dummy grenades from the trench and got the hang of it quickly. They climbed out of the trench, and after they had retrieved the dummies they were told they would throw live grenades after noon chow.

The after-chow exercise was pretty exciting. While the other squads were in defilade behind the trench, each squad would get its turn to throw live fragmentation grenades, one man at a time. The men hunkered down in the trench and watched each other. They heard the muffled cough of the explosions and the clatter of fragments in the trees. They saw guys shaking in anticipation as they let the handle fly off, heard the fuse start and waited to throw it. The officer was right there with them, and after a couple of near mistakes he herded Wallace's squad into a bunker and brought them out one by one. "We'll lose fewer men that way," he said dryly.

After everyone had thrown the live grenades to the satisfaction of the officer, he assembled them in the trench and paced back and forth on the rear parapet as he spoke to them. He reminded them again of the dangers associated with grenades of any kind: lob, don't throw, pitch it back or lay flat, let the handle fly off before you toss it. As he was talking he carried a fragmentation grenade in one hand and would shake it at the men to make his points. Finally he stopped pacing and stood at the lip of the trench, and as he talked he pulled the pin from the grenade. The men looked at each other and shifted uncomfortably. The officer continued talking but nobody heard him as they watched his hands. Suddenly, the officer let the handle fly off, fell to the ground and dropped the smoking grenade in the trench right in front of Francis Xavier O'Reilly, who bolted and in the process knocked over Ian as he was trying to reach the bomb. Some of the men ducked into the bunker, plenty tried to run and the others fell flat. Lewis got to the grenade and just as he was picking it up it went off. With a weak pop. No fragments. No coughing explosion.

The officer was back on his feet on the parapet, and he really chewed them out. "Half of you would have been dog meat if I hadn't poured the powder out of that thing. What you heard was just the detonator going off... if you heard anything. Don't you ever forget this exercise. Is that clear?"

"Yes, sir!"

"Corporal Shadwell," the officer called, and Shadwell climbed out of the bunker where he had put himself in anticipation of the exercise and stood beside the officer.

"Most of the men behaved pretty well. A couple of them tried to pitch it back... that man, and that one. A couple tried to run and a lot of them fell flat. And if my nose doesn't deceive me some others may have a different problem."

Wallace sniffed and could smell it, too. He looked around and saw Fix's face, redder than usual. Francis Xavier O'Reilly had shit his pants.

They made Fix and two other men with the same problem go off in the woods and clean up, but it didn't help much. The officer said, "Don't laugh at those men. It happens to the best of us. It's happened to me. And now you understand why you are advised to keep a tight asshole in combat.... particularly leading troops. Carry on."

They climbed back into the trucks and made sure that Fix and his two new friends would sit at the tail-gate with their butts in the breeze on the long ride back.

The rest of the men gabbed and chattered about the day. "I'm all for these trucks," Lewis said. "Getting places by shanks' mare has just about worn me out."

"Don't get too used to 'em," Ian cautioned. "Trucks are for dogfaces."

"Yeah," countered Perry, "just like all those great pieces of equipment we see in the training films. Tanks, trucks, jeeps, half-tracks and bazookas. We'll never see another bazooka. The Army gets 'em all. And hole-diggers, for Christ's sake! Only the Army has to call 'em something else that sounds more military. Automatic earth augers, for Christ's sake! For digging holes for barbed wire fence poles. I'll be lucky to have an entrenching tool. Jesus!" He spat over the side of the truck.

Wallace hit the sack right after evening class and tried to read. The light was lousy, but he dug out his *Soldier's Bible* and riffled the pages. He didn't know whether reading it would make him more confused or not. The pages fell open at the book of Leviticus, God's "Rocks and Shoals"—God's boot camp, thought Ian. An awful lot of dos and don'ts, and "unclean until the evens." Ian thought about the distressing nocturnal problems he occasionally had and presumed the other men did too. If they all lived by God's law as put down in the Third Book of Moses, there would be a great deal more bathing of bodies and garments and feeling unclean until "the even." Wallace didn't feel unclean and wondered if he should. Just nature doing its thing. He wondered if nature did its thing to Him. Probably not. Probably the only thing He ever did was pee through it.

What kind of thoughts were these! Tired thoughts. He flipped to Ecclesiastes. *"Rejoice, O young man, in thy youth; and let thy heart cheer thee in the days of thy youth, and walk in the ways of thine heart and the sight of thine eyes."* That's better, Wallace thought. He put the book back in his locker.

The bulletin board proclaimed that they would go to demolition school, in the field, on Friday. After extra-strenuous physical drill under arms they had chow and then clambered back into trucks for a ride to the boondocks. "Save that special seat for Fix," somebody said, and they all laughed.

The demolition range had bleachers on which they sat while the instructors lectured them on explosives in general and TNT in particular. They learned that dynamite was relatively unstable and that handling it too long could give you the great-grandfather of a headache. TNT, on the other hand, was very stable and could be handled easily. You needed a blasting cap or detonator to make it explode. A hundred yards from the men, on a stump, was a stick of dynamite and a quarter-pound block of TNT. An instructor with an M1 put on his sling and assumed the prone firing position. Looking back over his shoulder he said, "I'm going to hit the TNT first, then the dynamite. Watch."

He swiveled his head around, put the stock to his cheek and slowly squeezed off one round. The TNT block turned into a cloud of white dust. No explosion. The instructor shifted his position slightly and squeezed off the second round. There was an enormous explosion of noise, flame, smoke, dirt and wood. When the wind had blown away the smoke, the stump was gone.

Proper procedure and safe technique were demonstrated. The men learned about hellboxes, caps and a wonderful rope-like product called Primacord. Its chemical name was pentaerythritoltetranitrate. Wallace thought that was some word. It had an explosive speed of ninety thousand feet per second, and you could take down a tree with it. They practiced handling the caps with care, inserting them in the pre-cast hole in the quarter-pound blocks and wiring them to the hellbox, and then, to let everyone know that something was going off, they yelled the time-honored warning of the dynamiter: "Fire in the hole!"

After noon chow they blew some rough-timber structures apart, dropped a small bridge, leveled some trees (that would be used to rebuild the structures and bridge) and linked up twenty blocks with Primacord over a quarter-mile stretch of ground. A blasting cap was crimped to the end of the cord, and the wires run to the hellbox in a fox hole. As the platoon watched, the instructor twisted the hellbox handle and the universe was filled with noise, the ground shook and smoke, flame and debris shot sky-ward. It was very impressive.

"Wow!" said Fix, "what that would do to a pillbox!"

"Or anything else!" said Perry.

Lewis looked at Fix. "You're not in trouble again, are you?"

O'Reilly smiled at Lewis. "Up your gigi with a wire-haired cookie pusher, sideways," he said.

The platoon got back to the barracks about 1500, and Shadwell ran them through another "field day" before the evening meal. Inspection tomorrow, he reminded them, and for those who didn't fuck up there would be liberty. Wallace worried about what would happen at the Gayety when all the gang and their girls got there. He hoped liberty wouldn't turn into license.

Saturday morning inspection went off without a hitch, and the Musketeers stowed their gear and went to report to Shadwell with their clean shirts, field scarves and condoms. Wallace quickly shined his shoes to get off the parade ground dust before he went to Corporal Shadwell's quarters. He stood before the corporal while Shadwell checked out Ian's uniform, haircut and clean clothes. He squinted at the condom. "I'll bet you haven't used one. I bet it's the same one you brought in here the first time."

"This is my money-maker, Corporal."

"Whaddya mean, your money-maker?" asked Shadwell.

"I rent it out to the rest of the squad before they go on liberty."

"Get out!" said Shadwell, "and don't forget to go to the clap shack when you get back!"

Fly down, Death:
Call me:
I have become a lost name.

— Muriel Rukeyser
Madboy's Song

WASHINGTON 1943

IN SPITE OF IAN'S MISGIVINGS and a number of indiscretions, the party went very well. Wallace picked up some Senate beer on the way to Mount Pleasant Street and put the bottles and cans in a large tin wash tub with ice. He tied the church key (beer opener) to the tub handle with stout twine and made sure there were some empty corrugated boxes in which to throw the cans and bottles. He didn't want to spend Sunday morning policing the house.

Irene and Diana were already there when he arrived, and they said the other gals would be coming soon with their dates. Irene said she'd asked a guy from her office at the Navy Department to join them. It bothered Ian that he felt disturbed by this piece of news. What the hell was going on? Well, anyway it should be a good time. Diana said her date was "iffy"; he might catch the duty at the Pentagon, and she hadn't heard whether he was coming or not.

Around 1530 Fix arrived with his date, the Saber Lady, a gorgeous black-haired WAVE petty officer whom he introduced by her nickname, which didn't seem to bother her at all. Lewis showed up next with the Black Banana, who was a civilian, and some beer and introduced her as Mary O'Connor. She was short and lithe, blue eyed and blonde, and said she worked at State.

Irene told them all to come in and take off their coats or sweaters and help themselves to beer in the kitchen at the back of the house.

Diana put some swing records on the Victrola, and some of the couples were dancing in the living room by the time John Perry arrived. His gal was a tall, shy type whose clothing and demeanor shouted breeding and class. Irene took to her right away and led them off to the kitchen for refreshment. Perry's date was named Dorcas, and she drank some white wine that Perry had brought.

By 1700 all of the Gayety girls and their dates, assorted civilians and Army officer types, had arrived, as had Irene's "associate" from the Navy Department. He turned out to be a six-foot lieutenant junior grade in the Navy, his blue uniform decorated with a row of ribbons, one of which carried two battle stars. No one seemed to mind that the crowd was mixed enlisted and officers, and Ian marveled at the fact there were so many people from so many different backgrounds and parts of the country getting along so well. He doubted that he would ever have met many of these people had not the circumstance of war thrown them together at this particular time and place.

Wallace knew the party was working when he noticed that Dorcas, Perry's date, had taken her shoes off and that Irene's Navy guy had removed his blouse with its ribbons. A couple of trips to the corner replenished the beer, and then Fix said he knew a place where he could get some steaks and disappeared with the Saber Lady. Diana's date called to say he was stuck with the duty, and since Irene and the Navy were on the back porch enjoying the sunset, Ian asked Diana to dance.

Diana put her beer next to Ian's Lay-or-Bust on the mantelpiece and they danced slowly to Jimmie Lunceford's "Mood Indigo." Wallace started to talk, but Diana pressed close and put her cheek next to Ian's and breathed on his ear. Too close for comfort, thought Ian, and broke away a little only to have Diana swing right back in. He was on his second drink and felt warmly relaxed, so danced the way she wanted even though he was embarrassed.

Fix came back with an enormous bag of groceries, steaks, chips, rolls, tomatoes and the fixings, and before long a galley party was organized to fix the chow. Irene came up to Wallace and put her arm through his and asked for another Lay-or-Bust that he got for her. Her Navy friend sauntered over, and the three of them talked. Navy was named L. J. (Lonesome) Pine, a reservist product of the V-7 program at Virginia. He had a soft Southern accent and had served in the gunnery department on the U.S.S. *South Dakota*. He was now working for ONI (Office of Naval Intelligence). He was so smooth and polished that Wallace was uncomfortable with him. He could see that Irene was entranced. He went to get another Lay-or-Bust and overheard Perry saying to O'Reilly, "No wonder we don't see Wallace 'til he gets back Sunday nights."

"Sure beats the hell out of the slop chutes," said Fix.

"Chow down!" shouted a self-styled Army officer cook; the grub was passed around and people found themselves places at tables or on the floor. Wallace wound up on the deck in the square front entry hall next to the up-right piano. Lewis and the Black Banana sat on the piano bench and put their plates on the keyboard cover. Diana was on the floor across the hall. Irene and Lonesome Pine must have been someplace else.

When Dick Lewis finished his plate he asked the Banana to please get him a beer, lifted the keyboard lid and ran his fingers through a gifted arpeggio on the piano.

"Wow!" said Ian. "Come on and play us something!"

The Banana handed Lewis his beer. He took a slug, closed his eyes and accompanied himself as he sang a hillbilly tune called "The Box in the Baggage Car Ahead." Everybody roared approval, and he followed up with "That Little Old Letter Edged In Black."

"Hey, how about something we can all sing?" shouted Fix. Lewis played "Empty Saddles in the Old Corral" while everybody sang, and Ian caught Diana looking at him as he sang, *Where do you ride tonight?*" He looked away.

By now everyone had drifted into the hall and was sitting on the deck or leaning in the doorways. The space was filled with bodies, beer, cigarette smoke and music. Requests were shouted and songs were sung. Dead soldiers were passed overhead to the kitchen, and new drinks returned by the same route.

To the tune of "Bless 'Em All" the Marines sang: *"They sent for MacArthur to come to Tulagi, but Douglas MacArthur said no. He said there's a reason, this isn't the season. Besides, there is no USO!"* Then they told the story of Gunnery Sergeant Lou Diamond, who had dropped a mortar round down the stack of a Japanese destroyer, and to the same tune sang *"They say that the mortar's a very fine gun, oh what a story to tell. The barrel is rusted, the base plate is busted, the damn thing will blow you to hell."*

Faint-hearted applause from the Army, who contributed "One-Balled Reilly," and at that some of the couples drifted back to the kitchen and the back porch.

"Come on, Navy," said Lewis and relinquished his seat on the piano bench to Lonesome Pine who accompanied himself as he sang: *"The Captain he rides in a motorboat, the Admiral rides in a barge. It don't go a goddam bit faster, but it makes the old bastard feel large."* Much laughter. He then started a solo on: *"A capital ship for an ocean trip was a walloping window blind."* And Wallace climbed onto the bench with him, and they finished together: *"I'm off to my love with the boxing gloves, ten thousand miles away."*

"Know any limericks?" asked Pine.

"A few," Ian conceded.

"Tell you what," Pine suggested, "I'll start one, and if you can't finish it you owe me a nickel. If you can finish it you get to start one, and if I can't finish it I owe you a nickel. What do you think?"

Ian, who by now had put away more drink than he was used to, thought it was a reasonable challenge, and they began. This process cleaned out a few more couples, but the hardier ones stayed on and regaled themselves at the contest. The anatomical limericks came first and the two men stayed pretty even. Then Ian, remembering his night with the Episcopal priests, got started on excesses of the clergy and quickly took a substantial lead. Pine came back strong with some pretty ripe geographical stuff that left Ian in the dust and owing the Navy $1.20, at a nickel apiece.

Their throats were dry and their bladders were full, and the songfest broke up into small groups, dancing, shooting the breeze or disappearing. Some gal forgot to lock the bathroom door, and two guys busted in hoping to pee and found her sitting startled on the seat. Fix went out in the back garden to "kill weeds" as he put it and proceeded to pee on a couple who had stretched out on the ground for a breather. Feeling woozy, Wallace went to the third floor to stretch out for a minute and found the laundry door closed and locked. He went back to the first floor and out onto the front porch and breathed deeply to clear his head.

Couples were leaving, and Ian was astonished to see that it was 0100 Sunday morning. He turned to go search for Irene and bumped into Dorcas and Perry on their way out. Her ankle-strap shoes were buckled together and hung around her neck, and she was helping support Perry. "Loved your limericks," she said. "Simply loved them."

"Where are you going?" asked Ian. "There're no cabs around."

"Oh, a short walk. I've got an apartment over on Meridian Place. About four blocks. The air will do him good."

As they talked, Fix and the Saber Lady, Dick Lewis and the Banana joined them on the porch.

"Hey, Wringer," said Fix, "great party!"

"How about that piano player?" Ian said, pointing at Lewis, who actually blushed.

"And that limerick contest was something!" said Lewis.

"I wish I'd sung 'Cats on the roof tops, cats on the tiles,' " said Fix.

"Had to draw the line someplace," said Ian.

"Four Musketeers," said Perry, coming to life.

"Bet your ass!" said Fix, "and this sure beats swabbing decks and scrubbing buckets. And the slop chutes."

They put their arms around each other and pounded backs, then hugged the girls.

Wallace looked at Fix and said: "*Pax vobiscum.*"

Fix winked and said: "A little pax never hurt anybody!"

Ian laughed at the Latin pun, and Lewis, Perry, O'Reilly and company went on their separate ways.

Ian went back in the house to find Irene and Lonesome. He didn't see them on the first floor. The second floor was girl country. They wouldn't be there. He was reluctant to go to the laundry room on the third floor for fear he'd find the door still closed and locked. He didn't want to think about that. His room, for God's sake!

He went up anyway. The door was open and nothing seemed disturbed. He sniffed, and that didn't tell him anything either. He went back downstairs and found Irene standing alone on the front porch.

"Where's Pine," he asked.

"That was a great party, and I'm glad you asked your friends and their friends. I enjoyed them all."

"Cross section of America," said Ian. "Has Pine gone?"

"Yes," she said, "just now. And that's what I'm about to do. Go. To bed." She gave him a brief hug and went inside.

Wallace stood on the porch for some moments, disturbed, then he went inside, searched for stray bodies and, finding none, generally cleaned up and straightened up. He locked the front door and doused the first floor lights.

The bathroom was in use on the second floor, Irene, he supposed, and he went to his room. He took off his clothes, folded up the blanket and lifted the wooden lid from one of the tubs. He washed his hands and face, rinsed with cold water and with the water running relieved himself in the tub, aiming carefully at the drain. He sloshed out the tub with more water and brushed his teeth. Then he put his laundry tub bed back together, put on his skivvy shorts and stretched out with his hands behind his head and lay there in the dark.

I drank too much, he thought. Better watch it. But I had a good time. The Musketeers' girl friends turned out to be great. Why did they have those nicknames? I'll have to ask. Well, go ahead, think about what you've been avoiding thinking about. What about L. J. (Lonesome) Pine? I should like him, but I don't. He's a talented, good-looking officer with a war record, and he sees Irene every day. And I'm jealous.

He heard the bathroom door open and close downstairs.

Jealousy, he thought. Am I really jealous? Or am I hurt? What was it St. Paul said to the Romans? "Let us walk honestly as in the day, not in rioting and drunkenness, not in chambering and wantonness, not in strife and envying." Well, I sure as hell envy and have transgressed on almost all counts tonight. And, except for the hurt, it was fun.

He heard a click and opened his eyes. The door to his bedroom was open and Diana Bliss stood there in her night dress. He could see the soft outline of her body through the silk. "Wringer," she said, "are you awake?"

"Yes," Ian said. "And where did you get that name?"

"I heard the men talking. May I come in?"

"Go to bed, Diana," he said.

She walked in and hiked one cheek and thigh onto the tub. He could feel the warmth of her flank against his. She put her hand on his chest. He didn't want it to stir him but it did, and he was annoyed with himself. Here he was contemplating jealousy, pride and other carnal sins, and this woman comes to his bed and stirs him, as she had when she danced. How come? I thought all this was part of loving and caring. I'm learning, he thought, that the spiritual and the physical should be one, but are frequently two. Old Leviticus. Levitical law recognized the problem.

Diana moved her hand on his chest. "Do you know what's happening?" she asked.

"No."

"Do you know who was in here tonight?"

"No."

"Don't you want to know?"

"Go to bed, Diana."

"Do you like Pine?"

"I try to. Now, Diana, please go to bed. I'm Irene's guy. You've got my blood pressure up, and it's damned near daylight. Scram."

She looked at him for a long moment. Then she leaned over, her hair brushing across his face, her breasts brushing his breast, her cheek brushing his cheek. Then she straightened up and was gone.

He could not sleep for a long time. Frailty, thy name is woman.

He asked Irene about next weekend, Easter weekend, and the Cathedral service. She smiled yes, and he felt better and took off for Quantico in a railroad coach full of boisterous Marines and Army Engineers. By the time the train had left Fort Belvoir there were only Marines on the car, and half of them were asleep. As they pulled into the Marine base Wallace looked at dozing Fix and Lewis, leaned over and shouted at them: "RICHMOND!"

The two men leapt from their seats in panic only to see a few dozen Marines slowly standing up to detrain at Quantico. They called Wallace all kinds of a son of a bitch on the way back to the barracks.

The week was another tough one, but they were buoyed by the fact that they would receive their commissions in three weeks' time. They visited the Officers' Uniform Store at the PX and were measured for their new cord greens and beaver coats. They bought insignia and blitz cloths to make the gold second lieutenant bars fade to a salty shade as soon as possible. They argued about whether to buy chukka boots or regular oxfords and whether Kiwi wasn't better than Shinola. They had a lot of jokes about Shinola.

When the weekend came they boarded the trains for liberty. Some men were going to Washington, but others, like Perry, were going home. John would get to New York's Penn Station late Saturday afternoon, and he could catch a Patchogue train right there. He'd have the evening and Sunday 'til about 1500 to spend with his family.

O'Reilly was going to misbehave a bit on Saturday before he showed up at his parents' house in Bethesda to attend Mass with them and share their Easter dinner.

Lewis was going to the Black Banana's house, and Wallace was headed to the Gayety.

When Wallace arrived at Mount Pleasant Street it was a balmy, beautiful April afternoon. Irene and Diana were there alone, the other girls having taken off for the weekend. Ah, thought Ian. What does this portend? We'll see.

He suggested that they walk to the Rock Creek Park Zoo, down Kenyon Street and along Adams Mill Road. The girls put on sensible shoes, and they enjoyed themselves very much. The zoo was crowded, which wasn't too surprising considering the weather and the weekend. They saw the great apes and visited the monkey house, where one of the male orangs was rude. Irene didn't like snakes, so they avoided the reptile house but did see the birds and the big cats. Ian had never seen live tigers and lions before. A real occasion.

When they returned to the Gayety about five o'clock Ian worried what he ought to do about supper, or dinner as the girls called it. He'd saved most of his pay and had some of it with him, so he suggested they go out for dinner to someplace special. Diana said no, you two go alone, but they wouldn't hear of that, so Wallace got on the phone and called the only place he'd heard of, the Occidental. He was lucky and got a table for three, but it had to be early, at six-thirty. The girls were agog. They'd never been there before. It's where all the political, military and theatrical celebrities went.

"How did you do it?" asked Irene.

"Told them I was General Wallace and I needed a table."

"You didn't!"

"Sure I did. Let's go."

The girls were nervous about what to wear and what the maître d' would say when Pfc. Wallace asked for his table, but they all got on the trolley and went downtown. They alighted two blocks from the restaurant and walked to the door. The doorman gave them a funny stare, but Wallace informed him they had a reservation. Inside, the paneled walls were dark with age and covered with framed black-and-white photographs of the mighty and famous, the shakers and the movers. Wallace began to feel a bit self conscious, but the crowd was small and he felt he could carry it off.

Wallace asked for "mister" Wallace's table, to the relief of the girls, and they were seated. Ian noticed that he was the only enlisted man in the room. He decided he didn't care. The reason everyone was looking their way was because he was also the only Marine and was escorting the two most beautiful women by far in the venerable restaurant.

The maître d' took their drink order. Ian thought he'd better take it easy and ordered draft beer, and the girls had mixed drinks. A captain brought the menus as a waiter was serving the drinks.

Ian looked at the menu and paled. The prices were out of sight. He glanced up to see Diana looking at him with astonishment on her face. Irene, for whom money had never been a problem, continued to read the menu so she could make her selection. Wallace hoped he'd be able to cover the bill but decided to pick only those items which were relatively inexpensive, and few of those at that. The entire menu was à la carte.

The captain took their order—Irene ordered a full meal, saying that the walk to the zoo had done wonders for her appetite. Wallace felt like he was truly losing his. Diana ordered soup and a light salad, and Ian looked at her with gratitude. Irene was scanning the room to see whom she knew. Wallace ordered some fried chicken and a salad, and that made Irene's head swivel around. "Why, that's not enough for you!" she said, and Wallace replied that he really hadn't had chicken since he left the farm and it was just what he wanted.

As they waited for their food a tall civilian in a blue suit approached the table and said hello to Irene. He was in his mid-forties and was distinguished by gray at his temples. Ian stood up to be introduced but Irene forgot her manners and left Ian standing and Diana sitting there while she chatted. After an eternity the man looked at Diana and, holding out his hand, said that he was Lucas Duval, Deputy Assistant Secretary of the Navy. As Irene colored, Diana shook Duval's hand, and he then turned to Wallace. "I trust you have this situation well in hand, Private. I'm Lucas Duval."

Well in hand! If you only knew. Two girls on the same date and not enough money to pay the tab. He said instead: "Pfc. Wallace, sir, and I'm honored to meet you."

"Where are you stationed, son," asked the Deputy Assistant Secretary.

"Quantico, sir. Officers Candidates Class."

"When will you be commissioned?"

"Two weeks, sir, if I manage to keep out of trouble," said Ian with a smile.

"Just don't make any trouble for these ladies, and you'll be all right. Do you have family coming to the ceremonies?"

"No, sir."

"Too bad. Man ought to have someone he cares about see him become a commissioned officer of Marines. Well, if I can ever help in any way, remember my name…. Duval, Lucas Duval."

Duval walked away and Ian sat down thinking, mister, you could sure as hell help me right now.

The food was served, and Ian was quiet as he ate. Thank God the ladies had enough to talk about, pointing out this person or that as the place filled up. Ian was thinking that this was another learning experience, a growth experience. He tried to remember the prices of the dishes they had ordered and could not. Lord knows how much the drinks were. He'd never paid more than a dime for a beer. Sure looked like fifty cents here.

While they were having coffee Ian felt Diana's hand on his thigh. He looked at her but she was looking the other way. She moved her hand higher and shook his thigh a little. He felt sure that Irene would catch on or that everybody in the restaurant was watching. He sipped his coffee just as Diana pinched him and he almost blew the whole cupful across the table. "Are you all right?" Irene asked

"Hot," said Ian.

Diana moved her hand higher with insistence, and Wallace knew he'd have to put his hand under the tablecloth to stop her. What would Irene think? He slid his left hand under the cloth and slowly took Diana's hand in his. He started to push her hand off his leg when she turned her hand over and slipped a piece of paper in his palm and removed her hand immediately. He slowly withdrew his hand, glanced at Irene, who was again scanning the crowd, and peered at the paper in his palm. A small steel engraving of Andrew Jackson. He unfolded it a bit. A twenty-dollar bill.

Wallace looked at Diana, who closed her eyes and slowly nodded her head up and down. Then she looked away.

After paying the bill and leaving the tip they threaded their way through the crowded restaurant. Both Irene and Diana spoke to people they knew, and Wallace felt like a sore thumb. C'mon, he thought, let's get out of here.

They decided not to go someplace else for a drink, for which Wallace felt relieved, but to go home and relax. That had its dangers, too, Wallace realized, but at least he wouldn't be facing any more bills.

They put on comfortable clothes, and Ian made them drinks that they took to the back porch. "Early night for me," said Ian. "It's been a long week, and we talked about going to the National Cathedral for Easter service. I've never been to a cathedral service and would like to go. How about it? Are we on?"

Irene said she'd meant to tell him that Lonesome would be coming in the morning, and if Ian didn't mind they could all go to church together. Wallace felt as if he had been punched in the solar plexus, but he turned to Diana and asked: "Do you want to go?"

"I'd love to," she said and smiled an empathizing little smile.

Wallace excused himself early, and since he hadn't had a chance to be alone with Diana and thank her for her loan he went to the laundry and wrote her a note on a piece of brown paper bag he found there. He told her he was embarrassed, that he was overwhelmingly grateful and that he would pay her back after next pay day. He signed it "Hugs and kisses and see you in church."

Wallace got up early Easter morning, and after shaving, showering and shining his shoes he dressed and sat by the little window in the laundry and read the resurrection story from his *Soldier's Bible*. He chose the gospel according to Luke, the version he loved best. He started at the passage: *"And he came out, and went, as was his wont, to the mount of Olives."* Ian read intensely and as always was moved, losing track of time until he read *"and it came to pass, while he blessed them, he was parted from them, and carried up into heaven."*

He came to with a start and told himself he'd better part from this room and get carried down to breakfast. Irene was already in the kitchen having coffee at the table. She looked wonderful in her dress and hat. Sitting across from her was Lonesome with his uniform blouse over the back of his chair, sipping coffee. Was that a new ribbon on his uniform? Ian made a point of not being gauche about it, greeted them with a "Happy Easter," poured some coffee and joined them, feeling like an intruder.

Irene said she was going up to see what was holding up Diana and left. Lonesome asked Ian if he wanted part of the Sunday paper, and Ian took the first section. There was so little opportunity to see newspapers, no chance to hear the radio, no time to read the magazines that might come through the mail at OCC, that Ian read the Sunday paper voraciously every weekend. He hadn't learned of the German surrender at Stalingrad in February until he read an old *Time* magazine on the train to Quantico. He'd missed the U.S. Navy's victory over the Japanese in the Bismarck Sea during the first week in March because he didn't get ashore until two weeks after he'd scrubbed the buckets. Just the usual communiques today, though. How impersonal it was to read: "from all of these sorties six of our aircraft are missing."

He turned the pages and stopped at the casualty lists. The fallen were listed by state and by service, alphabetically. He ran his eyes over the lists lazily until he got to "MISSING AND PRESUMED DEAD... Connecticut... U.S. Navy... *Cooper, Avery S., Lt. j.g., USNR,*" jumped off the page at him. Coop? His roommate! Presumed dead as of 4 March '43. What was happening then? Where was he fighting? The newspaper was trembling.

"Something the matter?" asked Pine.

Ian thought for a moment and said no. He didn't want to ruin the day for the others and himself by casting a shroud over it in hollow sympathy for a man the others didn't even know. But he felt shaken and got up from the table and walked onto the back porch and bowed his head and tried to pray something. Nothing came. He'd had a letter from Coop a week, two weeks ago telling him how thrilled he was to be flying off a carrier. Couldn't tell him which one or where. But obviously it must have been somewhere in the southwestern Pacific. He felt a hand on his shoulder and turned to see Diana, radiant in her bonnet.

"O.K.?" she asked.

"Right," he said and took her back into the house.

They got to the cathedral early enough to be able to sit together on the hard little chairs that served for pews. Ian forced thoughts of Coop from his mind and concentrated on what was happening. The cathedral was filling rapidly, people were checking their bulletins. Ian took a book from the back of the chair before him. It was the *Book of Common Prayer*, totally strange to him. And many of the hymns seemed different from the ones he'd sung in church and choir.

He looked at the great aisles and remembered that, purposely, the architects had designed one aisle to be slightly angled, to give the building a distinction. But from where he sat Ian could not determine whether it was one of the aisles from the transepts to the crossing or part of the aisle from the great western doors to the choir and altar.

The organ prelude started, and though it was lovely Wallace did not recognize it. Then there was an enormous brass fanfare followed by the Dean of the Cathedral's echoing announcement from the narthex: "Christ is risen!" Ian had goose flesh.

The processional was "Christ, The Lord, Is Risen Today," and Ian had a little trouble keeping his throat from closing. Diana was watching him. Irene was whispering to Lonesome and pointing at someone. After the first lesson the choir sang the first anthem, "How Blest Are They Whom Thou Has Chosen." Oh, Coop, thought Ian, and struggled to control himself. After the announcements and the second lesson, Ian's favorite Easter gospel from Luke, the congregation sang "Thine Is The Glory" from Handel's "Judas Maccabeus." Ian got through that O.K.

The choir sang Lotti's "Surely He Hath Borne Our Griefs," and the sermon began. Ian had a hard time concentrating, but he forced himself to listen. In full, deep tones the Dean was reassuring the world that Christ's resurrection was our solace in this war against an atheistic enemy. Wrong, thought Ian. Well, right on the resurrection bit, but wrong on the atheistic notion. The enemy has a different theism, that's all. Ian focused on the minister's words, refusing to think about anything else. O.K. I am now back in control of myself. Wrong again.

The recessional was "For All The Saints Who From Their Labors Rest," and the people rose as the full organ played the first verse. When the singing started Wallace's throat simply shut tight. He'd never felt that way about the words of that hymn before and stood with his head bowed, staring unseeingly at the hymnal as he listened to the congregation and choir sing: *"And when the fight is fierce, the warfare long, Steals on the ear the distant triumph song, And hearts are brave again and arms are strong. A-le-lu-ia!"*

Moisture was welling in Ian's eyes, and he had to retrieve his handkerchief and wipe it away. He felt Diana's hand on his arm, and saw her look of concern as he pocketed his kerchief, so he gave her the best smile he could.

Wallace left the girls and Lonesome Pine in mid-afternoon. He'd had a moment alone with Irene and asked her to attend the commissioning ceremony, and she said that she was sorry but she couldn't get away on Wednesdays and that she was facing new responsibility in the Navy Department so didn't think she should play hooky. That depressed Wallace even more, so he thanked them all and said he had to get back. He left with feigned grace, two trolley tokens and a return trip ticket to Quantico.

"Why would he leave in mid-afternoon," asked Irene after Ian had gone.

"He was strange this morning," said Pine, "when he was reading the paper."

"And he was uncomfortable in church," said Diana, who got up and walked into the kitchen. She saw the paper on the table where Ian had dropped it. It was open to the casualty lists and she looked at them. Suddenly she put her hands to her mouth, straightened up and said, "Oh, my God!"

The letter Wallace wrote to Coop's mother that afternoon was difficult to write. He supposed he'd have to write others like it, but this was the first and certainly most meaningful one he'd write. He told her how he'd admired Avery (as his mother called him), how well they had got along together at college and what an example Avery had set for Wallace, both in scholarship and citizenship. Ian told her how proud and envious he had been when Coop had returned to college wearing his Navy aviator's greens and his gold pilot's wings. He told her that he always would think of Coop as his best friend. He hoped he'd be able to live up to the example that had been set.

Wallace lay on his bunk in the early evening light in the empty barracks —and wept.

CUMMINGTON 1943

THE BRIGHT WIND SNAPPED THE NATIONAL ENSIGN and the Marine Corps Flag at the staffs held by the color bearers as the platoons marched north toward the PX theater. The post band was just ahead of the color guard, playing "Semper Fidelis," and Wallace, as squad leader, first squad of C company, watched a sea of green fore-and-aft hats moving up and down in cadence as the candidates followed the band toward the place where they would be designated officers and gentlemen. Ian could see civilians standing on the sidewalks, men in suits and ladies in hats and gloves, parents, he presumed, or friends of the men about to be commissioned second lieutenants in the United States Marine Corps.

Some of us almost didn't make it, he thought. He remembered Easter evening after he had written Mrs. Cooper and fallen asleep on his bunk. He'd been awakened by the sergeant of the guard, who had said, "Tough shit, Mac, but you shouldn't have come back early. We're a man short in the guard room. One guy's got the GIs, so you're elected to sit in the guard room and log everybody back in."

Ian had put on his fore-and-aft hat and reported to the guard room, where they had given him a side arm and showed him the roster and how to log in the candidates from liberty. In addition to logging them in the guard, in the person of the sergeant and corporal of the guard, would conduct bed check.

Ten P.M. was the deadline, and as that time approached there was a Chinese fire drill in the guard room as dozens of candidates arrived and shouted their names in order to be sure they were checked in before time ran out. Ian got them all recorded, and then, checking the list, he saw that one name was unaccounted for: Perry, John.

What the hell happened, thought Wallace. He's too responsible to screw up. He chewed his pencil while the sergeant of the guard's party went off with clipboards, on bed check.

About 2020 John Perry appeared, breathlessly coming into the guard room, apprehensive as hell. "Jesus," he said, "the train was late and I had to take a cab from Washington. I'm glad you've got the duty. Put me down as back on time, will you?"

"Hey, John, you're asking me to do something wrong. I'd like to help you out, but you're twenty minutes late."

"Jesus Christ, Wallace, what the fuck difference does it make. I'm back, aren't I? I'm not AWOL. I can't control the trains, for God's sake. Log me in!"

"I've logged you in at 2020, and I'm sorry to seem to be a son of a bitch but that's the way it is."

"What a frigging friend you are!" shouted Perry and sped off toward the second deck.

The sergeant of the guard's bed check party returned and matched up their count with the log. The sergeant noted that Perry was logged in at 2020 and said to Wallace: "Good move on your part. We marked him as absent. Think we ought to turn him in?"

"I won't change the log, but maybe we ought to consider that he had to take a taxi all the way from D.C. because the New York train was late."

"O.K.," said the sergeant, and wrote "extenuating circumstances" in the margin.

The next day Perry was really worried that he might not get his commission and gave Wallace a hard time for logging him in late. Wallace didn't like being put under that kind of pressure, so he let Perry sweat and didn't say anything about the sergeant's notation.

Well, he thought, as they now marched toward the auditorium, the guard duty and the question of faking the log helped me to pull myself together. I really fell apart, and that's the last time I'll let that happen. There'll be too many opportunities for grief ahead, and I'm damned well going to handle them better than I just did. He nudged Perry, who was marching next to him, looked at him and winked. Perry smiled and winked back.

There were only four names lower down the alphabet than Wallace's, and he sat patiently as names were called and the men walked up to the stage. He wondered how many of these smiling men would be alive a year from now. As Wallace was leaving the stage he caught the flash of a bonnet at the back of the auditorium that he thought might be Irene's. His heart bumped. As they left the theater parents and friends were gathered on the steps and the sidewalk congratulating the officers, who were still in their enlisted uniforms, and Wallace scanned the crowd to see if he could locate Irene. No luck. He wished someone from his family could have been there, but his mother wouldn't travel alone, his grandfather was too old... and Irene was too busy. As he started toward the barracks to change into his officer's uniform and insignia, he heard a feminine voice call, "Wringer?"

He turned. There stood Diana Bliss, beautiful in her bonnet, with her red hair, her blue eyes, her freckles, her summer frock and her white gloves, her hands at her sides.

"Congratulations, Wringer," she said, and held out her hand.

He took it and in genuine appreciation and astonishment said, "Hey, Diana! It's great you could come. How did you get the time off?"

"Can't you tell I've got the flu?" she asked, and smiled.

"Come on back to the barracks and wait for me while I change, and then we can go to the PX cafeteria and get some lunch. Would you like to do that?"

"Yes, I'd like that," Diana said and took Ian's arm as they started toward the candidates' quarters.

Ian changed to his officer's greens and mirror-shined chukka boots, put on his visored hat with the distinctive French knot on the crown, made sure his new gold bars were exactly one knuckle's length away from the outside seam of his shoulder straps and self-consciously escorted Diana to the PX, returning salutes and "Good days" as they went.

The PX cafeteria was filled with new officers and their families, and Diana and Ian met many of them. Ian introduced Diana as "my friend" and got approving glances from a lot of the mothers—he blushed more than once. They bumped into the Musketeers and shook hands all around. The men were all pleased to see Diana and dug Ian in the ribs.

After Wallace had put Diana on the train for D.C. he went back to the barracks, packed his gear and moved, footlocker, sea bag and all, to the new barracks they would now occupy as second lieutenants in the United States Marine Corps.

After evening chow most of the men seemed to want to make the most of the privilege that accompanied their exalted rank and went to the Waller Building for a drink at the bar. Wallace went to his bunk and stowed his gear. He read the bulletin board and discovered that their ROC training was going to be much like the training they had already received. It differed only in being more intensive—there would be much more time in the field and much more exposure to command exercises. Each officer would pull officer-of-the-day duty as per schedule. Each officer would lead physical drill under arms as per schedule. Each officer would conduct close-order drill as per schedule. Each officer would participate in mock courts martial as per schedule. And on and on....

Wallace hit the sack and thought about the day. He didn't feel any different as a lieutenant than he had as a Pfc. He liked the pay better: one hundred fifty bucks a month, now. Not bad, even though some chief warrant officers got more. He liked the uniforms better, but knew he'd be in muddy, torn dungarees in the field most of the time. He liked the way Marines exchanged courtesy when saluting, though he didn't understand why you said "Good evening" shortly after noon. He felt a little sorry for himself, not having any parents for the ceremony, but then it had been nice of Diana to come. He only wished it could have been Irene.

The Marine Corps called it "command presence." The phrase loosely described the almost indefinable quality that made some men good leaders and some not so hot. There were leaders, and then there were drivers. The enlisted men tended to respond more favorably to leaders than to drivers. They grumbled when given orders by the drivers. They grumbled, too, when given orders by the leaders, for that is the nature of enlisted men. But they grumbled less and took pride in executing the orders well. And they tended to boast about their officers. In the matter of esprit, the Corps had staked out a generous claim and placed great importance on the contribution good command presence made to that esprit. Command presence got things done. The new officers were evaluated on command presence, and these evaluations had a great deal to do with their eventual assignments.

Wallace, Lewis and Perry were naturals in this quality. O'Reilly had to work at it. His perpetual smile and his crinkled eyes attested to such a high level of good humor that he was sometimes not taken seriously. This bothered him and occasionally flustered him. The problem was compounded by the fact that sometimes his voice broke when giving commands.

The Musketeers did as much as they could to help him out, especially in the matter of close-order drill. They tested him on marching movements of a body of troops and challenged him to tell them how to order a platoon to march around a building from point A, back to point A in the same alignment and facing the same direction, without giving the same command twice. He couldn't do it and worried about it all night before his turn to drill a platoon of the new officers the next day. He, and the others, would be scored by cadre officers on their efficiency and command presence.

Lewis sailed through his stint like an old salt. Perry was a little stiff but he didn't give any commands on the wrong foot or order the platoon to right shoulder arms when they were already at right shoulder arms. He did well. Wallace's big voice and his assurance about what he was doing daunted poor Fix, who watched the platoon perform like a veteran drill team under Ian's direction.

O'Reilly couldn't avoid his turn and started out with a mild gaffe. His voice broke on "Forward March!" and he was visibly upset. He got the platoon through some simple right and left column movements, some flank and oblique movements, and had the men at trail arms as they approached the waist high fence at the western end of the parade ground. Trail arms is a muscle tester, a ball buster, a quivering impossibility for any length of time. Fix was frozen as he watched the men approaching the fence with their right arms shaking and their rifle butts starting to bump the deck as they marched. He couldn't remember the command to get them out of trail arms. He was concentrating so hard he didn't even think about ordering the platoon "to the rear march." He suddenly realized they were two paces from the wire and shouted, "Over-the-fence! GO!"

The platoon scrambled over the wire and halfway assembled themselves and started to plod down the hill through the tall grass as Fix was trying to remember how to stop them and trying to disengage the ass of his trousers from the top of the fence.

"Platoon... HALT!" shouted one of the cadre officers, who walked up to Fix, heaved the seat of his pants over the fence and said, "You got 'em there.

You get 'em back!"

Red faced, Fix ordered "about-face" then "order arms." He looked at the men for a moment and shouted, "PLATOON!... Fall-out-on-this-side-of-the-fence and fall-in-on-the-other-side... NOW!"

By the end of the morning the platoon had been drilled and drilled, by the good and the bad and the indifferent. They had worked up quite a sweat—the backs of their shirts were black with perspiration and their eyes stung. They were standing at ease in the hot sun when the officer instructors put O'Reilly right back on the horse that had thrown him.

"O'REILLY! Front and center!"

Fix marched smartly to the officers and stood at attention. The senior instructor looked at Fix and said, "Take these people back to the barracks. In formation. See if you can get 'em to the right barracks, not someplace in Manassas or Belvoir. Their barracks. No detours and back in time for chow. Is that clear?"

"Yes, sir!"

"Carry on."

O'Reilly about-faced, and the platoon saw that he was purple with rage at having been chewed out in front of his peers. He was so mad that he shouted his commands with force and authority, venting steam. His voice didn't break and he counted cadence as if he'd been doing it all his life. The platoon gave him everything it could. The men knew O'Reilly was being watched by the instructors. O'Reilly didn't even notice them; his tunnel vision only allowed him to concentrate on his rage and bark out commands. The platoon really swung out and with the hot sun on their backs and the cool breeze in their faces they did everything Fix asked. Their hands were sore from pounding rifles all morning, but they slapped their pieces harder than ever when ordered. Their alignment was perfect. When they were halted in the company street behind the barracks they "left faced." At the command "order... ARMS!" sixty rifle butts smashed the deck in unison. A cannon shot! Fix suddenly came to and smiled. His order to "fall out" was greeted with a thunderous cheer. Men ran up to Fix and pounded him on the back. Wallace noticed the officer instructors grinning.

O'Reilly sat next to Wallace at lunch. He felt a little better, but the shame still stung. He looked at Ian and paraphrased the Requiem, "*Dies irae, ca-lamitatis, et miseriae. Tremens factus sum ego.*"

"No need to tremble before me," Ian said. "You proved you could do it, so it isn't the calamity you think. *'Audentes fortuna juvat.'* "

"Fortune favors the bold. I guess you're right. I was so mad I couldn't see straight. I said the hell with it and just goddam did it." He looked at Ian and his eyes crinkled. "It's nice to know a Protestant who understands Latin."

"The benefits of a liberal arts education," said Ian.

In June the National Symphony started its summer season of concerts on the barge moored at the Watergate. The audience sat on the marble steps that led down to the Potomac and enjoyed marvelous music under the stars. Irene, Lonesome Pine and Ian sat together, Irene in the middle, and listened to Richard Strauss's "Till Eulenspiegels lustige Streiche." Wallace attempted to explain this piece of "program music" to his friends, pointing out the various passages where Till was represented as doing one of his "merry pranks" and the passages where he was portrayed as contrite. He might just as well have been talking to the wind. Irene said she didn't like the discordant sounds, and Lonesome seemed to be more interested in talking to Irene about the Navy than listening to the music. People nearby "hushed" at them. Finally Irene and Pine got up and said they were going for a drink and would see Wallace later.

Ian stayed for the rest of the concert, quite aware that he and culture had been given the deep six by the girl he thought he had a date with. But there was no question, by the way Irene had pushed Ian's shoulder when he started to rise and by her "no, no, you stay here and enjoy the music," that he was being left in the lurch.

When the music concluded people slowly got up and wandered off. Ian sat looking at the water and watched the musicians pack up their instruments. Then he walked down Constitution Avenue past the Reflecting Pool to Seventeenth Street. He turned north past the Ellipse, walked by the State Department and turned right on Pennsylvania Avenue. He passed the White House, walked around Lafayette Square to Sixteenth Street and caught a Mount Pleasant trolley. When he got to the Gayety the door was unlocked and there were some lights in the back. He didn't think he wanted any small talk, and since it was quiet in the back he didn't know what he'd find. He went to the third floor, locked the laundry room door behind him to bar intruders—singly or in pairs—performed his ablutions and lay down on the laundry tubs. He decided he was pretty mad, mostly mad at himself for getting upset and feeling sorry for himself. He'd play it straight in the morning and not let anything show. A growth experience, he told himself. But he didn't like it. He was beginning to feel like an interloper.

Wallace caught the duty the next weekend. The duty roster showed that he was Officer of the Day from 0800 Saturday to 0800 Sunday. That put the kibosh on the weekend, so he called Irene and said he couldn't come up. She said that she was sorry and that she'd look for him the weekend after that. That made him feel better.

Saturday morning after chow Wallace took a little heat from the Musketeers as they were preparing for weekend liberty, telling Ian to take good care of the empty barracks and to make sure he knew his General Orders and all Post Regulations. Wallace was dressing, and after he put on his green trousers he saw the China khaki shirt and field scarf hanging in the locker. Why not, he thought, and put them on. Duty uniform of the day did not require blouses so he reported to the office in his green pants, fore-and-aft hat and China khaki shirt and tie. The outgoing duty officer gave him an odd look but turned over the web belt and holstered .45 caliber automatic. Wallace signed in in the day book and started his tour.

Wallace was alone in the office in mid-afternoon when someone walked down the passageway past the office, stopped, turned around and came to the door. Wallace looked up, and there stood a grizzled master gunnery sergeant, about forty years old, Wallace guessed. Probably he's passed more lighthouses than I have telephone poles, he thought.

"Excuse me, sir," said the gunny. "May I speak to the lieutenant?"

Wallace felt like a fool being called "sir" by this old salt, but stood up and said, "Come on in, Gunny. How come you're not ashore?"

The gunny came in. He was uncovered and did not salute, and Wallace offered him a chair. "Wore myself out last night at the NCO Club and needed the quiet of an empty barracks to recover. Probably get ashore this evening."

"What's on your mind?" Wallace asked.

"That khaki," the gunny said pointing at Ian's shirt. "I ain't seen any of that since Christ was in the brig. Where did you get it?"

Wallace was embarrassed, blushed a little and said, "I wondered this morning when I put it on whether I'd get myself in trouble over it, but figured no one's around so why not. I certainly didn't get this shirt in China, but I did get it from a couple of old China hands. A gift."

"Can I ask who give you the khaki?"

"Sure. Platoon Sergeant Dan Rose and Gunnery Sergeant Edward Ruditis. Down at Parris Island."

"Son of a bitch! Rose and Ruditis! Why I served with those two birds for two cruises and kept them out of more trouble than you could ever think of. My name's Pete Sigalos; Sigalos, Rose and Ruditis used to cut quite a swath on the Bund and some of the spots in Peking that foreign devils like us weren't supposed to know about. The Kou Rou Ji and the Dong Lai Shun. Got thrown out of most of 'em, too, but none of us was ever put in the brig. Ain't too many old China hands can say that! How come they give you the shirt? And what's your name, for Christ's sake?"

"My name's Wallace... Ian Wallace. And I'm a boot shavetail who shot pretty well at Parris Island. I think that's why Rose and Ruditis gave me the shirt. I think Rose made some money on my score, and I think Ruditis was pleased with the way I shot."

"What did you shoot?"

Ian colored slightly and said, "Missed 'possible' by one round. The last one. Ruditis was with me on the line, and I was using a rifle that the range armorer let me shoot with. Fella named Bojanowski."

"I know Steve Bojanowski. Good shot when he ain't hung over. Where'd your last round go?"

"Four ring. Ruditis said it touched the black, but it really didn't."

"Well, I'm glad to know anybody shoots that good. You deserve to wear that shirt. Those birds tell you anything about China duty?"

"Rose talked about it a little one day. But I don't suppose I'll see too much of the mainland. Looks like the islands for most of us. Did you see any Japanese troops when you were there?"

"See 'em! My God! they were thick as fleas. You got to remember that, not counting embassy troops, Japs have been in China, fighting in China, since '31. We was *in* Shanghai when the bastards bombed the hell out of the Chapei district and the native quarters of Shanghai in '33 and '37. We seen 'em strutting around Peking. Little men. Mean. Shoot you as soon as take a breath. Most folks don't realize the war over there has been going on for over twelve years already."

"Twelve years!" said Ian.

"Bet your ass, twelve years. Started in September '31 when the Japs took Manchuria and named it Manchukuo. Put a little bastard named P'u Yi in charge. Made him King in 1934. *King* for God's sake! They damned near come into Peking in '33 after taking the northern provinces. Got to the Great Wall, by God. They busted loose in the summer of '37: bombed and fought like hell and took any part of China they wanted. We was told to be on our best behavior, but I tell you it was hard not to bust some of the snotty little shits when we got the chance."

"Did you ever do that?"

"Sometimes. Needed the right spot, though. They traveled in groups in Shanghai, so you had to be careful. They had little respect for foreign troops, that's us and the Limeys and the Frogs, and no respect for any Chinese. Treated everybody like shit."

"You sure don't like 'em," Ian said.

"I seen too many of the snots. The gall they got! Why, they sank our gunboat in the Yangtze, the U.S.S. *Panay*, and what did we do about it? Not a goddam thing! Oh, complained a little, but that's all. And then in December '37 they took Nanking, and the goddamndest slaughter you ever heard of took place. The bastards let their troops run wild, and they killed over four hundred thousand Chinese civilians! That's damned near half a million! It wasn't that the Nips bombed the city. Oh no! They killed 'em one by one, hand to hand, bayonets, rifles, whips, swords. They raped 'em, blinded 'em, threw 'em in the river for target practice, doused 'em with gasoline and burned 'em, dragged 'em through the streets behind trucks and horses, machine-gunned 'em in wholesale lots, burned their houses with people in 'em. Smashed babies' heads against the wall or with rifle butts. We were madder'n stink but couldn't do a goddamned thing about it except spit at the Nips when we saw 'em in the street."

The gunny's face was red and he was breathing rapidly, but he continued. "By the fall of '38 the bastards controlled all the ports from Dairen in the north to Canton in the south, most of the railroads and all the important river traffic. The sons of bitches had a strangle hold on the Chinks, and they hadn't even declared war on each other yet! Talk about the Oriental mind! Hard to trust any of 'em. They'll tell you what they think you want to hear and think they're doing you a favor!

"And now the bowing, hissing bastards have got Hong Kong, Formosa, Indochina, the Malays, Philippines and too many Pacific islands to count. You ask me if I've ever seen any of the bastards! The Far East is crawling with them and their goddamned Greater East Asia Co-Prosperity Sphere! We're going to have hell's own time kicking 'em out!"

Sigalos stopped talking, still breathing hard and glaring at Wallace. Ian had never heard such a diatribe before and had learned a lot he'd never heard of before. He found his own pulse was up, and he was mad as hell. "Can they fight?" he asked, "Or have they just been up against a bunch of paper tigers?"

"Both," said the gunny. "They're tough as hell. Self-sufficient. Live off the land. Their gear is generally O.K. Small arms is .25 caliber. Bolt-action rifles, but good high-rate Nambu MGs. Don't know much about their artillery except for mortars, and they're good with them. They're good at night, as we found out on the Canal, and they got the best hat in anybody's army."

"Best hat?" said Ian. "What do you mean?"

"Forage hat," said Sigalos. "Little peaked felt thing with vent holes, chin strap for when you need it, soft visor to keep the sun outa your eyes, and a felt flap at the back, like the Foreign Legion caps. Keeps out the snow and rain in the winter and keeps your neck from being burned to a cinder in the summer. We oughta have something like that. Tin helmets don't stop shit. I know. I took one in the head on Tulagi."

The gunny leaned forward and showed Ian a long white scar just below the part in his hair on the left side of his head. Ian didn't know what to say. He felt he'd learned more with Sigalos than he had learned in all the Corps' lectures.

The gunny looked at his watch. "My God! It's seventeen-hundred! Time for chow down." He stood up and put out his hand. Ian rose and took the hand, and Sigalos said: "Thanks for letting an old timer bat the breeze with you. Seeing that old China khaki just turned on my memory. Didn't mean to carry on so, and hope I didn't spoil your afternoon."

He gazed out the window for a moment then looked Ian in the eyes and said: "Good luck, Lieutenant. And if you see any more old China hands tell 'em you know three of the best." He stood at attention, about-faced and marched from the office.

Wallace had a sandwich and coffee at the duty officer's desk and couldn't help thinking about what Sigalos had told him. He'd have to learn a lot more and talk to a lot more people to substantiate what he'd heard. He slept on the cot in the duty office, fully clothed, with his web belt and pistol and his fore-and-aft hat on the chair beside him. He stayed awake long after last call wondering about what he would be facing. He didn't think about Irene Gregg once.

He relinquished the duty at 0800 on Sunday to a disgruntled lieutenant who had returned from Saturday liberty the night before and was suffering from a serious hangover. Wallace wished him well and went to his bunk where he disrobed. He showered, came back to his bunk, rolled up in a blanket and went to sleep.

At noon he woke, put on his new lieutenant's uniform and his expert qualification badges and walked up the hill to the Waller Building where he intended to buy himself a good Sunday dinner. On such a beautiful late spring day the club was virtually empty. He decided he'd have a beer in the bar to celebrate the weekend and sat on one of the stools. Farther down the bar was a solitary stocky figure who was working his way through a whiskey sour. There was a stubby pipe in the ashtray in front of him. Wallace turned his attention to his drink and then sensed someone near him. He turned and saw that it was the officer from down the bar, a light colonel with rows of ribbons, Lieutenant Colonel Hume.

"May I join you, Lieutenant?" he asked.

Wallace started to rise, but Hume told him to keep his seat and pulled up the next stool. "My name is Hume," he said, "and while military courtesy is a fine thing, you'll find it is somewhat relaxed at the bar. You can say things here you probably would be ill advised to say somewhere else. It'll either be attributed to bad judgment with no offense taken or attributed to the effects of drink. If you're lucky they'll think it's the drink."

Hume sipped his sour, and Ian noticed the Annapolis ring on his finger. Hume noticed Ian's glance and said: "Yup. Trade school man. Canoe U. as they call it. Don't let it bother you. We're getting so out-numbered by you reservists, thank God, that we have to be nice to you."

"We've met before, Colonel, when I was a miserable candidate who couldn't button his blouse breast pocket."

Hume turned and looked hard at Wallace. Then he smiled and said, "Wallace, right? Do you still carry that little toothbrush?"

"No, sir," grinned Wallace, "I've turned it in for a pipe."

Hume roared with laughter, wiped his eyes and said to him, "What are you doing here on a Sunday noon?"

Wallace told him that he'd just finished the duty and Hume suggested that they eat together. Wallace began to feel uncomfortable, but once they had reached the table and ordered Hume quickly put him at his ease and conversation was very easy. Hume told him about some of his duty stations, including being gunnery officer on the U.S.S. *Alabama*, tours in various parts of the world, embassy work, recruiting duty. Ian asked him if he had served in China, and Hume said he had.

"I know three of the best old China hands."

"Who are they?" Hume said with scarcely disguised amusement.

"Dan Rose, Ed Ruditis and Pete Sigalos."

Hume was astonished. "How the hell did you get to know those old reprobates?" he asked.

So Wallace told him the story, including yesterday afternoon's experience.

"Yes," said Hume, "none of them was ever in the brig. I kept them out of it. They qualified, but they were damned good Marines, and we needed them. Took a little fancy footwork, but they never missed a day's duty. Good people. What Sigalos the strategist didn't tell you is that with Burma gone the Japs have cut off all the land and sea routes to China, leaving only air supply over what's called the Hump, the Himalayas, from India. Can't ship much in that way, so the Chinese don't have much to fight with. That means the Japanese need only about a million men to control the mainland, and then they can send more millions of men to the islands. Pete's had his bellyful of Japs as you could tell. I have too, really, but I suppose there'll be more. Plenty to go round, God knows." He paused and then said, "What are you going to put in for?"

Wallace had dreaded this question. It's one thing to talk to your mates about what you're thinking, but it's something else again when the question is put to you, even informally at the club, by a field grade officer who is high in Marine Corps Schools administration.

Wallace swallowed and replied, "I'm hoping to go to Sea School at Norfolk Navy Yard. Barring that, Flight School at Pensacola or a rifle platoon."

"You don't want to be wasted in a rifle company," Hume said. "You'd make a hell of a fine sea-going Marine officer. You're tall and seem to have the other qualifications. Good officers need sea duty on their records. It's great duty. The best. If you're really serious I'll put in my two bits on your behalf. Not that anybody's to ever know we had this conversation," he said, scowling.

"Thank you, sir. I'd appreciate that."

As they parted outside the Waller Building, Wallace gave Hume his best salute, which Hume returned, saying, "Wallace, remember to keep your pockets, and your lip, buttoned."

It wasn't until the Musketeers got back from liberty that Ian realized he hadn't thought about Irene for the entire weekend and that Sigalos's story had been confirmed.

When he made his mid-week call to the Gayety he got Diana on the phone, Irene was out. Wallace said he hoped to come up for the weekend, and Diana said that was fine, but then there was a long silence.

"Are you there?" Wallace asked.

"I'm here."

"Well what's the matter?"

"Irene won't be here this weekend. Do you still want to come?"

"Where's she going?" Ian asked.

"She's going to Lynchburg."

"Lynchburg? What the hell is in Lynchburg?"

"Ah, that's where Pine's family lives. She's going down with him, I think."

Wallace was silent while he digested that morsel. Irene had said she would look forward to seeing him this weekend when last they had talked.

"Do you still want to come?" Diana asked.

"I'd like that very much," Ian said. "Maybe you and I could have a date?"

"I'd like that very much, too."

The weekend went pretty well, though Wallace felt a little funny when he found somebody else's shaving gear next to his on the laundry shelf. He and Diana went out for dinner, and he learned she was from a different background than he was. A city girl from Cleveland, Shaker Heights she said, who was working in the office of her Congressman as an AA, administrative assistant. She found the work challenging and exciting though it frequently kept her busy until late in the evening. She'd gone to Antioch College, which Ian had always heard was a pretty avant garde school, and she'd majored in political science. This surprised Ian, who thought that most girls probably majored in languages, literature or homemaking.

They talked about the war, and Wallace was amazed at how well informed Diana was and how firm she was in her views. They walked to a bar on Wisconsin Avenue in Georgetown and listened to some Dixieland while they had a couple of drinks. They took a cab back to the Gayety, and when they said good night Diana gave him a hug and kissed him. Not a decorous little peck on the cheek, but a real humdinger, right on the lips. Oh my, thought Ian. Oh my, oh my.

Ian felt a little self-conscious on Sunday morning, but Diana was her usual easy-going self. They went to church together, and she took his arm as they were walking down the aisle. He was acutely conscious of her hip against his in the crowded pew. Keep your mind on the service, he told himself. *Honi soit qui mal y pense,* especially in church.

When Ian left for Quantico in the early evening, Diana gave him a good-bye kiss like the good night kiss the evening before and asked him if he could come up again next weekend. Wallace wasn't sure he could trust himself but couldn't bring himself to say no.

Diana was pretty much on his confused mind during the week. He tried to sort out his emotions and only found himself very mixed up about his feelings for Irene and Diana. Diana was certainly thoughtful, humorous, quick-witted and bright. She was attractive and desirable and apparently liked Ian very much. It certainly seemed that she would welcome his attentions. But he'd known Irene longer. They came from similar backgrounds. She was great fun, but....

"Do you know the answer, Wallace?"

"Sir?"

Daydreaming about the girls, in evening class on the subject of command, Wallace was totally unprepared to hear his name called.

"Do you even know the question, Wallace?"

Laughter in the ranks.

"At ease!" said the colonel instructor.

"The question, for your benefit Wallace, is this: We have assaulted a hostile beach and have progressed about six hundred yards inland. Our force is now pinned down by enemy howitzer fire from the other side of a mountain. We have no naval gunfire support, but there is a friendly submarine in the atoll's lagoon. It has a deck gun. As commander of the lead element you are ordered to put the submarine on the hill and take the enemy under fire. How do you do it?"

Wallace blushed and sweated and stood up and said, "Sir, I'd cut enough palm trees to make rollers, round up some cable and some vehicles to pull the submarine up on the rollers and——"

"Wrong," said the colonel. "Sit down. Does anybody here think he knows the answer?"

There was a long silence, and then a lieutenant in the rear of the classroom, a mustang, a former noncommissioned officer, said, "Sir?" and stood up.

"Think you've got the answer, do you? What is it?"

"Sir, the correct answer is: 'Sergeant, put the submarine on the mountain.' "

"Right!" said the colonel. "You birds remember that. And you, Wallace, remember to pay attention."

Wallace was interviewed by the company commander, Captain Sam Stryker, on Wednesday afternoon. Ian guessed the poor bastard did nothing but interview new officers. The men never saw him outside the company office; since the interviews took over an hour and since there were one hundred eighty men in the company the man must have been glued to his desk.

"Your record is pretty good," Stryker told Wallace. "You got high marks from your DIs at Parris Island. Captain Davis, Lieutenant Hynes and Tom Shadwell give you high grades for efficiency, initiative and bearing. Your written stuff has been four-point-oh in almost every case. You'd probably make an outstanding instructor here in Quantico. Have you given that any thought?"

Tough question, thought Ian. I'll have to answer this carefully. Don't want to insult this career officer. "Sir, I have thought about it a great deal and recognize how important the role of the instructor is. I have nothing but the greatest respect for the officers and men who bear the responsibility of training men to become real Marines. I must confess, however, that my first choice, if I were to have one, would be sea duty."

"Sea-going officers are usually regulars as opposed to reservists," said Stryker. "Have you given any thought to becoming a regular?"

"Sir, at the moment I'm in for the duration."

"I see," said the captain. "What other choices of duty do you have on your mind?"

The atmosphere just changed, Ian told himself. My comment about not becoming a regular just knocked me down a couple of notches in this man's estimation. Better watch out.

"Sir, I've thought about Flight School and, of course, a rifle platoon."

"Rifle platoon's your bottom choice, is it? Scared to go into combat?"

"Yes sir, I'm scared. And I'm scared about sinking ships and shot-down airplanes, but you asked me for my thoughts and that's what they are."

"Don't get snotty with me lieutenant, and don't think you're a hot shot regardless of what grades others may have given you. I'm the judge on your case, and what I say will carry the most weight. Is that clear?"

"My apologies, sir. It was not my intention to be snotty."

"Now that comes pretty close to insolence!"

"With all respect, sir, it is not my intention to be insolent. Please accept my apologies."

"All right, Wallace," long pause, "I'll accept them. But you watch yourself when you talk to superior officers in the future. Dismissed!"

What a son of a bitch! Wallace was steaming as he walked down the passageway. He didn't know that he had just acted in a way that would lead to anguish, pain, disillusionment and death.

On Thursday at mail call there was a letter for Ian, an unusual occurrence. He wondered if something had happened at home that required a letter to explain all the details. But the envelope was a pale blue square one with a red border on the envelope flap and an embossed Mount Pleasant Street address. What the hell, thought Ian, and opened the letter. It was from Irene. She said she hoped he understood her absence last weekend, but she'd had this fabulous invitation from Lonesome and she just couldn't turn it down. They'd had a marvelous time in Lynchburg and understood from Diana that Ian had come to Washington anyway.

What she really had to tell him, she said, was that she was entering the WAVES, Women Accepted for Voluntary Emergency Service. She was leaving Friday for the Great Lakes Naval Training Center, Great Lakes, Illinois, and she hoped he would write. Upon successful completion of her training she expected to be given a commission and assigned to the Office of Naval Intelligence. Please write, she repeated, and remember how much you mean to me. You and Pine are my dearest friends. I'm crazy about both of you.

Well, shit, Ian said to himself. She's already in the ONI as a civilian. Maybe the uniform and its glamour have seduced her. No. That wouldn't happen. Maybe if she's in the armed forces and she transgresses in the intelligence area they can shoot her. Bullshit. Maybe they only confide real secrets to Naval personnel. Maybe Pine and that jackass Deputy Assistant Secretary of the Navy Lucas Duval had talked her into it. Maybe the Navy pays her less as an officer than as a civilian. What the hell. She's gone and done it, I don't even get to say good bye, and she's crazy about me and Pine! Jesus!

Ian wrote Irene. It was a humorous keep-out-of-trouble letter. He thought of telling her to take some condoms on liberty, but wasn't sure that would go over too well, and promised to write when he could.

He continued to go to the Gayety on weekends, and he and Diana found that they were very comfortable together most times. Occasionally in the late evening Ian would become distressed when Diana sat on his lap and rested her head on his shoulder so that her nose was against his neck. Her soft warm breath and the feel of her body against his affected his blood pressure and at the same time gave him a feeling of contentment such as he had never known. They kissed affectionately but never let their obvious passion carry them away. He would return to Quantico with the most awful case of lover's nuts. But it was worth it.

The other shaving gear disappeared from the laundry shelf and Wallace felt like he was at home again. There was less stress and more laughter. Sometimes he cooked dinner for the gals and their dates. There was a lot of sitting around and just talking. It was relaxed and wonderful. Diana was interested in what interested Ian. She asked him about music, and he took her to the Watergate concerts and they talked about what they'd heard. They had long discussions about religion; while they never came to a meeting of the minds they respected each other's views. Diana was a dyed-in-the-wool high Episcopalian, and Ian suspected that her faith was rooted as much in the liturgy of the church as in anything else. If it comforted her, so be it. They talked about the bills pending in Congress and the politicking it took even to get bills out of committee. They discussed the third term question, and, though Diana was a staunch Democrat and Ian was Republican, they agreed it was strange that Wendell Wilkie received forty-five percent of the popular vote but received only fifteen percent of the electoral vote. An eighty-five percent electoral landslide for Roosevelt.

Wallace questioned Diana about life in Ohio and how she had arranged to get the AA job with her Congressman. What was college like? What did her father do before the accidental tragic death of both her parents? Brothers and sisters? They could and did talk for hours as they learned about each other. They liked what they learned. They liked what made them similar, and they liked and respected the fact that they differed in many ways. They were thrilled at the prospect of seeing one another on the next weekend.

Irene never answered Ian's letter.

Norfolk Naval Shipyard was not located in Norfolk, Virginia, Ian learned, but across the Elizabeth River in Portsmouth. It was an enormous ship-building and repair area covering acres of piers, machine shops, warehouses, foundries, barracks and housing. Most of it was paved in asphalt and had railroad tracks running down the roads and docks. Great gantry cranes growled up and down their tracks as they hoisted steel plates and beams, gun mounts and tubes from rail cars to the dock surface or to the ships being built or repaired. The noise of riveting and hammering was unceasing and the flare of welding torches lit the night with eerie flickering. The Yard smelled of hot steel, diesel fuel, rotting timber and salt air.

On the western flank of the Yard there was a red and green oasis, Marine Barracks, Norfolk Naval Shipyard. The barracks and housing had been built before the war and were constructed of red brick with white trim. The married officers quarters were large and commodious and lined the curving tree-shaded street that led from the west gate around the grass parade ground to the red-brick barracks and the building that housed the big Navy radio transmitter.

The post complement consisted of a permanent party, First and Second Guard Companies, which provided security at the Yard gates and docks, and young enlisted men and officers, the Sea School Detachment, being trained for service aboard the Navy's capital ships. These men would be assigned to light and heavy cruisers, battleships and aircraft carriers. On board the men would do guard duty, man the secondary batteries, do orderly service and make up the ships' landing parties. On most battleships one of the main turrets was also manned by Marines. To give the swab jockeys a standard to aim for, the Marines said.

Wallace, three other reserve second lieutenants and one regular second lieutenant, had received orders the second week in July that said: "When directed by the Commandant, Marine Corps Schools, on or about 14 July 1943, each of the above-named officers will stand detached from his present station and duties, will proceed to the Norfolk Navy Yard, Portsmouth, Va., and report to the Commandant, for duty at the Marine barracks, there." They were authorized a ten-day delay in reporting. Unofficial leave, Ian called it.

Great. And so much for that horse's butt Captain Stryker who'd given him such a hard time in his interview, telling him that only regulars were considered for sea duty! Only one regular was in this group, which made sense because the Corps was running out of them. They had to pick the cream of the reserve classes if they were to man the Marine detachments at sea.

Wallace had received his orders after a particularly satisfactory weekend with Diana, and he had called her at once. She was happy for him and had sounded relieved to know that he'd be only a few hours away and had been assigned to the duty he wanted. They had made plans for Ian to stop off at the Gayety on his way to and from his home in Cummington, Massachusetts, where Ian felt he must spend some time to demonstrate filial piety.

The disappointing aspect of the orders was that the Musketeers were broken up, as they knew they must be. Perry was delighted to be ordered to Pensacola for flight training. Lewis was ordered to Camp LeJeune, where he would be assigned to a rifle company. O'Reilly was disappointed that he was not ordered to Sea School. He drew duty with a guard detachment at Iona Island, a tiny Navy ammunition enclave in the middle of the Hudson River, just close enough to New York city to almost see it, but impossible to get there unless you could walk on water.

The Musketeers had a beery good-bye party at the BOQ the night before they all left for their various stations. They promised to write each other, and they said they'd all have to look each other up if they should ever get to one another's part of the world. God willing, they'd all get together after the war, too. They pounded each other's backs, shook hands and separated. After they had gone about three paces the men stopped and, as if on command, they each about-faced and, facing each other, came to the right-hand salute, which they held for almost ten seconds. Then they slowly lowered their hands to their sides, about-faced and parted.

The next morning as Wallace was preparing to walk to the depot, after having arranged to have his gear shipped to Marine Barracks, NNYD, Ports. Va., he picked up his small grip and started out the barracks door only to be accosted by Lieutenant Colonel Hume.

"Hello, Wallace," said Hume, returning Ian's salute. "Where are you headed? What duty did you draw?"

"On my way home, sir, for a few days and then to Sea School at Norfolk Navy Yard." Wallace didn't know whether to say thank you or keep mum. He decided that silence was the better part of discretion.

"Why, good for you! I'm delighted to hear that the Corps has for once shown enough good sense and judgment to send such an outstanding man to serve in the elite of the elite!"

That sounded a little like bullshit to Wallace, and he didn't know whether he was being put on or not. So he said: "I'm pleased, sir, and I'm looking forward to it. Permit me to say that I have enjoyed the opportunity to know you, and I appreciate all your advice and counsel."

That sounded a little like bullshit to Colonel Hume, but he figured he'd earned it. He put out his hand and said: "Good luck, Wallace. I hope that someday we may serve together. I mean that."

Wallace blushed and took the Colonel's hand. "Thank you, Colonel. I would consider it a great honor to be part of your command. And I mean that."

The ride on the Pennsylvania Railroad from D.C. to New York took forever. Wallace dreamed of his two days with Diana and wondered what going back to the farm would be like. What would his perceptions of that life be? What would they think of him? How quickly did he think he could get away without hurting feelings?

He changed trains in New Haven and took the New York, New Haven and Hartford Railroad north to Northampton, where he alighted and wondered at the sameness of the place he had left only seven months ago. He felt he had changed so much and assumed that the same rate of change applied everywhere else. He caught an aging International Harvester bus that was headed over the back roads to Pittsfield. Except for the driver he was alone on the vehicle. Ian helped the driver, who never said a word, and they unloaded some mail bags at Haydenville and Williamsburg. Then there was trouble.

The bus made its regular stop in front of the Whale Inn at Goshen but wouldn't start again. Wallace thanked the driver, who merely nodded his head, and found a public phone. No one answered at the farm, so he started to hike the remaining six miles through Lithia and Swift River to Cummington and home. God knows he'd hiked hundreds of miles since he'd gone away, but this seemed the toughest. He put his barracks hat on the back of his head, slung his uniform blouse over his shoulder, loosened his field scarf, picked up his bag and walked off. The hot July sun was merciless, and the thunder clouds were piling up over the mountains in the late afternoon western Berkshire sky. If I maintain a rate of one hundred twenty paces a minute I should make home in an hour and a half, he thought. Dust coated the shoes and uniform he had hoped would sparkle and impress when he arrived at the farm. His shirt turned black with sweat. He wondered if he was eager to get home or was fulfilling a family duty.

I'm different in so many ways, he said to himself, as he trod up and then down the hills of State Route 9. I should be excited, but I'm really dreading it a little bit. Keep up the pace, he said. No cars or buses passed him, and the western cloud bank grew and blotted out the lowering sun. At least it'll be cooler, he thought. I wonder where everybody was when I phoned.

Between Lithia and Swift River he got a ride on a farm wagon for a mile and was grateful except for the hay seeds that clung to his pants and the reek of manure that seemed to permeate his uniform. He double-timed the last two miles and arrived at the farm sweat-streaked, breathless, dusty and smelling of horse dung just as the heavens opened up and the storm, which had been growling and crashing with increasing intensity in the west, finally gave vent to its wrath.

The rain came down in gray wind-blown sheets as Ian leapt onto the front veranda and opened the door. The house was dark and had a very quiet, empty feeling. He called out, "Anybody home?"

No one answered, and he went to the kitchen. The table was laden with food of all kinds: cakes, pies, hams, fruit. There were bouquets of flowers standing in water in the sink. There were other flowers in vases in the parlor and dining room. What the hell, thought Wallace. I was going to surprise them. I didn't even tell them I was coming! But now nobody was here, so at least he'd have a chance to go see the hired man, who should be milking, and then he could change into some dry clothes. He threw a waterproof slicker from the back room over his head and dashed through the rain and mud to the barn, hoping the lightning wouldn't sour the milk. There were lights on over the stanchions where the cows were eating their mash. He saw rubber-booted feet under the ninth cow down as firm hands directed alternate streams of warm milk into the steel pail between the man's knees.

When he came around the stern of the cow, he found he was looking at a total stranger. "Where's the hired man?" he asked.

"Who're you to know?" replied the milker.

"I'm Ian Wallace. I live here."

"That's as may be," said the man. "But you don't look like no farmer to me. Look like a soldier."

Ian let that pass and said: "I just came home on leave. Where is everybody? And who are you?"

The man looked down at the pail as he continued to milk and said: "I'm Henry Allen. From Turners Falls. Friend of Mrs. Wallace. Just came over to help out."

There was a great rolling crash of thunder, and the lights flickered and then came on steadily again. "Well that's fine, but why is the helping-out needed?"

Henry Allen looked up at Ian and then back down at the pail again. "Well," he said, "there's been a death, and the folks and the hired man have gone to the burial."

Wallace felt a cold chill sweep over him as he stood in the steaming, fly-specked stable and the thunder roared outside. He didn't dare ask but knew he had to.

"Who's passed away?" he asked and held his breath.

"Must be your mom," said Henry Allen. "She must have got took with a stroke, three days ago. At the top of the stairs in the morning, and she tumbled all the way down. Doctor said there was nothing he could have done for her even if he'd been here. With the heat and all, folks thought it best to have the services now."

Ian's head was swimming. His mother. Poor, sad, withdrawn, tired woman. He hadn't even known. Three days ago he'd been in Washington with Diana. He should have come straight here.

"Understand your grandfather tried to phone you at the Army base, but they said you'd gone."

Wallace's throat was thick as he thanked Allen for telling him and for the help he was giving his grandfather. He picked up the slicker from the barn floor where he'd dropped it, threw it over his head and trudged back to the house in the teeming downpour. He turned on a light in the kitchen and dried himself off. He hung up the slicker and sat down at the scarred wooden kitchen table with his head in his hands, thoughts whirling through his mind and somehow wracked with guilt. He hoped he'd made her proud of him but she'd never mentioned it. He looked at the food and knew he should eat something. He hadn't even had any breakfast. He had no stomach for the neighbors' thoughtfulness, so he went to the ice box, a real ice box not a refrigerator, and took out the white enamel milk pail and poured himself a glass. When he tasted it, it was sour.

His grandfather wouldn't speak to him that night when he came home in the neighbor's automobile. He only looked a long look at him as he stood inside the door at the bottom of the front hall stairs. Tears welled up in his grandfather's eyes, already red from grief. He walked slowly past Ian and painfully climbed the stairs.

Wallace slept little, consumed by feelings of guilt, anguish and remorse. Toward dawn he rose, put on his old farm clothes, now too big for him, took an apple off the kitchen table and went out to the barn to help with the mucking-out and the milking. Henry Allen was gone, but Jed, the hired man, was there. He told Ian he was sorry about his mother and that there weren't no need to help. Ian thanked him and fell into his regular chore routine anyway. They finished up in less time than it usually took Jed alone, cleaned up and went into the kitchen where Jed's wife, Patience, a large, quiet, comfortable and unhurried woman, was stirring oatmeal. Oatmeal, thought Ian. The temperature's already in the seventies, and it's hardly daylight. Well, we farmers always need something to stick to our ribs.

Patience said she was sorry and was there anything special Ian would like for breakfast?

Ian said no, and just then his grandfather, looking older than God himself, limped into the room. He looked at Ian and smiled a weak, old man's smile and said: "I'm glad you're home, Boy. I was upset when I saw you last night. I was feeling sorry for myself and pretty damned mad to boot. It was a helluva day. But I'm glad you're here."

"Thank you, Grandfather," Ian said. "I only wish I'd been here earlier. I'd hoped to surprise everybody. Pretty thoughtless, and now I'm paying for it." He shook his head.

"No fault of yours. Things happen, and that's an end to it. We all wish it could have been different, but there is no sense in bucking God's will."

"You men sit down and have something to eat," said Patience. "And stop feeling sorry for yourselves. There's lots to do, and standing here in the kitchen ain't going to get it done."

They had their oatmeal with thick heavy cream and brown sugar, no coffee, but tea. The grandfather said, "You better go through your mother's things and see if there's anything you or Peter might want to keep."

"What about Peter? Has he been notified somehow?"

"I talked to the Army, over in Springfield and they said to talk to the Red Cross who would get a message to him. I gave a short message over the phone to a nice lady at the Red Cross who said she was in the Home Service Department, and she said that the message would get to your brother. Didn't know when."

"I'd like to visit the grave,' Ian said.

"Have to walk," his grandfather said. "The car's up on blocks what with gas rationing. Your Mom, bless her worried, grieving heart, is buried in Maple Grove cemetery in the family plot. No gravestone yet, but you won't miss it. It's the only fresh earth there."

Wallace went up to his mother's room where Patience was already putting clothes in boxes, cleaning out the closet, taking the sheets and blankets off the bed. She looked at Ian and said, "You don't have to go through all this stuff. I'll see that the clothes and things get given to some poor soul who can use them."

"The only things I'm interested in keeping are the pictures of the family and Mother's books. Can you put them in my room for me?"

"I'll do that, and you get on your way to the cemetery. It's a long walk, and it's hotter'n Tophet."

Wallace walked cross-lots to the graveyard—through the fields where the second haying would soon take place, through corn that was already shoulder high, through fields that lay fallow. He climbed the steep hill to the cemetery, clambered over the stone wall and continued on up through the old lofty maples to the family plot. He stood at the downhill end of the freshly covered grave and stared at the eroded gullies last night's rain had made in the mound and at the two wilted clusters of flowers that had been crushed by the downpour. He didn't know what to think or what he should do. Here lie the remains of the woman who bore you, he thought, of the woman I knew and loved as my mother and yet didn't know at all. May she find her peace at God's right hand. May all her worries be put aside. May her sons live up to her example of fortitude and hard work and do nothing to tarnish her good name. *"Yea, though I walk through valley of the shadow of death, I will fear no evil: for thou art with me; thy rod and thy staff they comfort me. And I will dwell in the house of the Lord for ever. Amen."* He didn't weep. I'm getting better at this, he thought.

Wallace asked Jed how long his grandfather had seemed so frail and was told that he'd been failing since shortly after Ian had been called to Parris Island. The letters his mother had sent had not mentioned any health problem his grandfather might have had. But then, in this family you don't talk about health. It's a private matter. And you don't talk about money, either. It's impolite. But I've got to talk with Grandfather, about both.

The conversation had been much easier that Ian expected. His grandfather said he was simply getting old. No specific complaints except that he couldn't get time to slow down. *"Eheu fugaces labuntur anni,"* he said. Alas, the fleeting years glide on.

As for money, there was no immediate problem. The farm would support him and the hired man and his wife. And there was a little income from an annuity. Ian was not to worry about the home front, his grandfather said. Just go do what you have to do, do it well and come home all in one piece. He said he hoped to hear from Ian once in a while, but he wasn't much of a letter writer himself. He'd try to let Ian know what was happening on the farm every month or so.

Wallace stayed at the house for two more days, helping out with chores and mending the tongue of the hay wagon. He wondered at how small his bedroom seemed and how unimportant were the memorabilia on his shelves. He felt more and more like a stranger. When he left, his grandfather seemed more like his old self. He'd beaten Ian at cribbage two nights in a row, and that helped. Patience told him not to worry about any of them. She might write once in a while herself. Jed just mumbled and was uncomfortable shaking hands. Ian flagged the old International Harvester bus and left for Norfolk via various trains and changes, with a stopover in Washington, where, he felt, he would more truly be at home.

Distrust all in whom the interest to punish is powerful.

— Friedrich Wilhelm Nietzsche
Thus Spake Zarathustra

NORFOLK 1943

THE MARINE CORPS AT MARINE BARRACKS, Norfolk Navy Yard, Portsmouth, Virginia, was a Marine Corps Wallace had only read about. It almost seemed as if it was still peacetime. The quiet, shaded drive. The green grass parade ground. Formal guard mount. Saturday morning parade with a sailor band. "Reading off" of prisoners convicted at summary or general courts martial. Wednesday "make and mend" (Wednesday afternoons off from duty, except those assigned, for sewing and general repairing of goods and clothing and the tea party that preceded the enlisted men's boxing match, which was held in the portable ring erected each week in front of A Barracks on the lawn, attended by all the troops and the officers and their wives in their hats and gloves).

The commanding officer, MB, NNYD, was a retired colonel who had been brought back into service to oversee this important post. A retread. He had been passed over for brigadier since 1936 and brought with him a grudge and cynicism that was only relieved when he bested the Navy Yard commandant at golf in their weekly shortened game on the perimeter of the Marine parade ground. Enlisted men followed the pair to replace the divots.

Newly reporting officers were expected to call at the commanding officer's quarters and leave their calling cards in the silver tray in the front hall of the colonel's residence. Not that they expected to be called to the commanding officer's quarters for social events, but it was the thing to do.

Wallace didn't have any engraved calling cards and didn't feel that it made a hell of a lot of difference to the war effort whether he left his card or not. He rapped at the colonel's door and left his warm regards and filled out a card that had blank spaces on it that was obviously meant for the indigent and incapable and those who didn't have the good upbringing or good sense to have calling cards with them. Down one, thought Ian.

Down two, he thought, when he was called in to be interviewed by the colonel himself, Colonel John R. Bentley, USMC (Ret.). The old colonel was tall, dignified, be-ribboned, with a prominent Roman nose and an "above-it" attitude that Ian could not describe. He asked Ian why he wasn't a regular and was pointedly unsatisfied with the reply. He summarily dismissed Ian, who was shown out of the colonel's office by a very old sergeant major named Brundage, who told him to read the Post Regulations on the bulletin board and not to fuck up like so many of the reservists they were getting now.

Wallace was assigned to quarters M9D, on the third floor of a marvelous brick building. He shared the quarters with three other officers, all of whom were veterans of Guadalcanal. Ian was awed at their ribbons and their reluctance to talk about their experiences. The apartment consisted of one head, a long hall, a living room, a dining room, a kitchen, a pantry and a porch looking over the grass parade ground from the third floor. The furniture was dark, chipped, store-bought government issue. There were no rugs on the wood floors. There were three bedrooms. Ian shared one with the only other second lieutenant in the apartment.

There were daily classes on Naval Etiquette, shipboard procedure, gunnery, Naval Law, landing parties, navigation, and mechanics of the Waterbury speed gear, the device which controlled the movements of the 5-inch 38-caliber gun, a heavy antiaircraft weapon mounted on the ships to which the Marines would soon report.

Wallace's brother officers from Quantico had been in different platoons there, but they soon became friends. One of those officers, Lieutenant Bosse, was having difficulty each time he came back from liberty and reported to sickbay for a little advice and counsel. He was told by the Medical Corps lieutenant commander in charge that he was suffering from a basic penis problem. He needed a circumcision. Duty assignments were reorganized, and Lieutenant Bosse was put in the hospital where the appropriate procedure was accomplished, and the lieutenant was put in a bunk with a sizable tent erected over his mid-section to keep the sheets from irritating his tender member. Wallace went to visit him in sickbay and Bosse showed him the bottle with the little squeeze-bulb spray attached to it which the doctor had given to him.

"What's that for," asked Ian.

"Got alcohol in it. Cools off the sensitive tissues," said Bosse. "It's hell if the thing erects or swells. Tissues split. Vessels rupture. You bleed to death. Through your cock!"

Ian was learning. "What do you do?" he asked.

At that point a gorgeous Navy nurse, Lt. j.g., swiveled by. Bosse lifted his sheets and pressed the spray bulb, directing the cooling mist on his apparatus. The spray bulb hissed and hissed. As she heard it, the nurse turned scarlet.

"I always give it a couple of extra shots when she walks by. Just to be on the safe side. And I like to see her blush."

"You know," Wallace said with a grin, "This operation usually signifies admission to manhood and is regarded by some as having the most profound religious significance. Do you feel spiritually moved?"

"Yes, it is a healing experience," Lieutenant Bosse replied.

Ian took Sea School instruction easily. The subjects were not hard (except for the Waterbury speed gear, and Wallace knew the answer for that one: "Chief, fix the speed gear.") and Ian felt he was learning the routines well. He stood his turn as assistant Officer of the Day and performed such other duties as were assigned to him in an exemplary manner. Major Munro, who commanded the Sea School, told Ian he would try to get him assigned to new construction. That meant being assigned to a capital ship before she was commissioned, and there were advantages to that. You became a plank owner. You didn't have to try to fit into an already established detachment, and you could help form up the one with which you would serve. The more experienced officers, like the men with whom he shared quarters, would be assigned as replacements to units already serving at sea. Their First Division patches and their battle ribbons were powerful credentials that would ease their way into an established outfit.

Despite all the excitement of his new experiences, as the weeks went by Wallace felt somehow out of the war. Left behind on a peacetime post. These feelings were occasionally shattered abruptly with events that brought the war much closer to home. The student officers were taken to the Naval Anti-Aircraft Range on the beach at Dam Neck, Virginia, where they watched crews serving the Bofors 40mm quad-mount guns, the 5-inch-38 gun and the Oerlikon 20mm machine-guns. The officers got to fire the 20mm weapons at target sleeves towed by slow-flying Stearman biplanes. The Mark 14 sight on the 20s was tricky in that you had to learn how to control the slew. In bringing the sight to the target it was necessary to swing by and return to the sleeve so that the sighting reticle would come to rest where you wanted it. Ian gained some notoriety by leading the target too much and chewing up the tow cable with his tracers, which seemed to arc slowly to the sleeve. By the time he saw where his hits were it was too late to compensate. The cable parted and the sleeve fluttered into the sea.

That afternoon, during their firing sessions, one of the Bofors blew up. Hot pieces of metal whirred by and "Cease firing!" was shouted over the bullhorn. Ian cleared his weapon and looked to his left. The nearest 40mm was a mass of twisted steel and smoke, its barrels pointing sky-ward at different angles. The gun deck was buckled and listing. Ian could see crumpled forms in dungaree blue on the tilted steel. Blood was running off the footplate in streams, pooling near another inert blue form on the concrete foundation ten feet below. Sirens wailed and ambulances, fire trucks and running figures converged on the scene.

A failed extractor, they said. The extractor on number two barrel had not pulled out the spent casing from the previous round and the subsequent round had been rammed into the already filled breech. Three dead and five wounded. Firing was halted for the day.

A week later the executive officer, a retread major named Lars Hovde, called Ian to his office and told him Ian was to be his liaison officer with the Royal Marine detachment on board H.M.S. *Indomitable*, now tying up at the docks. The commander of the detachment wanted to get his men ashore and had asked for permission to use the grass parade ground. Wallace was told to go to H.M.S. *Indomitable* and identify himself to Major Wynne-Pope and lead the British back to the Marine Barracks parade ground. He was told that the British could sign chits in the Marine Post Exchange after the parade, which Ian would subsequently present to Major Wynne-Pope for repayment.

The Yard office told him where to locate *Indomitable*, and he marched off, marveling at the heroic names the English used for their vessels. *Indomitable, Indefatigable, Invincible, Infallible!* How about *Insufferable* or *Inex-*

cusable? He chuckled and then stopped short, aghast at what he was seeing. Towering over him at the dockside was a monstrous aircraft carrier, its battle-gray paint chipped and rusted, the Union Jack whipping at its halyard and an enormous ragged and torn hole in its hull on the starboard side just at the water line under the island. Ian could see that the explosion had ripped the plates below the water's surface and that a number of gun mounts on the gallery deck had been uprooted. You could lose A Barracks in that hole, he thought. No wonder the Royal Marines wanted to get ashore. He wondered how long they'd been at sea.

The officer on the quarter-deck was dressed in white shorts and knee stockings, white shoes and an open-necked, short-sleeved shirt with shoulder boards, and a white cover on his brimmed cap. Ian had never seen such a uniform. The messenger standing at the quarter-deck was similarly attired except for the shoulder boards and cap. His rate was on his sleeve, and his hat was a flat white affair with a black headband and two black ribbons hanging down the back. The officer sent the messenger for Wynne-Pope, who shortly appeared in one-piece olive wool battle dress, British style fore-and-aft hat very much on the side of his head, webbing belt and suspenders supporting a shined leather holster and revolver, short canvas ankle leggings and black high-cut shined pebble-grain shoes. Black shoes! Ian was as surprised at that as he was by the white shorts.

Major Wynne-Pope courteously thanked him for coming and said if it would be all right he'd fall out the company on the dock and Wallace could lead them to the parade ground. "Chaps haven't had much of the chance to stretch their legs and sharpen up on parade. Thanks awfully."

As Wallace went down the gangplank he was struck by the odors of the ship. Burnt paint, diesel fuel, smoke, grease and what he thought might be rancid food. The whole vessel seemed dirty and tired. Even the officer and the messenger on the quarter-deck looked gray behind the ears and below where their shaving soap had stopped. Short of water Ian guessed.

When the company formed on the dock Wallace estimated there were about one hundred and twenty men and officers. The orders were screamed and unintelligible. To his surprise there was also a band, about twenty-five men with instruments and drums.

Major Wynne-Pope said: "Lead on!"

"Aye, aye, sir," Wallace replied and, lacking knowledge of what military niceties were required in the present situation, did an about-face and stepped out at one hundred twenty paces to the minute. He heard Wynne-Pope scream: "By the Right Quick March!"

The drums struck up a rather slower beat than Ian's pace, so he slowed himself to the tempo they had set. He turned and marched backwards and saw that he was leading the band, followed by the major and his company, Enfield rifles flat on their shoulders at the slope, arms swinging shoulder high as they marched. Wallace turned about and, to the beat of the drums, led the company across gantry tracks and stone paved roads to Marine Barracks and onto the parade ground at the north end. As they marched onto the field Ian noticed a pretty good number of Marines gathering in groups in front of A Barracks, watching. Officers in one group, enlisted men in another. To Wallace's embarrassment the band struck up "Rule Britannia." Ian did a quick right-flank movement, faced about and stood at attention as the detachment marched past. As Major Wynne-Pope passed by he threw a handsome British salute, looked at Wallace with a mischievous smile and screamed "EYES RIGHT!" and Wallace returned the salute as the men marched past.

As soon as the last rank had passed he heard a voice say, "Well that was hospitable of you!"

He turned to find Major Lars Hovde, the executive officer, laughing at him. "Bring the major and his officers to my quarters while their men are at the PX."

"Aye, aye, sir," Ian said and stood with the group of officers who watched in fascination the British close-order drill. They particularly admired the slow march. Wallace glanced over his shoulder and noticed some of the Sea School Marines trying to do the march themselves, with great difficulty.

The Royal Marines marched back and forth. Then they stood in ranks and did their manual of arms. And last, as their band played "From the Halls of Montezuma To the Shores of Tripoli," they lined up in company order facing their audience. Immediately after the last notes from the band, Major Wynne-Pope ordered three cheers, which they did by the numbers and with great enthusiasm. This was greeted by a roar from the Americans, much shouting and applause. The British stacked arms, the enlisted men went to the PX surrounded by their American comrades in arms, and the British officers accompanied Ian to the executive officer's house where cookies and soft drinks were served.

That night Wallace accepted Wynne-Pope's invitation to dine on *Indomi-*

table as the major's guest. He put on his best uniform, arrived at the appointed hour and was conducted to the wardroom. It was filled with laughing, chatting officers and blue with tobacco smoke. There were worn Oriental rugs on the steel deck and oil paintings and framed photographs of ships and officers on the bulkheads. The ship's silver stood in a fiddled cabinet. An upright piano was bolted to the after thwartships bulkhead. Wynne-Pope singled him out and introduced him to the ship's lieutenant and several others and asked what he'd like for a cocktail. Ian had forgotten that British wardrooms were wet but said with pleasure he'd enjoy a beer, if you please. The steward brought him a bottle and glass and Ian learned something else. The English drink beer warm.

After a meal of hardly palatable food, which literally reeked as it sat on the plate, during which Ian was embarrassed by being toasted, Wynne-Pope took him about the ship. Electrical cables snaked their way from the docks through the passageways, sledgehammers rang on steel plates and riveting guns made conversation almost impossible. Apart from the mess created by the work crews, Ian decided that the ship was simply quite filthy. No wonder it smells, he thought.

He learned that not only had Wynne-Pope lost eleven Royal Marines in the last torpedo attack, but also had lost his wife and daughter in the Luftwaffe's greatest daylight attack on London, Wynne-Pope said, on Sunday, 15 September 1940. He said he'd never forget the date.

"Where were you then?" Ian asked.

"In hospital. In Devon. Far away. Recovering from a bit of nonsense that happened at Dunkirk."

Wallace remembered that in late May and early June of 1940 an armada of tugs, trawlers, drifters, yachts, MTBs and destroyers had lifted over 335,000 British, French and Polish troops from the beach in the Dunkirk perimeter while under fire and air attack.

"And how did *Indomitable* get hit? Or can't you say?"

"Oh, we're all on the same side, after all. We supported the Sicily landings on 10 July and then crossed the Atlantic to pick up aircraft. Got pranged two days out, off the Virginia capes."

It was said so matter-of-factly that Ian wondered if he could ever be so casual about ill fortune.

Wynne-Pope apologized for the fact that his men had run down the stocks at the Marine PX but said that of course American cigarettes, lighters, watches, souvenirs *and* ice cream were simply not to be had on *Indomitable*. He gave him a check from the Royal Marine company fund, and after appropriate courtesies they bade each other good night.

Ian found a party in full swing at the apartment when he returned. The duty nurse at the Norfolk Naval Hospital had provided names to his roommates, and they were sharing their latest liquor ration with some attractive nurses they had never met before. Wallace excused himself and went straight to the sack, putting his head under the pillow to block out the noise. It seemed incongruous that he had just left a recital of tragedy and then found so much forced gaiety. He certainly felt closer to the war than he had felt before. When Wynne-Pope had been wounded and lost his family, Wallace had only just completed his freshman year at college. He felt guilty that so much of the conflict had taken place and he was yet to be really a part of it. He hoped the PX would be able to cash the Royal Marines' check. He drifted to sleep. No prayers.

Ian and the officers of the Sea School class visited other capital ships: U.S.S. *South Dakota*, just back from the South Pacific, her bridge decorated with over thirty painted Japanese flags representing enemy planes destroyed; *Richelieu*, freshly arrived from North Africa having joined the Free French, ready for refit.

What impressed them most about *South Dakota* was her computerized Main Battery Plot, her radar controlled 5-inch-38s, her war experience. In the October '42 battle of Santa Cruz, north of Guadalcanal, she had downed twenty-six enemy planes. Then in November in the Second Battle of Guadalcanal, she had lost electrical power at the start of the battle and had survived forty-two large-caliber hits off Savo Island. Unsinkable.

What impressed them most about *Richelieu* was her battle history against the British at Dakar in French West Africa in 1940, when a British naval force, supporting some De Gaulle Free French troops, attempted to take her from Vichy French control to prevent the Nazis from getting her. She suffered an air torpedo hit from a plane from the British carrier *Hermes* in early July and in early September had driven off the British despite taking a direct 15-inch shell hit. Her forward armament (two turrets with four 15-inch guns each) was most impressive as were her appalling sanitary facilities (a bulkhead with water running down it into a trough as a urinal, holes in the steel deck with raised footplates as crappers). Crew amenities were nonexistent.

Wallace wrote to Diana regularly, and she replied. He went to Washington when he could and looked forward to the day he could have Diana visit him, though nothing seemed to make it worth her while to visit this grubby port city even if he asked her. He much preferred to go to D.C.

Ian was sometimes roped into one of the nurses' parties and sometimes would make a date with a nurse and take her to the Starlight Roof at the Monticello Hotel in Norfolk. But he didn't really enjoy it.

One by one his fellow officers were assigned to ships, and new faces replaced the old. Ian finished Sea School, and while he waited for his assignment he was made assistant Post Exchange officer, a dull, paper-pushing job which he did well but didn't like. One of his chores was to check the Marines who ran the Yard gasoline stations. Except when he had the duty he would check the gallonage and the ration coupons at each of the many stations to make sure they balanced. He drove an old, tired, green Marine panel truck each evening to close the stations down.

He wondered what contribution he was making to anything, particularly when he got letters from Perry and from Lewis. He heard from Fix once in a while, but it was pretty obvious that Fix felt the same way about his assignment as Wallace did about his own. Bosse wrote rarely because he was already at sea.

In October the executive officer told him that he understood Wallace would be assigned to new construction, an Essex class carrier, U.S.S. *Franklin*. Ian was thrilled.

He learned that a Saturday night dance was to be held at the Officers' Club before the end of the month. Dress uniform was encouraged. This would probably be the only decent social event before he got his orders and he thought it might be fun for Diana, and for him, if he could borrow a set of dress blues. He inquired around and found an obliging captain who said he wasn't going to anybody's fancy party, and Wallace was welcome to borrow the uniform, mothballs and all. Ian tried it on, and it seemed to be O.K. except for the hat, which needed a new hat cover. He decided he could buy one of those for this one-time occasion and phoned Diana to see if she could come. She was thrilled and asked what she should bring. Ian told her to bring an evening dress and whatever daytime clothes she'd be comfortable in. The post legal officer and his wife had offered to have Diana stay with them in the spare bedroom.

Wallace made reservations for two for the dinner dance and was told he had to pick up his reservations no later than Friday before 1800. That worked out well, because he could close the gasoline stations and by making a two-block detour could pick up the tickets on the return trip to the Post Exchange.

He left the engine running outside the old warehouse that served as the club and rushed into the club office, where he identified himself and paid for and picked up his two reservations. He rushed back to the old truck, not wanting to raise suspicions at the PX office by taking too long to return. He shifted into first and sped to the corner of the woven wire fence that girded the Officers' Club swimming pool. As he turned the corner he noticed some fetching women in two-piece bathing suits preparing to leave the pool, and as he looked up the street he saw bearing down on him a bicycling naval officer also attracted by the same view. The officer in all his heavy gold braid was headed directly for Ian's fender, so Wallace hit the horn and the brakes, pulling as much to the right as he could without hitting the fence. His foot skidded off the worn steel brake pedal and smashed into the accelerator. The tires squealed in braking and then again in acceleration before Ian could firmly depress the brake pedal and the clutch. The naval officer's bicycle wobbled in consternation as the truck's rear doors banged open and then shut from the impetus of the pedals—he bounced off the left front fender and sent his white hat with scrambled eggs on the visor skimming through the air ahead of him!

Wallace brought the truck to a halt and leapt from the door to see the bicycler scoop up his hat from the pavement as he rounded the corner and disappeared. *Jesus Christ in the foothills! Who was that?* He drove back to the corner, but no one was in sight. He turned, and somewhat shaken, drove back to the office, where he made out his gasoline and ration coupon report.

As he left he noticed a buzzing collection of officers in the Officer of the Day's office and went in. He asked Major Hovde what had happened.

"Some dumb son of a bitch driving a Marine truck just ran over the Navy Yard commandant, Rear Admiral William Weatherwax! Down by the Officers' Club! And we're trying to find out who it was!"

Wallace felt like his belly had turned to lead. "Sir, I know who it was."

"Who the hell was it?" shouted Hovde, as all heads turned to look and a silence fell over the room.

"It was me, sir, though there was no run-over."

"What do you mean no run-over? Admiral Weatherwax says he was run over!"

"Sir, we were on a collision course, and I pulled as hard to starboard as I thought I——"

"Hold it!" shouted the executive officer. "The rest of you people get the hell out of here. Wallace, you come to my office. You," he said to the OOD, "don't you put anything in the Day Book until I tell you. C'mon," he ordered Wallace.

Wallace followed Hovde, not into his office, but down the steps to the front walk, and as the darkness fell they walked side by side to Hovde's quarters.

"Now tell me what the hell happened," Hovde said.

"Well, sir, I saw him coming and tried to brake, and the damned old truck gave me some trouble, and by the time I'd stopped he'd run into the left front fender and continued on."

"Did you try to go to his aid?"

"Yes, sir, I did. I jumped from the door just in time to see him pick up his hat on the fly and scoot around the corner. I was worried about all the gold braid, so I got back in the vehicle and tried to find him, but he was gone."

"How-the-hell-come you two didn't see each other?" asked Hovde as they went up the porch steps to his quarters.

"Sir, there were some ladies in swimsuits at the pool, and we may have both glanced at them. But I must repeat, sir, I was on my side of the road, almost into the fence."

Hovde didn't think to ask Wallace why he was anywhere near the pool, but instead chuckled at the vision of the admiral's hat sailing down the street as he ogled the women.

"C'mon in, Wallace, and I'll get us a drink and then I'll call Weatherwax at home and see if we can smooth this thing out."

Wallace was introduced to Mrs. Hovde, who laughed when she heard the story and said she wasn't surprised. The admiral was known to be quite a one for the ladies.

Hovde fixed each of them a neat whiskey without asking and phoned Admiral Weatherwax's quarters. After getting through the telephone guard, Hovde, who called the admiral Bill, told the Yard commandant that the young officer who closed the gas stations had returned to Marine Barracks and reported the incident. He said he was glad that there had been no injuries. He said he had the young officer with him and would take whatever action the admiral thought was warranted.

Hovde cocked the receiver by his ear and motioned to Wallace to listen.

"Well," said Weatherwax, "it's possible that our attention may have been diverted." He chuckled. "And it would seem a shame to go through a lot of rigmarole when there are other important things on our minds. It's also quite possible that I may have strayed out of the channel, and I don't believe we need to have that brought up. On reflection, it's pretty amusing, particularly since there was no damage to equipment or personnel. Here's what you do. You scare the hell out of that young officer so he'll keep out of the way of flag rank in the future, and we'll let it drop right here."

"That seems to be an appropriate solution, Admiral," said Hovde, "and we look forward to seeing you at the dance."

"You make sure you dance with Jane," said the admiral, and after a few more pleasantries they hung up.

"Are you scared, Wallace?" asked the executive officer.

"Shitless, sir," said Ian, quite comfortable with the word.

"O.K., let's finish the drinks and get on with the war."

Wallace picked up Diana and took her to the quarters of the post legal officer, Captain and Mrs. Jessup. Later they had dinner at the Starlight Roof in Norfolk and took the ferry back across the Elizabeth River to Portsmouth. Ian was glad it was dark so that Diana couldn't see all the "Elizabeth River whitefish" that usually floated on top of the water.

Saturday Diana watched the parade, and after lunch they sat on the third floor porch of Ian's quarters and talked until it was time to dress for the dinner. Ian thought Diana looked beautiful in her gown, and Diana was thrilled to see Ian in dress blues, with his Sam Browne belt and expert medals. They shared a table with other young officers and danced to the music of an all-sailor swing band that was very good.

Diana was very popular and danced with the other officers at the table and with Major Hovde and Captain Jessup. "They have very nice things to say about you," Diana told Ian.

Admiral Weatherwax and his wife put in a short appearance, and Major Hovde introduced him to Wallace when they were all on the dance floor, characterizing Ian as one of the Corps' better drivers. Weatherwax smiled and said he was glad to meet Diana, too.

Sunday, as Wallace was taking Diana to the train, they saw Colonel

Bentley and Admiral Weatherwax, followed by two enlisted men, playing their weekly golf game. The real war, thought Wallace.

Monday morning at 0800 Wallace became Assistant Officer of the Day. He performed the routine duties until about 1500 when the old sergeant major, Brundage, stuck his head in the duty office and growled, "Wallace, the colonel wants you in his office. Now!"

Wallace reported to the colonel's office, covered and armed as befits an officer with the duty. He knocked, took two paces forward, stood at attention, came to the salute and said, "Second Lieutenant Wallace reporting as ordered, sir."

Colonel Bentley continued to read some papers on his desk and left Wallace standing there for a good minute. Then he looked up, put his right elbow on the desk and pointed his bony forefinger at Wallace's chest.

"Wallace," he said, "I'm going to hang you! Get out!"

Ian, shaken, about-faced and returned to the duty office where Brundage was waiting for him with an official document. He threw it at Wallace, said, "Read that!" and walked out.

On post letterhead the document was from "The Commanding Officer to Second Lieutenant Ian Wallace, USMCR," and demanded an explanation why, in contravention of Article 206, Navy Regulations, Wallace had used a Post Exchange truck without authorization and had driven with an excessive rate of speed in the Norfolk Navy Yard on the date in question.

Wallace was furious. He'd been ordered to close the gas stations as part of his PX duties. No driver had ever been provided. He hadn't been driving fast. He phoned Major Hovde.

Hovde said the colonel had learned about Weatherwax's hat on Sunday at golf when Weatherwax told the colonel jokingly about the incident. When the admiral saw the colonel's reaction he phoned Hovde and warned him. The colonel had chewed out Hovde and the OOD at Office Hours that morning and admonished them not to say anything to Wallace. The colonel said he would take care of that himself.

Hovde suggested that Wallace call Jessup, the legal officer, for some guidance. Ian did that and the captain came in and looked at the papers.

"You'll have to reply by endorsement," Jessup said. "I can't tell you what to say, but I can see that you get it in the right form and order."

Jessup sat by him into the evening while they worked out the best way to present the truth of the case. Hovde dropped by and so did Major Munro of the Sea School. They were all pretty pissed off at the chicken-shit action of the colonel. Jessup pointed out that there were regulations which prohibited officers from driving vehicles. They all spoke up and said they'd all been driving Marine vehicles!

Jessup said that the colonel didn't have to look the other way if he didn't want to and could enforce post ground rules at any time.

"I know what it is," said Hovde. "He's pissed that I didn't tell him about it, that the OOD didn't report it and that he heard it first from Weatherwax, and the admiral could see that he didn't know a damn thing about it. So he read us off, and in order to make it a matter of record he's taking it out on Wallace! Then he can tell the admiral he's done his goddam duty!"

They worked on the endorsement until late and then had it typed and submitted in the morning. A second endorsement was fired right back from the commanding officer requesting further explanation of the unauthorized use of the truck, and further explanation of what the truck was doing in the vicinity of Kearny Avenue and Livingston Street could be included if the respondent so desired.

Wallace, Jessup and Hovde worked for several hours on the third endorsement, and it was returned to the colonel. Before the day was over the commanding officer's fourth endorsement required further explanations. Wallace slept little and in the morning his team put together a fifth endorsement and sent it in.

At noon Wallace received a document from the commanding officer, subject: Arrest.

Inasmuch as the explanation submitted with reference to so-and-so was unsatisfactory, Wallace was thereby placed under arrest for five (5) days, effective immediately. During his arrest he was confined to the limits of quarters assigned to him at all times, with the exceptions that he was authorized to absent himself from the quarters assigned him from 6:55 A.M. to 7:25 A.M., from 12:10 P.M. to 12:40 P.M., and from 5:00 P.M. to 5:30 P.M., during which periods he would secure his meals at the barracks and would report in person to the Officer of the Day at this barracks. [signed] John R. Bentley.

Copies of all the correspondence to: The Commandant, U.S. Marine Corps (with the request that the papers be filed with Wallace's official record); Commandant, Norfolk Navy Yard; Paymaster; Commanding Officer Sea School Detachment; FILE (2).

Wallace was stunned, but realized that it had been a losing battle all along. Nonetheless, he was very mad and very upset that the son of a bitch of a colonel could arbitrarily screw up his exemplary record. He was seething.

He went to the OOD's office and told him he was returning to his quarters under arrest. His orders didn't say he had to go to chow, only that he was authorized to, so he sat in his room and sulked. That didn't make him feel any better, so he paced. That didn't make him feel better, so he tried to read his Bible but felt so unforgiving that he threw it across the room. It smashed into the bulkhead and fluttered to the floor, broken and torn.

At about 1400 there was a tentative knock at the door. Now what the hell? thought Wallace. He opened the door, and there stood Mrs. Jessup with a tray on which were sandwiches and a thermos bottle of coffee.

"Jess said you didn't have any noon meal, so I thought you might be hungry," she said.

Wallace dissolved. All his hatred collapsed. His emotion exploded in laughter, and he asked Mrs. Jessup to come in. She said she really shouldn't, but would just stay for a minute to see that everything was all right. Wallace was hungry as a wolf.

That was the beginning of an astonishing week for Ian. He phoned Diana that evening, and they spent almost twenty expensive minutes on the phone while he reassured her that everything would be all right, not that he really believed it. He had visitors galore. They brought beer, booze, cake and cookies. His roommates offered to provide him with a Navy nurse date every night. The NCOs at the barracks during meals told him no officer was worth a shit unless he'd spent some time in hack. Jessup and Hovde came by every day, and occasionally Munro. Even Mrs. Hovde brought some cookies.

Wallace understood that they were telling him how they felt about his arrest and how they felt about the colonel, even though there was some risk at their open display of affection. He worried for them and he worried for himself. Copies to the Commandant, U.S. Marine Corps! *Jesus H. Christ!* And he'd better worry about Him too, and watch his thoughts.

On his first day after hack Wallace was walking through the passageway near the sergeant major's office when he heard Brundage shout, "Wallace!"

The hell with that, thought Wallace and kept walking. Brundage stuck his head out the door and shouted "Wallace!" again.

Wallace stopped, turned around, looked at the old sergeant major and said, "The hell with you, Brundage. I haven't heard a goddam thing!" And he turned and walked down the hall.

"Sir!" called Brundage.

Wallace turned around. "Yes, Sergeant Major?"

"Sir, there's an envelope for you in the OOD's office. Came this morning, sir," the sergeant major said with a smile.

"Thank you, Sergeant Major," said Wallace and went to the OOD's room.

The Officer of the Day handed him a tan official envelope. In it were orders, just dated yesterday, at Headquarters U.S. Marine Corps, Washington. "From the Commandant, U.S. Marine Corps. Subject: Change of station. When directed by the Commandant, Norfolk Navy Yard, Portsmouth, Va., you will stand detached from your present station and duties, will proceed to Washington, D.C., and report to the Commandant, U.S. Marine Corps, for duty at this Headquarters."

Report to the commandant? Good God. So soon. Why art thou cast down, O my soul? and why art thou disquieted in me?

We are the boys that fear no noise where thundering cannons roar.

— Oliver Goldsmith
She Stoops To Conquer

PACIFIC 1944

WALLACE HAD NEVER RIDDEN TRAINS VERY MUCH before he enlisted in the Corps. His travel had been limited to a narrow part of New England and his one trip to New York. Yet now, as the cars swayed over the rail links and switch points, he was pondering the number of train rides he had had in the past few months. All the way to South Carolina. Back up to Virginia. Up to Massachusetts and back. Down to Portsmouth and then back and forth to Washington. And here he was with new orders, headed across the continent to San Francisco via the Baltimore and Ohio; the Chicago, Burlington and Quincy; the Denver and Rio Grande Western; and the Western Pacific railroads, all in the same car.

They'd been bumped around in the middle of the night in St. Louis as the car was switched from the B&O to the CB&Q, which was annoying. But on second thought, Wallace concluded it was just as well that it was the middle of the night. The seventeen sailors of whom he was in charge tended to become adventurous during daylight stops. And, even though he'd told the chief petty officer to keep the men on the train, he fretted some at every stop.

Actually the swab jockeys in his charge were a pretty good bunch. Pretty responsible and reliable or they wouldn't have drawn this duty. Ian had been with them for a little over three weeks, and he thought he understood a little about each one. These seventeen were the survivors of a course that they and

Wallace had been put through, courtesy of the Office of Strategic Services, the OSS. Four of the original twenty-one men had failed to measure up, by failing to follow orders about not disclosing their real names, ranks or branch of service.

Way out in a tract of rough one-story log barracks deep in the Maryland forest known only as Area D, they had been given a party on the last night of their two weeks of "cloak-and-dagger" training. There they had sat, in their anonymous one-piece Army coveralls, wearing helmet liners with code names on the front, drinking beer, watching a dirty movie (if they chose to), singing songs and fraternizing with the instructors. It was a relief after two weeks of tension for the men. The instructor officers all played buddy-buddy and asked the men about where they were from, about their families and their branch of service. Four sailors fell for it, and when the group returned to Washington the four men disappeared. Back to their old outfits, Wallace presumed.

Looking out the train window in the dying January light Wallace could see the incredibly flat Kansas plains, deep in snow, empty and desolate. Occasionally a farm would flash by, all the lights on in the barn and maybe one light in the house. The kitchen, probably. He remembered the smells of the cows and the manure, the singular odor of the unseparated raw milk, the hay. And he remembered the kitchen smells and felt a momentary pang of homesickness and grief as he thought of his mother. He pictured her turning from the oven, red faced, straightening up with a pan of hot bread in her towel-covered hands. He could smell that bread, and it made his stomach growl with hunger.

How many more trains, he wondered. And how many more surprises. His transfer to Washington had been a surprise. His experiences since had been full of surprises, some good, some not so good.

He remembered he'd reported in to the Officer of the Day at Marine Head-quarters at about 2115 on a Sunday night. The officer, a major, logged him and then said, "Oh, so you're Wallace! Report to the Officer of the Day tomorrow at oh-eight-hundred."

"What's the duty, sir, do you know?"

"You'll find out quick enough for yourself when you get here in the morning. That's all I can tell you."

"Thank you, sir," said Wallace and left for the Gayety and Diana, disturbed by his reception and anticipating the worst.

He and Diana talked until the small hours; she tried to be reassuring, but none of her reassurances made going to sleep any easier. At least Irene wasn't around to make things more complicated.

On Monday Ian reported to the Officer of the Day at 0800 directly after colors. "Aha!" said the OOD, "so *you're* Wallace. You go down that passageway to Colonel Miller's office. It's on the right and he's expecting you."

Expecting me! Wallace went down the hall reading the little signs that stood out from the wall at the top corner of each office door. He found "Colonel Miller, Personnel Officer" and turned into a small outer office where a woman Marine corporal was seated behind a desk.

"I'm Wallace," Ian told her, and before she could reply a voice boomed from the inner office, "Send Wallace right in!"

Wallace had not felt butterflies in his stomach like this for a long time. Personnel Officer, for heaven's sake. He went in and stood at attention before Colonel Miller's desk, the big bull-necked colonel looked up as Wallace started to say the usual "Second Lieutenant Wallace reporting as ordered, sir," and the colonel said, "Glad to see you, Wallace," and stuck out his hand.

Wallace shook the proffered paw and the colonel told him to sit down.

"Do you know why you're here?" Miller asked.

Wallace suspected the worst, but thought he'd better not voice his suspicions so he said, "No, sir."

"O.K.," said Miller, "here's what you do then," and he proceeded to write something on a small slip of paper that he handed to Ian. Wallace looked at the writing. It said "Room 2732. Navy Building. Cmdr. Ledyard." Nothing else.

Ian looked up and asked, "May I know what this is about, sir?"

"They'll tell you when they think you need to know over at the Navy Department. Take the shuttle bus and it'll get you right to the building." He stuck out his big paw again and said, "Good luck."

Wallace got up, shook the colonel's hand, said, "Thank you, sir," and left.

The Navy Department was housed in D.C. on the eastern side of the Potomac in temporary quarters erected during World War I on Constitution Avenue between Eighteenth and Twentieth streets. The shuttle bus stopped at the Pentagon and then crossed the Arlington Memorial Bridge to Constitution Avenue and dropped Wallace and some other men at the Navy building. Ian mounted the stairs inside the building and asked a guard outside the office of the Secretary of the Navy where he might find room 2732. He was told which passageway to take and walked down the hall, carefully reading the black signs with gilt lettering that projected into the hallway from above each door: "Destroyers," "Submarines," and other arms. Watching the room numbers as well as the signs, he arrived at 2732, looked up at its shingle and saw that it read "Interior Control Board." I don't know what that means, he thought, but I don't like the sound of it.

He opened the door and walked in and found himself in a small gray room with a closed door to the left and another to the right. Directly ahead of him was a sliding gray panel above a shelf about waist high. A sign on the panel said "Knock." Wallace did that and waited an eternity for the panel to open. When it did Wallace was staring at a yeoman sitting behind a desk in what appeared to be a good-sized office with several other sailors and a couple of chief petty officers busy at typewriters or on phones.

"What do you want?" asked the yeoman.

"Commander Ledyard," Wallace replied.

"What's your name?"

"Wallace."

The yeoman said nothing but swiveled his chair around and delved into a filing cabinet while Wallace waited. The yeoman swiveled back and handed Wallace a stack of mimeographed sheets, stapled together.

"Go in that door to your right, fill these out and give 'em back to me." He closed the sliding panel.

Wallace went into the right-hand room and found only a couple of long gray tables and some folding chairs. He hung up his coat and hat on a wall hook, pulled up one of the chairs to the nearest table and studied the forms he'd been given. The heading "Interior Control Board" gave him no clue, nor did the questions he was asked to answer. His name, rank and serial number had been typed in the appropriate spaces. The other lines all asked about Ian's background, family, education, habits, language fluency (do I tell them French *and* Latin?), how many big toes his paternal grandfather had and on and on. Ian settled down to fill in the spaces as best he could, wondering why all this information hadn't been lifted from his personnel jacket. Maybe they were trying to trap him. Catch him in a mistake.

He felt sure of it when he came to the last of the four pages. The final question was: "If there is something relevant in your background not covered by the foregoing questions, describe it in the space below."

Hah! You won't catch me on this one. Ian laboriously detailed the story of his accident with Admiral Weatherwax and his subsequent arrest. He then signed the statement, put on his coat and hat, knocked on the panel and gave the papers to the yeoman. The sailor glanced at them, threw them in a wire file basket and said, "Be here tomorrow morning at oh-eight-hundred," and closed the panel. What the hell, thought Ian. It's only nine-thirty in the morning. He knocked at the panel again. The yeoman opened it and said, "Well?"

"I was told to report to Commander Ledyard. What about it?"

"You just did. He'll see your papers. Be back here in the morning." The panel closed.

Wallace spent the morning walking and preoccupied, worrying about what was happening. Everyone he knew was at work or at war, and here he was trying to find out how to kill time. He took himself to the Library of Congress between East Capitol Street and Independence Avenue and lost himself in the reference rooms and stacks, absorbed in the plethora of material on religious history.

The process repeated itself each morning. He signed an attendance sheet and was told to return the next day. One day he bumped into three Marine officers who were talking in the room with the long tables. He said, "Good morning," and they just nodded their heads and stopped their conversation.

On Friday he was told to be at room 2732 on Sunday at sixteen hundred hours. Nothing to do all week but check in, and now they want you to come in on Sunday!

When Ian arrived at room 2732 that sabbath afternoon there were two Marine officers and one Navy lieutenant in the room with the tables. They all nodded to each other and remained silent. Finally Wallace broke the ice and asked, "Does anybody know what the hell is going on here?"

"You haven't been told?" the lieutenant asked.

"Not one word."

The other officers looked at each other and remained silent.

One at a time the officers were called to the door by a chief yeoman. They were called at about half-hour intervals. None of them returned. Ian was last, and his adrenalin was hard at work when the chief summoned him and led him down the main hallway to an unmarked door. The chief knocked, opened it and said, "Wallace, sir," and stood aside for Ian to enter.

It was a large room with a desk at one wall and chairs all around the other three walls. A quick glance told Wallace that there was a lot of brass present, foreign and domestic, English and French, Chinese and American. All the chairs were occupied but the one at the side of the desk. Behind the desk sat the Chief of Naval Operations.

"At ease, Wallace," the CNO said. "Please sit down."

Ian seated himself facing the CNO. "We already know a good bit about you, Wallace," he said, "but in view of the duty you are about to undertake, a number of these officers would like to ask you some questions."

"Yes, sir."

"I'll start," said the CNO. He had Wallace's statement before him. He asked Ian a number of questions about his background, glanced at the last page and smiled the briefest of smiles—Ian felt the sweat trickle down his back. The CNO inquired about Ian's feelings about the color of a man's skin. Ian could honestly answer that he'd never given it much thought, but said that if a man was any good it didn't matter what color he was. Would he, Ian, object to parachuting in unusual circumstances? No. Would he object to or have any reservations about travel by submarine, or to landing from a submarine in a rubber boat. No, sir. Was he fussy about his food? An odd question, but no, sir. Other officers picked up the questioning. Could he operate on his own for extended periods without contact with other Americans? He thought so. Did he think he could live off the land? It depended on where the land might be, but he thought he could.

"*Vraiment, parlez-vous français?*" asked a French naval officer.

"*Je parle peu et bien,*" Ian replied idiomatically, "*si je veux qu'on me regarde comme un homme de mérite.*" The Frenchman raised his eyebrows.

"Are there any more questions?" asked the CNO. There were none, but the officers all seemed to be nodding their heads in agreement.

"Well, then, Wallace," said the CNO "did you volunteer for this operation?"

"No, sir."

"Then it is my honor to inform you that six weeks ago you and a very few other outstanding officers were carefully selected by the commandant of the Marine Corps for assignment to unusual and extra-hazardous duty. Congratulations." Six weeks ago! This has nothing to do with the Weatherwax thing! "These other gentlemen are here primarily to agree on the selections, and you have done well."

The CNO stood up and put out his hand. "You are to tell no one, repeat no one, about this meeting. You'll receive your orders shortly. Congratulations again, Wallace. That will be all."

Wallace shook the extended hand, about-faced and left the room. The chief yeoman was waiting in the hallway and told Ian to be at 2732 at oh-eight-hundred in the morning.

Wallace left the building relieved that his transfer to Washington was in no way associated with his arrest and that in fact he had been picked as an outstanding officer. Then why, he wondered, did he feel like he had just gone from the frying pan into the fire? He didn't know yet where he was to be sent. He didn't know what kind of duty he'd drawn except that it was *extra* hazardous. Good Lord, what could be more hazardous than being shot at?

He couldn't tell Diana anything about his meeting, and she was smart enough not to push the subject. She simply said she knew he'd tell her if and when he could.

On Monday morning instead of just checking in Ian was called into the inner office where he met Ledyard. Ledyard told him to collect twenty-one sailors from the other room and take them to Q Building. He told Ian that he and the sailors would be gone for two weeks and that they were to tell no one and to make no phone calls. What about the hotels and boarding houses where the men were staying? We'll take care of that; we know where they're all staying. What about toilet gear and clothing? You'll be given what you need. Ian wondered what Diana would think when he didn't show up and she didn't hear from him. She'd worry, and Ian thought it was insensitive of the Navy to insist on such secrecy.

"When you get to Q Building ask for Colonel Jones. He knows you by the code name Wally. Identify yourself and tell him you have the enlisted men with you."

Wally! Clever my foot! he thought as he rounded up his sailors and walked them to Q Building, a large, square, white stucco structure with a mansard roof, sitting behind a French picket fence. He identified himself to the civilian receptionist who connected him to Jones. Jones told him to take the men to room four in the basement where they would be met. The basement was light and airy and appeared to consist of five or six large class-rooms with one-armed writing chairs and blackboards. They went into room four and sat down and waited. With all the phony hocus-pocus Wallace correctly figured this had to be the OSS headquarters building.

In fifteen minutes a Navy lieutenant commander came in carrying a clip-board under his arm. He closed the door, pulled the shade over its glass panel, walked to the desk at the front of the room and leaned back against it.

"Men," he said, "this is the moment you've all been waiting for. You'll leave this room and go by train direct to Norfolk where you will embark. Once in the Aegean Ocean you'll be off-loaded to a coastal lugger and put ashore in Greece under cover of darkness. The bridge you've been trained to blow——"

"Sir," said Ian, standing up. "There must be a mix-up somewhere. We've had no training. We just got here."

"My God!" said the lieutenant commander. "Isn't this Group Charlie?"

"Group Wally," said Ian.

"Christ in the foothills!" exclaimed the officer, picking up his clipboard and rushing to the door where he bumped into an Army major just about to come into the room. The major came in and asked what *that* was all about. Wallace told him, and the major rushed from the room telling the men to sit tight. When he came back he said to forget they'd ever seen or heard anything until he, the major, started to talk. He explained that they would be going to a special training area—they would all have code names and wear Army fatigues and were to tell no one their names or ranks or any other personal information.

They were taken to a locker room where they changed to one-piece Army dungarees while their personal gear was labeled and stored. They taped their code names on the front of helmet liners, were issued little green cloth ditty bags with toilet articles and were herded into a 6x6 truck. The canvas tarps were secured so they could not see out, and the truck ground out of the yard. The men groused and bitched about not being able to notify anyone that they'd be out of touch for two weeks. They said their girls and parents would worry.

The special training turned out to be a rush-rush course in hand weapons, judo, knife fighting, explosive devices (pressure, release, push-pull) and night compass courses. Wallace had done it all before and found it hard to pretend it was all new to him. At one point the coast artillery officer who was instructing the small arms course couldn't get his M1 rifle back together. Wallace managed to suggest that maybe the sear pin should go in next. The officer looked at him with gratitude.

The experience was new to the sailors... or to most of them. Wallace didn't remember what rates they carried on their sleeves, whether they were left-arm or right-arm rates, but presumed they were specialists of some kind.

Some were pretty good with weapons, and one in particular was very good in the woods at night. Area D was on a broad river, which Ian suspected was the Potomac, though all they could see was the river and the rolling forested hills through which they made their single and group night compass marches. On one such maneuver Wallace teamed up with the sailor who seemed to know his way in the forest. They were the last pair to start a three-legged course. Each pair was to reach the objective, a set of fox holes and bunkers manned by school troops, sneak into the main bunker, sign the book and sneak back to the log barracks.

Ian and the sailor looked at the map and each other. "You know," said Wallace, "if we just cut straight across here instead of taking these doglegs we'd be home early. A little swampy there, but what the hell."

"I'm game," said the man, and they took off on their short cut. They got soaked in the swamp but reached the objective long before any other group, so early, in fact, that the troops had left their rifles in their fox holes and were playing cards in the bunker.

"That's a helluva way to stand guard," whispered the sailor.

"Tell you what," breathed Ian. "Let's quietly collect their weapons from the fox holes, hide them and then make a racket so they'll get out of the bunker, and we can get in and sign the book."

"You're on!" the sailor said, and they slithered from fox hole to fox hole dragging the rifles they gathered to the swamp's edge. They pushed all but one of the pieces under the water.

"Ready?" Ian asked. The sailor nodded. Wallace squeezed off three quick rounds and while the echo was dying put the piece with its mates. The troops came tumbling out of the bunker and soon were shouting at each other as they discovered their weapons were missing. Ian and the sailor slipped into the bunker, signed the book in the middle of the page, crept out and took the most direct route back to the barracks.

That had been fun, but the rest of the training was so much kindergarten. Wallace made the mistake of throwing a judo instructor to the ground, and found his bunk booby-trapped with a cherry bomb that night. Fortunately he'd checked the sack before he sat on it and disconnected the pressure device.

The final-night party was pretty transparent, Wallace thought. But then it fooled the four guys who spilled their guts when they got a little beer under their belts. Wallace couldn't wait for the whole affair to be over with. Probably it had been a good experience for the sailors, but Ian had been pretty bored, appalled at the incompetence of the instructors and astonished at the seriousness with which the OSS regarded its cloak-and-dagger approach to a simple training exercise in the woods.

Diana was very relieved to see him when he returned. Congressman Bensen had sounded out the Navy Department and told her that the Interior Control Board was part of Naval Intelligence and that sometimes short training disappearances occurred. Even so, she had worried. Ian thought her welcome home had almost made the absence worthwhile.

When he received his orders to go overseas he learned that he would be reporting to the Senior U.S. Naval Observer in China for unspecified special duty. China! The orders referred to his destination as PACT, which Wallace suspected was an acronym for Pacific Area China Theater. The orders stated that he would be provided with transportation, would be allowed per diem allowances as prescribed in Tables I and II of the letter of the Secretary of the Navy dated 11 November 1943 and was authorized to wear civilian clothes while on this special duty. Copies of the orders to: Chief of Naval Operations, the Quartermaster and Paymaster, Director, Naval Intelligence, Commanding Officer PACT, etc., etc.

He couldn't tell anyone where or when he was going. He sent a letter home telling his grandfather that his new address would be c/o FPO Box 990, Fleet Post Office, New York, N.Y., and that he would be out of touch for a while but would write when he could. He told Diana that he would be leaving soon, knowing full well it would be the next day. He gave her the new address and told her he would write her and that he would miss her terribly.

They were alone in the Gayety kitchen at the table. Diana looked at Ian and asked, "Did you ever have a steady girl?"

"Not really."

"How come?"

"Not too many girls near the farm. Just boys, with dirty fingernails and dirty minds. Most of them never finished high school. They quit to work on their family farm or when they were sixteen they quit to work in the factories in Holyoke or the armory at Springfield."

"What about at college?"

"Not much time. Not much money. Too many jobs. Too much study. Too many extra-curricular activities... too shy."

"Too shy!"

"Everybody else was so smooth. They'd all been to boarding school. They drove convertibles or station wagons. They knew how to dress and dance and how to play 'do you know so-and-so?' "

"How did you meet Irene?" Her name shocked Ian. He hadn't thought of her in weeks.

"Glee club," Ian said. "She drew my name as her escort at our first joint concert. And we saw each other at a couple of concerts after that. She was kind to me."

"You are a babe in the woods where gals are concerned, aren't you?"

"I'm painfully aware of that."

"I like Irene. She is sweet. That's the trouble. She's too sweet and she keeps tasting different candy. You. Then Pine. Lord knows who she's sweet on today!"

Ian knew why that didn't bother him. He looked at Diana and summoned his courage. "I think I'm sweet on you, Diana. I never felt like this before." He looked in her eyes.

She reached out her hand and touched his cheek. Then she leaned forward and kissed him gently. "And I'm sweet on you, Wringer. Only you."

Ian's heart pounded... "I don't know how to be very romantic," he said, "yet I know I'd like to be with you every day of my life. But I'm going away and that can't be. And I don't want to ask for promises. That doesn't seem fair. I just want you to know you fill my heart and my thoughts, and when I get back, if I get back, then I'll ask you for promises."

Diana gazed at him. "You don't have to ask for promises, Ian. I give them to you. When you get back, and you *will* get back, we can share our promises."

Ian thought his chest would burst.

Crossing the dark Kansas prairie with those same seventeen sailors, equipped with a passport stamped with visas for Egypt, Iran, India and China, and carrying orders directing him to PACT, Wallace nodded to the clack-clack of the Pullman car wheels as the train threaded its way toward Denver, Reno and Oakland. We're already a long way from Cummington, Massachusetts....

At Oakland they detrained, took the ferry across the bay to the terminal building at the foot of Market Street and went up the hill to the headquarters of the Twelfth Naval District. The enlisted men were sent to quarters at Mare Island, and Ian was sent to the Shaw Hotel, a block off Market Street. He found that he was sharing a room with a Navy j.g., a former member of the Secret Service who also was assigned to PACT. They checked in with headquarters daily by phone but otherwise were free to do as they wished until they were assigned transportation. Ian phoned Diana nightly with the understanding that the night he didn't call meant he was underway.

Wallace enjoyed the city and the bay, marveled at the Bay Bridge and the Golden Gate. His roommate, Tom Mooney, told amazing tales of his experience in the service, both at the White House and at Hyde Park, and of catching counterfeiters at gun point before being assigned to the Presidential body guard. Mooney phoned his pregnant wife every evening and then went out to the bars to collect his woman for the night. One morning Ian awoke to find Mooney in bed with him. A naked red-headed floozy was passed out on top of Mooney's bed. "Four times!" Mooney whispered.

The next evening Wallace couldn't get into the room. The door was locked, and Mooney wouldn't answer the phone. Wallace was furious. He phoned Diana from a public phone and then went up Market Street to see if he could get a room in another hotel, but was deterred by the sight of so many servicemen asleep in the lobbies, in chairs, on the deck, any place they could sleep in some little comfort. Many of them had pinned signs to their uniforms…. "Please wake me at 5 A.M.," and so on. Wallace found an all-night movie and went in and slept sitting up, in the company of a lot of other men who had made the same choice.

He left the movie theater about six A.M. and looked for breakfast. He needed a shave and to brush his teeth. His uniform was rumpled. He hoped he wouldn't run into the Shore Patrol. He stopped in front of an open restaurant: Bunny's Waffle Shoppe. Waffles, he thought, and maple syrup. A taste of New England. He went in and ordered California's simplest dish: a hot whole-wheat strawberry waffle with whipped cream.

He got back to the Hotel Shaw at eight in the morning and was able to unlock the door to the room. Mooney was snoring on his bed. The room was a shambles. It reeked of cigarette smoke and whiskey. There were dirty, lipstick-stained glasses on the bed-side table and the bureau. The ash trays were full. Wallace cleaned up the bathroom and then showered and shaved. When he came out to dress, Mooney was sitting naked on the edge of the bed with his head in his hands.

"Better get something to eat to absorb some of that poison," Wallace said.

"Eat! I can't even walk! Those women drained me dry, and I hurt all over. My nuts will ache for a month."

"Serves you right. But just the same you better have some breakfast."

"I've had breakfast," said Mooney.

"I'll bet," said Wallace. "What did you have?"

"A puke and a cigarette."

"Come on," said Wallace, and lifting Mooney by the elbow he guided him across the room, opened the entrance to the hall, pushed the naked officer through into the corridor, then slammed and locked the door.

Ian, Mooney, three other Naval officers and Ian's seventeen sailors were ordered to report to H.M.S. *Ranee* at Alameda Naval Air Station for transportation to the Far East. *Ranee*, CVE 46, an escort carrier built at the Seattle-Tacoma Shipyard and turned over to the British, was tied up at the station pier where cranes were loading her with P-40s and P-51s to be ferried to India. Large wooden cages, each containing a German Shepherd attack dog, were also being loaded into the forward end of the flight deck. They were the responsibility of one of the U.S. Navy officers.

On her shakedown cruise the British had managed to run *Ranee* aground near Port Townsend where Puget Sound joins the Strait of Juan de Fuca. She was ignominiously pulled off the mud by U.S. Navy tugs, her bow repaired, and she sailed for Alameda.

As Ian looked up at her from the dock he was reminded of H.M.S. *Indomitable*. Not as big, but the uniforms were the same strange ones he had seen in Norfolk, the hullplates were already chipped and rusting and she smelled just as bad. How can they take a brand-new ship and turn it into a honey barge so quickly, Wallace wondered.

Mooney, Wallace and two other officers were assigned to a cabin below the water line, in officers' country. One hanging locker, two double-decker bunks, a desk that folded down from the bulkhead, two steel chairs and a half-dozen bulkhead drawers. They left most of their gear in their footlockers and sea bags except for what they would need at sea. There was no place to stow shoes so Wallace put his in a metal waste basket next to the standing locker. They were assigned to specific duties when the ship went to general quarters, "action stations" the British called it. There were dawn and dusk action stations every day and at such other times as they might be threatened with attack. Ian was given command of the port 5-inch-38 gun on the port sponson under the stern of the flight deck. It and the starboard 5-inch were the ship's main armament. Mooney had charge of the seventeen sailors who would help pass ammunition to the 20mm guns on the gallery deck.

Mooney was boasting about what a sailor he was and what he and "his" men would do under attack when an announcement was made over the Tannoy: "We are now singled up and about to cast off. Bring in the brow!"

Mooney turned chartreuse, staggered from the bunk to the corner of the cabin and threw up on Ian's shoes in the waste bucket.

The officers were wakened in the morning by a steward who brought them tea before the call to action stations. A civilized way to fight a war, the officers all agreed, except Mooney, who couldn't keep anything down even in the calm seas they encountered between the Golden Gate and the waters south of Hawaii. They would be roused from their bunks with the call: *"Wakey, wakey, rise and shine, the day is fine!"* Then they'd scramble into their clothes and rush to action stations when the gongs rang, arriving in the cold blackness before dawn, shivering and remembering the hot tea in their bunks moments before.

Wallace conjured up mental images as he heard the British announcements and commands over the loud-speaker system.

"Middle watchmen fall in!" (splash)

"Darken ship!" (black paint)

"Cooks to the galley!" (into the longboat)

"Up spirits!" (ghosts on the quarter-deck)

The latter referred to the issuance of rum to all ratings at eleven each morning. The officers got their liquor in the wardroom. There was a chit system. All you had to do was sign the chit presented by the messman and pay up at the end of the month. Ian was told that Number One, the executive officer, "kept track of the chits to see who was over-indulging." Most of the British officers had a gin before lunch and a bit more before dinner. It astonished Wallace, who came from a dry home and a dry branch of service.

The British officers tried to be civil but found it difficult to accommodate themselves to the fact that they were running a ferry service, carrying American planes on an American built ship, to the U.S. Army Air Corps in *their* India, helped by American passengers, for heaven's sake. Ian made friends with a sub-lieutenant who was assigned to the ship from the Royal Canadian Navy Volunteer Reserve, the RCNVR. The stripe on his sleeve was not straight but wavy. The "wavy navy" the British called the reservists, not without some disdain. Damned glad we don't distinguish between regulars and reservists in our services, thought Ian.

The Canadian, Chaffee, became quite popular after it was discovered he could play the wardroom upright piano. There was much singing and drinking to his accompaniment. He and Wallace wrote a rude song about the ship's officers that was greeted with hilarity, and some of Chaffee's popularity rubbed off on Ian.

Number One made a point of standing Wallace to a drink before dinner one evening. The executive officer was RNR, as were some of the other department heads. Wallace asked what the differences were between the RNVR, the RNR and the RN.

"Why," explained Number One, "the RNVR are gentlemen trying to become officers; the RNR are officers trying to become gentlemen; and the RN are neither trying to become both."

Ian snorted appreciatively. "Are the duties different?"

"Not really. We all spend time making our idiot subordinates and the other ranks repeat orders so that we have some mild assurance that they may be carried out. Surely you've heard of Admiral Lord Rodney?"

"Sorry, sir, but no."

"Admiral Lord George Brydges Rodney is quite celebrated by our Navy as the man who insisted that all orders be repeated. At the peace of 1763 Rodney returned home with his squadron as vice-admiral of the Blue and upon entering harbor had the signal officer send a dispatch to his wife ashore. The message read: 'In today. Home tonight. Lots of love. Rodney.' The signalman waved his flags and the vice-admiral asked for confirmation from shore. The shore signals arrived and read: 'Home today. In tonight. Lots of rod. Lovely.' That's why all orders are repeated to this day," said Number One with his eyebrows raised.

Wallace enjoyed the story, apocryphal or not, and asked Number One what he had done before hostilities. He replied that he had been captain of a freighter in the guano trade between Chile and England.

"I should think you would prefer this duty to that," said Ian.

"Shit or soldiers, it's all the same to me," said Number One.

Wallace found that his command was in name only. The port 5-inch-38 was really run by Leading Seaman Crowther, a veteran of six years in the British

Navy who had had three ships shot from under him. At action stations he and Wallace would talk about their backgrounds. Crowther found it amazing to be talking to an officer that way. Wallace found it amazing to find out how little formal schooling Crowther had had and yet how smart he was. He'd had plenty of school on the 5-inch-38 he assured Wallace and answered Wallace's questions with accuracy.

They crossed the equator with no ceremony, and when they were almost due south of Hawaii at 4.03 degrees south, 154.59 degrees west, they had their first gunnery practice. The target was Malden Island, a small dot in the ocean that hosted a deserted British weather station. *Ranee* changed course during the firing so that both the port and starboard guns could fire. The port side fired first and as the ship changed course Ian's gun came on a dangerous bearing, elevated so much that there was danger the shell would hit the flight deck in its path; and the elevation mechanism jammed. The range to target had been cranked in and the gun was locked on, lifting and dipping as the ship went through the swells, but pointed at the stern of the flight deck. There was a shell in the breech which would have to be unloaded, a very ticklish proposition. The breech was hot from firing and they couldn't let the round "cook off."

"Sir," said Crowther, "I think we can unload through the muzzle."

"We're on a dangerous bearing and the cut-out switch won't let us fire."

"If you can get permission to unload through the muzzle, I can over-ride the cut-out switch and we'll shoot on the top of the swell."

Ian told the telephone talker to get permission from the gunnery officer to unload through the muzzle. Permission was granted. Crowther told the pointer and trainer to get out of their seats on either side of the gun. He put Wallace in the pointer's seat and leaned down and grasped the cut-out lever where it had disengaged itself from the firing pedal.

"Watch the muzzle, sir, and when it's clear of that catwalk under the flight deck, please yell 'shoot' and we'll get rid of this bugger."

The crew cleared itself off the sponson, and Wallace lined his eyes up on the barrel. The gun automatically adjusted itself to the target as it had been set to do. The ship's stern would rise with each swell, but Wallace could not see daylight between the barrel and the cat walk. If I don't call this shot right we'll blow the flight deck apart, ruin a lot of airplanes and probably kill this gun crew, Ian thought. We're going to have to unload this thing with the ramrod if we can ever get the elevating mechanism freed or un-stuck. Just then he saw daylight.

"Shoot!" he yelled.

Crowther pulled the cut-out lever and the gun fired, hurling its fifty-four-pound explosive-filled projectile out of the tube with an ear-shattering roar. The gun recoiled and spat out its used brass powder case, which clanged to the gun platform. While the smoke was blowing away Crowther and Wallace looked at each other. No blood. They looked up at the after-end of the flight deck. Still there, but the catwalk directly above the muzzle was noticeably concave where the shell had passed beneath it.

"All right," yelled Crowther at the crew, "Get these casings over the side and clean this mess up!"

They sailed down Cook Strait between North and South Islands of New Zealand and into Wellington Harbor. The harbor sat in a bowl among the greenest hills Wallace had ever seen. They were there for two days, and while no incoming mail came aboard Wallace was able to get his letters to Diana posted with the rest of the RN mail. He wondered what the British censor thought of his prose. On the first evening Wallace and Chaffee were invited to supper by an elderly couple in a community called Lower Hutt. The couple's home was spartan by anyone's standards. On the mantelpiece were pictures of the monarch, and three men in Anzac uniform. After a meal of lamb and potatoes Chaffee asked about the soldiers pictured on the mantel. Their three sons, they explained, all dead in North Africa.

Ranee sailed from Wellington through the Tasman Sea, Bass Strait, where she took gunnery practice on Wilson's Promontory while the sea birds rose in screaming swarms, and into the Indian Ocean just south of the Great Australian Bight. Ian thought he had seen rough water on the trip, but nothing prepared him for the mountainous swells of the Bight and Indian Ocean. The Roaring Forties, Chaffee told him. The wind blew all the way around the world from the tip of South America with nothing to stop it. It wasn't stormy. The sky was clear blue and the sun sparkled. The wind just blew like hell. The swells were so enormous that they dwarfed the ship. *Ranee* would slowly climb up the lee side of a swell, her bow would become airborne at the crest, she would shudder as the crest passed amidships. As the balance shifted her bow would plunge down the windward side, green water would come over the forward end of the flight deck drenching the first ranks of aircraft and her screws would beat wildly out of water as the engineer madly tried to control the revolutions of the shafts.

They had almost two thousand miles of this sea to traverse before they reached Freemantle, where they would pick up their escort, and everything had to be lashed down. Eating in the wardroom was almost an impossibility. The fiddles around the tables could not prevent the cascade of food and dishes from smashing to the deck during the biggest swells. Sea-sickness was common. The ship, which reeked of diesel smoke, rancid food and poorly cleaned heads, stank of vomit, too. And that made matters worse, inducing more sickness. Wallace loved the thrill of these seas and spent much time on the port 5-inch-38 gun sponson that jutted out over the side of the vessel, watching the waves and the response of the ship, yelling at the top of his lungs at the stomach-dropping sensation when the stern went over the top and plunged down the slope. Mooney, on the other hand, was lashed to his bunk where he sweated and retched, groaned and complained. A bucket was placed next to his head and secured to the deck. He would lean over and convulse, bringing up a string of thin slime. Wallace watched him in the throes of sickness and remembered how this incipient father had behaved in San Francisco. The Lord works in mysterious ways his wonders to perform, he thought.

"If something round and fuzzy comes up, swallow it. It's your asshole," he told Mooney.

In time they got to Freemantle, the port for Perth, and were met by their escort to India. They were to be accompanied by the RN cruiser H.M.S. *Gambia* and two County Class destroyers. After a day in port taking on stores they departed into the wide expanses of the Indian Ocean on their way to Cochin on the southwestern tip of India. Here they were in the territory of Japanese submarines.

For the first time the ship followed a zig-zag course, in company with its three escorts. *Gambia* ranged ahead, and the two destroyers shifted position from astern to abaft the beam, to trailing and criss-crossing. Ian supposed that was to confuse the listening devices on any Japanese submarine. Also, for the first time strict life-belt discipline was enforced. Topside you wear your life belt or get in trouble.

One afternoon the two destroyers ran a depth-charge exercise. Ian was below when it started, and as he buckled on his inflatable rubber girdle in his below-the-waterline cabin before going above to watch the exercise, he was surprised to hear the click-click of the depth-charge detonators before the muffled whump of the explosions. Topside, off-duty sailors lined the gallery deck to watch the little ships charge through the seas, smashing through the waves and heeling hard over when they turned at high speed. The command "darken ship" took on new meaning.

After the evening meal, which consisted of the last of the fresh vegetables loaded at Freemantle and some curious gray meat that ponked a little, Wallace played chess with Mooney in the cabin. He had just maneuvered Mooney into a hopeless situation that would lead to Wallace's first chess win ever when the gongs went off and the loudspeaker made a strident call to *"Action stations! Action stations!"* They'd never had other than dawn or dusk action stations, and Ian felt his stomach lurch as he donned his life belt and rushed up the ladder to the port 5-inch sponson. He was last to arrive, having the farthest to travel; the crew was already assembled and the gun cover had been removed and stowed. The pointer and trainer were in their respective seats and the gun was pointed outboard.

"What's going on," he asked Crowther. He couldn't stop his stomach from quivering and he was betrayed by his voice. Is this how I react to real danger? Is this what fear is? Come on! Take hold.

"Bridge reports a submarine on the surface." Wallace quivered. It wasn't chilly, but he was shivering. The gun crew was in shirt sleeves. While the talker informed the bridge that the gun crew was all closed up, Crowther went to the equipment locker and extracted a duffel coat and handed it to Wallace.

"Gets cold the first time, sir."

Ian threw the coat over his shoulders and put on the second set of headphones. He heard the gunnery officer, Guns, tell the starboard battery that the contact was on that side. Everything Wallace had ever heard about anti-submarine tactics told him that *Ranee* should be turning hard to port to put distance between herself and the enemy and to present the smallest possible target, her stern. Instead they were steaming as before.

"Starboard battery! With star shell... Load!"

Star shells! My God!

"Starboard is going to illuminate," he told Crowther. And illuminate ourselves as well, he said to himself.

"Commence! Commence!"

The starboard gun roared, its flash lighting the ocean and the cloud deck above. There was a "pop" at altitude, and the brilliant magnesium flare ignited and lit up the sea. Crowther and Wallace, who were craning their necks to see around the rear of the hangar deck, both pointed at the same time.

"There it is!" they said in unison as they saw the glistening black conning tower and the sluicing decks of the submarine. As they watched she started to submerge. The starboard 5-inch roared again, and another flare popped. Great plumes of white water sprang up, straddling the submarine, as the escorts charged in firing and shortening the range.

"She's under!" said Ian. He found he was sweating. The duffel coat had fallen to the deck.

"Cease firing!"

The beat of the screws retarded slightly, and Ian realized that they had increased revolutions during the attack and were now reducing speed to conserve fuel. No submerged submarine could catch up with this squadron unless it could cruise at twelve knots or better under water. None did.

He picked up the duffel coat from the deck and handed it to Crowther.

"Thanks," he said. "Stupid of me."

"It's anticipation and wonderin' what does it. Best to keep your mind on the job. You'll be all right next time."

They secured from action stations and Wallace returned to the cabin ashamed, but hoping to consummate his win at chess and to find out how Mooney had reacted to the incident. He got to the cabin first and found the chessboard and men strewn across the deck, victims of the motions of the ship. Serves me right, he thought. Pride goeth before destruction and a haughty spirit before a fall.

In the darkened cabin he stared at the bottom of the bunk overhead. Well, I knew about fright and wondered about fear and I guess I met fear tonight. I didn't like him but I think I looked him in the face. It's a bit like before the whistle blows, the pre-game feeling, but worse. I survived this little bit and can take the next, whatever it is. Keep your mind on the job, for to him who is in fear everything rustles. Remember, *"The Lord is my light and my salvation; whom shall I fear? The Lord is the strength of my life; of whom shall I be afraid?"*

When one knows thee, then alien there is none, then no door is shut.
Oh, grant me my prayer that I may never lose
the touch of one in the play of many.

— Rabindranath Tagore
Gitanjali

INDIA 1944

THROUGH THE INDIAN OCEAN Ian had tried to exercise each day by trudging along various parts of the ship. He circled the ship several times each day. One of his favorite spots was on the forecastle deck where he would hang over the bow rail and watch the prow hiss and cut through the sea, layering white spray and foam in ever-widening vees as the ship moved through the water. On some days there would be flying fish playing in front of the bow. On lucky days dolphins would play "catch-me-if-you-can." It was a wonder to Ian that none of the beasts was ever hit. They even seemed to smile.

One morning as Wallace hung over the bow rail he noticed that the water had lost its blue-green tinge and appeared to be turning a greenish-tan. There were no fish or dolphins. The wind across his face was sharp and hot, hotter than it had been when they crossed the equator. Looking ahead he could see nothing on the hazy horizon, but as he sniffed the air he sensed a hotness, a dustiness, a malodorousness, a fetidness, a heaviness that he had never before experienced. What they say is true, he thought. You can smell India before you can see it.

Headed by H.M.S. *Gambia* their escorts shepherded them into the entrance to Cochin with much clattering of signal lamp shutters and hoisting of signal flags. As Ian watched from the port sponson *Ranee* was carefully warped to the dock space port side to. The air was still. No breeze ruffled the water. Layers of heat rose shimmering from the black tarred surface of the pier and made its steel railroad rails seem to waver. An olive-green U.S. Army sedan waited at the dock, a captain and a sergeant leaning on the fender. Ian wondered why they weren't wearing shorts in this heat. He was certainly going to get some even if they weren't regulation.

Stubby coal-fed switching engines with only one set of drive wheels pushed short flatcars down the rails into position to receive the aircraft that would be off-loaded from *Ranee*. The engineers and firemen wore dirty white wrap-around loincloths and rags around their heads. They wore no shoes and Wallace wondered how they withstood the heat of the footplates. Used to walking on fire, maybe.

The brow was put over, and after port officials came aboard the American captain was welcomed into the wardroom. Ian met him and thought he was a cocky and unattractive man. He had come to sign the papers in receipt of the aircraft and to supervise their movement to a transition airfield. He was delighted to accept the offer of a drink from Number One and took a bottle of strong Australian beer. He was warned about its potency, its high alcohol content, but said he'd been a beer drinker forever and downed three of them. When he went to the flight deck to count aircraft it was just noon, and in the boiling sun he keeled over in a dead faint. That helps the spirit of Allied cooperation and the war effort in general, Wallace said to himself.

Orders for the Americans on H.M.S. *Ranee* were delivered, and Wallace learned that again he was to be in charge of the same seventeen sailors (one chief and sixteen EMs) on their rail trip to Calcutta. They packed up, and as they were debarking Tom Mooney rode him a little, telling Ian that the important people were being flown to Calcutta. Tom said he'd see Wallace in China. Ian asked Tom to let him know if he found out what the hell they'd be doing.

A British flatbed lorry delivered Wallace and his men to a rail siding where they were met by a navy-blue uniformed, brass-buttoned Anglo-Indian official of the National Railway System. Ian looked down the tracks but could see nothing but little rust colored goods-wagons with curved corrugated iron roofs. No passenger cars at all.

"What are we supposed to ride in?" he asked as the lorry pulled away.

"Oh," said the *babu-ji* in his clipped, sing-song English, "there will be better accommodation when the train reaches the Madras Line, sir. But for now it is my pleasure to show you how we have prepared for your travel."

He led Wallace and the men to a goods wagon. A set of temporary wooden steps had been hastily contrived to reach the sliding door.

"Steps, you see!" the babu proudly pointed and mounted them to the car.

Wallace followed. The wood floor of the windowless wagon had been swept clean, and there were boxes of GI field rations in one corner. A folding wood and canvas field latrine was at the opposite end of the car. It was like an oven.

"Food, sir, and sanitary facilities!" the babu pointed. "And when you reach the Madras Line a passenger carriage will be provided."

"And when do we reach the Madras Line?"

"Oh, soon, sir, soon," said the Anglo-Indian.

"What about water?" Ian asked.

"At the stations, sir, many stations. There one can have potable water, or tea, sir, even sweet Indian restoratives!"

A sure way to get the trots. How the hell do we shave and bathe in sweet Indian restoratives?

"The train will be leaving at precisely one forty-seven, sir. May I respectfully suggest you board, sir?"

Wallace looked at the railroad man, at the goods wagon and at his men. There was nothing he could do.

"All right you people, we've been assigned to World War I transportation.... *hommes quarante/chevals huit...* that means forty and eight, like your dads rode in France. We've got no choice, so climb aboard. It's only for a short trip, this man says."

"Oh yes, sir, to the Madras Line!" repeated the babu-ji.

Grumbling in the heat the men hoisted their gear to the floor of the car. Their simplest movement raised swirls of hot, dry dust that coated their sweat and clogged their nostrils. They clambered on, expressing their disgust with the accommodations and generally cursing Indian railroads, the British, the Navy, the heat and the sanitary facilities.

"Stake out a piece of the deck for yourself, and put your gear there. I wouldn't unpack anything but your canteens yet if I were you, because to get some air we're going to want to keep these mid-ships sliding doors open while we're underway. At the first station-stop we'll select a canteen party to collect water, and the rest will stay in the car to guard the gear and, I think, to keep other travelers out."

"Good journey to you, sir," said the Indian, and with a hardly perceptible bow he turned and walked off through the dust and the haze.

At exactly one forty-seven the American detachment learned what their train ride would be like. They were standing in the doorways to get fresh air when the train started. Indian trains were not equipped with springs nor with pneumatic couplings but with chains and heavy, flat-headed pistons that lessened the effect of the cars smashing into each other as the train slowed down or stopped.

They heard the high-pitched whistle and the clang of the cars ahead taking up the slack, but were in no way prepared for the dramatic jolt that assailed them when the chains on their car took the strain. The car jumped forward and smashed the pistons of the car in front only to be smashed in the rear by the car behind. The eighteen U.S. servicemen were hurled to the deck.

As the train lurched and banged and picked up speed ("I can run this fast," said one of the sailors) they decided it was best to sit on the deck and hold on to whatever they could. Ian set what he called "door watches" so that every one would get a chance to see out and breathe, although there was some question whether this was a good idea when the smoke and hot cinders flew in.

Above Wallace's space in the after port corner of the car a paper sign was shellacked to the wall. He read it:

South India Railway Co., Ld.
NOTICE
Anyone smoking, cooking or
having naked lights in horse-box
is liable to be prosecuted.
Trichnopoly, March 22nd, 1917
B. C. Scott
General Traffic Manager

Wallace ripped the notice off the bulkhead and stuffed it in his musette bag. He stood in the car door watching the jungle crawl by. So are the sons of men snared in an evil time, when it falleth suddenly upon them, he said to himself.

The journey was long, hot and exasperating. The train crawled through the shantytown tin-and-board huts in the outskirts of Cochin and went up the track to Trichur, to a junction at Shoranpur and eastward toward Trichnopoly. The train did not stop all afternoon, and as it turned east Ian wondered if it was planning to stop at all. The need for water was becoming imperative. So who do I speak to? Do I crawl over the hot iron car roofs like Buster Keaton in *The General* and when I get to the engine explain to the Hindu driver that we're thirsty? At least they were in the shade as the day progressed. They were passing through tall, fronded trees that cast shadows over the roadbed. There was less dust here, and the smoke was blowing forward of the train. The atmosphere smelled almost moist even though the monsoon, due this month, had not yet started. They occasionally passed primitive native Tamil villages of bamboo-walled huts with conical thatch roofs, beaten tan earth, nearly naked black people, and naked children chasing the train, yelling and throwing track ballast stones at their wagon. The sailors shouted back.

Just before dark the engine stopped on a dusty plain at a water tower to refill its boiler. Wallace jumped to the ground and walked forward.

"We need water back in our car," he said to the engineer who was coal black and covered with soot and oil.

"Not good water, *sahib*," the engineer told him. "When we are on Madras line is good water."

"Can't we get some boiled water out of the engine?"

The engineer and the fireman had a lengthy discussion, and the engineer turned to Wallace and said, "Is no way, sahib."

"What do you and the fireman drink?"

"Tea, sahib," and pointed to a leather bag shaped like a bladder with a cork in the narrow end, which hung in the cab window. "We bring with us."

"When is the first station-stop?"

"No stop at station, sahib. Only carriage trains go on station spur. We stop at station and peoples climb on roofs and under cars and on engine and fall off and be killed."

"Well, where will this train stop, and where will I get water for my men?"

"We stop in goods yard at Trichnopoly in morning, sahib. Then you see Station Master."

The engineer signaled that the conversation was at an end by climbing back to his cab as the fireman swung the water trunk back to its tower bracket. The engineer pulled the whistle cord twice, and the whistle emitted its shrill, high-pitched squeals. Who the hell can hear that, Wallace wondered walking back to the goods wagon. Probably that routine is in the 1917 orders of B.C. Scott, General Traffic Manager. The train started to move before he reached the car, and he grasped the outstretched arms of a couple of the men as the wagon went by and was swung aboard.

It rained heavily that night, and they organized a water collecting operation that involved straining the roof runoff, after they guessed the roof had been thoroughly rinsed, through a clean khaki shirt into a sloshed-out canteen cup, thence into canteens. They leaned out the door in their skivvies and howled at the sky as they got thoroughly soaked. They would have drunk the water even if it had come from the gutter.

Very early in the morning they arrived at Trichnopoly. The goods wagons were put on a siding, and the engine chuffed off. Wallace shook out a khaki shirt and trousers, put on his barracks hat and went in search of officialdom in what he hoped was a sufficiently impressive uniform. He found the Yard Master's office high in a tower overlooking the maze of tracks and switches and mounted the stairs.

"Yard Master not here before seven, sahib," he was told and was offered tea. He waited. As he looked out the windows he watched a switching engine couple itself to the goods wagons he had just left and slowly start to pull the train away.

"Hold it!" he yelled and asked the duty man what was happening.

"Moving train, sahib."

"To where? My men are on that train!"

"No people, sahib. That is goods train."

"Don't tell me goods train! My people are on the fifth car! See 'em in the door, waving?"

"Should not be people, sahib, not Europeans on goods train."

"Oh, for God's sake! We didn't choose this train. We were put on it! Stop the train!"

"When Yard Master Sahib comes he can stop trains. I cannot, sahib."

"Is there a problem here?" a voice behind Ian inquired. Wallace spun around to face an Anglo-Indian in a brass-buttoned dark-blue uniform.

"My men are on that train!" Ian said, pointing. "Where the hell are they going?"

"Ah, yes," said the official, "the Americans. We are moving the car to the station spur, sir, so the men can get off in preparation to boarding their own passenger carriage. If you will join me in a cup of tea I will escort you to your carriage personally and make sure that your accommodation is in every way satisfactory."

I'll join you in a cup of tea, Wallace thought, and if it's a big enough cup of tea I'll drown you and this whole railroad system in it.

Face, Wallace said to himself as he sat in the rail car now carrying them toward Madras. Talk about losing face! There I was in that yard tower shouting my lungs out and neither the duty man nor the Yard Master lost their composure. Maybe because of the night's experience and the assurances of that ass of an official in Cochin that we would get water at station-stops, I've stopped trusting these people. Maybe I haven't had a chance to trust them. They probably don't trust white people or other foreigners, either. They probably think it would be a good idea if the Japanese took over this country from the British, though there's fat chance the Indians would ever get it back for themselves. The Japanese would treat them worse than the English do, treat them like dirt just like they treat everybody else. But I sense a sullenness, almost a disdain here that I hadn't expected.

There were two Indian Rail Police on the Americans' carriage, dressed in khaki shorts and short-sleeved shirts, wraparound puttees and red pillbox hats. They were barefooted. The red caps are appropriate, like the porters at Grand Central, thought Ian, though they probably won't help us with our gear. The presence of the police, one stationed at each end of the wooden car, was to keep the hordes of Indians off the car at each stop. Unlike first class carriages, which had compartments with doors to the outside and to the passageways, this car had doors only at the ends, making it easier to control access. The carriage had obviously been used to transport troops before. There was a water spigot at the forward end of the car over which was the warning: "This Water Unfit for Drinking." Under this notice some soldier had written: "Unless Passed by an Officer."

The station platforms were madhouses of humanity. White-clad men (sheets-and-shirts Ian called the garb) and sari-clad women covered every inch of every platform, surrounded by their chattels wrapped in string-tied rugs, sitting on cardboard suitcases, carrying string bags of produce and babies on the hip, squatting on heels, arguing with vendors, cooking over little smoky fires, sleeping on the pavement, kicking the ever-present scrounging pye dogs, spitting red spit on the deck, rushing the car doors even before the train stopped, yelling with a stridency Wallace and the men found hard to believe. Several times the Rail Police had to resort to kicking as well as shouting and gesticulating to keep the natives out of the car.

If the stop was long enough Ian would send the chief petty officer and a couple of the men to the Stewart's Rail Cafe (Europeans Only) for bottled water and fresh fruit. These cafes were screened with gray muslin to keep out the insects and the fly ash from the engines. A *punkah wallah* sat on the platform outside the cafe sleepily pulling and releasing a rope, which caused the ceiling punkah to swish back and forth inside the cafe to provide a little movement of air in the oppressive heat. Returning with their purchases the forage party would fight their way through crowds of misshapen and mutilated beggars who called out, *"Baksheesh, sahib,"* through pickpockets and scowling natives who would spit at their heels. Even though Hindus were supposed to cleanse themselves early every day, preferably in sacred pools or holy rivers, the smell of rancid sweat and unwashed bodies was overpowering.

At many of the country stops crowds of natives would leap off the cars and descend the track embankment to answer nature's call. This was a solemn and complex ritual, for the Twice Born must use only his left hand and must cleanse the parts with water (one considered his home defiled if visited by foreigners who used only paper). Then shouting and scrabbling through the track ballast they would leap back on the train as it started to move. Ian understood why the empty C-ration cans were in such demand when they attempted to dispose of them at station stops. Indians would retrieve them from the waste bins, wash them and then conceal them in the voluminous folds of their garments.

The Americans didn't understand the caste marks and could get no helpful information from the rail policemen who appeared embarrassed to talk about it. Probably they were caste-less Muslims. The Americans did understand that an "untouchable" cleaned the head at various stops. They talked among themselves about the caste system and boasted that there was no such thing in the good old U.S. of A. Not much, thought Ian. We don't wear caste marks, but don't tell me there isn't a pecking order at home and most other places. But we can work our way out of our caste. Here you're born into it and stuck with it, even if the British are trying to have the system done away with.

They were plagued by mosquitos and slept with their heads wrapped in skivvy shirts so they could leave the windows open for whatever fresh air that would provide.

At Madras Wallace left the sea of humanity on the platform and went into the high, domed terminal building. The crowd was just as dense and noisy and smelly but seemed more so because there were so many people jammed into that immense, vaulted station. He found a news kiosk, bought the *India Times* and worked his way back to the car, glad to have negotiated the journey without serious mishap or thievery.

The newspaper headline proclaimed: "Japanese Invade Assam!" Ian learned that Japanese forces had left their bases west of the Chindwin River and crossed the Burma-India border with the apparent intention of taking the hill stations of Imphal and Kohima. The fighting in the Arakan, south of the new action, had been a diversion to tie up the British-Indian reserves while the enemy pushed into Assam. Intense jungle fighting was reported. The Government implored the populace to remain calm.

On the following day the train stopped for an hour at Cuttack, and the choice of refreshments at Stewart's was severely limited. They did get water and were surprised to see that some waiting passengers had apparently set up housekeeping on the station floor. Carpets or ragged rugs had been laid out with bundles put at the corners or piled in the middle. Cloth-shrouded sleeping forms littered these camp sites, but in every case one member of the group squatted on his heels and watched to make sure that there was no infringement on their domain.

The war news from Assam was not good. British and Indian troops had staged a tactical withdrawal to consolidate their forces. This in effect lengthened the Japanese line of supply while shortening the friendly supply route. At the same time, it was reported, an air-raid alert had been sounded in Calcutta, the first in some months, though no planes had appeared.

The cavernous Howrah station on the west bank of the muddy Hooghly river served the crowded metropolis of Calcutta, and on the sixth day from Cochin the train steamed slowly through the growing daylight and the poverty-stricken outskirts of Howrah toward the rail terminal, blowing its high-pitched whistle at every street crossing. The Americans stowed their gear and tried to look as shipshape as possible after six days and nights in the same clothes. They were met on the platform by a party of U.S. Navy personnel dressed in khaki, who escorted them as they lugged their sea bags and footlockers through the heavy, humid, hot morning to a U.S. Navy gray 6x6 truck in the teeming street outside the station. They heaved their gear aboard, Ian got in front with the driver and they negotiated the congested traffic: bicycles, horse-drawn *gharris*, military vehicles, pedestrians, open Sikh-driven taxis, buses, trolleys and sacred cows. They crossed the Howrah Bridge, passed down Chowringhee Boulevard and eventually came to a less congested part of the city where the enlisted men were off-loaded at a small U.S. Navy transient facility, a hostel called Camp Shea; tents, latrine pits, duck-boards, Lister bags and all the comforts of home. Ian bid the men good-bye, and the chief said that in retrospect the train from Cochin looked pretty good.

Wallace was delivered by jeep to a hostel compound for officers in Ballygunge, a shaded home with high ceilings, a courtyard and gardens surrounded by a stucco wall. He was shown his cot in a room on the second floor, where he dumped his gear. An Indian bearer came in and said he was Ranjit Jowai and that he would take care of sahib's needs. Sahib could pay whatever was reasonable. Wallace doubted that but learned that Ranjit would do his laundry, make his cot, air his bedding, bring *cha* in the morning, sew and mend and run errands.

"O.K.," said Ian, " how and where do I bathe and shave?"

"There is room for bathing, sahib. Come."

Ian followed the bearer down the hall and down the stairs at the back into an outdoor walled area with a slatted board floor and two shower heads protruding from the house bulkhead. Showers! He thanked Ranjit, who handed him a bath towel from a shelf and stood watching him.

What the hell, thought Ian. Am I some sort of freak?

"Well?" he asked.

"Your clothes, sahib. I will wash them."

Wallace felt like a fool. Stop making Occidental judgments, maintain your composure and demonstrate a little patience with the Oriental manner. He removed his filthy khaki uniform and Ranjit took it, underwear, socks, shoes and all. The water was barely tepid and the soap wouldn't lather, but there was more than a dribble of water and Ian luxuriated in it. He supposed there was some sort of water discipline, since the monsoon hadn't started, but no signs told him he couldn't stay as long as he wanted, so he scrubbed and rinsed himself three times before toweling himself as dry as he could in the humidity, wrapping the towel around his waist and going back up the stairs to his room.

As he approached his cot he was astonished to find that all his uniforms had been unpacked and put on hangers under the wall shelf, his small clothes were neatly stacked on the shelf, a clean uniform and socks and skivvies had been laid out upon the now made-up cot, and his shoes had been shined to a high gloss and stood side by side under his bed. Well, well!

Ian dressed and went to find the duty officer to report in and then to get some chow. He was famished. Ranjit showed him the office and where the mess was served, then disappeared. The duty officer was a very relaxed Navy lieutenant, a transient on his way to China.

"We know you're here," he said, "and after breakfast you can go to Church Lane and sign in."

"What's at Church Lane?"

"That's the office of the U.S. Naval Observer, Chungking, China. At least it's his India office. They'll be issuing you your orders for transportation over the Hump."

"And after we get over the Hump what the hell do we do?"

"Observe," said the duty officer, and went back to his magazine.

After an American breakfast alone in the mess, served by bearers, Ian went back to his room to collect his orders for endorsement by Church Lane. Ranjit Jowai was in the room with a khaki uniform freshly starched and pressed. Pressed underclothes had been placed on the shelf.

"What are those?" Ian asked.

"Your uniform, sahib," said Ranjit.

"But I just gave it to you!"

"Yes, sahib, but I wash, starch and iron while you eat," Ranjit replied without any change in expression. Ian guessed that in this humidity the clothes were dried under the hot pressing iron in order for them to be done so quickly. At least I won't run out of clean clothes, thank God.

He was taken to downtown Calcutta in the sidecar of an American motorcycle, painted Navy gray, but Ian could see patches of red where the gray had worn off and knew that this wasn't a Harley-Davison but an American make called Indian. Appropriate, like the red caps, he thought.

The motorcycle and sidecar bumped over the road as the driver expertly avoided the extraordinarily wild drivers of other vehicles. They skittered in front of a double trolley festooned with riders hanging on to the outside, turned left at the Victoria Memorial and went around the park where the Race Course was located. Wallace was interested to see that a dirt Spitfire strip had been gouged out of the infield of the track. Several planes were sitting near the end of the runway with their props idly ticking over. Other planes were in sandbag revetments around the perimeter.

More sandbags were in evidence as they came upon more government buildings. Blast walls were erected in front of most entrances and most windows were taped. Armed, turbanned Indian soldiers guarded the doors.

He turned in his orders for endorsement at 6 Church Lane and asked the chief yeoman when he'd be going over the Hump and what the duty would be.

"You'll probably be going over in two or three weeks. The goddam Army won't give us a space allocation for personnel on ATC (Air Transport Command), so we have to fly our people in on CNAC (China National Aviation Corporation). The Army lets us ship some gear on a low-priority basis but not enough to do what we want. So when you go we'll give you a bunch of "personal" weapons to carry. You'll be pretty loaded down."

"What about the duty over there?"

"It varies. Some detachments train Chinese guerrillas, some set up weather stations to monitor mainland weather that will be moving over the Pacific, some people are coast watchers, some operate hospitals. We work pretty closely with the OSS."

The OSS! Good God! Ian hoped he wouldn't be working with any of the incompetents he had encountered at Q Building or at Area D!

"What about a Navy officer named Tom Mooney?"

"Oh, he's at the Palace."

"What! The Palace?"

"The Palace Hotel, that is. He's living there."

"Doing what?"

"He's permanently assigned to this office as liaison with the British."

"Is he here?"

"No, sir, he doesn't usually get in before thirteen or fourteen hundred. Says he has to make his number with the Allies in the morning. I could call and see if he's still at the hotel, if you'd like."

"Please."

The chief yeoman called Mooney's room and was about to hang up after many rings when Mooney answered the phone. Wallace could picture him angrily stretching over some sleeping female form to reach the phone.

"Sir, it's Chief O'Hara at Church Lane. Sorry to interrupt (the chief knows, thought Wallace), but there's an officer here named Wallace who would like to speak to you."

O'Hara handed Wallace the phone.

"Tom? Did I break in on some important Indo-American operation?"

"Damn you, Wallace, every time I get a hotel room you screw things up. When did you get here."

"Just now. Can we get together?"

"Wait a minute."

Wallace could tell a hand was over the mouthpiece and could hear much mumbling, some of it quite loud.

Mooney came back on. "Just changed my schedule. How about lunch here?"

"Great. So long as I'm not expected to be doing anything else."

"Don't worry about it. All you transients have to do is check Church Lane by phone each morning."

Shades of Washington, D.C.!

"Be here at twelve and ask the concierge for me."

Wallace got the word and the local ground rules from O'Hara. He was also issued a .45 caliber Colt automatic pistol, three loaded magazines, holster, web belt, a bottle of Atabrine tablets and a mosquito bar. Wallace didn't understand what a mosquito bar was... maybe a place where mosquitos got a drink? No, it's a net to put over your sack to bar the insects from driving you crazy all night and possibly giving you malaria, dengue, hepatitis or the Chinese foot rot. Wallace was sorry he'd been flip.

O'Hara told him to bring his footlocker to Church Lane the next day and to put in it all the things he would not be taking to China. Keep your khakis, fatigues, boondockers, skivvies and small stores. Your greens, overcoat and the rest of the heavy gear is to be left here. The Navy would store it and get it to him when needed. Wallace also was to be issued clothing and other stores allowed to be carried as personal belongings on the airplane over the Hump, which he would need in China: army enlisted ODs, Navy storm jacket, long johns, gloves, additional summer khakis, new boondockers, bed roll, ground sheet, poncho.

Ian asked about mail, and O'Hara told him all mail went to the Senior Naval Observer, Chungking. He'd get it when he got there, if the Army chose to fly it over.

As they talked the low growl of the air-raid sirens began, climbing in dissonant two-tone pitch, reaching a high crescendo as O'Hara said, "Better watch this!" and led the way to their second-story window.

Wallace's gut began to quiver again, but he followed O'Hara to the window as did the rest of the personnel in the office. No one fled to an air-raid shelter. It was almost as if they were going to a circus. The streets below were in chaos. White-clad natives were fleeing to the park's many sand-bagged trenches. People were leaping from trolleys, taxis, trucks, buses, gharris, bicycles and rickshas to run for cover. At the race course Spitfires were thundering down the airstrip to get into the air to provide air cover for the city.

"What are we supposed to do?" asked Wallace.

"We're supposed to go to the basement, but we usually stay here and watch. Somebody has to stay here for security reasons, so we all stay. Just as safe here as anywhere else. The bombers rarely get this far, the basement is jammed with sweating Indians, and you wouldn't catch any of us in those park trenches for anything! Indians all think we're made of money, and I guess we are by their standards. Get your throat cut as soon as say scat."

It seemed sensible to Wallace, who craned his neck out the window to watch the contrails high above. Two groups of three arrow-straight contrails were approaching from the east while curving single contrails were reaching up for them. They heard the cough of heavy antiaircraft batteries and watched the exploding puffs below and in front of the approaching Japanese flights. The Spitfires got above and behind the bombers, which Wallace could now see were twin-engine Mitsubishi G4Ms, Bettys in aircraft recognition parlance, and were commencing to attack the formations. The bombers bored on, even as one slowly started to lose altitude, smoke pouring from its starboard engine. Ian could hear the distant tat-tat-tat of the machine-guns, the droning of the Japanese bombers, the screaming of the Spits' Rolls-Royce Merlin engines, and it excited him. His quivering was gone, and he found himself shouting with the other Americans to "get the bastards!"

A second Japanese plane was hit and, as they watched it burst into flames, turned slowly on its back and fell from the formation spinning wildly, centrifugal force spewing pieces of flaming wreckage in all directions. It exploded with a thunderous, reverberating roar a thousand feet below the attackers, but the enormous burst disabled a following Spitfire and it limped away, loosing altitude and trailing heavy smoke. Wallace saw the enemy formation turn away and looked questioningly at O'Hara.

"They've dropped their pills. You'll hear 'em soon enough," the chief told him.

Shortly they heard muffled crumps from the southwest, the direction of the King George and Kiddepore docks. Very little smoke was to be seen, and Wallace was surprised.

"Long way away," said O'Hara, "and some of those eggs probably landed in the Hooghly. I don't think they give a shit if they hit anything, They really want to keep the native population in panic. Slows down the war effort. The locals hate the British and us for bringing our Japanese war to their doorstep. Did you know that the Congress Party is considered by some to be hoping for a Japanese victory? And have you heard of the Indian National Army? Indian soldiers who deserted and are now fighting for the Japanese against their former rulers. This is a screwed-up place and air raids help keep it that way."

The all-clear sounded, and Wallace got directions to the Palace with the advice to wait a few minutes for things to calm down and then to wear his pistol as he walked the relatively short distance to the hotel.

"It's damn near noon, so stay on the shady side of the street if you can," said O'Hara. Wallace looked out the window and saw that the sun was pouring straight down and thought he'd have to go from awning to awning. Still, he'd probably be wringing wet by the time he reached his appointment with Mooney. The temperature at street level must have been one hundred ten degrees Fahrenheit.

Though no bombs had fallen on this district, Wallace noted that a number of shop windows were broken and that goods and merchandise were strewn about on the sidewalks, guarded by tall, turbanned Sikh police. The crowds were pushy and noisy, trying to reclaim their vehicles, rushing back to their stalls and offices or to the piece of sidewalk they called home. Wallace imagined that some of the merchandise missing from the shops would be for sale from sidewalk rugs before evening.

White, hump-backed cows ambled across the roads and across the pedestrian pavement, adding their excrement to the red-spotted paving that the natives continually colored with their red spit. Are they all tubercular? Ian wondered. He brushed the flies from his face and pushed his way through beggars crying "Baksheesh, sahib." The people noise was deafening.

The lobby concierge at the Palace phoned Mooney, calling him "sir"—not sahib—and told Wallace to wait in the bar, please. Ian found a spot at the bar and ordered a bottle of beer that arrived warm. As he was drinking it, he surveyed the room. Mostly British officers and what he supposed were civil servants. A few WAAF officers. No civilian women. The room was dimly lit, with electric ceiling fans stirring the air. The walls were darkly paneled and hung with framed photographs and prints of military ceremonies and historical happenings back to and preceding the visit of King George V and the Delhi Durbar. Mooney walked in, dressed in a tropical shade gabardine uniform with service ribbons and highly polished mosquito boots. He spied Ian, walked over and before speaking to Wallace said to the barman, "Send the leftenant's drink to my table in the dining salon."

"Yes, Mooney sahib," said the barman.

Ian raised his eyebrows at that and at Mooney, who said, "How good to see you, Wallace."

He's not only starting to look British, he's even starting to sound British, Ian reflected.

Mooney ordered for them. Gin and tonics, to start, and curried lamb. The waiters wore white tunics with green sashes, tight white trousers, green cloth sandals and small pink turbans. The busboys were dressed in similar clothes but were identifiable by their lack of sashes and turbans. The mâitre d' was in a tuxedo. What a war.

Wallace tasted his gin and tonic, bitter and sweet at the same time, and asked Mooney about it.

"In the last century, to fight malaria, European families took quinine water as a tonic each day. It was pretty awful, so they would carbonate it as you would with a soda cartridge. Then some smart bloke got the idea of sweetening it with gin, at least for the adults. It was known as gin and quinine then, but as a taste developed for the drink it gradually became known as gin and tonic, a rather less medicinal sounding cocktail. Do you enjoy it?"

"It is, as you said, an acquired taste. I'm sure I'll get to like it." This man's gone British in a little over a week!

"Tell me how come you've been stationed here in Calcutta," said Ian.

"Well, you see when I learned that Americans in our China group were to be kept from combat——"

"No combat?"

"No combat, dear boy. And, you see, when I learned that I said to myself, why not make my contribution to the war in the comfort of Calcutta rather than the discomfort of Chunking. After all, O'Hara was running this office and is rather what the British refer to as 'other ranks.' We needed someone, really, to liaise with the English officialdom on their own level. And with the U.S. Army, of course. My experience in the Secret Service dealing with foreign dignitaries at the White House and at Hyde Park stood me in good stead once I called it to the attention of the proper authorities."

Proper authorities! Political pull, you mean. Well I'll be a sad bastard, Wallace said to himself.

"It's good to know you'll be here in case there's some special support we'll be needing," said Wallace, and took a large mouthful of curry. He almost choked. His nose ran, his eyes watered and his throat burned. He grabbed his beer and gulped it down.

"Should have warned you about that, old boy. Sorry." said Mooney.

"And what about this fighting in Assam," Ian asked. "How much of a threat is it?"

"One can't tell, really. Our people seem to have slowed them down a bit. But it does upset the native population and Government House are worried." (*are* worried!)

"What do you think are the Japanese objectives?"

"I think it's quite transparent that they'd very much like to put our staging fields for the Hump out of commission. One way to do that would be to cut the rail line that supplies the fields. They could be trying to take Dimapur, which is a railhead just northwest of Kohima… that would constrict the supply line to China and possibly free up some enemy troops for service elsewhere."

"What airfields are those?"

"Why, Jorhat and Dibrugarh, in the Brahmaputra valley, just south of the eastern Himalayas. Where your plane will be stopping to drop off, pick up and to refuel. Dibrugarh is the last stop before the mountains."

"How did you learn all this so quickly?" Ian asked.

"Crash course. The locals said if I intended to be any help I should know the lay of the land and the present strategic situation. They were kind enough to brief me quite thoroughly."

"So, what advice do you have for me while I'm in Calcutta?"

"I should certainly enjoy myself, if I were you, barring being out on the streets at night. Talk to others who've been there about what to take. And do go to the Tailors' Temple on Jhowtolla Road and get yourself a proper kit for this climate, old boy," said Sir Thomas Mooney, USNR.

The following day Wallace was issued his new gear, and, to his delight, O'Hara told him he'd been able to get hold of Wallace's mail through a friend of his at the Army Postal Service. It was a fairly sizable bundle, and Wallace was anxious to take it back to Ballygunge and read it. But O'Hara said that Mooney had called earlier and wanted Wallace to meet him at The Calcutta Swimming Club for lunch, and gave Wallace the directions, adding that he'd better take a taxi. Taxis, driven by huge Sikhs, were safe and very reliable. Wallace left his bundle and new gear to be picked up later and departed for he knew not what.

The Calcutta Swimming Club turned out to be not only that but also a cool and convenient place to meet and conduct business during the heat of noonday. The building was light and airy, shaded by palm trees, floored in tile and with many punkahs moving the air. To the rear of the clubhouse was a large palm-lined courtyard garden with an enormous blue-white marble pool all set about with tables, chairs and gaily striped umbrellas. Bearers were moving among the tables serving drinks and light luncheon. Wallace spotted Mooney, who had garnered a table, and joined him in the shade.

"You're soaked," said Mooney. "Here's the temporary membership card I've organized for you. Take it and go to the men's dressing room, just there," he pointed, "and the bearer will give you a bathing suit, towel and locker. Better have a dip. I've already had one."

When Ian dove in the pool he was shocked. The water temperature was only a few degrees below the air temperature. He'd not contemplated swimming in hot water. He lolled about for what he considered was a polite length of time, left the water, dressed in his freshly pressed uniform (!) and joined Mooney at the table.

"This is great," Ian said. "How much do I owe you for your trouble?"

"Only ten rupees. Pretty reasonable. But then it's only for a week."

Wallace thought he could certainly spare three bucks for this kind of comfort for a few days. He hadn't spent any money in months.

Mooney must have read his mind. "After lunch I'll drop you off at the tailor shop, and you can spend some of those dollars that are burning a hole in your pocket."

"Is that where you got that uniform of yours?"

"You bet. After the baby was born I decided to splurge a little on myself in celebration."

Wallace had forgotten to ask! He wondered if Mooney had thought about it himself or had had it brought to his attention by a letter from his wife.

"Boy or girl?"

"Another girl. I'm sure as hell going to have to pay for a lot of weddings. This one is Teresa. Red haired. Certainly hope she's mine."

Wallace was overcome by Mooney's display of pride and emotion. Well, the hell with it.

"Speaking of red," Ian asked, "what is the matter with so many of the Indians? They spit red saliva or blood or something all the time."

"Betelnut. They chew betelnut. Its supposed to be a stimulant. Gives them a sense of well-being, they say. But it turns their teeth black and rots them. Frankly, if I had to live the way they do I'd probably chew the damned stuff myself. Not very sanitary all the same."

Wallace was annoyed yet pleased that Mooney had a car and driver. He resented Mooney's assertiveness and arrogance, yet the car made Ian's travel a lot easier. They dropped him off at the corner of Jhowtolla Road and Syed Amir Ali Avenue and drove away with a casual "Keep in touch" from Mooney. Ian found a sign that read "Tailor's Temple, Civil & Military Tailors" over a door in a narrow whitewashed building. He went in and was measured for khaki shorts and a bush jacket. And what about mosquito boots? Ideal for tucking the trousers in to keep the mosquitos off the legs and other parts in the evening, he was told. He was measured for boots, and was told that all would be made up for him by morning. If he had only come earlier he could have had them this evening.

He took a taxi to Church Lane, told it to wait, collected his mail and gear and went back to Ballygunge, not opening his letters in the car but waiting until he was back at his cot, comfortable and alone.

Following an admonition from Ranjit to "always shake out bathcloths, sahib... beware of vermin, sahib, vermin," he stood under the dripping, tepid shower and contemplated what he had learned from his mail. He was upset in one sense and gratified in another. He had first read his mail from Cummington, then mail from friends and finally letters from Diana. Like saving the frosting when you eat cake.

Patience had written two letters about a month apart. In the first she reported that all was going well, that his grandfather seemed to be in reasonable spirits and that they had had a letter from his brother, Peter, who was in

Italy with the Fifth Army. The second letter said that Peter's wife had moved from New York to Cummington to help care for his grandfather and to do whatever she could on the farm. It would save on the rent money she had to pay in the city, too. Ian sensed that there was a little feminine resentfulness on the part of Patience, who had had the run of the farm even when Ian's mother was alive. The only other news was that the furnace had broken but they hoped to get it fixed soon. Ian could picture them huddled around the old kitchen stove to keep warm on the cold winter days and nights. He hoped that the pipes hadn't burst. It worried him.

He had a letter from John Perry, who was in a hospital in Hawaii, injured but recovering. Perry said he'd heard that Lewis had been killed in action on Kwajalein in early February. Perry had crash-landed in the sea on a training exercise after his engine quit. He said he hadn't heard from Fix.

Diana's letters were warm and comforting. She told him how much she missed him and how she looked forward to hearing from him. She said it was strange to have the Gayety so empty. None of the old crowd was there anymore. New faces, new guests. She said her Congressman, Daniel Bensen, was wrestling with the question of whether to run again in November or to get a Navy commission. She said she loved Ian heart and soul.

That will keep me going no matter what, he told himself.

He accompanied two transient Navy officers to a cinema downtown to see Noel Coward's *In Which We Serve* that evening. They went armed. They were impressed by the film and by the fact that the entire audience rose and sang "God Save Our Gracious King" before the performance. The fact that there was an interval between the short subjects and the feature, during which one could go to the lobby for lemon squash, was another bit of cultural education. After the film the streets seemed strangely quiet and deserted. The audience crowded itself under the marquee, reluctant to move into the street or down the sidewalk. No cars passed by. In the distance they could hear shouting and the growing murmuring roar of a crowd. They heard a rattle of gunfire and saw tongues of flame shoot above the rooftops blocks away.

"This is no place to be," said Ian and, leading his two Navy companions, he darted down the street to the corner and turned right, away from the noise and toward the Race Course. They encountered a barricade manned by Sikh soldiers who let them through. The English officer in charge told them that there was a bit of unrest in the native quarter (native quarter!) but that the matter was well in hand. The Americans went to the RAF mess Quonset hut where the pilots stood them to a beer. After an hour an RAF lorry, driver and guard were organized and they left the airstrip for a roundabout trip to Bally-gunge, picking up three other Americans who were urgently looking for transport along the way.

Under his mosquito bar, after having assured himself that the whining insect he heard was outside the netting, Ian considered the day. He'd learned a great deal, not only today but also in the week or more he'd been in India. He hadn't had any conception that India was so crowded. Oh, the Tamils he'd seen from the train in southern India, the ones in the conical bamboo huts in the forests, weren't living like sardines in a can. They looked relatively free and able to do as they pleased. But the crowds on the station platforms, in the rail cars, in the waiting rooms, on the streets, in and hanging onto trolley cars and buses, living on the sidewalks—constantly bickering and scrapping! Per-haps that was what had happened tonight. Hindu versus Muslim. Or Indian versus British. Or Sikh versus Hindu. No Buddhists involved, he was sure. He wondered how so many millions of passionately devoted worshipers of so many differing religions could possibly coexist. Each group intolerant of the others, except probably the Buddhists.

He thought back to his comparative religions courses and tried to re-member what little he could. The Tamils, descendants of ancient Dravidian people, were the most numerous people in the south of the subcontinent and relatively friction free, he presumed. But the Hindus, who worshiped Brahma and a host of other deities like Shiva, Kali, Indra and Vishnu, and were devo-tees of the caste system and the practice of suttee and purdah, despised the Muslims and the Sikhs. The Muslims said there was only one god, Allah, and Mohammed was his prophet, and were ready to die for their beliefs, hope-fully taking a couple of Hindus or Christians apiece with them.

The Buddhists seemed to look at their navels a lot as they tried to achieve Nirvana and weren't particularly warlike. Gautama Siddhartha had set them the example selflessness and virtue, right living and peace of mind. That had cost them popular support as the law of Karma, the transmigration of souls and the general medley of superstitions and faiths gave way to Hinduism, a triumph of aboriginal Dravidic India. Buddhists were relatively few in mod-ern India. Ian thought any right-thinking Buddhist wouldn't get into a street riot.

The Sikhs were relative newcomers, having been around for only three centuries or so. There weren't as many of them, but they all seemed tall, humorless and threatening, despite their belief in purity of life and toleration. Wallace knew it was a monotheistic religious and military sect. The beards and turbans were impressive. Maybe that was why there were so many Sikh policemen and Indian Army men. The British certainly relied on them a lot, it appeared.

How on earth had the English controlled this diverse population for so many centuries, Ian wondered. Guns, he supposed, and trade.

How would Mooney survive in this maze? By guile and subterfuge, political pull and using bountiful American goods to make a little cash on the side in the black market. What the hell, if the Army won't fly the Navy's stuff over the Hump why not put it to good use. He'll probably get himself decorated for being a lubricant in the gears of war.

And what about the news that Americans were not to be allowed in combat? That meant he'd be relatively safe, he supposed, but certainly conscience-stricken. Peter has been through North Africa, Sicily and now Italy. Avery Cooper is dead, shot down in the shark infested Bismarck Sea in March. Poor Dick Lewis is under a little white cross in some military cemetery on a god-forsaken atoll in the Pacific. Perry's in the hospital, or maybe out now and flying tactical ground support for Marine infantrymen, or combat air patrol over some airstrip or tangling with Zekes over Rabaul. Maybe, he thought, just maybe there is a way around this combat proscription. First we'll have to find out what the ground rules are. Then we'll see. You're starting to sound pretty bloodthirsty. Well, we'll see, we'll see.

And Diana, bless her heart. There is always Diana. There always will be Diana. His heart ached at the thought of her. Bless her and keep her well and safe from harm, he prayed God. What god? Whose god? In the land of so many gods how do you know who to pray to? To the only God you know, the one universal Father of all mankind, revealed supremely in Jesus Christ our Lord and present with us to guide, comfort and inspire. O.K., God, I can use all the guidance and comfort you can spare. A little inspiration wouldn't hurt, but mostly how about some guidance to ease this conscience of mine?

Mooney called Ian one morning and asked him if he'd like to do a little sightseeing with the car and driver. Wallace was surprised that there was time enough for Mooney to do that and fuel enough to squander on such frivolities. But he jumped at the chance. They drove to the docks where they could see the rusty freighters unloading war supplies, manpower providing the heft that would have been done by machine at home; to the Indian Museum; to the Parasnath Jain Temple where Mooney made rude remarks about the sculptures. Even though Ian explained about the religious symbolism of the *linga* and *yoni*, Mooney could not keep a straight face.

Last on the trip was a visit to the burning *ghats*. Ian suspected that this was the place Mooney had really wanted to visit in the first place, to satisfy his morbid curiosity. The driver said he'd just as soon wait at the car, so Mooney and Wallace went through the stone columns and arches on the banks of the Hooghly to a strip of hard earth where two fires were burning and another was being prepared. Ragged groups of Hindus stood about staring at or chatting about the shrouded corpse being laid on the stacked wood. Wallace felt uncomfortable being there, a foreign intruder at a solemn ceremony. Mooney was fascinated and kept pointing and talking in a loud voice as fire was made and the body began to burn.

"Let's go," Wallace said.

"Hold it!" said Mooney. "Maybe somebody will commit *suttee*!"

"You're sick," said Ian, "and besides, it's against the law now." He turned and walked back to the car, sickened at the sight and aware that the two of them had spoiled a ceremonious moment for the mourners.

"You're a Catholic, aren't you?" Ian asked Mooney when the j.g. had returned to the car and they were under way.

"I guess so. At least I was brought up to be one. Don't practice it much."

"Well how would you feel if some Hindus came into your Catholic church during a High Requiem Mass and talked and pointed and laughed?"

"Oh, I don't know. I always used to laugh to myself when I watched the priest, you know, the celebrant, finish off the communal wine and then do the dishes right in front of God and the congregation."

Wallace had attended only a few Catholic services but had always been impressed at their solemnity, the distinguished Latin liturgy and the somber medieval music. Most of the Catholics he knew were very devout. Well, he was learning not to judge the many by the few. And he decided he really thought Mooney was a genuine first-class A-number-one dyed-in-the-wool son of a bitch.

He asked Mooney, "What do you know about the Chinese? All I know is what I read in the papers," and was surprised at the outburst he provoked.

"Don't believe any of that shit!" Mooney almost shouted. "The papers only publish what they're told, and the U.S. is trying to put the best face on a rotten situation. I learned more about the Chinese when I was in the Secret Service than I have since I joined the Navy."

Wallace could believe it. He'd had no briefings of any kind on the military and political situation in China; no instruction on how to behave; no rudimentary language or cultural training.

"How did you learn about them in the Secret Service?"

"I was assigned to the Secret Service detail guarding Madame Chiang Kai-shek the last time she came to the U.S. to raise money. She and her crowd stayed at the Waldorf Astoria. They'd go out and plead for money and then come back and gamble with it! Right there on their floor in the hotel. Poker, dice, anything! No accountability. And was she ever a haughty bitch! Not like you read in the papers... Wellesley graduate, sister-in-law of Sun Yat Sen, Christian and all that. She treated us like dirt and treated her Chinese worse. There were factions among her own bodyguards, and she didn't trust anybody. Not that I blame her. I wouldn't have exposed my back to any of them. And dirty! Spit on the floor. Pee in the corner. Didn't know how to use the bathroom.

"I asked the agent-in-charge if it was like that in China when he went over to set up the arrangements. He said the backbiting was unbelievable, the factions undecipherable, the sanitation unspeakable. He said Chiang was more interested in keeping the Communists out of government than fighting the Japanese. He keeps the provincial governors and the war zone commanders in line by doling out arms and military stores, but he has revolts all the same. And there are still war lords and bandits doing whatever they want, mostly in the mountains. India is a comparative paradise."

Heaven and earth are not humane.
They regard all things as straw dogs.*

— Lao-Tzu
The Way of Lao-Tzu

*Straw dogs were used as sacrifices and then discarded.

SZECHWAN 1944

WHILE THE 155,000 MEN OF GENERAL MUTAGUCHI'S Fifteenth Japanese Army were hammering at Imphal and Kohima, Wallace received his orders to report to the Senior U.S. Naval Observer, Chungking, China. Wallace hoped that the British-Indian Army would keep the Japanese at bay at least until his plane made its stops at Jorhat and Dibrugarh. He didn't fancy being drafted off the plane at one of those stops and being put into the thin red line. The news was not good on that front, but he knew that if the airfields were under fire the plane would not leave.

He considered the equipment he had been issued to carry on the plane as his personal gear: 2 jackets, utility; 3 trousers, utility; 3 shirts, utility; 2 caps, utility; 2 shoes, field; 2 gloves, work; 1 jacket, field; 1 bag, special clothing. His winter gear, rain parka and winter parka, rain trousers, winter sweater, long johns; heavy socks and shore artics would be drawn in the field. In addition to his .45 he also had been issued a Smith and Wesson .38 caliber revolver, ammunition and holster, a .45 caliber Thompson submachine gun with sling and three loaded magazines in their pouches, and a .30 caliber carbine with sling and five loaded magazines. He would stuff all the clothes in his sea bags but he had to wear the weapons. He thought he would clank as he tried to walk. When he was weighed before he boarded he supposed the scales would rupture.

Wallace was the only Naval Group person assigned to the CNAC flight of April 12. His ticket certificate said that the fare was Rs 1500, and with the value of the rupee at about thirty cents U.S. it meant the Navy was spending four hundred fifty dollars to get him over the Hump. It seemed like a great deal of money to Ian.

He was driven out Barrackpore Trunk Road to Dum-Dum Road, where the weapons carrier turned left toward Dum-Dum airport while his arsenal rattled and clattered on the bed of the vehicle. For the first time he saw the daily collection of corpses from the streets where famine had had its way. He'd heard of that but never seen it, because the collections were in the early morning. Death seemed to come at night rather than in the hope and activity of the day.

All he knew about his trip was that he was apprehensive about his first airplane flight; that his orders merely said that he would "further proceed, when directed on or about 12 April 1944 to Chungking, China, and there report to the Senior U.S. Naval Observer for duty," and that according to a note on a Calcutta Swimming Club Refreshment Order he would be met at Chungking by someone named McInerny. He knew also that the flight stopped to refuel at Kunming, in Yunan, on the eastern slope of the Hump, before proceeding to Chungking.

Wallace clambered from the weapons carrier and slung his armament on his shoulders. He picked up his two sea bags, thanked the driver and started to turn away only to notice that the driver was saluting. He hadn't seen a salute since he left *Ranee*, but he tried to return it and dropped one sea bag and the TSMG. He noticed the smile on the driver's face and knew that the bastard did that every time to make the officers feel like horses' asses. He also heard soft chuckles from some waiting men standing at the foot of the fold-down steps behind the wing root of the silver DC-3 that would take them to China. The craft was marked with a large Kuomintang blue and white sunburst, and in English and in Chinese characters it proclaimed itself to be "China National Aviation Corporation."

Two men in squashed, visored caps, khaki trousers, white shirts with epaulets and wings over their left breast pockets walked past Ian toward the plane, talking. They were very tanned white men and sounded Australian. Ian didn't know why that made him feel better. He was wringing wet in the heat, because he was wearing a field jacket that he was told he'd need on the other side, because it would be cold. Rather than carry it, he had worn it and now regretted that decision as he struggled toward the official who was collecting tickets on the other side of the scale at the foot of the fold-down steps.

Most of the men waiting to board were in military dress, Chinese and British, and some were American civilians, as best Ian could make out. He took his turn on the scale, watching the agent shake his head. He dropped the TSMG again as he stepped down and heard one of the British officers say, "Oh, God! Not another Terry and the Pirates!"

Ian was last to board, because they needed to weigh everyone else to see if Ian could carry all his gear on the flight. He clambered up the three steps, edged himself sideways through the narrow door and side-stepped up the sloping aisle, bumping other passengers with his load as he did so. The only empty seat was next to a British officer who was wearing tropical kit—shorts and shirt—with a military sweater in his lap.

"Make yoursel' at home laddie," he said with a distinct Scottish burr and helped Ian unload and stow his impedimenta. Wallace finally seated himself in the aisle seat with his weapons between his knees and introduced himself to the Scot, who professed to be delighted to hear Wallace's name and said they might be distant relations. His name was Alec Bruce. Wallace was embarrassed not to know what the pips on Bruce's shoulder straps stood for and had to ask.

"Captain," he said, "assigned to the British Military Attaché's Office at the embassy in Chungking. You're with that hush-hush Navy Group, right?"

"How do you know about them?"

"Och, man, this is my thirteenth trip over and I've seen a good many of your people. And besides, at the embassy we're quite up on what's going on."

"I wish you'd tell me," said Ian, "I'm totally in the dark."

But then the engines started to turn over and catch, blowing blue smoke to the rear and making talk difficult. Bruce showed Wallace how to attach his lap strap and shouted that after the plane got off the ground they could chat. Wallace didn't know how. The engine noise was deafening.

The plane taxied to the end of the runway and ran up its engines, tested its control surfaces and sat waiting for clearance. Ian could see jungle around the airport perimeter. Then the idling engines slowly revved up until the roar was thundering and the plane was vibrating. Wallace was just wondering why the plane didn't move when the brakes were released and the aircraft lurched and started to creep down the runway, slowly picking up momentum, blowing huge clouds of pale brown dust in its wake. Wallace was counting the seconds before the wings overcame gravity and began to worry when the twenty-five-second mark passed. He stared at the seat back in front of him and prayed. Agonizingly, slowly, the plane lifted. Wallace was startled by the thump of the retracting landing gear and saw jungle pass beneath the wing, no more than twenty feet below. And then he thought that the engines were dying as the vibrations and the noise suddenly lessened. He grabbed the arms of his seat and looked at the Scotsman.

"Prop pitch and power just changed," he said. "Don't need all that power now that we're up. Gives you a bit of a fright the first time, though."

"My first flight and it shows, doesn't it?"

"There's a first time for everybody. But you're lucky. You're sitting next to a career courier who'll be happy to point out the sights and the ins-and-outs of air travel. I hope, by the way, that you relieved yourself before boarding. The facility in the back is rather cramped and medieval, though better than most of the privies in the Flowery Land."

"The Middle Kingdom?"

"Where'd you hear that?"

"In training camp. From an old China hand."

"Yes, the Middle Kingdom. The Chinese have long considered themselves the center of the civilized world, and people outside the Flowery Land are barbarians, or devils, foreign devils. They refer to their country as All That Is Under Heaven, too. The Chinese word for their country, you know, is *Chung-Kuo*.... Chung meaning central or middle and kuo meaning country."

"Where does the word China come from then?" asked Wallace.

"China is a western word, I've been told, and its root is in the name of the first empire, Chin.'

"Have you studied Chinese history?"

"Not quite. But you do pick up things just as you are picking them up now."

"It certainly would have helped if the U.S. Navy had given us some briefings about where we were going and what we were to do and how to deal with the people."

Alec Bruce thought for a moment and then said, "I don't know what advice to give you except to keep your eyes and ears open, learn everything you can including the language if possible and don't look down on the Chinese.

Treat them as you would treat others. I try to remember that I am a guest in their country, but many people make the mistake of treating the Chinese contemptuously. Then they wonder why they never get a straight answer."

Ian thought the advice, even though delivered a bit pompously, made good sense. He could imagine the trouble one could get into if one behaved toward the Chinese like some people treated the Indians... the "Europeans Only" syndrome. Or like people treated Chinese in America... good only for cooks and laundrymen.

"What can you tell me about the 'hush-hush' Navy Group, as you call it?" asked Wallace.

"Well, some of it is conjecture and some of it our people have picked up from their Chinese opposite numbers. To some of it we have been alerted officially."

Wallace remembered he had seen a British officer in the room when he had been interviewed by the CNO in Washington that long-ago December Sunday afternoon. And also, the British had provided transportation across the Pacific and Indian Oceans, hadn't they? So don't be so surprised.

"I rather imagine," Bruce continued, "that I should let your command inform you of what you need to know. At least I can say that we understand some of your types are in bed with the Tai Li organization, Chiang Kai-shek's Bureau of Investigation and Statistics.... an odd name, really, for an espionage and counterintelligence organization."

"Espionage?"

"Right. Tai Li is a spymaster and runs networks in free and occupied China. They say his agents are thugs and assassins and primarily interested in eliminating enemies of the Kuomintang and rather less enthusiastic about operations against the Japanese. Though they say he trusts your Observer and is helping in that effort. Otherwise he's reported to be a practicing xenophobe, like most Chinese. That's why they call us barbarians."

Working with thugs and assassins! Chinese thugs and assassins! I wonder what the reporting relationships are and who can trust whom?

"Your General Stilwell," Bruce went on, "refers to the Tai Li organization as the 'Chinese Gestapo.' "

Marvelous.

"I'm quite sure you'll enjoy your stay in Happy Valley, that's what your people call your headquarters, providing you don't mind a bit of corruption, laziness, inefficiency and bigotry."

Bruce lit a cigarette and gazed out the window. He's not very bitter! Ian thought, but, good-Christ-in-the-foot-hills, I hadn't bargained for this kind of a tour. Maybe "extra-hazardous duty" was an inadequate description.

The CNAC flight put down at the Jorhat strip, raising a cloud of dust from the steel matting on the runway. The plane pivoted at the end of its run and taxied back to a fuel truck. The pilots killed the engines and opened the door from the flight deck. The first pilot stopped in the opening and said in a loud voice that no one should leave the plane during refueling. They were anxious to get under way as soon as possible and didn't want to waste time looking for the odd sod who'd gone into the jungle to piss.

How civilized, thought Wallace.

The two men worked their way down the narrow aisle, opened the door and let down the steps. Immediately the plane became an oven. The hot air rushed in, and the sun broiled the aircraft's skin. Sweat popped from every pore.

Alec Bruce asked Wallace to let him into the aisle, and with difficulty the British officer made his way to the door, where Ian could see him chatting with someone on the ground. The sweat was pouring off Ian's nose and chin. His clothes were sodden. He felt a little rush of light-headedness, not quite a petit mal, a little flicker of fear that he'd be trapped in this furnace and pass out, a little flutter of claustrophobia. Take hold of yourself, he ordered.

At least Bruce was getting a little fresh air by the door. The veteran Hump-runner knew all the angles but sure as hell didn't share them.

Wallace leaned over the empty window seat and watched as the fueling hose was disconnected from the wing tank. A service man, naked to the waist, climbed on the wing and measured the fuel with a dipstick. The hose was reconnected and more fuel was pumped in. Shortly there was an over-flow, and as the man shouted and signaled several men rushed up with a two-wheeled fire extinguisher and aimed the funnel at the spilled gasoline. Ian could smell the fuel. He heard a man gagging in the row behind him. He looked up to see Bruce standing in the aisle.

"The simplest way to do this is for you to move to the window seat," Bruce said, "and besides, I've seen all the bloody scenery anyway. Move over."

Wallace heaved himself over the arm rest dragging his weapons with him, and Bruce, in his tropical shorts, sat in the aisle seat.

"My God, did you shame yourself? This seat is soaking wet!"

"Your choice," said Wallace, smiling.

The Englishman looked hard at him and then laughed. "Right-o," he said. "The gen is that we probably won't stop at Dibrugarh. That's why all the fuss about the fuel. We usually top off at Dibrugarh and fly fuel-light from here to there so we can move some cargo. Not today, however. Spot of Jap air activity near Dib. Don't want to get caught on the ground. So Kunming is the next stop."

I hope, thought Ian. All we have to do is fly over Dibrugarh on the upper reaches of the Brahmaputra; over the Himalayas, the world's highest mountains; over the gorges of the Mekong and the Salween rivers; the southern-most bend of the Yangtze; over the Nu Shan range southeast to Kunming on the shores of lake Dian Chi; and find the air strip in the dark—avoiding Japanese fighters the while, he mused.

Below them the jungle receded, to be replaced by less vegetation in the upland foothills. From time to time Ian could see little plumes of blue smoke rising from small clearings or from the forest itself. The plumes got fewer and fewer as the plane continued its uninterrupted climb over the rising land. Ahead, over the wing, Ian could see a deck of clouds that obscured any view of the mountains. The engines droned and throbbed and he dozed, while confused thoughts drifted through his semiconsciousness. I am going over the Hump to get killed so that all the Muslims, Hindus, Tamils, Sikhs and Rajputs can continue to bicker and slaughter each other in freedom; so that the political factions, the war lords, bandits and river pirates in China can continue to butcher, rob and rape the peasants of the land in the name of All That Is Under Heaven. I am flying over the Backbone of the World to protect my grandfather's farm in Cummington and to avenge the loss of my best friend Avery Cooper and my musketeer Dick Lewis, but not by fighting Japanese since no combat is allowed. I am flying the world's most dangerous airline to join forces with Tai Li and his collection of cutthroats and torturers, of ruthless thugs and assassins. But does he become my ruler by my serving under him? No, the Lord redeems the life of His servants; none of those who take refuge in Him will be condemned.

The plane dropped suddenly, and Wallace's weapons flew toward the overhead only to be caught just in time by the awakening Marine as he clutched the slings and brought his arsenal back to his lap. He felt that his belly was still several hundred feet above him as his lap strap pulled at his thighs.

"Just popped out of the overcast," said Bruce, "but there must have been some fighters about, so we've popped back in."

"How do we know whose fighters they were?"

"None of ours hereabouts, and besides, better to be out of sight in any event. No one can hit you if they can't see you. The thing is, of course, that we'll have to pop back out again or land on a rather precipitous mountainside."

Outside Ian's window gray mist streamed by and tiny droplets of condensation streaked across the pane. As he watched the light increased and the mist lessened. Suddenly the plane burst into clear blue air above the cloud deck, and Ian was exposed to the breathtaking view of steep snow-covered escarpments bathed in the pink light of the setting sun.

"Almost over the top now," said Bruce. "We usually top out at about eighteen thousand feet and go through a col between two much higher peaks. Then it's downhill all the way to Kunming."

Ian noticed that he was short of breath and that Bruce's cigarette, though still between his fingers, was out. As he watched, Bruce brought the weed to his lips and struck his lighter, which flamed weakly as he puffed to relight the tobacco. After a couple of puffs the glow on the tip went out again.

"Not enough oxygen to support the fire," Bruce informed Wallace. Ian remembered that at ten thousand feet Army Air Corps pilots went on oxygen. He supposed the Australian pilots up forward wore masks.

They went over the top in a blaze of blue sky, glistening air-borne ice crystals, pink and white light on the snow, and rocky black and gray shadows. Bruce pointed to a great scorched avalanche area on the rocky mountain wall to their left. "Tanker didn't make it. Probably in the fog and ice."

Some B-24s, Ian knew, had been stripped of their bomb bays and had fuel transport tanks installed so they could serve as flying tankers to supplant the fuel drums other transports flew over to supply the Flying Tigers. Flying coffins.

"Since it's your first trip, it's necessary to celebrate the event in appropriate fashion," said Bruce, worming a small silver flask out of his kit. "Rather like crossing the equator, you see. Have to have a spot of this to make it official."

Bruce twisted off the cap as the plane started it's descent on the eastern slope and the darkness of the mountains' shadows quickly covered them. He shook the flask and smelled it's contents before taking a pull.

"Ah!" he said and handed the flask to Wallace. Ian also smelled it. Neat Scotch whiskey. He put the flat little silver bottle to his lips thinking "Over the teeth, behind the gums, look out stomach here it comes," and took a small swallow. In the rarefied atmosphere of eighteen thousand feet there was an explosion in Wallace's innards, a watering of the eyes and an instant feeling of euphoria coupled with a sense of dislike for the man next to him, who was watching Ian's performance with a wide grin.

With a thicker Scot's accent than usual Bruce said, "High altitude makes the Brown Infuriator go a lot farther. Easier on the pocket book."

Ian's ears popped as the plane continued its descent. He could see tiny lights from time to time, orange and spread far apart. Fires in nomads' camps, protection from the evil spirits of the night and from the tigers that were said to inhabit still the primitive forests and plateaus below. We must be under the clouds, Wallace thought. No stars were visible. And then ahead he could see a small string of weak lights on which the plane lined up. He could feel the plane flare out as the power was cut and the thump as the wheels touched down. The aircraft traveled a little distance before the tail wheel settled down and the plane slowly rolled before braking on one wheel and coming about to taxi to the collection of huts Wallace could just make out in the dark.

The engines stopped, and the pilot came to the door. "Only Kunming passengers may debark," he said and went with his co-pilot to the rear door and let down the steps. There was a general shuffling as the debarkees struggled with their belongings and slowly made their way out the door.

"Bugger this," said Bruce, and heaved himself up and went to the rear and stepped out. Ian, cramped for so many hours, stood in the aisle and stretched. What the hell, he thought, and went to the door and stepped down the three steps. He couldn't see Bruce in the dark. A heavy form loomed before him and spoke to him in rapid and assertive Chinese, pointing to the plane. When the form got close enough Ian could see it was an extraordinarily fat Chinese, dressed in a black buttoned-to-the-neck-with-cloth-buttons banker's cloak that fell to his shoe tops, wearing a brown fedora hat and bedecked with an official patch of some kind sewn to his chest. As Ian was putting on his field jacket to ward off the unexpectedly cold air, the Chinese shouted at him and pointed at the plane.

"Just wanted some fresh air," Wallace said.

The Chinese was much quicker than Wallace thought he could have been, carrying so much weight. He surprised Ian by putting his paw on Ian's breast and shoving, hard, propelling Ian backwards into the plane's steps where he fell. The Chinese stood over him and yelled, pointing. Two soldiers, in mustard colored padded uniforms, wrap-around leggings and cloth shoes, with the longest rifles Wallace had ever seen came up and pointed their long thin bayonets at him. He struggled to his feet, dusted himself off and went back to his seat on the plane.

Welcome to Far Cathay.

"Glad it was you and not me, old boy," said Alec Bruce on the flight to Chungking. "That was one of Tai Li's chaps, one of the nicer ones, and two of his *pings*, soldiers, that is. Fortunately I'd just nipped under the wing to kill the weeds in comfort, so to speak, and wasn't seen. Ah well, being able to wee without my legs bent and my head cocked over was worth the risk. And the show was marvelous." He slapped Ian's knee.

The landscape below was totally dark, and Wallace didn't see any signs of habitation until they were almost ready to alight at Chungking. Looking out the windows he could see little specks of light on either side of the airplane. Strange, he thought, to see lights at the same altitude as the wings. As he watched, lights kept creeping higher than the descending craft. He sensed Bruce watching him.

"What's happening?" he asked.

"Chungking's surrounded by water on three sides—it's where the Kialing Kiang and the Yangtze Kiang meet—and it's built on the sides of steep hills. The air strip is in the middle of the Yangtze on Penghu sandbar, and the city rises above the level at which we land. It's uphill all the way from here."

Wallace quickly discovered what Bruce meant by his last remark. After having said adieu to the Scot, Wallace found McInerny on the other side of the passenger barrier and turned his sea bags over to the coolie McInerny had with him. This poor man, naked but for faded black pants wound round his waist, and folded over, bare-footed, with callused shoulders and a bamboo pole, lashed Wallace's gear with bamboo rope that he looped over the ends of his pole. With a grunt he lifted his load and started off. "We follow him," said McInerny.

Wallace looked up and saw that they were at the foot of the longest flight of stone steps he had ever seen. They glistened in the dim light and the cold, misting rain. McInerny carried one of Wallace's weapons, the .30 caliber carbine, but Wallace lugged the heavy one, the TSMG, and they started up. The steps were slippery and Wallace was careful how he placed his feet. He started to count.

McInerny, whose dark-blue Navy utility jacket bore no insignia of rank, said, "It's best to do a cadence and just put one foot after the other without breaking cadence even though some steps are higher than others. That way you don't tire so easily."

Ian was huffing. He'd lost count of the steps. He stopped to catch his wind and watched the coolie keep plodding upward, nonstop. I've dealt with two Chinese and lost face twice, he thought.

At the top McInerny told him there were one hundred and thirty three steps. Didn't tell him before because he might have wanted to stay at the bottom, ha ha. Enlisted man for sure, said Ian to himself. They ought to have steps like these at Parris Island.

They heaved the heavy gear into McInerny's jeep, guarded by a Chinese in a padded uniform but carrying a .30 caliber U.S. carbine and wearing a GI web belt.

"One of ours," McInerny explained.

They climbed in, the ping in the back seat with his carbine in his hands, and started off slowly to Happy Valley. The streets, paved with large, thick stone slabs, were wet, steep and slippery. Little light seeped out of the buildings they passed but Ian could smell the unmistakable smoke of charcoal fires.

"They use charcoal for everything," said McInerny. "Cook over it, burn it in *huo-puns* in the middle of the room to keep warm, even burn it in a rig they attach to their trucks and buses and distill the smoke to make fuel. We use it to heat our tents, too. Gotta be careful, though. Damned stuff burns up a lot of oxygen, and you can get a carbon monoxide headache that would make you think you got an axe in your skull right down to the ears."

Wallace stored that piece of expert advice and noticed the change in smells as they left the thirty-yard-high city walls behind and moved into the countryside on a rutted, muddy dirt road. The new smell was fetid—sweet—sickening.

"Rice paddies out there. You can't see 'em but you can sure smell 'em.

After a while you don't notice."

"Whew! What is it?" Wallace asked.

"Shit," said McInerny. "They save all their crap and fertilize the fields with it. That's why you never eat anything that ain't been cooked and never drink water that ain't been boiled. Save their piss, too. Ladies set their hair with it, they say."

The jolting ride seemed endless, but shortly after midnight they stopped at a path that followed a little brook up into the darkness.

"*P'eng-yu*, here, will help you with your gear. P'eng-yu means friend. I call 'em all that. Don't have to remember their goofy names. I gotta stow this vehicle down here with the others and take out the distributor cap or we'll never see this jeep again. Takes me a few minutes. You follow P'eng-yu. He'll show you where to go. I'll probably see you in the morning."

P'eng-yu carried Wallace's carbine and one of the sea bags. Wallace, draped with his TSMG, .38 revolver, .45 automatic pistol, his musette bag and his other sea bag on his shoulder, climbed up the slippery path behind the Chinese, keeping his eyes on the man's dim straw sandal-clad feet as best he could in the dark. He kept slipping and wondered why the little short man in front of him in the straw sandals was having no trouble. He could hear the stream off to the left and smell paddies down there, too. They climbed for more than a quarter of an hour, and then the ground seem to level out a bit.

P'eng-yu stopped, turned to Ian and spoke in Chinese: *"Na bien sz ni-te chang mu,"* and pointed.

Ian felt, rather than saw, a large building to his left, dark, with upturned eaves. He strained his eyes and could make out a long, two-floor edifice with a tile roof. It was dark. Up the hill to the right, where P'eng-yu was pointing, was a set of steps carved in the dirt that led to two levels of tents in rows. Pyramidal tents, ghostily illuminated by light that filtered out under some of the flaps. Only two or three tents displayed any light at all. Small wonder, thought Wallace. It's after midnight, God bless us all.

P'eng-yu led Ian to the last tent on the top of the two levels and threw Ian's sea bag and carbine in under the flap. He turned around and did a caricature of a western salute, said, *"T'sai gin,"* and disappeared.

Ian lowered his own burdens to the ground and untied the tent flaps that he could reach by putting his hands through the overlapping canvas layers, wondering why he didn't get any help from whoever was inside and had left the light burning. The flaps parted and Wallace swung his gear into the tent and stood up to find that there were six folding cots set up, but only one was occupied.

On that one occupied cot sat a man in a sweat shirt and skivvy drawers clipping his toenails by the light of a hissing Coleman lantern. He looked up at Ian.

"I heard you were coming, so I stayed up," said Francis Xavier O'Reilly.

"Deo gratias!" said Wallace.

Ian lay in his moldy, cold blanket and listened to the rain drum on the roof of the tent. He figured he had just gone back in time from the twentieth century to the middle ages, or earlier. Fix had beaten him by two weeks and had been just sitting around waiting for assignment. O'Reilly had flown from the East Coast of the U.S. and had arrived via Cairo, Tehran, Karachi and Calcutta. He had stamps in his passport to prove his route. Fix had heard of this obscure duty and had volunteered for it in order to get off Iona Island in the Hudson River. He couldn't tell Ian what their specific duty might be but did tell him that he would probably get the gung-ho talk from the executive officer in the morning.

Swell, thought Wallace. Inspire me to work with a bunch of cutthroats to protect my way of life. Make me feel like I'm doing something worthwhile. Make me proud to write my grandfather and tell him how I am carrying on the family tradition of distinguished military service. Make me flushed with conceit so I can honestly tell Diana I'm doing something important. Make me truly believe that I am going to make a real contribution to ending this war and avenging the loss of my best friends. O Lord, thou God of vengeance, how long shall the wicked exult?

The building Ian had seen dimly in the dark was Naval Group's administration center, radio shack, mess hall and "recreation room." It consisted of one enormous two-story hall with round tables and hard wooden chairs for meals and with some other nondescript tables and settees for "recreation." Tattered, out-of-date magazines littered the seats. The kitchen was to the rear, and the offices and radio shack were in small rooms to one side. Though the OSS ate with them, Fix said, they had their own building just down the valley. Fix thought there was a little friction between the OSS detachment and Naval Group, a tug of war for command and for policy and plans development. As of the moment it seemed that each group was going its own way.

Two meals a day were served and were served Chinese style: bowls and chopsticks. Wallace wasn't used to vegetables and rice and maybe a little soup for breakfast, but Fix told him he'd better learn how to adjust, because this is the way it would be in the field, if they were lucky. Lots of interesting food, Fix said, including a strange gray gelatin that tasted like running down hill with your mouth open in the fog: "Nothing Pudding" they called it.

The Group executive officer called in Wallace for his briefing just after his first meal. Ian was amazed how small and crowded the offices were compared to the room he had just left. There seemed to be four yeomen typing at back-to-back tables, an office for the exec and an empty office for the CO. Wallace could hear a radio key at work in the only other room. Outside, a Wisconsin two-cycle engine with a bad muffler was driving the generator that supplied what little electricity was needed to illuminate the offices and run the radio.

Commander C. C. Spofford showed Wallace to a chair and opened a file in front of him that he read for a moment and then looked up. "I'm sure you are like the other men who are assigned to this duty and you wonder what is going on. Well, I'm going to tell you a little about what we're up to, but not more than you need to know and no more than the Japanese know already. If you get yourself caught we don't want you to disclose sensitive information. Don't think they can't get it out of you. They can."

He paused, shook a cigarette out of a pack, offered one to Wallace, who declined, and lit up.

"Our mission is to work with the Chinese in a group called SACO, the Sino-American Cooperative Organization. The Chinese half is the Tai Li bureau. We're commanded by Captain Milton Miles, though you won't see much of him. He's on the move all the time. The camps, Chungking, Washington, Calcutta, Delhi—trying to keep it all together. Our assignment is to establish centers for training and equipping Chinese and get them acting as guerrillas behind the Japanese lines. At the request of the Generalissimo and Tai Li, no Americans will be exposed to combat. We tend to think it's a 'face' thing. They don't want their troops led by foreigners, and they don't want to lose face by losing any of us. We observe and suggest."

Daddy, what did you do in the big war? I showed yellow men how to kill other yellow men and ate Nothing Pudding.

"We do other things as well," the commander continued, "but since that is none of your concern, the less said the better. You'll be involved in one of the columns, as we call the Chinese commando groups. And your record indicates that you should do well. You come very highly recommended, by one man in particular."

"Who's that, sir?"

"A regular officer. Marine captain, name of Stryker, Sam Stryker. He says," Spofford looked at the file, " 'this officer is highly qualified for extra-hazardous duty.' Where did he know you?"

"Quantico. He was my ROC company commander."

"Well he thinks very highly of you."

Bullshit! The son of a bitch was responsible for putting my name in front of the commandant, just to get even! Wallace was surprised at the strength of his own emotion. He thought he'd outgrown that sort of thing.

"In a few days," Spofford continued, "you'll be assigned to one of the columns and provided with transportation. Better start to learn the language as best you can. The Chinese interpreters, the *fan yi kuan*, eat with us and will be enthusiastic about helping you. You'll have an interpreter with you in the field, but if you get separated it helps to know how to get by."

"What about the coast watchers, the hospitals and the weather stations?" Ian asked.

"Goddam it!" Spofford exploded. "Who the hell told you that we were involved in that sort of activity.?"

"Common knowledge in Calcutta, sir, and on the plane coming over I was pretty well briefed by a British officer who seemed to think that the whole thing was a bit different."

"What do you mean by 'a bit different?' "

"Well, sir, he thought we were pretty naive about our workings with Tai Li and even a bit more childish than the OSS. He called the OSS 'Oh, So Social.' "

"It's true that there are a great number of highly qualified, well educated men from recognized eastern universities and a number of very well known society figures in the OSS who have volunteered for our special kind of duty, but it in no way falls to the credit of your British friend to disparage the work of this group. After all, the only thing the British are fighting for is the restoration of Empire."

A great statement of Allied understanding and cooperation, Wallace mused.

"Sir, what do I know if I am put to the test?"

"You know absolutely nothing!"

Wallace left the commander's office feeling like he was part of a game, yet no one had explained the rules to him. This was almost worse than the OSS. Everybody thought it *was* a game. They sat here on their fat behinds and played with pins on a map, while the real conclusive war was being fought in Europe and the Pacific.

Fix and Ian slid down the long mud path and the slippery steps to the rutted roadway where Ian had left the jeep the night before. The reek was unbelievable. Fix told Ian he'd get used to it. Six hundred million Chinese had learned to live with it. And die because of it, Ian thought.

Where the creek crossed the rutted road there was a small gray town, gray mud walls, dark gray tile roofs, light gray charcoal smoke coming from under the eaves and thick, gray rectangular stone paving the space between the roofs that overhung the common sewer running through the middle of what would otherwise be called a street. The ditch was stone lined and fed from the deposition of night soil emptied into the street to ooze its way into the common duct leading to the stream that ran through the village and down to the Yangtze Kiang. The human waste was collected at the end of the street for use on the paddy fields.

Fix led Wallace past small open-fronted shops, followed by a flock of little Chinese children, sewn into their winter padding. The children shrieked and pointed, fascinated to see two foreign devils, especially one with such a lack of grace as to have red hair.

"*Yang kueitze! Yang kueitze!*" they shouted.

Fix stopped suddenly, turned around and took off his overseas cap. The children stopped and recoiled, putting their hands to their mouths. O'Reilly looked at the children sternly. He was being watched by a crowd of gray-clad elder Chinese.

"*Wo sz yang kueitze.*" I am foreign devil, Fix said forbiddingly. Then he pointed at the children, smiled and said, "*Ni-men sz hsiao kueitze!*" You are little devils!

The elders tittered, and the children hid their faces and ran.

"A crowd will collect around us wherever we stop. We're curiosities. They'll talk about us, knowing that a foreign devil couldn't understand what is being said. The first few phrases I learned the villagers simply refused to understand. Their eyes told them I was a barbarian, so their ears refused to hear. Only after I had come here several times and displayed cash did the merchants begin to listen."

"How much Chinese do you know?"

"Just a little... how are you?... good-bye... how much/too much—that's all one phrase when you're buying something—and I know how to count. Come on, let's buy you your brass basin or you'll be unclean for the rest of your tour." Like the tribe of Levi, thought Wallace.

They stopped at a small metal-monger's shop and were instantly surrounded by curious citizens. None of them was tall enough to reach even Ian's shoulder. No one touched them, but they were so close it was difficult to move about. The odor of stale clothes and bodies was strong, almost overcoming the pervasive smell from the paddies and the street. Fix pointed to a small spun brass bowl about four inches deep and maybe twelve inches in diameter.

"That's what you'll bathe in and shave from for the rest of your natural life," Fix said and then spoke to the proprietor with the "how much/too much" phrase, and after some expected haggling paid for the bowl and handed it to Ian. "Don't lose it, and you owe me one hundred eighty-seven dollars, Chinese."

Wallace could not make himself sit around reading out-of-date magazines, like many of the other men, or play bridge just to kill time. Together he and Fix arranged to study the language four hours every day. Wallace made his own English–Chinese dictionary, writing out the Chinese words the way they sounded to him. Transliteration the interpreters called it. The interpreter who helped every day laughed at Ian's futile attempts to master the tones. Wallace supposed you could call his attempts pidgin Chinese. But he persevered, and he and Fix practiced on each other and the interpreters every day, trying to limit the amount of English they would let themselves speak. They were learning *P'u-t'ung-hua*, a Peking dialect like Mandarin and supposedly taught in all Chinese schools, so that in some distant day people from one province could understand people from another. The interpreter spoke some Cantonese, *Kwangtung-hua,* to them one day and they couldn't understand a word of it. It is a language of immense dialectal diversity, they were told.

On their long excursionary hikes in the countryside they spoke to farmers and shopkeepers using their P'u-t'ung-hua with growing success. They learned that *hao pu hao* meant "good, not good?"—a way of asking "how are you?" The answer was either *ding hao,* very good, or *pu hao*, not good. Ian absorbed the fact that when old China hands said "here's how" over a drink or a greeting, they were really saying *hao.*

They wondered if it would ever stop raining and misting, and warm up. On the first sunny day in weeks, they got a ride to Chugking in the Navy jeep and walked the precipitous stone steps of the capital's streets, astonished at the custom of Chinese men friends walking together holding hands. Wallace thought of the old Dwight Fisk phonograph recording of Noel Coward's "Fairies at the Bottom of My Garden." The casual way men would urinate into the gutter on a crowded street appalled them. Many of the older women tottered along on feet that had been bound when they were children. Lily feet. And nose picking! Everybody picked: old, young, men and women. The children just let their noses run down across their upper lips, with an occasional wipe of the hand, but their elders went on real exploratory excursions and would examine the results. Ian and Fix noticed that there were several schools for the disposal of the yields of such journeys: seat-of-the-pants wipers, flingers, ball rollers, eaters and draggers—drag it across anything. And after all, kerchiefs cost. Fingers are free.

Fix and Ian were not curiosities here. There were many barbarians on the streets of the capital of Kuomintang China.

Way out in the country on the mud road back to the compound, with McInerny at the wheel of the jeep, they passed a string of ill-clad Chinese farmers, coolies and other males roped together from neck to neck by one continuous strand of bamboo rope, their hands bound behind them, guarded by padded-uniformed Chinese soldiery.

"Prisoners?" asked Ian.

"Recruits," said McInerny. "The recruiting parties go into the country-side and lasso who they can, and if there isn't enough money to buy out or enough PI (political influence) to beg off you get marched off to basic training. You thought Parris Island was tough? You ain't seen nuthin'. Whips, spread eagles, water treatment, family threats, shit for food. No wonder they ain't got no loyalty to the regime. They run the first time they hear a shot. If they's lucky they get to take their weapon with them. Join up with bandits, maybe. Weapons are premium here. Most folks only got sticks. If you play your cards right you can become a pirate general yourself. Depends on how mean you can make yourself. Loyalty don't mean shit. Survival is all."

A levy, for god's sake! Thoughts of British press gangs of the seventeenth and eighteenth centuries coursed through Ian's head; of American seamen impressed by the British during the War of 1812; of Northerners during the American Civil War who bought substitutes to send to war in their stead. He wondered if these men would ever see any of the members of their families again. Probably, if they didn't get killed in training or in some pell-mell retreat, they would wind up even more bitter and hardened in a province where they could only speak one language, force.

The recruits shuffled by, rope cutting into their necks, getting occasional whacks from rifle butts, looking at the ground. Some wore cloth shoes, some wore straw sandals. Most were barefoot. You'll be sorree, thought Ian.

He wondered if the barefoot men had thought to assuage the tempers of evil spirits by tying the strings of their worn-out straw sandals together and slinging them over the single wire that stretched between the leaning electric poles lining the road. The lines were festooned with sandals near the city. Less so in the country.

O'Reilly and Wallace were depressed as they sat on their cots in the tent they shared. Ian quoted William Ernest Henley's "Invictus":

> *Out of the night that covers me,*
> *Black as the Pit from pole to pole,*
> *I thank whatever gods may be*
>   *for my unconquerable soul.*

O'Reilly picked it up:

> *In the fell clutch of circumstance,*
> *I have not winced or cried aloud;*
> *under the bludgeonings of chance*
>   *my head is bloody but unbowed.*

"I am the master of my fate; I am the captain of my soul," Wallace put in. "Bullshit," said O'Reilly.

"You are all expected to go," said Spofford, the executive officer. "It is meaningful of them to ask us, and it would show a lack of grace and understanding if we did not attend. Also it would cause them, and us, much loss of face. We have never been asked before."

Spofford was talking about the Chinese spymaster Tai Li. The Americans had been invited to an address by the Generalissimo to be followed by entertainments. Tai Li himself had issued the invitation, the command. The G'mo expected full attendance. One did not fuck around with either the G'mo or Tai Li, the executive officer explained. Wear your best uniform and don't say a goddam word or laugh or snicker. You just might learn something.

They dressed in pressed khakis, field scarves, overseas caps and field jackets. They trooped down the hill to the Chinese compound where they were ushered onto hard bench seats in the rear of an immense, dim auditorium with a stage at the front. The room was packed with Chinese officers of all ranks. Blue smoke drifted through the air toward the peaked tile roof. A color guard of Chinese soldiers in whipcord uniforms and shined riding boots stood at center stage.

There was a strident command, and the audience came to its feet shouting, with hands raised in what was almost a Fascist salute. Ian was appalled. Chiang Kai-shek marched onto the stage surrounded by bodyguards, some in uniform, many in civilian clothing. He returned the upraised-arm salute. The audience fell quiet and seated itself. Chiang, a short, slight man, stood on a box behind a podium and addressed the throng. He spoke for over two hours, often interrupted by throaty roars of approbation from his officers who leaped to their feet and shouted in unison with their right arms lifted forward in salute. Shades of Nuremburg, Munich, Berlin! Almost *"Seig heil,"* Ian thought. He dared not look at Fix nor any of the other Americans.

Following the almost endless speech of which the Americans understood nothing, they were treated to entertainments by the Chungking Opera Company. Programs dimly printed on brown rice paper were handed out. Except for two lines of English, a courtesy to comrades in arms, the programs were printed in Chinese characters. The two lines in English were the titles of the works they were going to enjoy. Chinese operas, in the pentatonic scale, all-male voices including the female roles. Ritualistic. Classic. Sticks with hair on the end were horses. Fighting was stylized, no touching. Much shouting accompanied by screeching two-stringed violins. Ian could more or less follow the plot lines in "Tsao Tsao's Narrow Escape," but had some difficulty with "The Beggar's Marriage." Cultural misunderstanding, he mused.

In his sack, under the mosquito bar, he pondered his brief experience in the Middle Kingdom. He thought he had been prepared for the worst from his conversations with Mooney, O'Hara and Alec Bruce. They don't know the half of it. Starting in India and now in China, he had asked himself over and over: how can so many people live in such misery? How can it be that there is so much more horror in the world than I have ever been led to believe. How can God permit so much wretchedness? Is there a God? Lord, I believe; help Thou mine unbelief.

"*Ching pao* coming," said Fix, as he walked into the tent one noon.

"What's ching pao?" Ian asked.

"Air raid," said Fix.

"How do you know? I didn't hear any sirens or anything."

"Alarms are visual," Fix told him. "Come here and I'll show you."

They left the tent and went up the hill behind it, where Fix pointed to a tall, thin bamboo pole. At the top of the pole, pulled up by a halyard reeved through a primitive block, was a round paper ball, much like a paper lantern. Other paper balls were fastened to the base of the pole. A young Chinese ping squatted nearby, looking intently to the east.

"That's a one-ball alert. See those other poles way off there?" He pointed and Ian spotted many more poles on top of hills to the east and south, where the enemy would come from.

"How does it work," he asked.

"There are Chinese spotters near every Japanese air base. They watch planes leaving and raise one ball. Other spotters see it and do likewise. All line of sight. Doesn't take but a few minutes to cover the country. When the planes' direction is figured out another ball goes up, just on the hills in the direction the planes are taking. As the planes pass over, up goes the third ball. If you're lucky they keep on going. Look!"

They watched the Chinese ping hastily run up the second ball.

"Two-ball now," said Fix. "Means they're coming this way."

Ian felt the familiar buzzing in his stomach. "What do we do now?"

"Nothing now," Fix told him. "But when that third ball goes up, we hightail it for the caves. Up there behind the compound," he said, pointing.

Ian could see a number of padded figures trotting to the caves already as he and Fix ambled down the hillside. They stuck their heads in the tent next to theirs and said, "*Ching pao!*"

The men looked up from their tattered magazines and one of them said, "How many balls?"

"Two," said Fix.

"Fuck it," said one man as several of the others started to rise. "They're headed for Chungking. They'll fly right over here. Lemme know when it's three-ball," and he returned to his magazine.

Fix and Ian and a small group of other Americans sauntered across the hill toward the caves as the third ball was hauled up. They increased their pace but did not want to seem to be in a hurry. Wallace could hear the beginning drum and throb of distant engines. He stopped, shielded his eyes and scanned the sky to the southeast. He saw them. Just specks, quite high. A lot of them.

"Too many to waste on us, " said Fix. "They'll head for the big time."

He and Wallace and a number of other Americans sat on the ground in front of the caves, now quite crowded with Chinese from the compound, and watched the planes go by overhead, unmolested.

"Where the hell is the flak? And where the hell is the Fourteenth Air Force?" Ian asked.

Spofford, the exec, said, "The Fourteenth, and the CACW, are still mostly flying P-40s, and those outriders up there are Zekes protecting the Bettys. They eat up P-40s. CACW is responsible for defense of Chungking. A matter of face, defending the capitol. There'll be a little flak closer to town. But not much."

The planes droned past in waves. Toward Chungking little puffs of gray smoke began to appear in the sky. The concussions arrived much later. Shortly, clouds of black smoke and brown dust began to bloom over the city, blotting out much of the sky. The air throbbed and rumbled.

Spofford cursed and spat. "Better to lose a few thousand civilians than risk the loss of some Chinese planes and pilots!"

Ian looked at Spofford and saw a different man from the one who had been so tough with him at their meeting only a few days ago. Some veil had been lifted behind his eyes, and his true self was on display.

"Bastards are saving them to fight the Communists," Spofford said. Then he saw Wallace staring at him, and the veil dropped. "Their choice," he said, "and we don't know all the circumstances and reasons."

Wallace risked a remark. "I'm just a new boy, but that sure looks like a piss-poor effort at defense."

Spofford turned a stern glance at him. "Straw dogs," he said, and the veil lifted a bit. "The civilians are sacrificed and discarded to preserve the circle of protection that Chiang feels he must have against all his enemies, local and barbarian. Watch. He'll send up a few people from Peishiyi to harass those Nip planes on the return route. Gain a little face and blame the lack of success on others. *Ma-ma fu-fu!*"

"What's that mean," Ian asked.

"Supposed to mean "so-so," and that's all you can say about this effort. Literally translated it means "horse-horse tiger-tiger"—neither the one or the other. Makes you think, damn it! They're supposed to be the tigers and fight and we're supposed to be the horses and do the work, but it seems like there's a hell of a lot of horse-horse and damned little tiger-tiger. Shit!" He glared at Ian and realized how he'd exposed his feelings. The veil dropped, and he looked away.

Four lonely CACW P-40s with blue and white Kuomintang sunbursts on their wings toyed on the edges of the returning formations. Wallace could hear the stutter of machine-guns, but the Japanese, preserving fuel for the return trip, didn't break formation, and no planes on either side were shot down.

Ma-ma fu-fu! Was this what it would be like in the field?

In time of peril, like the needle to the lodestone,
obedience, irrespective of rank, generally flies
to him who is best fitted to command.

— Herman Melville
White Jacket

HUNAN 1944

O'REILLY AND WALLACE RECEIVED THEIR ORDERS to report to NAVU2, Naval Unit Two, or Second Column as the Chinese called it, in a village named Nanyo, north of Hengyang in Hunan Province, the rice bowl of China. South of Tung Ting Hu, one of China's largest lakes, Nanyo was near the Siang Kiang, a river which flowed north through Siangtan, Changsha and on into the lake. The province was filled with paddies, flat along the river and terraced as the land rose to mountains both to the east and west. The Communist leader Mao Tse Tung had been born in the village of Shaoshan near Changsha, Wallace knew.

The important Hankow–Canton railroad followed the general course of the Siang Kiang. The Japanese held the northern terminus of the line at Wuhan, but there were rumors of a major offensive to be mounted at any hour by the Japanese to control the 686-mile rail line all the way to Canton. Such a corridor would effectively split southern China, isolating the Chungking regime even more.

Fix and Ian flew to Kunming, courtesy of the U.S. Army, and there learned that they would be couriers for a cash shipment to the Naval Group office in Hengyang. They watched as eleven dirty, gray U.S. mail bags were loaded with bundles of Chinese currency printed in Philadelphia. They accompanied the bags in a weapons carrier to a C-47 in which was already loaded a P-40 engine on its way to the airstrip at Hengyang. They hurled the mailbags aboard along with their gear and weapons, made themselves comfortable lying on the cash and waited.

A young, thin, red-headed second lieutenant climbed aboard wearing a one-piece flight suit and asked if either of them had flown in one of these things before. Just a little, they told him, and he said that was enough and would they mind helping? The pilot's name was Charlie Jarvis; together they lashed down what was lying loose. Jarvis showed them how to close and latch the fuselage cargo doors. As they moved forward Ian asked: "Who's the co-pilot?"

"Ain't nobody but me," Jarvis said, "unless one of you guys wants to sit in the right-hand seat."

Ian was right behind the pilot so he slipped into the co-pilot's position and strapped himself in. Fix sat on a little fold-down seat. Ian looked at the array of dials and switches and was baffled by them all, until Jarvis pointed out that there were almost two of everything, one set of gauges for the port engine and another set for the starboard engine. "Just don't touch anything unless I ask you to, O.K.?" Jarvis ordered.

Ian and Fix watched in fascination as the pilot went through his preflight routine, noting that most of the knobs and switches were worn and free of paint from much use. Bare metal showed everywhere. As Jarvis ran up the engines, one at a time, Wallace noticed the fastenings on the windshield frame vibrating. Looking out the starboard cockpit window at the engine, it seemed to him that it was a-drip with lubricants and black from exhaust. He hoped the pilot knew what he was doing.

Jarvis taxied the plane to the end of the mesh-covered dirt runway, locked the tail-wheel, checked the flaps, pushed the throttles forward and took off. Jarvis told Ian to pull up a red handle by his seat. Wallace looked for it, but all he saw was bright metal. "That one," said Jarvis, pointing.

Wallace pulled it, and the undercarriage came up and thumped. He remembered how that had startled him when they had taken off from Dum-Dum for the trip over the Hump. Getting used to it, he said to himself. But don't get cocky.

"We may not make Hengyang today," Jarvis told them. "Gotta drop off some spare parts at Kweilin. Depends how long we have to wait around to get unloaded and refueled."

They flew at about five thousand feet, which put them only fifteen hundred feet above the highest ridges between them and Kweilin. Course ninety degrees. Due east. From time to time Jarvis would fiddle with the mixture levers, and Ian could detect changes in the engines' sound. "Want to fly it?" Jarvis asked. "It flies by itself if you don't screw around with it too much. Gotta be gentle on the controls."

He lifted his hands from the controls and said to Ian, "She's all yours."

Ian grabbed the right-hand control yoke and jammed his feet onto the pedals. The plane yawed and started to dip.

"Easy does it!" said Jarvis. "Follow my motions," and he put his hands back on the controls. Ian did that and kept his eyes roving from the turn-and-bank indicator to the attitude indicator to the altimeter to the horizon and found that Jarvis used very little control, adjusting only when air currents made the plane drift off ninety degrees magnetic. At one point Wallace looked over at Charlie Jarvis and saw that he was reading a magazine. Fix was dozing.

They dropped off altitude as they approached the Li river and threaded their way through the most astonishing mountains Ian and Fix had ever seen. Although Kweilin is only five hundred feet above sea level, it is in the midst of thousands of peaks, most of them perpendicular—a fairy land of mountains rising from a flat green, paddied plain.

"How the hell do you fly in here in bad weather?" Ian asked.

"You don't if you can help it. Damn overcast settles right down on these peaks. The Chinese think it's beautiful and write poetry about it and paint pictures. But us poor damn throttle jockeys have to grope around hoping we find some way to land. There's three bomber strips and a fighter strip, and we have to find one of 'em before we find Solitary Beauty peak or God of Longevity Mountain."

The C-47 slowly settled toward Yang Tong, the Kweilin runway to which they were cleared, gently kissed the smooth stone surface and rolled, while Jarvis was careful with the brakes. He said something about old tires. Old everything, thought Wallace. They parked the plane in a rough dispersal area not far from the Base Operations tent. Fix climbed down and put chocks under the wheels, and Jarvis and his new co-pilot went to find someone to unload the spares and to organize refueling.

They waited for hours, and with good reason. Fifteen B-24 bombers of the 373rd Squadron, 308th Bomb Group (H) from Yangkai were being armed and refueled for a mission, and all hands were busy. Wallace and Jarvis made their number with the Base Ops commander, a very young first lieutenant named Goddard, and were told to help themselves to coffee and settle down. Jarvis drew a mug of joe, and Ian drew two and left the tent.

"Where you going?" the pilot asked.

"Out to our armored car to give him who safeguards our money something to stimulate his bladder."

The three men watched in fascination as the lumbering four-engined bombers lined up on the taxi-ways, blowing clouds of dust from the crushed stone runway and waiting for the signal to take off. The Base Ops officer stood in front of the tent with a microphone in his hand conducting the action. One by one the planes thundered off, formed up overhead and disappeared toward the southeast.

"Canton?" Ian asked.

"Right. White Cloud. Big Jap air base. They'll get there after dark and plaster it. Concrete runways there, and if they lay 'em down right the base will be out of business for days. Dirt runways are better. Easy to repair. A little dirt and some new mat and that's it. You gotta pour concrete and let it set. Keep your fingers crossed."

They ate American rations in the mess tent, staked out their bunks in the transient tent and shot the breeze in the dark, waiting for the bombers to return. Ground crews began to assemble. A couple of ambulances rolled up. Clouds began to gather on the peaks. The radio remained silent. Goddard paced back and forth. As they watched, the stars disappeared and a layer of mist spread from peak to peak over the airstrip. They strained their ears for the sound of engines.

"If they don't get here pretty damn soon that cloud cover is going to cost us some planes. Maybe all of 'em. It's getting thicker." Goddard's worry was plain.

Sometime before 2300 the drone of engines was discernible way off to the south. The sound grew and grew until it was almost overhead.

"Hit the runway markers," ordered Goddard, and two strings of low, weak lights dimly illuminated each side of the strip. He called the flight leader over the microphone: "Can you see the runway lights?"

"Negative. Can't see shit, and we gotta get down. Got some wounded need help. We'll circle for a while with the landing lights on so we don't kiss each other. Maybe it'll break up."

Fat chance thought Wallace. Those clouds won't be gone until the sun works on them in the morning. By then fifteen planes and one hundred and twenty men would be dead in rice paddies, smashed into mountainsides or lost in the river.

Fix asked Goddard and Jarvis what the strange looking glow was, moving over the eastern end of the runway.

"That's from somebody's landing lights, by God! That deck must be too thick to see the runway but thin enough for searchlights! Sergeant! Fire up that searchlight weapons carrier and get it down to the east end of the strip." Goddard looked at some charts. "Point that thing due east at an elevation of thirty degrees. You got that?"

"Yessir!" roared the sergeant as he and two other enlisted men jumped on the vehicle and tore away.

"Flight, we see some lights through the overcast," radioed Goddard. "We're going to illuminate your glide path to the down-wind end of the strip. Thirty-degree down angle. Holler if you can see the light."

"Roger, base."

The weapons carrier halted in a cloud of dust, and the people at the Base Ops tent could hear the men on the searchlight yelling curses as they cranked and cranked trying to get the auxiliary generator started.

"Come on! Come on!" grunted Goddard.

Then they all heard the generator engine cough and catch and smooth out, and the light blazed on, painting a large oval of blue-white light on the cloud base.

"Ah, base, we got your light," crackled the radio. "Looks like Times Square. Coming in now. Crank up the ambulances."

Wallace was tense as he watched the bombers break through, fly down the brilliant beam and sweep over the searchlight to land. He counted. Fifteen. Three of them were pretty chewed up. The ambulances and the stretcher bearers hurried to them as they shut down their engines.

"Some pilots!" said Wallace.

Jarvis shook his head. "Now you know why I fly freight."

In the transient tent Wallace lay on the hard canvas cot under the mosquito bar and marveled at what he had seen. He thanked God that the planes had all returned and "seen the light." He wondered if he would be as cool as the flight commander when his personal balloon went up. He wondered about home, half a world away. He wondered about Diana and when he would hear from her. When did he write her last?

They flew to Hengyang the next morning, after off-loading the spares, fueling up and saying good-bye and thanks to Goddard. Goddard told them that the pilots' reports at debriefing indicated the concrete runways at Canton had been destroyed. Good news.

Aloft, off to the port side, they could see the Siang Kiang winding between peaks and ridges in its twisting northeasterly flow. A little more than halfway to their destination they were approaching Lingling, at the confluence of the Siang and the Tao Shui. As they flew on with Fix in the right-hand seat they could see the river straightening out to the north of the city and an emergency airstrip north of the river. Charlie Jarvis throttled back some and started to descend toward the river.

"What the hell?" shouted Fix. "This can't be Hengyang!"

Jarvis said nothing, and Wallace stood up between the seats to see what was happening. Jarvis had a grin on his face as he brought the plane down almost to water level. The prop wash lashed the river and punished some small *shan p'ans*, sampans, as the plane roared toward an arched stone bridge that spanned the Siang.

"What's going on?" shouted Wallace.

Charlie Jarvis just grinned and leaned forward over the control yoke. Fix started to reach for the control column and Jarvis yelled, "Leave it alone!"

There were three arches supporting the bridge, which was filled with pedestrian traffic, carts, ponies and charcoal-burning trucks. A small arch held up each end of the bridge and a slightly larger one underpinned the center span. Charlie was headed right for it.

"Jesus Christ in the foothills!" screamed Fix, gripping the arm rests. Wallace lashed himself in as the plane slued some in the down drafts and river winds. Wallace was sure the props were almost touching the surface of the water. The plane skidded a bit again, and Wallace's stomach slid the other way. The arch rushed at them growing wider as they neared. Ian was sure Charlie would lift the C-47 over the span. He watched Jarvis's wrists, gently firm on the wheel. No pull to his lap. Wallace looked up and the bridge was upon them. There was the shattering, echoing howl of engines as the plane roared into the shadowy archway followed by a burst of sunlight as it raced into the clear. Jarvis lifted the aircraft over the panicked boatmen, who were madly poling sampans and rafts toward each shore.

The pilot turned and smiled at them.

"Have you ever done that before?" yelled Fix.

"No. I always wanted to, but never had the excuse before. Just because I don't fly a B-24 doesn't mean I can't thread the needle with this old tub. Nothing to it." He was grinning, ear to ear.

Wallace sniffed. "O'Reilly," he shouted, "did you shit yourself again?"

The two-hundred-air-mile trip got them to the Hengyang field about 1030. They made a long approach to the strip high on the east bank of the Siang Kiang, across the river from the city itself. The ground fell off to the river for about a quarter of a mile through bamboo trees to the west and was fenced in by mountains a few miles to the east. The single dirt runway was lined with revetments for aircraft protection. The revetments were empty. Everybody upstairs. The men could see freshly filled bomb craters on the strip.

Jarvis eased the old bird down gently, made dust when he touched and rolled toward the tile-roofed single-story mud hut that flew the wind sock and sprouted antennae. They were halfway down the strip, still making knots, when the port wheel caught a freshly filled crater, sank in, hit the far lip and blew the port tire. The plane swung hard left and the pressure buckled the right landing gear, which folded up beneath them as they continued their high-speed slide sideways through the dust. Jarvis hit switches as the props bit into the earth, braking the plane to a grinding, tearing halt just off the left side of the runway, facing back toward Lingling.

"I told you it wasn't so tough, didn't I?" smiled Charlie.

Fix and Ian pulled their eleven mailbags of money through a hole in the fuselage, while Charlie talked to a ground officer who had arrived in the "follow me" jeep. They could overhear some choice remarks about what a swell job had been done on refilling the bomb holes and a sharp response about how good pilots avoid them.

Soon a U.S. Navy jeep arrived with a courier from the Hengyang SACO liaison office to pick up the money and the men. While they were loading the bags aboard the vehicle, a twin-boomed P-38 whined in to a perfect touchdown. It taxied up to them, and the engines were cut. Charlie joined Ian and Fix as the ground officer went over to the P-38 and stood by while an enlisted man put a small metal ladder against the fuselage.

"Photo recon plane," said Jarvis.

The P-38 canopy was raised; the pilot looked out and made "thumbs down."

He climbed down, and they overheard him say, "They didn't hit a god-dam thing but countryside. They plowed the paddies in beautiful patterns, but that goddam concrete runway is still in operation. They took off from it to chase after me! Wait 'til you see the pictures."

O'Reilly and Wallace threw their weapons on the bags in the back of the jeep, and one bag burst sending printed-in-the-U.S.A. Chinese *yuan* scattering down the runway. It took them fifteen sweating minutes to collect it all, stuff it back in the bag and secure everything with line.

Wallace looked at the collapsed C-47, the thumbs-down P-38 pilot gesticulating with the ground officer, the torn bag of cash. He thought of last night's mission. "Well," he said to Fix, "you can't say that the good ol' U.S. taxpayer ain't gettin' his money's worth."

"You bet," said Fix, nodding at the C-47, "and look at all those unexpected spare parts Charlie brought."

After the jeep was poled across the Siang on a bamboo platform lashed between two sampans, they drove to the dusty center of the town. A metropolis, thought Ian. Some of the buildings, though rickety, were three and four stories tall. Some bomb damage. Many soldiers and a lot of street corner pillboxes. They turned the money bags over to the liaison man at the SACO office and got a receipt in full only after they had counted the loose bills from the burst bag in front of him. Then they piled back into the jeep and threaded their way through the teeming, noisy streets around the low, slitted concrete pillboxes at every corner, dodging the occasional scampering Chinese, who dodged just in front of the jeep in hopes the jeep would run over his pursuing evil spirit, to the north gate where a couple of Chinese ping guards sat smoking and playing cards, paying no heed to hordes of pedestrians or wheeled traffic that noisily surged through the narrow opening in the city wall.

Outside, the jeep headed north toward Nanyo on a dirt road that had been ditched crosswise every twenty yards or so. Ian estimated the ditches to be three feet deep and about ten feet wide. The edges of the ditches had been rounded by road traffic so it was just possible to drive on the road, but at a crawl. These barriers didn't slow the local foot traffic that simply carried its yo-yo pole burdens on the hard-packed earth path on the downhill side of each shoulder, trotting with chickens swinging in bamboo cages, with trussed, screaming hogs hanging upside down by their lashed hooves, with mountains of green cabbage piled high over the wooden-wheelbarrow pushers' heads, with hundreds of pounds of gray mud bricks hung from each end of shoulder poles, with household bedding and pots, with infants lashed to the backs of tottering foot-bound women, cursing and sweating in the hot dust and spitting at the Americans as the jeep roller-coastered slowly into and out of the ditches.

"Two questions," shouted Ian to the driver, over the whine of the high revving engine and the growl of the jeep's low-gear transmission.

"Shoot," hollered the driver.

"How come these ditches, and how come most of the foot traffic is southbound?"

"The ditches were dug about a week ago to slow the Japs when they get here. We were told today that they're on their way. That answers your second question about the southbound traffic."

The NAVU2 compound was just north of tiny Nanyo village, a poor, dirty place, and was situated in an open flat area surrounded by paddy fields and hard-packed tan earth. Ian could see what he presumed had been a crude shooting range and butts. The compound itself was the same mud-gray color as most of the village buildings. Shaped in a U, the building had two floors, a curved-tile sloping roof and across the open end a wall with a spirit gate. A battered jeep was haphazardly parked near the gate.

"Go on in and ask anybody for Commander Birdsall. He's expecting you," said the driver. "I'll get some of the house-boys to bring in your gear."

O'Reilly and Wallace stepped over the high doorsill, comfortable in the thought that no evil spirits could follow them and went into the courtyard. It was empty. The main part of the building was straight ahead, wings coming forward from each end. A rough plank walkway had been erected along the inside perimeter of the compound, and at the corners crude stairs led to a rough-plank balcony which served the second-floor rooms. Curved-tile eaves overhung the balcony. They went straight ahead to the door of the center building and entered a rude dirt-floored room with a small high window in the rear wall. As their eyes became accustomed to the dim light they could see a naval officer sitting behind a rough wooden table glaring at them.

"Don't Marines teach their officers how to report properly?" spat the officer. "Get out, and try to do it right this time!"

O'Reilly and Wallace did a smart about-face, weapons clanking, and marched out the door. Outside they could see a number of Americans leaning over the balcony railing watching the performance. They halted and looked at each other in disbelief.

"Holy shit!" said Fix.

"I guess you could call him that," said Ian, "but I think we better do as he says. You're senior, O comes before W, so you're in charge."

"About-FACE!" barked Fix.

"Forward HARCH! Detail HALT!" Fix reached out and knocked on the door jamb.

"What is it?" came from inside.

"Lieutenants O'Reilly and Wallace reporting for duty, sir!" yelled Fix.

"Enter!"

They marched in and stood side by side at attention, covered, since they were armed. Birdsall, a lieutenant commander in sweat-stained khaki, got up from behind the table, walked around it and stood in front of them. He looked each one of them in the eye. I wonder how many times he's been passed over for promotion, thought Ian.

"Give me your orders," Birdsall said.

They handed him their manila envelopes, and the commander left them standing at attention in the stifling room while he returned to his seat and opened and read the men's orders. He looked up.

"Couple of fuck-ups, huh?"

Judge not others that ye be not judged, thought Ian.

"Well you hadn't better fuck up around here or I'll have your guts for breakfast! Get out!"

They about-faced, marched into the sunny yard and saw a Marine gunnery sergeant approaching. He stopped, popped them a snappy salute and said, "If you'll please follow me, gentlemen." Fix and Ian looked at each other, raised their eyebrows and followed the gunny up the corner ladder to the second deck where he showed them a room. It was small with one tiny paper-covered window, just room for two board cots and two small tables for their washbowls. No chairs or stools. No door in the opening. Their gear had been thrown in the corner.

Wallace turned. "Gunny, my name's Wallace, and this is Lieutenant Francis Xavier O'Reilly. How about telling us your name and what the hell is going on around here."

It wasn't really a question so much as a gentle command.

"Well, sir," said the gunny in a strong Maine accent, "my name's Asa Wells, gunny, as you can see. I'm a regular, and this is my second China tour but it ain't at all like the first."

He's being careful, Wallace thought. Got to figure us out before he gets too cozy with the officers.

"What's the complement here, anyway?" asked Fix.

"Sir, there's a small group of enlisted here and three officers. The enlisted men are mostly Navy, couple of us are Marines, all of us supposed to be specialists. The Navy officers are Commander Birdsall, who's camp commandant, Lieutenant j.g. Tom Pearson, who's exec. The Marine officer is First Lieutenant Barnabas Rebstock, USMC, training officer. About twenty of us in all."

"What do you do?"

"Sir, it's not my place to brief you. I'm supposed to take you to the exec for that now." He paused, assessing the two new officers. He seemed to make up his mind and said, "If you want the straight poop as I see it, I'll be glad to shoot the breeze with you later. I'll show you the exec's office now."

They followed him to Pearson's tiny room–office–radio shack where a khaki-clad yeoman was pounding on an ancient typewriter, a chief radioman was leaning back on the hind legs of a rickety chair listening to Morse radio traffic from a small TBS radio set, and where Tom Pearson was playing solitaire on a small wooden table.

"Hey! Welcome to Fox Yoke Two!" he said, putting out his hand.

This is more like it, Wallace said to himself, shaking the man's hand.

"What's Fox Yoke Two?" he asked.

"That's phonetic alphabet for the nickname everybody but Bunghole Birdsall calls this place."

I'm going to like this man, Ian thought. Fox Yoke. FY equals fuck you, and Two equals too! Fuck you, too! And Bunghole Birdsall! He smiled and looked at Fix.

"Well, I hope we're glad to be here, but we're sure as hell in the dark as to what it's all about."

Pearson sized them up. They looked like pretty good sorts, so he decided to give it to them straight.

"Come on, let's get out of this vale of tears and get some fresh air."

He led them out of the compound to a place that must have been the firing line of the crude range. They sat in the shade of some bamboo trees on hard, wooden short-legged stools.

"NAVU2 is part of the SACO network of outposts where Chinese guerrillas are supposed to be trained. The Chinese are under the command of regular Chinese army officers but report to the Tai Li organization, Chiang Kai-shek's Bureau of Investigation and Statistics. That's the Chinese half of SACO. The recruits are dragooned from the countryside and dragged in at the end of a rope. We clean 'em up, train 'em to shoot (and even then they can't hit a bull in the ass with a steam shovel), teach 'em a little about demolitions, show 'em how to fuck up a train with nothing but a little track ballast, talk a little about hygiene (a waste of time), equip 'em and supposedly get 'em started harassing the Japanese behind the Jap lines."

"Where the hell is everybody?" asked Fix. "I don't see any Asian hordes around here."

"Column Two's training is over, and the column has left. Gone north, up Changsha way. Good man's in charge of 'em. Fella named Ho. General Ho Lin Shui. He's got some ma-ma fu-fu officers and noncoms and fifteen hundred rag-tag men equipped with M1 carbines, TSMGs, S-and-W .38s, Colt .45s and a few hundred pounds of granulated TNT. No radios. Communicate by runner. It stinks."

"Then what the hell are we doing here?" Ian wanted to know.

"You guys are going to observe how they perform, but you can be damned sure they'll spend as much time keeping you out of fire-fights as they will trying to start one or running from the possibility of one."

"Don't think much of them, do you?" Fix remarked.

"Shit!" said Pearson.

"You people!" A shout came from the compound. "You people haul your asses in here right this goddam minute. Do you hear me?"

Birdsall stood on the sill of the spirit gate, hands on hips and glowered at them. They stood up.

"Don't run," said Pearson as he ambled almost insolently toward where the commander stood. Fix and Ian tried to look as if they were striding but kept even with Pearson.

"How long have you had the pleasure of serving with that gentleman?" Ian asked.

"Six months. Since December. Right goddam here!"

"And what about the other guy, Rebstock? What's he like?"

"Not too bright. Regular USMC, if you'll pardon the expression. Mustang. Butchers the King's English. Hasn't learned a word of Chinese. Been a first lieutenant for years."

They reached the gate, and Birdsall said, "Officers meeting," and motioned them to follow. They assembled, all five of them, in the mess room, little larger than the other spaces they had seen, and sat on uncomfortable benches around one of the rectangular tables, shuffling their feet on the dusty floor. Birdsall sat at the head of the table.

"Lieutenant Rebstock, meet your two new officers." Your two new officers! What the hell!

O'Reilly and Wallace rose and shook hands with a forty-ish heavy-set balding man whose belly hung over his belt too much and who had broken red veins on his cheeks and nose. He said nothing.

"Well, this is it," said Birdsall.

Oh, for God's sake! thought Ian.

"What intelligence has been telling us would happen has happened. I can confirm what we heard as rumor yesterday. Chungking advises that the drive the Japanese started in April into Honan Province between the Yangtze and Yellow rivers has now turned south, aimed at the communication centers of Changsha and Hengyang. Their objective seems to be to stop Fourteenth Air Force attacks on the their supply lines by taking the air bases in eastern and central China."

He paused and looked about the table, savoring his moment. He looks, thought Ian, like one of those men who always seem to have a secret and who make others feel insecure because they don't know it. Wallace bet that Birdsall shared this manner with few others and was simply condescending to everyone. He wondered if this trait was a measure of self-perceived superiority or of insecurity.

"The enemy also is losing his sea lanes and needs the railway. His operation is code named Ichigo, which means 'number one,' and we're going to stop it!"

Holy Mary, mother of God! thought Fix. With what?

"Lieutenant Rebstock, you and your party will leave tomorrow evening, go north and link up with General Ho. You will do everything in your goddam power to see that those miserable pings we equipped do something besides run away! Is that clear?"

Rebstock stood up, at attention. "YES, SIR!" he bellowed.

These guys think they're in the movies or on display at Marine Barracks or that an all-seeing God is about to make out their fitness reports! Fix hit Ian with his knee. They didn't dare look at each other.

"Rebstock," Birdsall looked at a list, standing as he read from it, "you will take only what you and your people can carry, with the exception of some stores and ammunition for General Ho's people. Your detachment will be these two new officers, Gunnery Sergeant Wells, Gunner's Mate First Class Fugakis, Chief Radioman Steger, Chief Motor Machinist's Mate Treviso, Corpsman Tony Pagani, Chief Shipfitter Tobias and Corporal Samanov.

"Your fan yi kuans will be Paul Pong and Adam Lo. That makes twelve of you altogether. A compact and talented group that should be able to keep itself in the way of the Japanese and supply us with intelligence and Ho with guidance.

"You will depart tomorrow based on the verbal orders I will give you. Do any of you people have any questions?"

"How do we travel, and where are we headed, sir?" asked Ian.

"Lieutenant Rebstock will give you all that information when he's ready to. You two are dismissed. Pearson and Rebstock, come with me."

Fix and Ian were left standing, while the other three went from the room. Pearson looked back over his shoulder, rolled up his eyes and tapped his temple with his forefinger.

O'Reilly and Wallace waited a moment, unsure of what to do, and then went out into the compound to look for Gunnery Sergeant Asa Wells.

Barnabas Rebstock held a detachment meeting later in the afternoon, and Fix and Ian got to meet the other men on the detail. They were a competent looking bunch, and as each man stood and told his name and rank for the benefit of the new officers, Ian would note Wells's nod of approval, or tilt of his head, from the corner of his eye. Everybody got the nod except Corporal Samanov. When Rebstock rose to speak, Wells gave no reaction.

They were told to weed out their gear, take only what they personally could carry, make sure they took good broken-in shoes, get extra ammo if they thought they were short and pack their Chinese civilian clothes.

"We don't have any of those," Ian said.

"You will by tomorrow," Rebstock answered. "Tailor's coming after chow, and you'll have 'em before breakfast."

"Where are we going and how?" Fix wanted to know.

"I'll tell you when we're underway," Rebstock said, pacing. He was sweating profusely, smelled of alcohol and was wearing his side arm. Ian thought the man would have worn a steel helmet, too, if he'd had one. After a number of platitudes about going into the field, honor and example setting, he closed the meeting.

Outside, Ian asked Wells what he and Fix should take as their gear. The gunny accompanied them to their tiny space and helped them chose the few articles they would need: mosquito bar, poncho, a second pair of shoes, plenty of socks, some skivvies, khaki shirt, trousers, fore-and-aft hat, wash rag, razor, toothbrush, brass basin and weapons. Cram the gear into a couple of musette bags and wear 'em like ass packs.

They sat on the deck and shot the breeze with the sergeant, who told them they probably wouldn't wear the civilian clothes unless they got into a tight pinch. Just insurance. He said the detail was good people.

"What about Samanov?" Ian asked.

"Goes off half-cocked too much of the time. All he's interested in is loose shoes, a tight pussy and a warm place to shit. Him and Fugakis is at each other a lot, and neither of 'em listen good. Makin' 'em pay attention is like tryin' to push melted butter up a wildcat's ass with a hot awl!" He spat on the deck.

Wallace admired the man's descriptive simile. He used to hear that sort of country talk from Jed, the hired man, and hadn't heard much of it since he left the farm. He asked about Rebstock.

"Barney Rebstock." Wells thought for a moment and said, "Talking about officers ain't good joss. 'Specially to other officers. But you could tell this afternoon that he gets into the ching pao juice pretty heavy. I knew him on my first cruise out here. Gung-ho and phony. First John then, too. I can't figger out how Barney and Bunghole got this duty, though they both been here before. Barney was battalion supply officer, and I hear Bunghole was on Yangtze river patrol. Born with a hair up his ass. Neither of 'em been home since the thirties, they say. Don't think either of 'em is smart enough to pour piss out of a boot with instructions printed on the heel. Most places I been, the closer to the action you got, the less chicken shit you got. Not here. These guys are scared, I think. Useless as tits on a boar hog."

Wells looked embarrassed and shut up.

"Did you know Dan Rose or Ed Ruditis or Pete Sigalos or a colonel named Hall?"

"I sojered with those birds in Shanghai, and once in Tientsin I run into a major named Hall. A fireplug. A bulldog. Chewed nails and spat tacks. Kept me out of the brig."

"That's him," Ian said.

"How come you know them names?" Wells asked.

"Friends of mine," Wallace exaggerated.

"Goddam," said Wells, as Ian and his friend O'Reilly went up a couple of notches in Wells's estimation.

A very short, nervous and flighty tailor measured them for their Chinese clothes. The simple faded blue garments, pants and shirt, were to be made right on the premises and be ready by morning. They'd twist rags around their heads for hats, like many coolies did. Fix asked Chief Radioman Steger, who was also getting measured, why he thought the tailor trembled so much.

"Scuttlebutt is that they deep-six these guys after they've secured from tailoring. For security reasons. The tailor must have heard the same rumor."

After chow, toward dark, Wells asked Steger if it would be all right for Wallace and O'Reilly to go up on the roof with the radioman, and Steger told them to come along. Not knowing what was going on, the two officers climbed up a rickety bamboo ladder and through an opening in the tiles onto a small wooden platform where they shared tight space, legs hanging over the edge.

"What's going on?" asked Wallace as he watched Steger open a canvas pack and remove a small radio.

"This here's an SSTR-1 radio. Ain't worth a shit, but I can raise Heng-yang with it. I talk to a guy at the airstrip and tell them if they got visitors coming. Japs fly right over here on their way down."

"How do you know it's Japs?" Fix asked.

"You just listen and you'll find out."

They sat for what seemed like hours, while a pale moon came up and ground mist sifted in from the river. Steger cocked his head and said, "Listen!"

At first they could hear nothing at all. Then, faintly, off to the north they could hear the drumming sound of an approaching aircraft. It sounded like a twin-engine plane that was out of sync.

"Betty—G4M" said Steger. "But even the single-engine jobs, the Vals and the Zekes, have that distinctive Jap engine sound. It ain't exactly a warble, but it ain't smooth either. Not like ours. After a while you can tell planes blindfold just by the sound of 'em. B-25s, B-24s, P-40s. P-38s a piece of cake. Has its own whine."

Ian remembered the sound when the photo recon plane had come in at Hengyang earlier in the day.

"P'eng-yu base, this is Fox Yoke. Ching pao! Ching pao! Do you read me?"

The set crackled while they waited for a reply.

"Fox Yoke, I read you about three by three. Whaddya got?"

"Ah, base, we got one bandit southbound overhead about now. Sounds low. Give yourselves about five, seven minutes. Copy?"

"Roger, Fox Yoke, we copy. One bandit in about five minutes. Hope they don't keep us up all night."

"What did he mean, 'all night,' " asked Fix.

"Oh, they usually send one over every ten, fifteen minutes. Keep it up for hours. Sometimes they quit by midnight."

The trio swatted at mosquitos and watched to the south for some sign of activity. They saw a few faint flashes on the horizon.

"We're too far off to see much more than that unless they hit fuel storage or a plane or start a fire in the city. Mostly they go for the strip, though."

After the third plane passed, about forty-five minutes later, an enormous glow lit the southern sky and stayed there for a good half hour while two more planes, guided by the fire, passed overhead.

They heard the ladder rattle. "Relief comin'," said Steger and they wormed their way down the slats and made way for Corporal Samanov, who had drawn the next watch.

"Don't go to sleep, and don't drop my radio, punk," said Steger.

"Fuck off, Chief," said Samanov and climbed up the ladder.

Wallace lay sweating under his mosquito bar and listened to the incessant whining of the insects and the occasional throb of aircraft engines. He felt oddly removed from the slow-motion hostilities. Like watching a movie. Sort of exciting but no threat. Maybe tomorrow would be different. They were going north, toward the oncoming Japanese. Up Changsha way.

The next day they were buzzing with excitement. The morning radio transmission from Chungking told them that the Allies had landed on the European continent the previous day. That news and the prospect of action had their juices flowing. The morning was consumed getting gear organized by the compound gate. Crates of ammunition, combat packs, musette bags, radio gear and some few medical supplies were stacked just inside the wall.

"Who the hell is going to carry all that?" Ian asked Wells.

"Got a few coolies comin' with us. And some of General Ho's men will take over the ammo."

But the coolies didn't show up, nor did any of General Ho's pings to guide and accompany the Americans north toward the advancing Japanese. Radio messages indicated that the G'mo was worried about Americans getting into combat and that plans were on hold. Then they were told to go ahead, only to have the order countermanded on the next transmission. Bunghole's frustration was taken out on the men. The men argued about why the fuck the Fourteenth Air Force could be in combat and they couldn't. And Rebstock seemed to spend a lot of time alone in his room.

Finally, after twelve days of start-and-stop, Chungking gave them the go-ahead on June 18. Wallace noted that it was Sunday and hoped it was a good omen. Bunghole was telling them to get their asses in gear and shove off before the order was rescinded, when a laboring, charcoal-burning stake truck wheezed to the gate. Two Chinese, armed with M1 carbines, wearing U.S. web belts on their dirty mustard-colored uniforms rode in the bed of the truck leaning over the roof of the cab. Another soldier rode next to the driver. As the truck backed toward the gate, the men in the compound could see a small group of half-clad coolies huddled on the floor of the truck bed.

The truck stopped, and the soldiers ordered the coolies off at gun point.

The driver got down and was herded to the wall, where the third soldier kept him covered with a Colt .45. The interpreters, Paul Pong and Adam Lo, and the soldiers got in a shouting match, but soon the coolies began loading gear aboard the truck, motivated by the occasional shout or whack from a rifle butt.

"Just cause they shout don't necessarily mean they's mad at each other," said Pagani, the corpsman. "Maybe they's deef. When they's really sore, they scream and fight with they feet. Fella with the .45's an officer. He don't need to shout at that driver. Gun shouts for him."

Lieutenant Rebstock arrived at the gate, and the enlisted men turned away. Ian and Fix saluted and said, "Good morning, sir."

Rebstock returned the salute and stalked outside the gate with Adam Lo and spoke through the interpreter to the officer guarding the driver.

"We'll be loaded and out of here by 1400," Rebstock said when he returned. His breath stank. Ian looked at his watch. Only 1100. And how could it take so much longer to load those few stores, he thought to himself.

"Sir," he asked Rebstock, "how about chow? I don't see any going aboard that truck."

"We'll eat off the land, Lieutenant," Rebstock replied. Ian wondered if Rebstock knew his name. "Gather around, you people," Rebstock ordered, and the detachment shuffled through the dust to the shade of the wall.

"We're going north by river steamer," he announced. "The gear will go to Hengshan, where the boat is at, on this truck with the coolies and the guards. We'll walk to Hengshan and board soon as we get there. Gotta get underway pronto so's to get down river far as possible afore dark. We're headed for Changsha, where we'll off-load and link up with Ho and with Joe Chance. Changsha's been attacked twice by the Japanese, between April and October 1939 and September to October 1941. Beat off both times, they were, by a fella named General Hsueh Yueh, the Tiger of Changsha and his Fourth Chinese Army. They'll hold 'em back this time too.... Chance runs the radio net up there, and he'll have the latest word.... And today's a historic day... the Allies started the second front in Europe two weeks ago, D-Day, and now we're finally going up against the Japs, our D-Day." He looked sternly at each of the men in his command. "You people be at this here gate at 1300 ready to step out."

"Hot damn," said Fix, "over in Europe we're starting to push the Fritzes around, and here we are just about to get pushed around ourselves. Maybe they'll clean up over there quick and come help us clear out this mess."

Bunghole, Birdsall, Tom Pearson, three enlisted men, the one interpreter left behind and the house-boys stood on the balcony shading their eyes against the glare and watched as the column sweated mightily on the path through paddies that led to Hengshan. Another of Ho's soldiers led the way. Ian wished he had some kind of forage cap like Pete Sigalos had told him about. The hot orange sun, burning through the mist, broiled the back of his neck and put sweat in his eyes. At least his feet were in good shape from all the hiking he and O'Reilly had done in the mountains southeast of Chungking. He took out his only handkerchief and tied it around his forehead to catch the sweat. He turned up his shirt collar to keep the sun off his neck. He watched as the other Americans followed his example. Except for Rebstock, who was limping noticeably as he struggled at the head of the column, trying to keep up with the Chinese soldier in front.

It took them an hour and a half to reach the mud bank at the edge of the Siang Kiang in the malodorous little village of Hengshan. The truck with their gear was just laboring to the bank of the river. At the bottom of a long flight of stone steps to the water, anchored about fifteen yards offshore, was a rusty steel *ch'i ch'uan*, a steam boat about sixty feet long, with a small wheelhouse, a tall, pitted, peeling stack held in place by rusty cables, its scarred wooden decks reached by an unstable floating bamboo gangplank. Pale gray coal smoke drifted up from the stack in a thin plume. The engine slowly thumped.

Two Chinese squatted barefoot in their greasy trousers tending a cooking pan over hot charcoal on the fantail. Two Ho soldiers stood outside the deck house, and two more stood amidships pointing their carbines into the hold where the coal, the machinery and the stokers were.

"Jesus," said Chief Motor Mac Treviso, "good thing we're going downstream in this bucket!"

The brown silt-filled river swirled and eddied by the hull of the boat on its way north to Siangtan, Changsha and Tung Ting Hu. Don't want to fall in that, thought Ian. Wells, standing next to him, put in words, "Shit-brindle color. Good reason for it, too."

One of the men on the fantail scraped out the cooking pan into a tin container, dangled a gray cloth in the river and then swabbed out the pan with it.

The Ho soldiers on the truck shouted at the coolies, and a small crowd of villagers began to watch the proceedings. One soldier beat the coolies to get them started carrying the gear aboard the boat, and the other two soldiers went into the crowd and came back with two other men shuffling in front of the soldiers' weapons. Several tottering bound-footed women in gray rags screamed and wept and clutched at the soldiers. Ian watched in horrified fascination as the soldiers knocked the women down with their rifle butts. Most of the detachment was looking the other way, on purpose. What the hell are we doing here! Wallace asked himself.

As the coolies and the two peasant villagers carried the gear aboard, Wallace noted one of the Ho soldiers counting loads. The carriers splashed across the slithering, swaying bamboo, piled the goods aft of the large open hatch and trotted back to shore for more. Double-time both ways. After a time the Ho soldiers herded the coolies to the stern, except for two men who ran to shore for the last loads. When they brought the gear aboard they, too, were pushed to the rear and guarded by the soldiers.

Rebstock led the Americans and the interpreters aboard; the two deck hands who had been doing the cooking began to operate the anchor winch. The soldiers cast off the gangplank. The crowd on the shore and the coolies on the fantail started to scream. One of the soldiers fired two rounds over the heads of the crowd, which fell to the dirt.

As the boat got slowly under way, one of the villagers on the stern leapt overboard and started to swim ashore with clumsy strokes through the roiling water. A soldier raised his carbine and took aim at the man's head, not twenty yards away. He was squeezing the trigger when Ian knocked the weapon down with a sweep of his arm, and the round roared into the water behind the swimmer. The soldier whirled around as Ian wrenched the carbine from his grasp and tossed it to Fix. Ho's man glared at Ian and let out a string of Chinese curses. Ian stood still. The man's spittle hit him in the face. Wallace watched as the shore receded and the exhausted villager dragged himself up on the bottom stone step.

Then Wallace took the weapon from O'Reilly, removed the magazine, emptied the chamber and handed it back to the soldier.

"Tell him," Ian said to Adam Lo, "that I'll give him his ammunition before we go ashore."

"Wallace!" bellowed Rebstock from the wheelhouse. "You get your ass up here right this goddam minute!"

Ian ran forward, and Rebstock stood him at attention and read him off before God and everybody, ending up with, "that soldier lost face because of you, you stupid son of a bitch! That's Chinese doin's, and you keep your goddam nose out of it! What they do is their own affair! Get forward! And you, O'Reilly, stand aft and keep an eye on the gear and that pissed-off ping!"

Rebstock turned and went into the wheelhouse and sat on a stool next to the captain of the boat. The captain stood at the wheel directly in front of a Ho soldier with a TSMG, cocked, pointing at his back, and conned the chugging boat north, down the surging waters of the Siang Kiang.

Wells, Steger, Treviso and Tobias joined Wallace, sitting on the foredeck planking.

"The others is back with Mister O'Reilly," said Wells. The men had their weapons across their knees. They looked at Wallace and imperceptibly nodded their approval of what he had done.

River traffic, shan p'ans mostly, petered out the farther north they got. After several hours, they noticed now there were no people working the paddies and none of the mud farmhouses had smoke coming from under the eaves.

"Don't like the looks of this," said Treviso, the chief motor mac. "Seen it like this on the *Panay* in '37. Goin' up the Yangtze. 'Fore the Japs raped Nanking. Somethin's up."

"Locals know sumpin' we don't, most likely," said Wells.

Wallace was tempted to ask Treviso about the *Panay* incident, but was smart enough to realize that if the chief wanted to tell about it he wouldn't have to be asked. He turned to Wells.

"You a country man, Asa," he asked the Down Easter.

"Ayuh. Norridgewock, near Skowhegan."

Noncoms normally didn't like this kind of friendly shit from officers, but this man seemed different.

He looked at Ian. "Why d'ya ask?"

"Takes one to know one," said Ian.

"No shit. Where you from?"

"Farm in the Berkshires. Dairy cows. Some crops. Not much but work. Did you farm?"

Wells gazed at the brown river. "Lived on one, but mostly did chores for others. Picked up what odd jobs I could. Ma died when I was nine and then the old man got to drinkin', so when I could I joined the 3-Cs, the Civilian Conservation Corps, and lived in a barracks in the woods. Regular food and a little pay. Nowhere to spend it, though."

"What did you do in the 3-Cs?"

"Loggin', swearin', fightin' and tryin' to keep the queers outa my bunk. Joined the Corps after a year. Look there!"

Wallace looked where Wells was pointing. The boat was coming out of a sweeping curve of the river, and there a mile ahead climbing up the hills on the west bank of the Siang was a small city.

"Siangtan," said Tobias, the chief shipfitter. "We rigged some shan p'ans with .50 caliber machine-guns back in March right there at the bottom of them stone steps. Probably sunk now. Guns musta vibrated right through the bottoms. Told 'em they would."

North of Siangtan on the east side of the river they could see smoke billowing into the early evening sky. Rebstock climbed from the wheelhouse and joined them. He called for Adam Lo as the boat began to veer toward Siangtan's steps.

"Tell that son of a bitch we're going to Changsha! We don't stop here!"

Lo went into the wheelhouse, and the men could hear a loud argument. The boat continued its course toward the steps.

"What the fuck is goin' on," shouted Rebstock.

Lo came out of the wheelhouse. "Captain say too dark before get to Changsha. Can't navigate. We stop here."

"Goddam it——"

"Sir," interrupted Wells, "they's somebody wavin' at us from them steps."

Rebstock took out his field glasses and had a look.

"Don't recognize 'em, but they're wearin' our gear. Better take a peek. Adam, tell that no-good captain to come in slow." He turned to the men on the foredeck, motioned them down, removed his .38 from its holster and walked aft to the men at the rear. Wallace could hear the men moving to cover about the deck.

Wallace and Wells peered over the side toward the steps.

"Nobody takin' cover there," said Wells.

They watched the four men on shore as the boat slowly edged toward them. One of the men was tall. He towered over the other three. They were all waving, and Wallace could hear some shouting. All the men on the foredeck raised their heads.

"Why I'll be goddamned," exploded Steger. "That's Joe Chance. He's supposed to be up at Changsha runnin' the radio there. Good man. I trained 'im."

The shore and steps were ominously empty except for the four mustard-color figures. No Chinese could be seen at the top of the long flight of slippery steps nor in the narrow streets that led uphill from the top of the stone blocks.

The captain reversed the engine, and the boat slid broadside to the bottom step while the two deck hands threw lines to the men with Joe Chance. The lines were passed through great iron rings set into the stones centuries ago. The shore party threw over a dented metal gangplank, and Joe Chance jumped aboard.

"Who's in charge," he asked Steger.

"I am in charge, by God, and what the hell are you doin' here!" shouted

Rebstock, emerging from the wheelhouse.

"Lieutenant, they've tooken Changsha." Wallace saw Rebstock go pale. "We got our asses out just in time. Had to deep-six the radio gear and almost got caught. I was right in the middle of the Chungking sked, relaying five-letter groups from Column Three when the Chinese army bugged out, thousands of 'em! Goddam officers had taken all the trucks and their wives and household gear and skedaddled already!

"I kept sending 'til the Japs were comin' down the street, then signed off in the clear tellin' Chungking we had unfriendly company. These three men," he pointed to the Ho soldiers on the shore, "helped me push the radios into the water, and we sashayed out the back, borrowed an empty sampan and this is as far as we got before it sank. That smoke up yonder is farms and villages burning. Can't be more'n a battalion of Nips and some artillery, but there's nuthin' between us and them but brown water."

"You seen anyone else hereabouts?" asked Rebstock. "We're supposed to be met."

"This town's empty. Closed up. Shut tight. Everybody's vamoosed."

"Well, ah, let's see.... " said Rebstock, not knowing what to do with his hands.

"Looks like some movement on the east bank, Lieutenant," said Wells, who had been scanning both sides of the river, uncomfortable at being so exposed.

Rebstock spun around and glassed the far bank. "Gettin' too dark to see much. I guess we could stay here and go back up river in the A.M. Take you, too, Chance, and your people."

"Not me, sir," said Chance. "Fuckin' boat is too convenient a target. I'll take my chances holed up in some mud house up top, where I can get out the back end."

"Sir," suggested Wallace, "why don't we get this stuff ashore for Ho when he comes. We'll have a better look at the lay of the land in the morning. And the boat is a hell of a target. We'll do better in the countryside."

Rebstock seemed at a loss, so Wallace nodded to Wells, who took Adam Lo aft to get the coolies organized with the help of the soldiers. The coolies were shaking with fright. The soldiers beat them and got them started hefting the gear.

Wallace looked at Rebstock, who was again looking through his field glasses at the far bank. His hands shook. No booze for hours, Wallace thought. Or is it something else?

Wallace turned and said to Fix, "Hey, p'eng yu, how about you and Wells and Chance and his guys go up into the town and find us a place, high up. Outskirts if you can. Send somebody back to show us where, and I'll get this stuff ashore. Steger, you go with' em. Take your radio gear and see if you can pick up any friendly traffic. D-Day, guys. Over the side."

"O.K.!" said O'Reilly.

"Right!" said Wells.

"Aye, aye, SIR!" said Steger and hopped to it.

Wallace looked for Rebstock and found him behind the wheelhouse taking a pull from his canteen. Boiled water? Hardly, thought Wallace.

"Sir," said Wallace, looking at the first lieutenant, knowing why he was frozen in that rank, knowing why he looked as if all his flesh had just sagged and his bones had just dissolved, "time to go ashore."

He took the first lieutenant by the elbow and gently led him to the gangplank, across the water, up the slippery steps where they followed the coolie train up the steep hillside, through the dark, empty, narrow, shuttered streets. Rebstock limped on each foot, and his breath came in great heaving, reeking gasps.

They quartered themselves in what Adam Lo and Paul Pong said had been a bank. High above the river, two stories with big rooms and thick walls, all the furniture gone, but just too far out of town to have been a commercial establishment. Somebody's villa, probably. The walled-in compound was on a narrow dirt road that led to mountains in the west.

They put Rebstock in a big first floor room where he lay down on the floor and went to sleep, shivering. Wallace rigged a mosquito bar over him. They ate some cold rice, and Wallace set up the duty watches. He and Wells went out into the back of the compound, overlooking the river. In the dull glow of fires to the northeast they could make out the boat still moored to the steps, could see the coolies huddled under a straw-roofed shed against the rear wall, guarded by two of the Ho soldiers as Wallace had ordered.

"Whaddya think, sir," asked Wells.

"Well," said Wallace, "there doesn't seem to be much point in getting back on the boat. Easy pickin's if those are really Japs on the far shore. I think we better high-tail it out of here to the west into the mountains, and we'll send some of these Ho men to see if they can find the Second Column.

Then we'll join up. Steger tells me we only got one-way communication, 'cause the damn SSTR-1 can't even raise Hengyang. We get Chungking's signal, All-India Radio, the BBC and station KRHO in Saipan where a Japanese lady is playing swing music and giving us the Japanese version of the news in English. So we won't be in the dark about what's happening in the world, just in the dark about what's happening right goddam here!

"I'll get Rebstock's map and one-time code pad, we'll send a message at our next scheduled time whether anybody answers or not, and we'll read the Chungking traffic to see what we can learn. Then we'll get away from this river. Too popular."

"Aye, aye, sir," said Wells.

O'Reilly and Wallace shared a mosquito net hung over blankets thrown on the deck of a second-floor room in the back of the villa. Fix was cleaning his .45 by the light of a small, shielded candle stub. He sang softly:

> *Bunghole is a friend of mine,*
> *I can bang him anytime,*
> *For a nickel or a dime,*
> *Fifteen cents for overtime.*

He stopped and looked at Ian. "What about Rebstock?"

"I don't know," Ian replied. "I went through his gear and got his map and his one-time pad. He was watching me but didn't say a damn word. Just closed his eyes as I started to leave the room. He can't walk, won't talk, didn't eat. We'll have to carry him somehow."

In the middle of the night Ian was awakened by Wells shaking his shoulder. "Ching pao, sir. Sounds like an Aichi, a Val. Just one, but he may drop some eggs, so I thought you might want everybody out in the ditches. No sense gettin' beaned by a mud brick in here."

"Right, Asa," Wallace answered. "Get 'em out. I'll be right there."

Wallace poked Fix, who grunted. "Ching pao, buddy," he said. "Get your ass in gear."

He poked Fix again, and Fix grunted and started to snore. Wallace stuffed his feet in his boondockers and shuffled to the rear window as the uneven throb of the Aichi's engine came closer and closer. It seemed to pass directly overhead. Wallace wondered if he could see exhaust and leaned out, to be greeted by an enormous orange-white flash and concussive roar, followed by a hail of flying debris rattling against the walls, whistling past his ears through the window opening. He ducked to the floor and shouted, "Fix!"

He looked around, and in the glow of flames from the rear of the compound he could see Fix leaning against the door jamb.

"What are you waiting for," said Fix. "Let's go!"

The two men raced down the stairs and out onto the road in front of the compound. The rest of the detachment seemed to be lying in the muddy ditches next to the road, while the plane lazily turned at the southern end of the town for another pass. Wallace batted at the swarms of mosquitos that threatened his nose, mouth, eyes and ears. He could hear slaps and curses from the ditches.

"Better get down, sir," said Wells from his piece of ditch. "That first egg was a lucky hit. No tellin' where he's goin' to spray 'em next."

Wallace sat on the edge of the road and listened as the Val labored back over the town closer to the river. There was an explosion near the waterfront followed by a small but persistent fire. The plane turned again, at the northern end of Siangtan, and started its return trip.

"A regular Washing Machine Charlie," said Wells. "Keep us out here all night."

"Is everybody accounted for?" asked Ian.

"Don't know about the Chinese. But our folks is all here. Except for Lieutenant Rebstock. He wouldn't move. Just cussed me out. So I left him. The interpreters is here, too, though it's hard to tell. Darker'n three foot down a bear's throat."

Wallace pondered that piece of wisdom, rose and went back into the compound. He was back in five minutes, during which time bombs burst at random on the little city. He was guiding Rebstock, who limped beside him.

"I saved this spot for you, Lieutenant," Wallace said in a weak effort at levity. Rebstock didn't respond, but sat on the road with his arms around his knees, rocking back and forth.

Wallace laid down near Wells, with his handkerchief over his face to keep off the mosquitos and listened to the growing and fading drone of the Japanese airplane and the thud and crack of the occasional bombs that fell. Has to be more than one plane, he thought. Aichis don't carry that many bombs. Probably they're running relays. He wondered what should be done by daylight. He seemed to be in charge. He wondered how that had happened. Osmosis, maybe. He chuckled. Never thought I'd be able to laugh in a situation like this, he thought. Even forgot to get the buzzing and the quivers. Thank God for that. Oh, yes, God, thank You and forgive me. I've been forgetting You. Please don't forget me and these Thy sons who seem to have become my responsibility. And guide our reactions to all the viciousness and cruelty that we see among our allies as well as our enemies.

He told Wells that whoever had the watch should wake him at four ack emma, unless the ching pao was over earlier, and drifted off to sleep.

Before the false dawn at four A.M. the planes had left, and Wallace thought he'd better make an inspection of the grounds and buildings. The detachment had returned to their mosquito nets and were snoring inside the building. Wells accompanied Wallace to the rear of the compound with Adam Lo. Two coolies lay dead in the dirt near the ashes of the shed under which they had been guarded. The ground around them was dark with their blood. The rest of the coolies and their guards had fled. Down at the steps by the river the great iron mooring rings hung slack. The steamer had left.

"Where do you think they've gone?" Wallace asked Lo.

"Coolies go south or to mountains. Soldiers look for General Ho, I think."

Fat chance, Wallace said to himself and led the way back to the building. Gunner's Mate First Class Fugakis had the watch and was arguing with Corporal Samanov about the merits of Chinese versus Indian women. Their views were diametrically opposed, and they vigorously supported their arguments by generous use of four-letter epithets.

"Knock it off," ordered Wallace. The two looked at him as if he had trespassed in some private preserve.

"Where are the Ho soldiers?" Ian asked.

"Back room. Two of 'em. The rest of 'em musta run when the ching pao started."

"Get 'em, Adam," Wallace said to Lo.

Questioning revealed that one of the soldiers had lived some one hundred li to the west of Siangtan before he "enlisted." So he says, Wallace thought. Ian had tried to follow the questioning, but his ear was not quick enough nor his vocabulary wide enough to follow what was happening. The soldier volunteered to guide them to the west. I don't blame him; gets him out of the line of fire, Ian thought.

"Tell him," Ian instructed Adam Lo, "that we're going west, and we're going to have to live off the land or off what we can buy. There'll be no requisitioning at the point of a gun and no head bashing with rifle butts or anything else. Is that clear?"

After some colloquy, during which Ian saw Wells watching the two Chinese and nodding, Lo said the soldier understood.

"O.K., Wells, you muster the troops and bury those chests of Ho ammo in that bomb crater out back. I'll get Rebstock on his feet and see what kind of petty cash he's carrying. We'll meet out in front in ten minutes and get out of here before it gets too light. Step on it!"

Wallace squatted by Rebstock with the map and told him he thought the proper course of action was to head west to get away from the river. Head for a town called Shihtan, some fifty miles west, if the map (Carte Internationale du Monde, Paris, France, 1925) could be believed. Make it in two days, maybe, with a stop at Siangsiang. Buy some chow at the first settlement or village we come to. Rebstock stared at the map, unseeing.

"How about the petty cash department?" Ian asked, rummaging in the lieutenant's musette bag and coming up with four bundles of large denomination Chinese yuan. He put these in his own bag, stuffed Rebstock's netting into the officer's pack and pulled him to his feet.

"We all saw you walk last night, so please put one foot in front of another and we'll get there."

Rebstock didn't move.

"Sir, we've got a bunch of men out there that we're responsible for, and they're waiting for us. Please come."

Rebstock stood where he was, swaying slightly.

"Then, sir, I guess I'll have to leave you behind," said Wallace and turned for the door. As he left the compound he heard Rebstock following him with a limping shuffle.

They were high above the city when the sun came up and they were treated to a demonstration of Japanese gunnery. From across the Siang Kiang several batteries of artillery opened fire on the empty and defenseless town, sending skyward geysers of earth, dust, tiles and smoke. The thunder was constant. Fires were started, and soon a pall of smoke and dust covered the entire city. As the detachment crested a last hill, Ian looked back and through the glasses could see Japanese infantry embarking in small canvas boats and commandeered shan p'ans, crossing the river to the west bank.

The road petered out to a track and then a narrow path that wound through steep hills. No farms, no paddies. Ian could tell they were generally headed in the right direction. The merciless morning sun on his back told him that. They descended to a valley with a little stream at the bottom and followed the path, hoping to find some clear water, rounded a bend and found a farm compound.

Here they ate, boiled water for their canteens, paid the *lao-pan* and left, much to the relief of the peasants.

They spent the night in another farm compound, after buying a thin meal of cabbage soup and assuring the farmer and his family that they would protect them from the monkey people if they came.

Next morning Ian asked the Ho soldier where Siangsiang was. Two hours he was told. At the end of two sweating hours Rebstock collapsed, and no Siangsiang was in sight, though the land had flattened some and there were farms and paddies. They pulled into a farm compound, sat in the shade and palavered with the peasant. Yes, he could make a litter for the sick man. Two bamboo poles and the man's blanket. One would have to pay. Certainly. And someone to carry the litter? The peasant's two strong sons would carry until nightfall. Again one would have to pay.

They never reached Siangsiang, slowed by attacks of dysentery affecting all hands and by rumors at the farms that the monkey people had sent a column there. They cut northwest through the hills.

Resting at the crest of a small mountain overlooking a ravine to the south, Wallace detected movement along the stream at the bottom. Where the water came out from under trees he saw a closed-up column of brown clad men carrying rifles and bayonets, wearing tin hats, leading mortar, machine-gun and pack laden horses and following a Japanese flag.

"Everybody down and shut up!" hissed Wallace, who slid to his belly, freeing his .45, chambering a round and peering at the column through the blades of tall grass in front of him. Next to him Paul Pong was quivering uncontrollably. Wallace put out a hand to steady him, and Pong shrieked at the touch, leapt to his feet shouting with terror and ran toward the Japanese with his hands held high.

The column stopped in its tracks, looking up the mountainside, then deployed, men throwing their rifles to their shoulders.

Wallace's synapses reacted like lightning. Can't let Pong get caught—

we're in enough trouble without that—knock him down and get out. He raised his Colt, and with both hands resting in the grass, not breathing, squeezing—sighting at the interpreter's fleeing back low down—and squeezing more, fired, hitting high as Pong ran down the steep slope. The round hit the interpreter at the base of the skull, and his hat flew off in a chunky red mist as he fell head downward and slid, to booming reverberations of the shot as the sound caromed from side to side of the ravine.

Wallace rolled to his shoulder, saw Adam Lo staring at him in disbelief, and called to Wells, "Get these people moving, on the deck. Around the crest, not over it. I'll meet you on the other side."

Not waiting for a response, Ian wriggled down hill through the tall grass and stunted pine brush to Pong's body, which he stripped of all identification, web belt, pistol, papers and insignia. He yanked off Pong's GI shoes and hurled them into the tangle. He turned and crawled back toward the summit and heard rifle fire, the flat crack of a .25 caliber Arisakas. If it was directed at him he couldn't tell. He followed a fold in the earth around the nose of the ridge, got into concealment and looked back. Some of the Japanese were laboriously trying to climb directly up the slope through the scrub, avoiding the path and having a tough, slow time of it.

Wallace looked for signs of his detachment as he trotted down the reverse slope. He followed a track and suddenly saw Wells and Steger through the pine and bamboo. He came to a breathless halt.

"Where are the rest?" he asked Wells.

"Mr. O'Reilly has took 'em on down, carryin' the lieutenant. Told 'em we'd catch up with 'em by that path down yonder," Wells said, pointing.

Wallace was shaking. "Do we have any Ho soldiers left?"

"Two," said Wells, "last I saw. One of 'em the guide."

"Wants to get home," said Wallace. "So do I. Let's go "

They trotted downhill through the bamboo forest, their equipment thudding and slapping at their haunches, braking every so often to look and listen. Toward the bottom they came upon a little path that led to the northeast, and they followed its fairly level course to the larger path Wells had pointed out from the crest. At the juncture they stayed in the trees and looked for O'Reilly and his group heading west. Suddenly around the bend at a dog-trot came a squad of Japanese soldiers. The Americans hunkered down and didn't move. The Japs came to the small path, halted, looked up it, argued, and then continued their trot toward the west, disappearing around the ridge.

"Do you suppose they're chasing Mr. O'Reilly?" asked Steger.

"No," said Ian. "Look up the path."

There, to the east, pounding along to the west hard on the heels of the Japanese, were Fix and his people, sweating and out of breath. Wallace and his men stepped out into the path as the others arrived.

"Jesus, are we glad to see you!" wheezed Fix. "We dumped Rebstock twice coming down and that slowed us up. There's a squad of Japs somewhere behind us."

"Lucky you slowed down in the woods," said Wallace. "Gave the Japs time to get in front of you. They just passed here. You were right behind them."

"My God!" said Fix.

"O.K., people, into the woods outa sight and take ten," Wallace ordered. "Fix, how about you and Adam Lo join me and Wells."

The four men drifted into the bamboo out of sight from the path. Adam was uncomfortable being with Ian, the man who had killed his fellow interpreter. The shakes were catching up with Wallace now, so he sat down with his elbows on his knees and his chin in his hands so the shakes wouldn't show.

"Adam," he said, "I am sorrier than you will ever know about what happened up there. Sorry that Paul broke. Sorry that I had to do what I did. Sorry it was him or us. And I'm sorry to have hurt you and spoiled what could have been our friendship. Do you understand?"

Lo looked at the deck for a while and then spoke. "Paul lose his family at Nanking rape time. He very much fear Japanese devils. He try to give up to save himself." He looked up through the bamboo fronds shimmering in the afternoon sunlight. "Japanese would hurt him bad, he talk, then they kill him. Better this way, I think. But bad any way. You do what you have to do."

Wallace listened, surprised. Maybe this was a case of "*pour encourager les autres*."

"Is that guide still with us?"

"Yes."

"Does he know where we are?"

"I get him." Adam disappeared and came back with the soldier, who squatted down on his ankles.

"He say we two hours from Siangsiang."

"Shit!" exploded Wallace. "We've been two hours from Siangsiang forever!"

"He say different direction now. Southeast. Next village Shihtan. Tomorrow maybe."

"Well, that's some help. It's where we're headed anyway. I don't think the Japs will come that far west of the river. Maybe we can get some news there. Maybe Steger can raise Camp Two."

"Maybe pigs have wings," said Wells.

They headed off to the west with a Ho soldier as point to keep a lookout for the monkey people. Rebstock's litter was passed from one pair of men to another as the time passed. Rebstock had fouled himself over and over again in the litter, and the stench was revulsive.

Near dusk they approached a high hill with a little *chiao t'ang*, a temple, nestled in a pine grove on the top at the eastern edge of a ridge.

"Shihtan at end of mountain," Adam said. "Tomorrow."

They entered the two-room shrine, obviously unvisited for years, and flaked out on the floor, exhausted and starving. Wallace set the watch and called Tony Pagani, the corpsman, to help him. Together they carried Rebstock's litter outside. They stripped the lieutenant and buried his clothes and litter blanket. Wallace and Pagani poured a little precious water from their canteens on a pair of Rebstock's clean skivvies and scraped the dried slime and feces off him. Wallace thought he'd puke.

They put the man in a clean set of khakis from his pack, put his boondockers back on, and Wallace talked to him. He got no answer. He told Pagani to go inside. When the corpsman had gone Wallace tried once more and got no response, so he slapped the lieutenant hard, across the face. Rebstock opened his eyes.

"Now, sir, there's no more litter and there are no more clothes. We're all pooped, and I'm sure you've recovered enough of your strength to help out, 'cause we can't carry you anymore. Let me see you stand up and try to walk."

Rebstock didn't move, so Wallace hauled him to his feet and guided him into the temple while the men watched. "The lieutenant will be walking with us tomorrow or staying here. It's up to him," Wallace told them.

"We don't know what's happening out there, but we gotta keep heading west and put some distance between us and the Japs. We'll bed down here tonight and leave before dawn. Maybe everything will be all right when we get to Shihtan. Sleep with your holsters unbuttoned, your gear at hand and your shoes on."

Steger tried to raise any friendly ear on his little radio but got no response to his repeated tapping of the key. They scanned the dial and got some faint cracklings, then a BBC news program that faded in and out. They learned that Hengyang had been surrounded. Where is Camp Two now, they wondered.

In the small hours of the night Tobias had the watch. The chief shipfitter wondered what the hell he was doing in this god-forsaken spot when he became intensely alert at a sound in the woods downhill from their billet. He heard it again, and it sounded like people carefully moving through the brush. He slid to Wallace, who lay awake oblivious of everything but his conscience and his guilt. Tobias put his hand over the lieutenant's mouth and breathed in his ear, "Company comin'!"

"Let's get 'em all moving. Make sure they take their gear. Out the back and follow me."

The two men moved silently to alert the other sleeping forms, and like wraiths they all gathered their equipment and packs and slipped out the rear. Wallace had to pull Rebstock up, with his hand over his mouth. "They're coming," he told him. "It's up to you whether you go or stay."

Wallace turned to leave, and Rebstock grabbed Ian's belt from the rear and followed him out.

They followed the ridge line, groping in the hot darkness for footholds, hanging on to the man in front so as not to become separated. Ten minutes into their trek there was the concussive crash of grenades and a spatter of rifle fire at the chiao t'ang, which caught fire and served as a beacon for the men as they stumbled away, down the mountain.

At dawn they were on the nose of a ridge overlooking a small mountain village. They looked carefully for enemy signs and saw none. Adam Lo volunteered to go in and find the *shih chang* to see if the mayor could tell them whether the way was clear. He would either walk slowly back or wave them in.

Lo changed to his coolie clothes and slipped away. They watched him through the glasses as he reached the path and walked toward Shihtan village.

"Hope he comes back," said Wallace.

"I think he will," said Wells. "I been listenin' to him talk with the other

Chinese, and I figger he's straight with you."

"You savvy this lingo?"

"Yessir, but I just don't let on that I do. Talk it, too, if I have to. Better for everybody not to know, though. Gives me an ace in the hole."

"That's good to know. You're another weapon. I'll keep it under my hat, for damn sure."

"What you goin' to do about Barney-boy, there," Wells asked, jerking his head toward Rebstock.

Wallace swiveled to look. Rebstock sat staring at his filthy, crusted, bloody bare feet. He'd slept barefoot and left his shoes back at the temple.

The mayor took them into his compound and gave them hot water to wash by, boiled water for their canteens, and a meal of rice and vegetables. He called in a couple of barbers to trim the scruffy Americans and a Chinese doctor, who soaked Rebstock's feet in some herb concoction and bound them tightly with rags.

Wallace offered to pay the mayor, who declined, explaining in English that he was a graduate of the University of Michigan and that this was little enough for him to do to help repay the kindnesses he had experienced in America. Ian thanked him in his poor Chinese, and the shih chang beamed. Wallace told the man he hoped the Americans could rest for a bit at Shihtan. The mayor said, "Do not wait for the almonds until you have no teeth."

Ian thought that was the polite Chinese equivalent of "get while the getting is good," or possibly "gather ye rosebuds while ye may." They'd have to move soon. That was certain.

A barber had Ian's shoulders under a smelly gray cloth and was operating the hand clipper when Wells looked out the compound window and said, "Hi! What's this? *K'u li* train comin' so early in the morning?"

Adam Lo and the Ho soldier joined Wells at the window, watching the line of blue-clad coolies struggle up the steep path approaching the village, grunting under the loads at the ends of the yo-yo poles. The train stopped outside the village.

"Don't like this," said Wells. Wallace and the mayor joined the people at the window. The coolies were suddenly galvanized into action and threw the carrying baskets over, spilling rice and retrieving mortars, rifles and grenades.

"*Jih-pen bien-yi!* Japanese plain-clothes soldiers!" hissed the mayor.

"Everybody get your gear and get out the back!" yelled Ian.

There was a mad scramble for packs and pistols, and the men raced out the side of the building where the enemy couldn't see them. Wallace tried to get the mayor to come with them as he watched Rebstock sprint out on his wounded feet. The mayor bowed and said thank you, but no, he was shih chang and would stay in his village. Wallace checked to be sure he was last man out and dove through a rear window as the first mortar round landed on the roofs.

The poor, ragged villagers swarmed into the street to flee and were met by rifle and machine-gun fire. More mortar rounds were landing on the tile roofs, and the crowd surged toward the west screaming and shoving. Ian found himself alone in the village cemetery behind a burial mound, in defilade, but where he could see the horde of villagers running down the western path between the paddies in panic, clutching babies, bedclothes and such other household goods as they could throw on the ends of yo-yo poles. As he watched, some other Japanese, in uniform, descended from the woods a half mile down the way and set up a machine-gun. They didn't open fire but slowed the mob and seemed to be looking at each peasant as the crowd squirmed between riflemen on each side of the path.

Bullets whined through the graveyard and kicked dirt, showering Ian with soil from the top of his hiding place. Jesus, he thought, have I spent all my life to wind up like this? He looked for a way out between the mounds down to the little brook at the foot of the short slope. Maybe get to the brook and work down it, he thought. As he contemplated the route he saw a group of Japanese, in uniform, settle themselves on the bank of the brook and survey the burial ground. Wallace's hopes sank.

Explosions continued behind him, one very close. He turned, saw smoke billowing out the rear window of the mayor's compound and then watched the shih chang fall out the window in slow motion, leaving a broad smear of blood on the wall as he slid to the ground. A helmeted Japanese soldier appeared at the window and fired three deliberate shots into the still, crumpled figure.

Wallace was shaken. He watched the fleeing peasants, wondering how he could join them and escape. Ridiculous. He was a foot taller than the tallest peasant, fair of skin and blue of eye. He heard his name between gusts of weapons fire. It seemed to come from his right from behind another mound.

"Who's there?" he called.

"Wells, goddamit! Behind the mound with the wilted flowers on top."

Wallace scanned the burial ground and found Wells's hiding spot two mounds away. Hell, he thought, no sense in dying alone, and bellied through the grass to the fresh mound, rounded it and found the gunny taking off his clothes.

"What are you doing, for Christ's sake!" asked Wallace.

"Gonna call in some of that insurance and put on my coolie uniform. Try and join that mob there and get out somehow."

Ian struggled into his coolie clothes, stowed his khakis and tied his tattered wash rag around his head. "Well, let's go out in the same uniform."

Wallace looked at the checkpoint down the path and saw that the Japanese were pulling strong male peasants out of the crowd and making them squat under guard. He now understood the Japanese tactic: surprise with unopposed plain-clothes troops; no time for villagers to evacuate and empty their godown storehouses; intimidate with regular troops; use the locals to carry the rice back. He also saw other uniformed Japanese soldiers running along paddy dikes parallel to the main path. Several male villagers tried to escape through the paddies and were caught and bayoneted.

Then Wells and Wallace looked at each other, looked at all the soldiers at the foot of the graveyard, at the checkpoint, in the paddies, heard them in the village looting and firing and realized it was no use. In no way would they let themselves be captured. A strange sense of calm descended on the two men. No more fear, because there was no uncertainty. They decided to throw fingers to see who would shoot whom first before putting the gun in his own mouth. They felt unfazed at the prospect, just disappointed that it had come to this.

Wallace reached out his hand and said, "You're a good man, Asa, and I'm glad I got to serve with you."

"It ain't like the old Corps, but you sure as hell is good people, Wallace."

He took Ian's hand and his grip suddenly stiffened. "They're gone! Down at the end of the graveyard. They've gone!"

Wallace craned his head around. The soldiers had disappeared. His fear returned. His stomach churned. His adrenalin pumped. His breathing, so calm moments before, came in breathless little gasps.

"Come on!" he said to Wells and the two of them wiggled from mound to mound dragging their gear until they got to the stream. Nothing there but bootprints and cigarette butts. They took off their shoes and stowed them, slathered mud on their clothes, feet, exposed skin and hair, and trotted down the stream, bent over, looking for a way to join the mob. In the gully where the stream entered the highest paddy there were four fresh corpses. The men stole two conical straw coolie hats, two yo-yo poles, threw their gear into the baskets at each end of the poles, ripped the shirts off two of the men and threw the rotting garments over their equipment, shouldered the poles and, with knees bent, trotted into the mob and down the path to the checkpoint.

Fix was out of breath. He'd never run so fast or so far in all his life. He'd kept stopping to let the others catch up, and then he'd urged them on. They'd gotten down the path mingled with early escapees from the village before the Japanese had set up their checkpoint.

Now, a mile from the checkpoint but still in view of the enemy, Fix led his group off the path at a turn, uphill into the bamboo, and spread them out into a loose perimeter.

"We're a liability to those people," he said pointing to the refugees, "and we'll draw attention and fire. Keep your eyes peeled for Japs and watch for the missing. Who's not here?"

"Wells and Wallace," said Fugakis.

"And Rebstock," said Samanov.

"Hell, he was with us a minute ago. I seen him come up here into the trees. A regular sprinter," said Corpsman Pagani.

"Fugakis," said Fix, "you and Samanov go up into those trees and find the lieutenant. If you can't find him in five minutes get your asses right back here. We'll wait that long for Wallace and Wells."

Fix squinted through the trees back up the path and saw Japanese soldiers herding off a platoon of peasants. Smoke rose from Shihtan. Fleeing Chinese continued to run through the checkpoint and, after they got by it, to take to the paddy dikes and run toward the hills. He heard an airplane engine and saw a lone Nakajima Ki-43, an Oscar, slowly circling over the town, attracted by smoke. The Japanese at the checkpoint saw it too and quickly picked up their machine-gun and ran into the woods.

The plane slowly tipped over on one wing and banked toward the path, righted itself as it lost altitude, leveled off and opened fire on the milling peasants as it swept over the track. Figures tumbled into the paddies, fled into the muddy fields, crumpled on the path—unmoving.

"Oh, you goddam sonso'bitches!" screamed O'Reilly. "You filthy goddam no good cocksucking sonso'bitches!" he shrieked, shaking his fists at the sky. He turned aside and, hands on knees, vomited, straightened up and wiped his mouth on the back of his hand, looked at the men and shouted, "Any you people wanta puke, be my guests."

He stomped to the edge of the bamboo grove and eyed the deserted path and the bodies strewn along its way. He saw no Japanese soldiers except the rear guard beating the rice-bearing coolie train as it left the village toward the east. He heard nothing but the faint undulating drone of the vanishing Nakajima and the keening of the wounded and the grieving.

Bring Water, bring wine, boy!
Bring flowering garlands to me!
Yes bring them so that I may try a bout with love.

—Anacreon
Fragment27

KWANGSI 1944

HALF A WORLD AWAY FROM SHIHTAN'S DAYLIGHT, the darkness of the late June night blanketed the District of Columbia. West of the Capitol thunder grumbled near the headwaters of the Potomac. Blackout was in effect, sobering the night, relieved only by pale flashes of distant lightning and the weak probing of hooded headlights, as occasional automobiles prowled their way through empty streets.

In her new apartment on Kalorama Road, Diana Bliss woke with a start, sitting straight up in bed, clutching the damp sheet to her breast in the humid Washington darkness. Her heart thudded, and she was covered with goose flesh as she shivered despite the heat of her bedroom. Her breath came in rapid little gasps. In the darkness her vision was of a body face down in water, dark blood seeping from its head, slowly turning the water pink. She remembered her dream: the body was rolled over, and through the water Ian Wallace stared up at her with unseeing eyes as blood ran from his nose and mouth. She screamed and put her head in her hands and sobbed. Oh God, God, God! Oh, God! She rocked back and forth, tangled in the sheets, tears flowing, the taste of salt in her mouth. She dimly heard the occasional and muted sounds of traffic in the street outside and slowly brought herself back to reality. Take hold of yourself, she said, shivering. She turned on the bedside lamp and by its dim light went to the living room cupboard where she kept her small supply of liquor and poured herself a short whisky in a tumbler. She shivered again, and before she drank she returned to her bedroom and put on her terry-cloth robe and her slippers. Still shivering, she returned to the living room and sipped her drink. Its warmth flowed over her breastbone and made a little comforting glow in her belly. Her fingers relaxed their tight grip on the glass.

She looked in the wall mirror and saw a disheveled red-haired freckle-faced woman with red-rimmed blue eyes looking at her in terror. She looked at her drink and finished it in a gulp. It burned its way down her gullet. God, she thought, I hope I'm not going to lean on this for help in trouble. Heaven knows there's plenty of trouble coming… Ian gone and out of touch (can I really remember what he looks like after only five months, she wondered?). They should have exchanged photographs. She was annoyed at herself for not thinking of it. But how could you, in the rushing pace and thrust of wartime departure. She hoped he remembered her blue eyes and what it felt like to hold her (she remembered that). And her employer and long-time warm, loyal friend Congressman Daniel Bensen was about to accept a commission in the Navy for active duty on a warship. Navigation officer he'd said, because of his experience sailing E Scows on the Great Lakes. Diana knew she'd have to face dealing with Bensen's replacement. Hopefully he'd want to keep her on to acquaint him with the ins and outs of the Washington and Congressional scenes. More trouble.

And if the new Congressman didn't want her, what then? Perhaps Lucas Duval could help. He was the Deputy Assistant Secretary of the Navy for whom Irene Gregg had worked and whom Diana had met at that memorable dinner at the Occidental when Diana had slipped Ian twenty dollars. And Duval had testified on landing-craft matters before Daniel Bensen's War Contracts Committee. Bensen had followed up that connection to help assuage Diana's concern about lack of communication from Ian. Duval had given the Congressman a letter for Diana that she had received this morning. She took it from her desk and read it again:

> Dear Miss Bliss:
> Congressman Daniel Bensen has relayed to me your concern about lack of communication from your friend Ian Wallace. I do recall meeting you both when you were with Irene Gregg one evening. Wallace reported to his command for duty in late March. Prior to his

arrival he was delayed some time in India, and our Naval Mail Clerk was instructed to forward his mail to him there. However Wallace had departed for China before all his mail could reach him. The lack of adequate transportation and communication in that part of the world interferes with timely receipt and dispatch of mail, unfortunately. It will be of interest to you to learn that Wallace is now stationed in the field. His health is good. Being in the field his mail will take a little longer to get in and get out as I am sure you can understand. Do not hesitate to contact me if I can be of further service.

    Sincerely,

    [signed] Lucas Duval

Why doesn't that make me feel any better, she asked herself. Why do I feel so threatened, so deserted? What happened to the crowd at the Gayety? Why don't I like my new apartment? Because it's empty, and you're scared and feeling sorry for yourself.

Her body suffered a little spasm as the image of the bloody face flashed through her mind. She looked at the telephone and at her watch. Not too late, she told herself and dialed Daniel Bensen's home number. He answered on the second ring. She pictured him: tall, black haired and brown eyed, in his shirt sleeves, eight blocks away, sitting with papers and documents in his lap, alone in his bachelor flat. He had been so thoughtful of her, so helpful. She wanted comfort. Company.

"Hello," he said. Diana didn't know what to say.

"Hello, who's there?" he asked.

He heard her whisper "Diana."

"Are you all right?" he asked.

"No," she said.

"Stay put," he said, "I'm coming right over."

Diana put the phone down, wondering what she had done.

When Bensen got to Diana's apartment, the door was unlocked and he found her sitting on the living room sofa rocking gently back and forth. She looked up with tears in her eyes and said: "Oh, Daniel."

He sat next to her on the sofa, put his arm around her shoulders and stroked her hair. She leaned against him and his muscular body gave a sense of strength and reassurance to her.

"What can I do?" he asked.

She lifted her face and looked in his eyes. "Oh, Daniel," she said, "I'm so frightened."

He put his cheek next to hers, slippery with her tears, and she put her arms about him, still rocking slightly. He moved his head back and looked at her and lowered his lips and kissed her gently. She let out a long sigh as they kissed and held him, then slowly drew him down with her on the cushions. His hand found her neck and lingeringly caressed it. His hand slipped into the opening of her robe and stroked her breast. She arched her back, parted her lips and touched his tongue with hers. He groaned a little groan, sat up and carried her to the bedroom. She threw the damp sheet back and dropped her night clothes. "Oh, Daniel," she said, and curled down to the bed, waiting and shivering, reluctant and wanting, aching for comfort and for care.

When Diana awoke alone in the small hours of the morning, she felt curiously relaxed yet at the same time visited by a transient sense of guilt. She could no longer see Ian's bloody face, only the face of Daniel Bensen hovering over her, comforting her, consoling her, loving her. I wanted to give myself to Ian, she told herself, and my first gift is to Daniel, the man I spend every day with and whom I have known for ages. He is so kind and considerate, and I've only known Ian for a few weekends, for a few months, yet how do I console myself for being so self-centered that I needed comfort rather than constancy? How is it that I feel very little remorse? How can I love two men? she asked herself.

When she woke again she felt rested, unthreatened by her dreams of the night before, at peace with what she had to do. She was quite sure of herself for she had almost always been able to cope, to do the needful. She was not a manipulator, but was considered to be straightforward, sometimes outspoken, occasionally blunt, and certainly with a mind of her own. She had been the only female on the Student Council at Antioch; she had almost defied her parents before their deaths in the flaming auto accident by saying that she was going to Washington to work for their Congressman; she had got the job by herself; she had voted Democratic in a Republican district; she had organized the Gayety; she had warned Ian about Irene; she had gone to his commission ceremony; she had helped him through his arrest and reassignment; she had fought the Congressman's fights in the political intrigues of Washington. She was quite sure of herself.

She rose and prepared a breakfast of powdered coffee, toast and margarine (no bacon, she was out of ration coupons), dressed for hot weather, picked up the newspaper outside the door as she left for work and went to the streetcar stop on the corner of Kalorama Road and Sixteenth Street, NW.

She read the news as the trolley swung southeast on Massachusetts Avenue at Scott Circle and headed for Union Station: buzz bombs in England; Allies struggling through the hedgerows of Normandy; Americans and British armies well north of Rome on the Italian boot; the Japanese still putting up fanatic resistance to the Second and Fourth Marine divisions on Saipan despite the formidable success of the Navy in the Battle of the Philippine Sea; and in China Changsha had fallen to the Japanese offensive started in Honan in the spring. The news stiffened her resolve to shed the indecision that had haunted her for days.

She left the car in front of Union Station and joined the crowds of government workers flowing down Delaware Avenue toward Capitol Plaza and their offices in the Capitol building, the Supreme Court and the Library of Congress. Diana crossed the Plaza, warm in the early morning sun, headed for the House Office Building between C Street and Independence Avenue, climbed the stairs and walked down the hall to Daniel Bensen's office.

The secretary and LA (legal aide) were not yet at their desks in the outer office but Diana could hear Bensen in his office on the phone. She put her purse in her desk drawer, dabbed at her damp forehead with a tissue, waited until she heard the Congressman hang up and knocked at the glass panel of his door.

"Come in! Don't stand on ceremo——" his words cut off as he saw Diana enter.

Her heart did an extra systole (she hadn't expected that) when she saw him leaning forward in his shirt sleeves in the muggy heat, hands on his desk. Before he could speak, Diana summoned her forthrightness: "Thank you for helping me last night, for coming over and for your company. I don't want you to feel uncomfortable, I just want you to feel happy that you helped me."

"I hope last night won't interfere with our, ah, friendship. Our——"

"Oh, no," said Diana, "You comforted me and helped drive away the dark and an unfamiliar sense of insecurity that I've felt for too long… not knowing about you and when your commission would come; what I should do about my work; where Ian is; no parents to turn to. You made me feel secure and I'm grateful."

"Thank God," said Bensen, resisting the impulse to go around the desk and hold her. "You helped me in ways you couldn't know, until now."

He held out a tan manila envelope with Navy Department indicia on the corner. The address label read: Lt. Cdr. Daniel Bensen, USNR, House Office Building, Washington, D.C. "It was delivered just before you came in, and I was on the phone to Lucas Duval about it just now."

Diana felt a little faint. "What were you talking about?" she asked, hoping a little hope that maybe he had tried to get some kind of delay.

"I reminded him of his offer to help you if you wanted a new job. He told me yesterday he was looking for a confidential secretary, and I just suggested that since my orders have come and since you have top security clearance he interview you. He'd like to see you at ten this morning."

Diana sat down, somewhat breathless. "So soon," she said. "I suppose congratulations are due, but I'm a bit taken aback. I hadn't really expected this right now."

Bensen came and sat in the chair across from her and took her hands. "Please don't mind my calling Duval for you. It's just that with the session winding down, with the election of my successor not happening until November, I thought you'd better have some choices available. And I have to leave Wednesday."

"My resolve this morning," Diana said stiffly and with all her strength, "was to tell you I'd like to see Duval rather than waiting here for the Seventy-Ninth Congress to meet. So thank you. But my God, Wednesday! That's the day after tomorrow!"

The Deputy Assistant Secretary of the Navy's Office was on the second deck of the Navy Building in the old, temporary World War I construction facing the Mall. Despite the heat Diana refused the offer of government transportation and walked the half mile to her appointment, arriving damp and early. She was asked to wait and was surprised when Lucas Duval came in from the hall, not from his office. "Meetings, meetings," he said and welcomed her to an office that was a far cry from the spartan preserve of her junior Congressman. Paintings of Revolutionary sea battles hung in heavy carved gold frames on the walls. Brass shell casings were used for waste baskets and ash trays. Heavy maroon draperies guarded the windows. From a large leather frame on Duval's mahogany desk Franklin Roosevelt smiled out at her from under his crushed fedora while his sentiments about Duval were scrawled across the bottom of the photograph in FDR's casual style.

The interview went extremely well, and Duval was the embodiment of gentlemanly courtesy, assuring her that the job would require absolute discretion on her part and that he would do what he could to see that the transition from one office to another was made as easy as possible. After a day and night of emotional surprises, Diana was relieved that the matter could be so quickly and amicably arranged. The only sensitive moment came when Duval asked her why she had not chosen to be a uniformed member of the armed forces. She told him quite frankly that she didn't think she could stand being herded together with a bunch of women in a barracks smelling of disinfectant and being assigned to some menial job. She thought she could do a great deal more here in Washington in a reasonably meaningful job. Duval said he understood and agreed with her.

He asked her to come to work as soon as she could phase herself out of her present responsibilities, possibly Monday? Diana said that the LA and the secretary could handle constituents' matters, the only chores left now that the session was ending, and she would like to come in this Thursday if that was all right. Duval was pleased, they shook hands and Diana left, feeling refreshed and relieved.

A number of Daniel's Naval Officer friends threw a farewell party for him at their cellar apartment on Wisconsin Avenue in Georgetown. The flat was affectionately called the Bombshelter, and the lease had been passed from hand to hand and officer to officer as assignments and duties had shifted and changed. The present group was a mixed lot, but all shared the common experience of overseas combat. Some worked for BuPers, some for BuShips or BuOrd. Those with service in Europe called the flat *l'Abri*. Guests who had not served overseas referred to the place as the "Beaushelter." One out-of-his-element officer, a major, wore the green and pinks of the Army Air Corps with the CBI (China-Burma-India) patch on his shoulder and a chestful of ribbons under his pilot's wings. He called the place *Ai shui jiao fangzi* (love-sleep-house). He was the brother of one of the Navy officers.

As the evening got noisier and wetter, Diana found herself talking with the CBI pilot on leave before reporting to a stateside assignment. He said his name was Ben Bickford. She queried him about the CBI theater of war and learned that he had been mainly in the Burma jungles, ferrying supplies to General "Vinegar Joe" Stilwell's people near Myitkyina. Diana asked how long he had been overseas and he said thirty-six months. She asked him how he stood it for so long.

"Why," he said, "every evening at tea-time those of us who are still left stand in a circle flipping our lips with our forefingers while we chant 'The jungle doesn't bother me! The jungle doesn't bother me!' " He roared with laughter and went to fix their drinks.

Bensen took Diana home to her front door at about eleven-thirty. They kissed chastely, clasped each other for a spell, thanked each other, promised to write each other, kissed and clasped again, and Bensen left.

Diana went inside, kicked off her shoes and flopped down on the sofa. Such a week! So many changes. So many new faces. So many new emotions!

Had one brief moment of fear and fragility meant she had "cheated" Ian? I worry about Ian. I worry about Daniel, she thought. Though I'm saddened by Daniel's departure, I'm thrilled and happy for him. So many things settled. Some big things unsettled. Should I worry about myself, my fecundity? She prayed she would not have to have that worry, too, God help her. She felt she was on an emotional see-saw.

Yet she was excited at the prospect of her new work and by the people she'd met. There was so much news, she'd have to write Ian. She'd meant to ask Ben Bickford, the CBI pilot whom she'd said she'd see again, if there were jungles in China. She wondered what Ian was doing.

Camp Two had moved from Nanyo just before the Japanese arrived. Lacking operational intelligence of any kind, Bunghole Birdsall had hired a charcoal-burning truck the day after the detachment had left. He radioed Chungking that he was moving, loaded the truck and the jeep and drove through crowds of refugees to Hengyang with Pearson, the three sailors and the interpreter, all armed to the teeth and whacking the knuckles and arms of frantic Chinese trying to climb aboard.

There followed an arduous journey to the west of Hengyang as part of a column of U.S. Army Air Corps trucks, jeeps and weapons carriers evacuating such equipment and personnel from Hengyang airstrip as couldn't be flown out. They moved in a cloud of dust on a narrow dirt road, hampered by broken-down Chinese vehicles, by swarms of peasants fleeing to the west on foot and by the need to stop and refuel from the fifty-five-gallon drums of high-octane gasoline carried on the Army's 6x6s.

Bunghole's charcoal-burner gave out the second day west of Hengyang, and his group had to transfer to Army vehicles and load as much of their gear as they could on their jeep. The rest of the equipment they pushed over the side of the road, to the pleasure of the refugees who picked the truck and its contents clean.

The column drove through She-tien-chiao, fifty miles by air but one hundred road miles from Hengyang. They stopped to the west of town and forted up like a western wagon train to keep from being overrun by either hostiles or friendlies.

Birdsall told his radioman to maintain his nightly effort to contact Rebstock's unit and to maintain his schedule with Chungking. Poor transmission and reception in the mountains, but they heard from headquarters. No response from Rebstock.

When they decoded the message from Chungking, they learned that they were to establish a new Camp Two at Hungkiang. That meant traveling another seventy miles to Paoching, eighty more to Tungkow, fifty more over the Suehfeng-Shan mountains to Ankiang and then thirty last miles to Hungkiang.

They accompanied the Air Corps convoy to Ankiang, where they parted company. The Air Corps drove west to the air strip at Chihkiang while the remnants of NAVU2 struggled south, all gear and personnel teetering on one tired jeep. The three-hundred-thirty-mile trip had taken nine days.

At Hungkiang, a scrubby mountain town just east of the Kweichow Province border, they were met by a small cadre of Americans who had taken over the local two-story school building as billets for the unit. The chief storekeeper, in charge until Birdsall's arrival, handed envelopes to Bunghole and Pearson.

Lieutenant Commander Birdsall was ordered to report to Church Lane in Calcutta as liaison officer with the U.S. Army and the British. The chief storekeeper told him that it was rumored he would replace a man named Mooney who was going stateside under a cloud having to do with diversion of supplies, misuse of government funds and a problem with the daughter of a high-ranking colonial official.

Birdsall left at once, with delight. Pearson watched him go with the same emotion. Bye, bye Bunghole, he thought.

Tom Pearson was promoted to full lieutenant and made commander of Unit Two. He called the unit together and told them how he planned to work and welcomed suggestions. He said their first chore was to set up training facilities for a new Chinese unit. The second chore was to find Rebstock's detachment.

That evening he went to the radio shack and stood by as the operator worked his key, sending Rebstock's call sign over and over. He couldn't raise them.

"Send the message anyway. Maybe they'll copy and at least know where the hell we are."

O'Reilly watched the vanishing Nakajima, watched some of the peasants pull themselves from the mud, clutching bloody bellies, dragging legs, groping blindly. Some of them simply sat back down on the path. Some headed back to the burning village. Some continued toward the west. Fix went back in the trees and heard Fugakis and Samanov arguing about who had found Rebstock. They never quit, mused Fix.

Rebstock leaned against a thick bamboo tree, eyes closed, trousers soiled, feet bloody. Fix walked up to him and asked, "Can you walk?"

The lieutenant nodded.

Fix went to the edge of the grove, thinking, well, we'll give them a few more minutes. Can't wait too long, though, or it will be getting dark. He looked at his wrist watch and was astonished to see it was only eight-thirty in the morning.

He watched a string of peasants approaching, tottering and carrying their poles clumsily. The two peasants at the end were making bad weather of it. Their carrying baskets were bumping into their shins and calves. Their conical straw hats were pulled over their cast-down eyes. One man was bleeding from the side of the head. They were taller than the others. Fix gasped.

When the last two men were opposite him, O'Reilly jumped from the forest and yelled, "Hao pu hao!"

The two men stopped, looked at Fix, dropped their poles, swept off their hats, and the bloody one shouted, "Ma-ma fu-fu! Ma-ma fucking fu-fu!" and sat down on the path.

The rest of the unit erupted from the trees shouting, "Ding hao! Ding hao!" rushed to the path, swept up Wells and Wallace and their gear and dashed back into the trees. Wallace, with blood pouring from his head wound, saw Rebstock sitting at the foot of his tree and said, light-headedly, "Don't put me near him."

Pagani surged up with his corpsman's pack, got Wallace down, saw the long bullet gash in his scalp and the missing top of the ear, wiped away blood, sprinkled sulfa powder, and bound a pressure bandage around his head. Each time Wallace tried to talk, Pagani told him to shut up until he was through with him. He gave him water from his canteen and turned to Wells.

"You hit anywhere? Can't see nothin'."

"Nah, just shiverin' like a dog shittin' razor blades," Wells said breathlessly. "That sumbitch's legs is longer'n a country mile, an' he don't scare for shit. Walked us right through the fuckin' checkpoint before that fuckin' meatball showed up. Then we dove in the paddy shit, and he took one in the head. Did you clean 'im up good?"

"I'm all right, Gunny," Ian said. Then, after a burst of nervous laughter, he said, "This sure beats the hell out of sucking the business end of a .45."

They rested for a time, then Wallace insisted on getting the soggy map out of his gear so they could see what they had to do next. He unwrapped the map from around the soaked one-time pad, and they all gathered near and saw they were northeast of Paoching. Ian thought they should go to this fairly sizable city, probably one hundred fifty miles from Hengyang, by way of a town named Kushui, an out-of-the-way place hopefully free from Japanese excursions.

Ian pulled his boondockers from the carrying basket, dried his feet with a pair of socks and put his boots on. He strapped on his webbing and pistol and called for his pack.

"It ain't here," someone said.

"Gotta be," Wallace replied. "You got my map from it." He looked around.

"Adam," he called, "where's that Ho soldier guide?"

All hands then looked, and neither the guide nor the musette bag with the money was to be found.

Wallace damned himself for carelessness. Should have known, he told himself. There was enough yuan in that bag for a family to live on comfortably for the rest of their lives.

He stood up, a little dizzy. "All right, people," he said, "we're on our way. No mama, no papa, no flight pay, no per diem. We can't buy anything, so we gotta get it the hard way. But, by God, we're going to find our people. Saddle up."

They skirted Kushui, not liking the look of things there, found an empty farm compound (why was it empty? Ian wondered) and bedded down, hungry. Wells scouted a bit and found a tethered goat kid left behind by the previous occupants. He also found some snails and a large iron pot. They built a fire indoors on the floor and boiled a stew they would forever remember as Shit Soup.

Lowti was largely deserted, but they were able to steal some rice, eggs and cabbage at night. Wallace was against taking food at gun point if it could be avoided.

They came across the dead remnants of a Chinese detachment that had been ambushed. The corpses were black and the air was thick with an ocean of flies. Pagani, the corpsman, tied a rag over his nose and mouth and wandered among the corpses, brushing at his face. From a distance the men watched him inspect some of the dead. He turned one over with his boot and picked up something that looked like a stovepipe and a heavy canvas satchel.

As he returned, Wallace could see that the stovepipe was an ancient Lewis gun, a slow-firing, fully automatic weapon, rounds fed from a pan affixed to the top of the receiver. Wells turned to Ian and said, "A real *chi kuan ch'iang!* Them things used to be mounted on the top wing of SE5s and Nieuports in the World War! I fired one once on the range outside Shanghai!"

The gun was filthy but operable. The canvas sack contained three more pans of ammo. Wells cleaned up the gun with oil and patches from his carbine, got the front bipod functioning and said he hoped to get to use it. Fire-power does wonders for one's confidence, Ian told himself.

They stopped in the hills north of Paoching and did their nightly attempt to send and to listen on the radio. This night they heard their call sign: Baker Baker Queen Five. Steger got excited and called Wallace, who hovered over the man as Steger wrote down the five-letter code groups addressed to them from Fox Yoke Two. "BBQ5 acknowledge" demanded the radio. Steger's fist worked. "Do you read BBQ5?" Nothing.

"Shit!" said Steger, tearing off the sheet of code groups and handing it to Wallace. Ian got the water-stained one-time pad and by the light of a little tung-oil wick, after figuring out what the date was from the first five-letter group, found the right code sheet and laboriously decoded the message.

He got out the map, looked at it and called the men together.

"We just heard from Camp Two," he said. "The new camp is located in Hungkiang, here," he said, pointing to a spot on the left of the map. The men leaned forward to see in the dim light, looking at the distance from Paoching.

"Holy shit!" said O'Reilly.

Mornings later, before dawn they stopped in the woods on a hill across the river from Paoching. They were leery of the place. Last night the town had been quiet. No lights. They waited for dawn to see whether they could cross the river and maybe find a telephone or a bus. As the light grew they could see that they were across from a barracks-like building with curving eaves and a dirt parade ground that reached from the building into the swirling, brown river on a little peninsula. They heard shouted commands but couldn't tell what they were. Wells and Wallace looked at each other.

"Do you know what I think?" said Wallace. "We're too late. Those are Japanese." He nodded across the river.

"No, sir," said Wells, "if them is Japs we're just in time," and he patted the Lewis gun.

Wallace asked Fix to take the men farther back into the trees and a little more to the west and to wait until sun-up—and if Ian and Asa didn't show just after that, he and the men should skidoo.

Fix looked hard at Ian and said, "You need somebody to pass ammo. Treviso or Tobias can handle the men."

Wallace thought an officer should remain with the men but relented as he looked at Fix and saw the intensity in his eyes. He's as pissed as Wells and me. "O.K., set it up and come on."

They lay in the trees with the chi kuan ch'iang between two trunks, its bipod resting on fallen leaves. Wells was behind the sights and Wallace and O'Reilly lay on either side of him with a pan of ammunition each.

Just before sun-up a platoon of Japanese soldiers, in uniform pants and sandals and naked from the waist up, trotted onto the field, rifles at high port, yelling cadence. They stacked arms and lined up three ranks deep in front of an officer, facing across the river. They started to do exercises by the numbers, shouting in time as they did.

"What the hell are you waiting for!" Ian spat.

"Come on, Asa," whispered Fix.

"Fuck 'em. Let 'em get a little pooped first," Wells said hotly.

The sun rose, shining directly into the monkey soldiers' eyes. Their torsos glistened with sweat.

"Now!" said Wells and squeezed the trigger. The old gun thudded and bucked as Wells slowly found the range and traversed the parade ground. The troops scattered, stumbled and fell. Wells reversed direction and ran out of ammunition. He knocked off the empty pan, and Ian locked on a new one. Wells pulled the charging handle and opened fire again. Some of the Japanese had made it to the building during the lull in the firing, so Wells hosed the windows, then did one more sweep of the parade ground and said, "Thank you, gentlemen, and let's get the fuck outa here!"

On July 26, five weeks and two days after they had left Nanyo and with three hundred fifty miles or so behind them, eleven ragged, starved, bacteria ridden, bandaged and be-whiskered men trudged into Hungkiang carrying one of their number in a makeshift bamboo litter and found the school.

A khaki-clad gunner's mate sat on a bench in front of the school cleaning Cosmoline from the workings of a TSMG. He looked up as the men came toward him.

"Holy Jesus!" he said. "Who are you?"

"We're Camp Two detail returning from detached duty, son," said Wallace. "Please tell Commander Birdsall we're here."

"Ain't no Birdsall here, fella. Lieutenant Pearson's the commanding officer."

Thank God, Ian told himself. "Go get him."

The next day Pearson called him to his office. Ian went in and sat down.

"You're the shadow of your former self," Pearson said.

"Can't help it," said Ian. "Picky eater. And I was supposed to be eating in the Chinese officers' mess, but the sons of bitches never showed up so we lived off the land. What the hell happened?"

"Can't find out. We were told Ho's assignment was changed and that your group was to return, but we couldn't raise you on the radio. You did a great job getting back.

"I also want you to know that Rebstock has been shipped out to a U.S. Army Surgical Field Hospital. He'll probably lose both feet. He got hold of some juice before he left and got up enough Dutch courage to dictate this. It's addressed to the Commandant of the Marine Corps, via the Commander U.S. Naval Unit Number Two and the Commander of U.S. Naval Group, China."

Pearson handed Wallace a typed sheet. Ian read it:

Subject: Second Lieutenant Ian WALLACE, USMCR
Commendation to be entered in the record of.

1. The subject-named officer was assigned to duty with the Headquarters, Second Division, Chinese Commando Army, and was a member of that Command during engagements with the Japanese as shown below:

21 June 1944 – Near Siangsiang, Hunan, China
23 June 1944 – Shihtan, Hunan, China

2. The subject-named officer performed his duty in a proficient and military manner and showed himself to be calm and courageous during these engagements.

3. It is requested that this commendation be entered in the record of the subject-named officer.

BARNABAS REBSTOCK
1st. Lieut., USMC

Absolute bullshit! Scared to death, I was. Didn't say anything about Paoching, Ian noted, which is good because we're not supposed to be in combat and also because the Japanese went on a killing rampage in that town, avenging their losses. Wallace looked up.

"I don't believe this" he said. "Sounds like he was running things. He was so out of it he didn't know shit from apple butter!"

"I've heard it all," said Pearson. "And so has anybody else who's got ears. The yeoman at first refused to type the goddam thing. But I said 'do it,' and it got done. It's Rebstock's faint-hearted way of saying thank you for saving his ass and not bringing charges against him. Didn't have the balls to say it to your face. Rebstock's last and only courtesy.

"And I've got more news for you... you don't get a Purple Heart because we're not in combat. And, third, you are hereby ordered to Nanning, Kwangsi Province, down by the Indochina border, to establish and take command of Camp Five, U.S. Naval Group China. Any questions?"

Wallace crumpled the commendation into a tight paper ball and said to Pearson, "Bend over. Subject-named officer wants to get rid of this."

Ian lay on his sack in fresh khakis. His belly protruded, filled with good chow. He belched, purely to show proper appreciation for the good meal. Fix, who was writing letters on the next cot and humming "Winnipeg Whore," looked up and said, "Pig!"

"You bet," said Wallace. His head still throbbed, and he sported an enormous scab along the left side of his head. The top of that ear was gone. They'd done a little debridement today to clean it up and make it look better and less ragged. The new bandage hurt now that the local anesthetic had worn off.

He'd read his mail, what there was of it, and it was all disheartening. His grandfather had passed away months ago, and Jed and Patience had to look elsewhere for work. They didn't know what would happen to the farm. They hadn't heard from Peter's wife nor from Peter; and please take care of yourself.

Headquarters Marine Corps, under direction of the Commandant, wanted to know where his missing fitness reports were, last of same having covered the period 1 October 1943 to 7 December 1943. In accordance with Article 137, U.S. Navy Regulations, 1920, and ALNAV 156-1943 submit to your reporting senior form N.M.C. 625-A&I for forwarding to this Headquarters immediately to complete fitness records. That last period covered the escapade with Admiral Weatherwax. Marvelous. Let 'em wait.

Diana's letters were wonderful, but he worried about her, because Congressman Bensen had accepted a commission in the Navy, and Diana was now working for Lucas Duval in the Navy Department and wasn't sure how well she would do. Hurry back, oh, hurry back!

He thought about her and wondered how many days she had been out of his mind, pushed aside by more immediate and pressing matters. Bad, he thought. That's bad. But even as he thought so, from the corners of his mind in crept the anxiety that had plagued him for weeks.

How you doing, prospective minister? he asked himself. Great, just great. Killed my first man. A friend, at that. Lied about it and said merely that he'd been killed in combat. Everybody else lied about it, too, to back me up. Partners in crime. Lied about Rebstock and didn't bring any charges... just couldn't ruin the man any more than he'd already ruined himself in the eyes of those who had been there.

And how are you to be judged according to Deuteronomy, one of the Pentateuch Books of Law? How judged according to the commandments of the Lord brought down by Moses from Mount Sinai in tablets of stone, written with the finger of God? Well, let's see... I'm O.K. in the God department, no other gods though I've been tempted... no graven images, either... I seem to be taking the name of the Lord in vain with every other breath... I fail miserably in remembering the sabbath and haven't even known what day of the week it was, much less keep it holy... I honor my father and my mother, if I remember to think about them... I've killed, helped to kill and caused killings, and I should feel worse about it than I do... no adultery, yet, though that has some physical appeal about now... stealing? pretty good at that and getting better... is lying about Pong and Rebstock bearing false witness?... and have I been coveting!... not necessarily my neighbor's ox or ass, but certainly his food and his shelter and anything else we needed, with an occasional late-night thought about his maidservant.

How did you score, he asked himself. Flunked seven; passed three. Give it a little time and you can probably flunk them all. Are we getting bitter?

Hengyang was still holding out, though surrounded, when Wallace and his group left for Nanning. They would proceed to the south by truck and train far from the scene of current battles. Nonetheless, the atmosphere was saturated with gloom, foreboding and hopelessness. The Chinese were publicly boasting of how long they would hold out at the sites of the American air bases, but already Lingling was gone and Kweilin was about to be threatened.

The line of movement for Ian's group was west to Tuyun by truck, south by train to Liuchow where another American air base was located, and south by truck and jeep to Nanning, site of another small American air strip.

The roads were crowded with fleeing bureaucrats, students, merchants and opportunists. The southbound train, made up of flatcars, boxcars, ancient passenger carriages and coal cars and pulled by a big Czechoslovakian Skoda engine, was packed with verminous foul-smelling troops of the Ninety-third Chinese Army. Only about one in five seemed to be armed, and all of the lower ranks looked to be about fifteen years old. Most of them had scabies, and many suffered from the granular excrescences of trachoma that threatened to seal their eyes shut. They carried cotton tubes of rice over their shoulders like blanket rolls.

Wallace and his people had a small part of one passenger car to themselves. The glass had long since gone from the windows and hot gasses, smoke and coal ash poured in from the engine's stack. They were guarded by a party of Tai Li pings completely equipped with American arms and clothing. Wallace could feel the animosity between the shabby soldiers of the

Ninety-third and the Americans and their "running dog" guards.

"Nobody leaves the car," he ordered the U.S. personnel. He also suggested that Adam Lo, the interpreter, stay with them at all times.

The tension-filled, halting ride seemed to go on forever. The Americans were fortunate to have K-rations for chow, but their Chinese associates fended for themselves.

The car's latrine was unspeakable, consisting of two steel footplates on either side of a hole cut in the car floor in a tiny partitioned area at the end of the car. You could see the railroad ties passing beneath when you were standing up, and you could feel the wind on your bottom when you had to squat. You also had to be careful where you stepped. Ian was reminded of the crappers on the Free French battleship *Richelieu* when he'd visited her in Norfolk Navy Yard.

"It sure is hell on the knees, squatting like that and trying not to capsize as the train sways," said Ian.

"Yeah," said Wells, "it's hell on the knees all right, but it can be shit on the ankles!"

The truck ride from Liuchow to Nanning was hot and dusty on a road originally built when the only wheeled vehicles were wheelbarrows. Still plenty of them, some with sails, but the ride was less threatening than the train trip. They spent two nights in Chinese wayside "inns," learned about lice and bedbugs and to sleep with one eye open. They lost some gear from one truck when a guard dozed off but otherwise made the journey uneventfully.

The Americans remained in good spirits, laughing and skylarking. All of Ian's command had volunteered for the assignment. He'd been touched when, one or two at a time, the men had sought him out and said they understood he was going south to set up camp and could they please come along. Wells had been first. Then Steger. Pagani the corpsman and Tobias the shipfitter. To his surprise the constant arguers and bitchers, Fugakis and Samanov, came to him together and asked to accompany the group, explaining that they were both good gunnery instructors.

"You two are always at each other's throats," said Wallace. "Why do you want to stay together?"

"He'll fuck up if I'm not along," said Fugakis.

"Gotta keep an eye on him or he'll wind up in the clap shack," said Samanov.

Now, seated on the bed of the dusty, bumping truck, they were arguing, as usual. Wallace listened as the debate ranged from weapons to women to intellectual prowess.

"If you weren't brain-dead you would be fuckin' dangerous," said Samanov.

"You're so dumb you oughta go back to Magnitogorsk!," said Fugakis.

"They're smarter in Magnitogorsk than they are in Theologos!" Samanov retorted, looking away.

A couple of geographers! Wallace realized that these men had been together for a long time and knew each other well. He was glad they were along.

Fix would not be coming. He'd stayed in Hungkiang to train another group. But other men and officers would arrive after Ian had set up shop, flown in from Kunming, and Wallace wondered how they would get along with his "veterans."

Nanning was a flat city on a curve of the Yung River about one hundred miles northeast of the border of Tonkin, a protectorate of the French and part of French Indochina. Tonkin had been under Japanese military control since September 1940, after the fall of France. Hanoi, the capital, was another hundred miles to the southwest. The rest of the loosely associated countries known as French Indochina—Cochin-China, Annam, Cambodia and Laos, each of which also sent delegates to the Consiel Surperieur des Colonies in Paris—were now in the hands of the Japanese as well. Tonkinese, Annamese and French influences were apparent in Nanning, Wallace had been told. Despite Japanese capture of the city during their Southern Kwangsi Campaign in 1939-40, little Japanese influence could be seen.

To the east the Japanese controlled most of Kwangtung Province, including Hainan Island. Wallace estimated that he had Japanese forces no farther than one hundred miles away in the south and the east. He'd have to keep his eye peeled to the north, where the Japanese were bearing down on Kweilin and would obviously try for Liuchow. If Liuchow fell the only way out would be up the West and Yu rivers to the mountains of Yunan Province, hopefully to Kunming.

He supposed that Nanning was a target of the Japanese as well, since their objective was to knock out all the American airfields in central and southern China. Nothing seemed to be standing in their way. Oh, Chennault had promised that his AVG (American Volunteer Group—the Flying Tigers) would defeat the enemy, but even after the AVG had become the Fourteenth Air Force with it's associated improvement in equipment and supply, General "Vinegar Joe" Stilwell, Commander of U.S. Forces in China, was being proven right: you can't hold airfields without ground protection. And the Chinese were providing little of that.

We'll deal with it as it comes, Wallace told himself.

The first evidence of French influence manifested itself in the quarters that had been arranged for the Americans, the interpreters and the Chinese officers. Sheltered by tall palm trees, a deserted hospital built by the French was turned over to the unit. In its own large compound just outside the city, the quarters consisted of tile-roofed one-story buildings connected by covered walkways and separated by neglected gardens. There was a kitchen building and a bath building as well. The kitchen was a high-ceilinged room with the usual earthen stoves, though with no latrines in the corner as in some Chinese dwellings. The French, with an eye on gastronomy, had kept the kitchen and the shit house apart. The bath building had an enormous earthenware jug and spigot at the high end of a long, sloping, thigh-high flat trough where one could put one's brass basin in order to wash, and then dump the dirty water.

The second evidence of French influence was manifest in the persons of two Free French Marine sergeants who lived in one of the small buildings in the compound, whose messages to their superiors went out over the Camp Five radio via NKN Chungking and whose mysterious and lengthy absences were never explained. Doing something in Indochina? Ian wondered. He now understood the presence of French uniforms at his interview with CNO that Sunday months ago.

The Indo-Chinese influence revealed itself in Wallace's house-boy, an Annamese named Nien. Supplied by the Tai Li organization, Nien would see to Ian's needs—and probably report on my shortcomings, Wallace thought. Nien spoke Cantonese, some French, Viet, some Japanese and a little English. He was a slight boy of eighteen with sharp features and without the pronounced Oriental fold at the eyes. He told Ian that his cousin had been taken by the Japanese and was a servant of the general who ran the Haikou prison camp on Hainan Island. Ian had been told that Hainan was known as the Devil's Island of China before the war, a place of exile, the edge of the earth, harboring wild tribesmen, snakes, bugs and evil spirits. What must it be like now?

Ian and Nien conversed in a workable combination of French, sign language and pidgin English. Nien taught Wallace and Wells a smattering of Japanese, military terms mostly. He was a pleasant boy and had mysterious connections that sometimes produced interesting surprises. Most rewarding of the surprises was the Tonkin beer that he procured for the Americans. How the beer got out of Indochina he would not say. He kept it cool for them in the huge bathhouse water jug.

Wallace was pleased to have command, but quickly realized that the responsibilities were irksome. Too much paperwork. Too many trivial bickerings to deal with. Inability of the Chinese to keep a schedule. Arguments with Chungking about supplies and transport. Arguments with the Air Transport Command about tonnage into Nanning. New officers to integrate into the unit, Doctor (Lt. j.g.) Louis Boyd, USNR, and Second Lieutenant Ted Wise, USMCR.

Doc turned out to be a great addition and demonstrated his savvy by not pretending to know it all. Ian overheard Doc asking Corpsman Pagani for advice and suggestions, after which Pagani became Doc's biggest supporter.

Wise, on the other hand, thought he was smarter than a tree full of owls and got off on the wrong foot with Fugakis and Samonov, who knew more about weapons and training Chinese than Wise did. Wallace solved that one by asking Wells, a recognized "old China hand," to make a few tactful suggestions to the enlisted men. The men set up a couple of situations that were beyond Wise and then bailed him out without loss of face in front of the Chinese.

The fifteen hundred Chinese recruits were under the command of a General Chen, who never showed up. The general's work was done by Colonel Tseng, a bright, sharp, attractive young man, a graduate of Whampoa, Chiang's Chinese military academy, and the French military academy at St. Cyr, who spoke French and some English. He and Wallace got along famously, except for the lateness of the pings for all training exercises.

The operations officer of the Nanning Air Base was a Texan, a first lieutenant about Ian's age, who shared his frustrations with Ian over beer during evening get-togethers. His name was Tod Thompson and they became good friends.

Camp Five's weapons and demolitions arrived, and Thompson donated some trucks to help deliver the crates from the air strip to the Navy compound. When Thompson saw crates of granular TNT and rolls of Primacord being thrown off the trucks, he said to Wallace, "I'll relieve you of some of that when I have to blow my strip."

"You think they'll come?" asked Wallace.

"They'll come."

Wells couldn't find the blasting caps that were listed on the manifest, and they had to radio Calcutta via Chungking for more. In reply they were told that caps had been packed in the TNT powder in crate number ten. Wells and Wallace almost fainted.

On Thompson's suggestion Ian had slit trenches dug on the compound grounds. While the bombing of Nanning had been sporadic before, the Fourteenth Air Force expected that hostile Japanese air activity would increase in support of the Ichigo campaign.

Wallace fumed over the need to prepare twice-monthly War Diary reports covering personnel, intelligence, plans and operations, supplies (an inventory of everything, including the amount of ammunition delivered, expended and on hand, by caliber), military situation, transportation, communications, radio intercept, aerology, medical and health, finances—nine pages, typed just so.

It also galled him to be the only officer to work the little coding machine... both encoding and decoding. It took several hours each day.

These duties prevented him from being in the field observing training exercises as much as he wanted to be, and he had only a second-hand feel for how things were progressing. He was uncomfortable with how the war was progressing in the China theater, however.

On Sunday, June 18, Changsha had fallen. Where had the Tiger of Changsha gone? Yet on July 9, Marines had wiped out the last resistance on Saipan. On Tuesday, August 8, Hengyang fell to the Japanese, despite a heroic effort by General Hsueh's Tenth Army with no support from Chiang or Stilwell. But on August 25, the Allies liberated Paris. He felt he was truly on the other side of the world, and his side was rapidly turning upside down.

Japanese air raids on the Nanning strip increased in frequency, occurring nightly when the sky was clear. The Japs simply found the bend in the river and dropped their eggs next to it. Couldn't miss. The local power company, which still provided electricity after dark, would signal ching pao by dimming the lights. Once for alert. Twice for on the way. Three times and out until after the all clear. The men would sit in their slit trenches and slap at mosquitos, hoping no stray bombs would find them. Wallace was beginning to quiver again, but attributed it to the ceaseless dysentery that was causing all hands to lose weight.

One late evening after a prolonged raid that had sent up great columns of fire from the air strip fuel dumps, Wallace sought a little comfort from his Bible and couldn't find it among his manuals and training materials. Idiot! he said to himself. Have you taken on the God of War and forsaken the God of your fathers?

On September 3 the Allies liberated Brussels, and on September 12 the first Allied units crossed the German border near Luxembourg. On Friday, September 15, the Americans had to blow up their air base at Kweilin. On September 20 the commanding general of the Chinese Ninety-third Army, which had been sent to the defense of Kweilin and whose troops had done more looting than fighting, was executed by the Kuomintang.

Receipt of stateside mail was rare, and Wallace yearned for word from Diana. In her last letter she said she had moved from the Gayety to a smaller apartment on Kalorama Road. Ian had been sending his letters to her new address. He wondered if they got there.

One evening he was decoding a clutter of radio messages, not reading the tape as it came from the hand-operated Haggelin machine, and he felt a strange prickling at the base of his scalp. He stopped turning the little crank and ran the tape through his fingers. There was a message addressed to him personally from the Chief of Naval Operations. It offered the Navy's condolences on the loss of his brother, Peter! The next message in line was the usual "We regret to inform you... killed in action... northern France..." Some idiot in Chungking had messed up the message queue. What a way to find out. He felt numb and tried to pray without much success. What do you say except the trite phrases that have been said so many millions of times in this war? But he felt enormously diminished, hollow-chested and guilty. Where are you Peter Wallace? Where are you Dick Lewis? Where are you Avery Cooper? Are you at the right hand of God?

Chungking told him the military situation was deteriorating and asked if he could speed up his training schedule and the issuing of arms to Column Five. More of an order than a question, so they doubled up on training schedules.

Wallace noticed the beginnings of civilian flight from Nanning as he was driving to visit Thompson at the air strip. More merchants had shuttered their shops. Fewer vendors were at the roadside. People with bundles of household goods were trotting along the shoulders of the rough unpaved dirt road to the west. He asked Thompson what he knew and was told that Thompson had been ordered to prepare to blow his installations. Thompson said that if he just waited long enough the Japanese Air Force would destroy the whole place for him. Wallace promised him five thousand feet of Primacord, and Thompson said he had something special with which to pay for it.

When Wallace delivered the reels Thompson gave him something guaranteed to answer the question they all got in the mail from their buddies in other theaters: "Is it true what they say about Chinese women?" He was handed an eight-by-ten photograph of a young Chinese woman, naked from the waist up; the photo had been retouched by the Thirty-fifth Photo Recon Squadron lab so that the woman's mouth was vertical instead of horizontal.

The Japanese advanced westward from Kwangtung into Kwangsi, headed for Nanning, and Wallace sent Wise and an interpreter with a Chinese detachment up the Yung River to Poseh to scout a new location for Column Five. The American unit was reduced to a skeleton crew after Wallace had men flown out to Kunming through arrangements brought off by Thompson. Ian, Doc, Wells, Steger, Fugakis and Samanov stayed behind to wind things up before returning to Camp Two. The Japanese were closing on Liuchow, and the Americans hoped to get out before communications and the road were cut.

Nien came to him and said that his cousin had appeared from Hainan. His cousin said that the American pilot prisoners at Haikou camp might be sent north by train, depending on how the war went. Wallace asked to talk with the boy and learned that not only did the lad understand Japanese, but was able to read and had read the characters on a contingency plan. Hostages, he said. The Japanese wanted hostages in the homeland, and the safest way to get them there was by rail on the mainland. The seas were now too dangerous.

How could one find out when the train was to leave? Nien replied that there were ways, many spies, like the aircraft warning net. Wallace doubted that anyone in the Chinese military establishment would give a hoot to risk lives to free foreign devil prisoners, but got excited at the thought of perhaps being able to do something useful after all.

"Who can tell me about the train? Where it will be? When it leaves? Where it's headed?"

The boys looked at each other and jabbered in Cantonese. Then Nien turned to Wallace and said, "Tai Li."

Colonel Tseng and his officers wanted to give a banquet for the remaining Americans to thank them for their training and the arms they had been issued. The colonel asked Ian if he and his compatriots would like to visit the Flower Boats on the river for a special Kwangtungese dinner as guests of the Chinese officers. Wallace thanked the colonel, and a date was set.

They drove through a rainy dusk to the gray building on the river bank, where Colonel Tseng waited for them. He led them down the slippery wide flight of stone steps to the floating dock, on each side of which were tied carved mahogany and teak boats with high-rising sterns and paper lanterns. They followed the colonel across a gangplank into a brightly lit room that ran the length and width of the boat. The room was dominated by a long table surrounded by silk covered chairs, two deep. The table was laden with fruits, wine carafes, wine cups. New *k'uai tzu,* chopsticks, were at each place.

The fifteen Chinese officers were spaced out, standing behind every other chair and all hollered "Hao! Hao!" as the Americans entered. Ian and his crew were seated between the Chinese officers, and no sooner had they sat down than a group of Chinese girls in silken robes buttoned to the neck, slit to the hips and sleeveless, came in, and one stood behind each man. They carried cruets of hot *mao tai* wine.

"Your *tai piau,*" Tseng said, pointing to the girl behind Wallace who poured Ian a cup of hot wine.

"What's a tai piau?" Ian asked.

"Like a representative or a servant. She will serve you. She will feed you if you like. She will also drink your toasts if you desire."

That sounded like a great idea to Wallace, who recognized the danger of Chinese toasting. *"Kan pei!"* was the rule. Dry cup. And when someone proposed a toast to you it was required that you drink with him. The Americans were outnumbered by the Chinese officers by more than two to one. He'd need his tai piau.

"Additionally, your lady will perform any other service you may fancy," Tseng pointed out. *"Une fille d'ésprit, compagne de voyage, fille de soir. Une coccinelle.*"

Orioles and swallows ready to spread grace and favor, to make clouds and rain, Ian understood. He looked at his tai piau. Dark, short, straight hair. Fair, clear skin. Good teeth. Deep brown eyes and a pretty smile. About five feet two. A child? Looks cute, he thought. Then he remembered what Wells had told him about the little white card he carried in his wallet. When you hold the card up next to the skin of a Chinese girl and they are the same color, it's time to go home. He chuckled, for the first time in days.

The food came in great platters and bowls, course after course. They were served *hsiang su ya tzu* (fried duck), *la tzu chi ting* (diced chicken with pepper), *pai chi kuei yu* (Mandarin fish with white sauce), *ch'uan chi yu t'ang* (carp soup—Ian gagged a little), *hai yu niu jou* (sliced beef with oyster sauce—Wells wondered where the oysters came from), *ku lao ju* (sweet and sour boneless pork), *chia ch'ang tou fu* (fried bean curd with mushrooms and onions), *hsia tzu ch'un sun* (bamboo shoots with shrimp eggs), *feng kua tung ku t'ang* (chicken feet soup with mushrooms) and hot white rice wine. Ian shunned the chicken feet and showed off by eating greasy peanuts with his chopsticks, one at a time. The toasts were endless, and Ian didn't want to lose face, so he drank every other one. At one point he asked his tai piau for her cup, but she wouldn't let him smell it. She's drinking hot water, he thought. And probably the Chinese men are, too. An old trick. He looked at Wells, who winked at him and slowly poured his drink into the fish when no one was looking.

Fugakis and Samanov were feeling no pain. "When're we gonna fuck?" shouted Fugakis, the diplomat.

"Whadideye tell ya, Lieutenant," hollered Samanov. "Headed for the clap shack for sure!" He slapped Ian on the shoulder and his tai piau on the rump and swayed off the gangplank and up the steps with her to the gray building at the top of the bank. Others followed, Chinese, Americans and tai piaus. Wells was last, and Wallace hadn't yet risen. Ian's tai piau stood behind him massaging his neck.

"You stayin' here, parson?" asked Wells. "Probably better than doin' it on them stone *kangs* up there."

Asa left with his girl, and Wallace was alone with a woman-child who would do whatever he might wish. He was a little addle-headed, but resisted when the girl tried to pull him toward the gangplank. He woozily understood that it was a matter of face for her, loss of face if she didn't satisfy her client.

He also woozily understood that it was loss of face for him if his men didn't think he performed. Instead of going down the gangplank and up the steps to the hard stone kangs, he led her to the rear deck, a sort of porch with a railing and roof. Two silken chairs and a table with a bowl of seeds beckoned him. He sat down and waved his arm at the other seat. The girl sat down in his lap, sliding her silk behind into his privates and her arm around his neck. Sweet Jesus! What do I do now, Ian wondered, as flushed desire struggled with chaste conscience.

The girl put her tongue in his ear, and he reacted and squirmed. Oh, the lips of a strange woman drop as a honeycomb, and her mouth is smoother than oil! Then she took seeds from the little bowl and began cracking them between her teeth, blowing out the hulls. She cracked a dozen of them, looked at Ian and smiled. Then she kissed him on the lips and tongued seed after seed into his mouth. He chewed them and they were sweet. He put his head back. Stay me with flagons, comfort me with apples, he thought, for I am sick of love.

The tai piau put his hand on her silken gown. He caressed her child-bosom and slid his hand to her stomach. His head rolled and his mind slid. Thy belly is like an heap of wheat set about with lilies and thy two breasts are like two young roes that are twins.

The girl undid his shirt buttons and ran her long fingernails down his chest. Load and lock! She undid the top of his trousers and his fly and trailed her fingers across his belly. Ready on the right, ready on the left, all ready on the firing line!

She pulled his trousers to his feet, knelt between his knees and blew softly on his bobbing stalk. She drifted her nails under his plums. Unlock!

She lowered her head on his lap. His toes tingled and curled, waves of spidery sensation crept up his legs and arms, his belly warmed and fluttered and his soul shivered, his calves tightened, the sensation surged from his belly and his legs and met in the middle. She moved her head. Commence firing!

Ah, he thought dreamily, soaring on the lubricous wave, an exchange of seeds.

The men were pretty raucous on the way back to the compound, but when they got there Doc lined them all up and gave orders in no uncertain terms. There will be a clean sweep-down, fore and aft, he told them, that he would personally oversee. They got their brass basins and soap and lined up at the trough in the bathhouse with their pants around their ankles, washing their genitals.

While washing himself Doc shouted, "Any of you people who went wet decks tonight line up right here at the shrine of Saint Sulfanilamide!"

He waved a silver tube of ointment that three of the lovers used. Wallace wondered if he should use it. What could he catch? Gingivitis? Chinese foot rot? Trench cock? Or the Chinese mocus from the evil demons of the night air? Well he'd had vaccinations for cholera, smallpox, typhoid, typhus, yellow fever and plague, and he decided to sweat out the chances of getting the dread genital fungus. Purge me with hyssop, and I shall be clean; wash me and I shall be white as snow.

He wondered if he was still a cherry. Well, technically he was, anyway. He wondered if he had been faithful to Diana or had he broken another commandment? If so, all I have to do is make graven images and probably I'll have broken them all.

In the morning a letter was delivered to Ian written in Nien's own careful English. Ian read it:

> My lieutenant
>
> I come now for saying good bye to you and your friend, because I have to evacuate Nanning in the brevest delay. Before I hoped to serve you until you leaving Nanning, but the chief of military intendance had locked me out. In serving you, I have made up with you a little beer trade in order to get a small capital after. I have bought these beers 160$ a bottle, and to my locking out, it remained to me 120 bottles, but now with regard to the order of quickly evacuation of Nanning there is a great crack of prices. Under the present order of evacuation, I am no money presently, because all I have was been plant in beer trade. So, I pray you and your friend to help me by buying my beer at the price which seems convenient to you. So making, you help me very much.
> Sincerely Your obliged.

Wallace went in search of his house-boy and found that the local militia was outside the gates sending the Chinese servants and cooks away shouting that they must leave Nanning.

Colonel Tseng was no help when Ian went to thank him for the previous evening. He told Ian to forget it, Nien was pulling a fast one. Probably didn't have any beer. Just trying to get some American money, playing on their well-known charity. Ian thanked him but felt bad. He wanted to believe Nien and pay for the beer, but there was no way. And he wanted to believe in Nien's cousin's train.

Wells and Wallace took five cases of unissued TNT and the few remaining reels of Primacord to the air strip and gave them to Tod Thompson in exchange for three fifty-five-gallon drums of hundred-octane gasoline. The base was nearly deserted. Bomb craters pocked the runway, buildings were smashed, revetments blown away. Aircraft carcasses had been pulled to the side of the runway to make room for the transports that were evacuating personnel and equipment. Fighter missions were still being flown, but Thompson didn't know how long that would last. Everybody was getting itchy.

Wallace and Wells wished Thompson *"Bon chance"* and drove the jeep and quarter-ton trailer back to the compound. With the other Americans they loaded their 6x6 truck and the jeep trailer with everything but their bedding and the big radio. They endured a very heavy air raid that night, bombs spraying everywhere, some landing in the compound on barracks the Chinese had moved out of that day when they left for Poseh.

In the morning they ran their regular radio schedule with Nan King Nan, Chungking, broke down the radio, stowed it in the 6x6 and joined the stream of Chinese refugees fleeing the city.

"Haven't we done something like this before?" Wallace asked Wells.

"Bet your ass," said Wells from behind the wheel of the jeep. "I'd sure as hell like to be someplace else."

"If you could be anyplace in the world, Asa, right now, where would you want to be?"

"In Maine. Down in my barn."

"What would you do if you were down in your barn?"

"Why, I'd go up to the house and go to bed."

They left Nanning on October 4, while the war on fronts in other parts of the world was being won. Since the start of Ichigo in April the Chinese and the

Fourteenth Air Force had been unable to stop Japanese General Shunroku Hata's fifteen divisions and five independent brigades from taking most of eight provinces, a population of one hundred million and the last lines of communication to the coast, and killing half a million soldiers in the process. Ichigo's momentum and the Chinese military's inability or lack of desire to stem it, by committing well-equipped troops guarding the Communists in the north, made one wonder if the Japanese army might settle on the mainland for good even if the home islands were lost.

The road to Liuchow was a hundred miles of dust, bullock carts, water buffalos and southbound refugees. The Americans blew the horn and shouted for room on the narrow track.

They spent the first night at a little roadside hamlet called Pinyang, planning to sleep in the vehicles. There was constant murmur and rumble and shouting as crowds of refugees passed through or thrashed in their sleep by the side of the road. Wallace eased himself out of the truck before dark and stretched his legs. He was surprised to see a small building with a sign in English: China Inland Mission, Bridgeman Chapel. He went to the door, and before he knocked he could hear a voice speaking inside. He carefully pushed open the wooden door and found himself in the rear of a small chapel. There were a half-dozen rows of benches, four Chinese sitting on them, a white lady seated in the front and a pinch-nosed, white-haired man in a loose fitting blue Chinese gown preaching in Kwangtung-hua from a little pulpit.

Wallace seated himself at the back. He couldn't understand the dialect but picked up occasional references to Jesus. He studied the faded painting of Jesus wearing his crown of thorns on the wall behind the missionary. Eventually all hands said "Amen," and the white lady fired up a little pedal-operated harmonium and she and the preacher sang "In Christ There Is No East or West" in Chinese while the congregation stood silent.

At the end of the hymn the preacher held up his hand and pronounced a benediction in the native tongue, and the Chinese scurried out the side door. The missionary and the lady came to the back of the chapel and stopped in front of Wallace. Ian thought the minister looked as if he smelled something bad and couldn't find it. The expression on the lady's wrinkled face was blank.

"Are you Reverend... ah... Bridgeman?" Wallace inquired, remembering the name of the chapel.

"Bridgeman! My name's Wesley, an unfortunate name for a Presbyterian. Bridgeman! Don't you know who Bridgeman was?"

You don't even know who I am, thought Wallace, and you're asking me riddles. "No, sir, I don't, but apparently I should."

"I don't know what else you can expect from riff-raff and soldiers," said Reverend Wesley and turned to the woman. "Go see that those heathen don't ruin the meal." Ye servants of God your master proclaim! thought Wallace.

The woman shuffled off. "My wife," said Wesley, "and who might you be?"

"Just a man going from Jerusalem to Jericho," Ian replied.

"Well, I recognize the reference but I can't play the Samaritan. Hardly enough food for me and my wife, let alone our four servants. You'll have to find succor elsewhere."

"Perhaps my unit could spare some food for you, and transportation to a safer place," Ian said.

"The Lord will provide," said Wesley, cocking his head back and looking at Wallace down his nose.

"The work of the Lord is done through man," Ian replied.

"Don't you presume to preach to me! I've been here for forty years, and the *Lord* will protect *my* going out and *my* coming in!"

"Well, sir, I thank you for your hospitality." Ian started to leave and then turned and asked Wesley, "Who is Bridgeman?"

"Who is Bridgeman! Elijah Bridgeman founded this mission in 1829 for the American Board of Commissioners for Foreign Missions. That's who Bridgeman is!"

"Thank you for telling me," said Ian. Then he couldn't resist saying, "Your congregation probably has your meal ready."

But Reverend Wesley hardly heard, for he was already headed for the side door.

Well, Ian told himself, I know who Bridgeman was, but I am nameless for that missionary. I hope, at least, my name is in the book of life.

Forty years. Four "converts." Servants. Rice Christians. Wallace was depressed. He climbed back in the truck, made a place for himself and tried to go to sleep. He couldn't take his mind off the missionary. How could a man profess the Christian faith and be so inhospitable and mean of mind? What kept him here? What will happen to him and his wife when the Japanese come? Certainly his four converts will skedaddle. I'd better go back in the morning and force him and his wife on the truck. I'll tell him I'm God.

At daylight Ian and Wells went to the mission and found it empty. The harmonium and the painting of Christ had disappeared from the chapel. The little manse in the compound by the side door was empty. The mud stove in the cook room was cold.

"God beat us to it," Wells said to Ian.

The trip took three dusty, hot days, and they arrived at the American air base at Liuchow towing the jeep and trailer. The jeep's gear box was gone.

They were assigned to the barracks set aside for transients, but spent most of three nights in slit trenches outside while the Japanese bombed the base incessantly. Wallace got so frustrated that he emptied his .45 at the sky.

Their last message in Nanning had told them to go to the new Camp Two location, Chenyuan in Kweichow Province some hundred fifty miles west of evacuated Hungkiang. As he and Wells walked to the base transportation office to see about gasoline, Wallace wondered if it would ever be worth unpacking his gear again.

No gas available, he was told, and besides, the roads north to Tuyun and Kweiyang were hardly passable—ditched—choked with refugees, retreating Chinese soldiery, bandits and fifth columnists who were spreading fire and panic along the route.

While Wells watched and listened, Ian argued, cajoled and threatened until the transportation office gave in and gave Wallace a chit for his vehicles and arranged a little space on a rail car for Ian's unit. Steger turned his radio over to the Air Corps, they collected what they could carry and were trucked to the Liuchow railhead, a phantasmagoria of screaming peasants, bicycles, wheelbarrows, soldiers, bullocks, ponies and yelling Chinese minor officials.

They shoe-horned their way onto their car and watched as refugees climbed on the car roofs, clung to the car sides, hung between the carriages and underneath on the wheel frames, even tried to climb on the engine's hot boiler. Ragged, shouting, shoving refugees with their pitiful goods wrapped in straw climbed on the engine cab roof and the coal car. They sat precariously on the narrow steel walkplates over the drive wheels and on the cowcatcher. Ragged Chinese soldiers beat civilians for space, and finally some armed pings went to the locomotive cab and ordered the engineer to start, over the objections of the distraught, screaming stationmaster. The soldiers summarily shot the stationmaster and pitched his body from the train. The great Skoda engine chuffed, spun its wheels and then slowly started north.

The train ride was another nightmare, worse by far than their trip south on the same line months ago. They were stopped by crowds at each village, and the soldiers would throw poor peasants off the train to be replaced by those who could afford exorbitant fees. They were stopped by bandits, and a fire-fight erupted between the soldiers on the train and the ragged brigands who had thrown logs across the tracks. Dozens of passengers were killed before the bandits were wiped out, the logs removed and the train resumed its crawling journey. Dozens of other passengers were killed when the train traversed the first tunnel. The screams of the crushed and falling refugees could be heard above the clacking of the wheels and the confined huffing of the engine. The cars emerged into daylight, and after the smoke had cleared from the car the Americans saw blood dripping from the frames of the glass-less windows.

Three days later they fought their way off the train at Tuyun and found the 6x6 Camp Two had sent for them. It had been waiting for two days and was about to depart. McInerny, whom Ian remembered from Chungking, was at the wheel.

"Where the fuck you people been? On some goddam joy ride?"

Wallace stepped to the running board on the driver's side, reached in with both hands and grabbed the surprised McInerny by the shirt front, yanked him out and hurled him to the dirt.

"Take your own goddam joy ride," Ian said pointing to the train, getting in and firing up the engine, while his men cheered and threw their gear in the back of the truck. McInerny tried to climb aboard but the men laughed and pushed him back down as Wallace put the truck in gear and started to move ahead. In panic McInerny ran through the dust after the truck, choking and yelling. Wallace slowed enough to let McInerny reach the back of the truck where hands pulled him roughly over the steel tailgate.

"Tell you sumpin', Mac," Wells said. "It don't do to fuck around with this one-eared lieutenant. I and him have sojered together for a while and took some shit, and I can tell you that smart-ass motor mechanics get him up tight... tight as a bull's ass in fly time and twice as mean. Better remember that." The rest of the unit laughed, and McInerny spat dust over the tailgate.

They reached Chenyuan after dark, climbed the long stone steps to the compound on the hilltop and checked in with Pearson. Wallace thanked his men for being a damn good professional bunch with whom he was proud to serve, and went to find Fix and flake out.

They had arrived in Chenyuan on Friday, November 3. On Friday, November 10, Liuchow fell.

To undertake executions for the master executioner (Heaven)
is like hewing wood for the master carpenter.
Whoever undertakes to hew wood for the master carpenter
rarely escapes injuring his own hands.

— Lao-Tzu
The Way of Lao-Tzu

HUNAN 1945

DIANA BLISS LET HERSELF INTO HER APARTMENT and turned on the little lamp on the entrance hall table. It shed its weak pink glow on the small silver tray where the cleaning woman had put the little pile of mail, picked up from under the slot in the door. Diana didn't notice it as she looked at herself in the oval gold-edged mirror over the table. The light from the lamp below was flattering. She looked radiantly lovely and felt that way. Her blue eyes were bright, her color was high from the chill November wind she had struggled against from the trolley to the door, her red hair was becomingly windblown. She had had a grand evening, sharing it with Daniel Bensen and some of his shipmates and their girls. Since resigning his House seat to accept his commission in the Navy, Bensen had been three months at sea on a light cruiser in the North Atlantic with fairly frequent calls at East Coast ports where Diana could meet him. He was now passing through Washington on his way to new construction on the West Coast.

Any uneasiness Diana and Daniel might have felt had been dispelled promptly months before, when Diana had said, "thank you for your help and thoughtfulness," the morning following their night together. Fortunately she had not found herself in a "delicate condition" the month that followed. It had been either all business during his last two days in office or warm, affectionate friendship on the occasions when they were together socially. Their letters to each other were newsy and cordial, devoted but not intimate. The only discomfort Diana experienced during the evening had been at Union Station when she bade Bensen good-bye as he boarded the train for California. Diana had a sense of deja vu as she remembered a similar scene way, way back in January.

Remembering Ian's departure brought her a little pang. She should be writing him more. But the demands of her job with the Deputy Assistant Secretary of the Navy and the socializing she had been doing with Bensen when he was in port or with Ben Bickford, the CBI pilot now stationed at Andrews Air Base outside D.C., and with the men at *l'Abri* when Bensen was at sea occupied most of her time. In her mind-of-her-own way she saw nothing wrong with going out with these men. They were good friends. Oh, sure, there was a little kissy-facey and huggy-body, but nobody ever really tried anything. It was camaraderie. They respected her relationship with Wallace. Her arms-length affection for Bensen was known only to Diana and Daniel.

She knew her activities stole time she might have otherwise spent writing to Ian more frequently, but in her new position she had been able to uncover a considerable amount of information about U.S. Naval Group China and knew how impossible it was for Wallace to get mail for very, very long periods of time. She supposed she rationalized her relatively infrequent letters by the fact that Ian would only get mail every three months or so. And that was about the time that elapsed between letters from Ian to her.

She'd also learned what Ian was doing and had been relieved that no combat or danger seemed to be involved, until a recent memo which crossed Duval's desk indicated that SACO Americans would soon be allowed and urged to fight. That worried her.

She also worried about the internecine struggle between Naval Group and the OSS, and other commands as well… Fourteenth Air Force, ATC (Air Transport Command), the American theater commander, and the Chinese Army and bureaucracy that moved like molasses in January. She thought congressional politics were pretty heady and enjoyed the game involved. There was a certain amount of name calling, but that bounced off politicians' thick skins like so much rainwater. The politics of the military at war, however, the interservice rivalries, were shocking. She did not consider herself naive, but the infighting had been news to her.

Diana was dismayed to learn that the OSS-SACO marriage of convenience had fallen apart. OSS coveted SACO's supplies flown over the Hump and wanted to use them as inducements to get quicker Chinese action in conjunction with OSS operations. The OSS tried to dilute the value of intelligence gathered by SACO and the Tai Li organization, feeling that the U.S. should gather and evaluate intelligence on its own. The new OSS unit AGFRTS (Air and Ground Forces Resources and Technical Staff), organized as a part of the Fourteenth Air Force, was in competition with Naval Group in supplying intelligence, setting up activities behind enemy lines, providing targets and rescuing pilots.

U.S. Theater Commander Vinegar Joe Stilwell hated the Naval Group for its independence and wanted the Group to report to him. More frequently than not SACO supply shipments over the Hump were diverted, delayed or "lost" and complaints to the theater commander fell on deaf ears.

Even in Washington the Army and the Navy were tilting over Naval Group China. The Army couldn't seem to understand why it was necessary for the Navy to have armed Americans ashore on the Asian mainland.

Diana hoped that Ian, in the field, was unaware of what transpired on the home front and in the rear areas. It was enough for the men in the field to worry about themselves let alone to wonder what was happening at command levels.

Now Diana looked down at her mail, and the top letter made her heart do a little roll-over. The letter was dated in mid-August and the "passed by Naval Censor" stamp bore Ian Wallace's initials. Diana wondered whether that was cricket, to censor your own mail. But then, his few letters were always circumspect, and Diana could only imagine where he might be and what he was doing. She carried the mail into the kitchenette and sat at the dinette under the overhead light. She took a deep breath and opened Ian's letter, wondering again why she was almost afraid to look. Was it because she was beginning to notice a shortening of Ian's patience, a loss of forgiveness and an unwillingness to search for understanding of cultures new to him? What had happened to tolerance? There seemed to be an edge, a shrillness, sometimes a stridency, creeping into his comments. His desire for retribution for Japanese behavior seemed thinly masked.

This letter told her that he was fairly well, though he had lost a little weight. He said he had seen a lot more of the country (this was underlined) than he had expected to and that his legs and lungs were great. His ability to speak Mandarin was improving, though he felt much more comfortable in the company of a reliable interpreter. He recognized a few of the ideographs, of which, his interpreter told him, the cultured man knew at least thirty-five thousand. He joked about being unlettered in this part of the world. The letter became more anecdotal as he related some of the escapades of Asa Wells and Fix O'Reilly, and his growing fondness for the two men showed through.

He cautioned her that the mail might be interrupted for a spell longer than usual and said he hoped to make the hiatus worth the effort. The one thing that kept him going, he said, were his memories and dreams of her. Not his God, nor anyone's god, anymore. Her.

Diana was shocked. Was this the philosopher? The student of religions? The minister-to-be?

These musings about his innermost feelings were revelations with which he should not have burdened her. She was burdened enough sharing her affections, however chaste, with Bensen and with Wallace. Ian could not know the astonishing burden Diana felt.

The cold gray days of November settled in on the Chenyuan camp. The NAVU compound, one long two-story barracks-like stone building and one old school assembly hall, sat high above the village at the top of a long flight of stone steps, the only flat place for miles. The village of perhaps fifty dwellings shouldered itself between the little river and the precipitous mountainside, sending its blue charcoal smoke slowly into the fog and low cloud that continually shrouded the peaks and ravines. It was damp. There were no troops to train. The little roadside town afforded few diversions, except for the Peach Blossom barbershop/bath house and two open-fronted restaurants that catered to the occasional passers-by. It was rumored that one could get laid at the barbershop. One of the sailors, Hartley, came down with the clap and was confined to quarters, proof that a determined man could find it if he looked hard enough.

The same man subsequently went over the wall one night and was reported by a Tai Li guard to be in the village doing it again. Wells and Wallace were detailed to bring the man back and went to the barbershop where Wells spoke with the *lao pan*.

"We seek the American who makes the two-backed beast," Wells said. "He is unwell, and we take him to the doctor."

"Well enough to pay and perform despite the weeping willow," said the proprietor. "He pays for his privacy."

"He'll be paying for something else," Wallace said to Wells, "if we don't get him out of here."

"Then we, too, pay," said Wells to the barber, and cash changed hands.

The lao pan showed them to a dark, evil-smelling room with damp straw on the dirt floor, where two pockmarked women sat on heated stone beds. Another small room to the side was shielded by a thin gray cloth at the door that provided only visual privacy. Grunts and groans came from inside. Wells went to the door and flung aside the cloth. Hartley was lying on the heated kang, pants at his feet, being ridden by a woman who had rucked her padded garment up to her waist. Hartley's eyes were closed, and he grunted as he thrust with his hips. Sweat ran down his face.

Wells grabbed the woman and pulled her off. Hartley opened his eyes and shouted, "Fer Chrissakes, Gunny, I ain't even finished! Goddamit, git outa here and git yer own!"

"You are finished, you shankered swab jocky. Pull up your damn pants and come on. You keep doin' this and you'll get so damn weak you won't even be able to push a sick whore off a pisspot!"

Hartley stuffed himself back in his trousers and then saw Wallace. "Jesus Christ, Lieutenant, you ain't gonna put me on report, are ya?" he yelled.

"Keep your voice down, Hartley, and come with us. You are in deep shit."

They escorted Hartley through the dim barbershop, where Asa and the proprietor exchanged politenesses, Asa assuring the barber that Wells and Wallace appreciated the courtesy demonstrated by the establishment and that they would be pleased to return and partake of the bath at some future date.

They took Hartley by the elbows, propelled him up the muddy, rutted street and up the stone steps leading to the compound.

"What'll they do to me, Lieutenant?" Hartley asked.

"If you're lucky they won't have to cut it off," said Wallace. "But I imagine you'll never be able to piss right again unless you learn to play the flute."

Doc told Ian that Hartley was beyond his help and that he'd have to be shipped out to Calcutta for treatment.

"Why do they do it, Doc?" Ian asked.

"Hartley said it. 'Stiff dick don't know no difference.' Some of them never learn. Some of them don't want to learn." Here the doctor paused... "As for me, I'm learning... learning every day that what I was taught in medical school applies to a different time and place. Learning that I have to practice by what little medical judgment I have and by my wits. Helluva school."

Wallace lay in his damp blankets and wondered what he'd learned that would ever stand him in good stead after this war was over. Something about human nature, maybe? Something about cruelty; about poverty; about death; about lust; about fear; about deceit; about disease; about despondency?

"Fix," he asked his bunk mate, "what the hell are we doing? Who the hell are we working for? Why the hell are we here? We train all these people and give them weapons, and then they disappear. What the hell do they do?"

"Aha! Are the scales falling from your eyes?"

"Not like Saul at Damascus; but how much truth is there in the rumors I keep picking up about this lash-up and the rotten bunch we seem to be associated with? And how in God's name will our puny effort make any difference in the great eternal scheme of things?"

"What have you heard." asked Fix.

"Oh, that we serve as a virtual branch of the secret police under Tai Li; that the people we train are used for counter-insurgency work rather than fighting the Japanese; that Stilwell hates Miles's guts because we're independent and don't coordinate with the other services; that we're arming coastal pirates; that we operate a police training school run by former Secret Service and FBI guys with attack dogs—we brought over some dogs on our ship and Mooney was an ex-Secret Service agent. Just enough smoke to suggest fire. What do you think?"

"I've heard a lot of that shit, too; that we're serving a political role to save Chiang's ass; that we're undermining the efforts of the OSS; that we're allies with the Blue Shirts, Tai's assassination goons, smuggling and spreading terror among the guys who oppose the Nationalists."

"Pearson says that the reason Chiang likes Chennault and Miles and not Stilwell is because he's using them to modernize his own organization—his air force and his gestapo. Makes you proud doesn't it?" said Ian.

"But by God," he continued, "I've got to do something! You nor I nor nobody else is going to reform this rotten country, and we can't fight them and their rottenness because they're on our side. But, sure as God made little green apples, I'm going to take a swipe at the Japanese one way or another whether we're allowed in combat or not. I'm going to go after that prisoner train and get those men out."

"If you ever hear of the train again," said Fix. "What did Pearson say about it when you broached the subject?"

"Told me I was full of shit. Said that kind of rumor wasn't hard intelligence and don't be a damned fool."

"Tell you what you do," said Fix, "ask Miles. He's coming here next month. He's so enthusiastic about any action, he'll probably let you go for it. You heard about combat, didn't you?"

"What do you mean?"

"Why, just a couple of weeks ago, mid-October I think, he sent an ALL-SACO message about it. You must have been on the train from Liuchow."

Fix rummaged in his papers and produced a flimsy message copy and handed it to Ian.

Wallace read the radio dispatch; "Permit all American personnel to observe, assist and participate in all types of operations. This is the green light you have been waiting for. Good hunting."

"So we can finally go to war," said Ian.

The Japanese turned north after they took Liuchow and headed up the rail line toward Tuyun and Kweiyang. The Chinese armies disintegrated and fled with the refugees streaming north.

Soldiers raided peasant farms and tore down rafters for firewood to cook by and to get warm, one of the typical reasons the military occupied the bottom rung of the Chinese social ladder beneath the scholars, the farmers, the artisans and the merchants. The countryside was dotted with roofless mud houses, walls standing starkly in the gray landscape.

The weather deteriorated and air missions were rare because of the fog and rain. "Rainin' like a cow pissin' on a flat rock!" said Wells.

There was stage-one panic in Chungking and talk of moving the government to Kunming. But then the weather and the long supply lines brought the Japanese offensive to a halt south of Kweiyang. Nanning's strips had gone, and Chihkiang and Kunming were the only forward air bases left.

The Americans were upset about news of the Battle of the Bulge in Europe starting in the middle of December. It seemed as if the whole Allied effort was in jeopardy. But suddenly their thoughts were centered on another matter. They were told that an operation would be mounted against the Japanese in Hunan Province after the first of the year. Americans would accompany members of the Fourth Column on a two-pronged raid. Miles, now a commodore, would explain it all when he arrived. The camp buzzed with anticipation.

Good God, thought Ian. Everybody knows about this. The barber. The whores. The shopkeepers. The peasants. The Japanese.

"Hey! Pagani! You got a Bible?" Corpsman Pagani looked up to see Chief Motor Machinist's Mate Treviso standing in the door of his cramped quarters.

"What the hell you want with my Bible, anyway?" Pagani asked.

"Some of us asked Lieutenant Pearson about a Christmas Eve service, and he said to ask Lieutenant Wallace to do it. Only the lieutenant don't got his Bible anymore. Lost it in Nanning. He says 'You find me a Bible, I'll do a little service.' So how about it? You gonna let the lieutenant borrow your Book?"

"Jesus Christ!" said Pagani.

"That's right," said Treviso. "His birthday. You gonna do it?"

"Yeah," said Pagani, and searched through his gear. He came up with a well-worn King James version, heavily thumbed at "The Song of Solomon."

"Tell him not to drop it in the mud," he said throwing the volume to the chief.

"What a sweetheart," snorted Treviso, and stumped off to find Wallace.

The ingenuity displayed by the men amazed Wallace, Fix, the doctor and Pearson. The men took over the "dining hall" and wouldn't let the officers help or tell them what was going on. All that Wells and Treviso would say was that the officers would see what the men had been up to at Christmas Eve service. They also said they were rigging up a Christmas dinner for Christmas day. Real stateside chow.

After the second, and last, meal of the day on Sunday, December 24, most of the enlisted men disappeared into the hall carrying various objects hidden under blankets or shrouded in crude brown Chinese paper. Wallace went to his room to brush up his remarks, re-read the lesson from Luke and memorize the prayer he had laboriously constructed, without really having his heart in it, but with a lot of help from Ecclesiastes. He finally closed his eyes and said out loud, "I have been remiss in my worship and my thoughts. I have violated Thy commandments. I have sinned without caring. Whoever You are, I'd appreciate it if You would make me worthy enough this evening to help the men feel something of the spirit of this time, to help burnish their memories of years past and families at home, to help them reveal to themselves the fiber and inner strength they must call up in the days ahead and to cast off the contempt they feel for so many of the people of the world who are not like them."

He opened his eyes and then closed them again and said, "Amen."

At 2330 the men met the officers at the door to the hall. Ian could sense an air of anticipation as he approached the group. They were like children in their eagerness to show accomplishments to their parents.

"Merry Christmas, Asa," Ian said with his hand out, and then shook hands and exchanged greetings with all the men. Then the men led the officers into the hall. Ian stopped dead in his tracks. Rough chairs had been arranged in rows, with an aisle down the middle. A box with a blanket over it had been put on a blanket-covered table at the end of the aisle and the Bible rested on this altar. Two small candles burned on either side of the box, and a carefully constructed packing-crate wooden cross hung from the ceiling behind the box. In each window a saucer of tung oil supported a tiny flickering wick. Red and white paper streamers went from rafter to rafter. Evergreen sprays were over the windows and a wreath of bamboo fronds with a red cloth ribbon was at the door. And at each end of the table stood a Christmas tree decorated with twisted Primacord garlands, small cloth bows of Chinese fabric, little paper lanterns and C-ration can tops cut into stars and angels. Ian wondered if he'd be able to speak.

The officers were shown to seats in the front row as some men found seats and others genuflected and crossed themselves before sitting down. Lieutenant Pearson opened the service with thoughtful remarks about bridging the miles between here and home with our thoughts and hoping that next year we'd all be with our loved ones. Then he asked Wallace to do the lesson and prayer.

Ian stood behind the box and thought, what a hell of a place for an incipient agnostic to be. Me, who wanted to be a minister, now a doubter, conducting my first service. He read from the Book of Luke, chapter 2, verses 1 through 19: *"And it came to pass in those days, that there went out a decree from Caesar Augustus, that all the world should be taxed."*

By the time he got to *"And suddenly there was with the angel a multitude of the heavenly host praising God, and saying, Glory to God in the highest, and on earth peace, good will toward men,"* he wondered how he was doing and looked up to see that rapt attention being given to the words by his small audience.

He finished at verse 19 saying, *"'But Mary kept all these things, and pondered them in her heart.'* Let us pray."

There was a shuffling in the group as some men bowed their heads and others knelt in front of their seats. Ian noticed Chief Tobias ('God is Good,' in Hebrew) standing at the rear, uncomfortable and feeling out of place.

Ian began: "Dear Lord, *'to every thing there is a season, and a time to every purpose under heaven; a time to be born, and a time to die* (not yet, he hoped); *a time to plant, and a time to pluck up that which is planted; a time to kill* (let that cup pass from me, he said to himself), *and a time to heal* (do you hear that doctor?); *a time to break down* (not in front of this bunch), *and a time to build up; a time to weep* (how can you help it when you see the state of Thy world), *and a time to laugh* (we need more of that); *a time to mourn* (what good does it do?), *and a time to dance; a time to cast away stones, and a time to gather stones together; a time to embrace, and a time to refrain from embracing* (do you hear that Hartley?); *a time to get, and a time to lose; a time to keep, and a time to cast away; a time to rend, and a time to sew; a time to keep silence, and a time to speak* (even for a hypocrite?); *a time to love, and a time to hate; a time of war, and a time of peace.'*

"Dear Lord, reassure us by the remembrance of the birth of Thy son Jesus that there may be a time when nation shall not rise against nation; when Ye may judge between nations and they shall beat their swords into plowshares and their spears into pruning hooks and nation shall not lift up sword against nation, neither shall they learn war any more. Scatter the peoples that delight in war and trample underfoot those who lust after tribute. Shed forth Thy blessed peace upon us Thy servants and yet endow us with strength so that we may be valiant in the trials to come; make us tolerant of the differences of others as Thy son was tolerant of sinners and of all those who strayed from Thy ways. And may the souls of those of our families and friends who have gone before us or whom we have lost in this war join the company of saints at Thy right hand. *Requiem aeternam dona eis, Domine, et lux perpetua luceat eis*. Grant them eternal rest, O Lord, and let perpetual light shine upon them (this piece for Fix and the other Catholics). Let us remember them in our silent prayers."

Ian paused and peered under his eyelids. All heads were bowed, including Tobias's. He, himself, remembered his family and departed friends with sadness, wondering if their souls were with the saints. "And hear our silent prayers for those dear to us with whom we cannot share this moment, but who are always in our hearts."

Ian thought of Diana, and her image made his chest turn over. He wondered whether he was wishing or hoping or praying about her.

"And teach us to pray as Thy son taught us, saying: *'Our Father, which art in heaven... '* " Ian peered at the men again as they mumbled the prayer, mixing 'debts' and 'trespasses.' He noticed that Tobias had his hat on and was doing a prayer of his own.

" *'...but deliver us from evil; for thine is the kingdom, and the power, and the glory, for ever and ever. Amen'* "

Wallace paused in silence for a moment, then said: *"Sanctus, sanctus, sanctus Dominus Deus Sabaoth. Pleni sunt coeli et terra gloria tua. Hosanna in excelsis.* Holy, holy, holy, Lord God of Hosts. Heaven and earth are full of Thy glory. Glory be to Thee O Lord. Hosanna in the highest. Amen."

As the heads were lifted up, Wallace said, "It hardly seems like Christmas without a carol. Let's all go stand on the steps and sing."

He led them to the steps of the hall and began "Silent Night," and the words and tune were picked up by the others. Their music drifted into the foggy mist. The smell of charcoal smoke and night soil enfolded them. Hardly balsam and pine, thought Ian as he glanced next to him and saw tears coursing down the cheeks of Pagani while he sang. Some of the house-boys and Tai Li soldiers came out of the main building and watched and listened to the quaint barbarian custom. Ian was reminded of a more innocent time at Amherst, when he and his fraternity brothers would sing on the porch in the evening and the traffic would stop to listen.

The men stood in line to thank Ian and wish him a merry Christmas and to say thank you. He felt like a pastor at the church door. A fake parson. Tobias was last and said, "I was glad you used words from the old Bible and not just the new. Hearing words from the *Hagiographa,* The Writings, made me feel more a part of it. And you were courteous to the Catholics, too. Thank you."

"The spirit of the Season of Light, Chief. Happy Hanukkah."

Fix was sitting on his bunk waiting for him when Ian got back to his sack. He was drinking mao tai and spitting some of it at the charcoal *huo pun,* watching it flare up. "You were terrific. You sure you don't want to be a priest?"

"Come on, Fix, knock it off. If that performance made guys feel good, so much the better. It made me feel lousy because I don't know where my head is taking me these days."

"Don't know whether you're a minister or a Marine, right? Whether you're a horse or a tiger, huh? Well I'll tell you something: stop thinking about it in your head and start letting your heart tell you what's right and wrong and don't worry about a jealous God. Do your duty and ask for forgiveness later. I may have been brought up in Codfish Flats and been called a Mackerel Snatcher by the other guys, but we Catholics have it all over you Protestants. We can confess our sins and our doubts and be given absolution. You people are in eternal fire even before you die and go to Hell.

"I'm not much of a Catholic, as I've told you, but I believe that the work of God is done through man and that's the reason we're supposed to propagate the faith. But in the meantime we've got to press on, regardless, so we can get back to the business of spreading the word. And don't forget what Gunnery Sergeant George Daniel Rose said: 'There's always some dumb son of a bitch who don't get the word.' Most of those sonso'bitches seem to be on this side of the world, so we're seeing millions of 'em. Do you think you can remember that, get on with the fucking war and ask for forgiveness later?"

In the dark, chilly room Fix glared at Ian and spat mao tai at the glowing coals, which blazed momentarily, casting flickering shadows on the wet stone walls.

"I'll sure as hell try," said Ian and rolled over on his cot. But he couldn't sleep. He was perplexed in the lonely chambers of his mind and heart. Am I a Christian? Am I working for Fascists? He thought of the sights he had seen on the Siang Kiang in the flight from Shihtan and from Liuchow. His mind wandered through the mazes of Taoism, Confucianism, Buddhism and ancestor worship. He drifted to the Confucian *Analects*, the *Book of Odes, Shih Ching*. What had happened to the humanistic system of ethics? What of loyalty, reciprocity, dutifulness, filial and fraternal affection, courtesy? How about friendship and good faith? Where is the natural moral order that says man fully realizes himself in the perfect fulfillment of his role as subject, father, son, friend, husband? How can we work with a people who were never taught not to tell lies, not even as children? Deceiving people and telling lies are great arts—part of the ancient Chinese technique of rule and of keeping face. But why am I shocked? I was shocked when I learned that the Golden Rule in Jesus' Sermon on the Mount was a paraphrase of Confucius from the *Analects* and Aristotle from *Diogenes Laertius*. And where does the Christian ethic fit in? And where am I, and what am I doing? It *is* hard to kick against the pricks, as Jesus said to Saul in The Acts, and as Aeschylus admonished in "Agamemnon."

For Christmas dinner Treviso had inserted himself in the Chinese kitchen and had baked two large geese in the stone oven, which had previously served as a kang. He also baked sweet potatoes and boiled some Chinese cabbage. Using doughy gray Chinese rice bread, he made croutons in boiling hog fat, sprinkled them with ginger and stuffed the geese with them an hour before the meal to keep them from getting too greasy. They had local *jiu-tze* (oranges) and *hua sheng ping kan* (peanut cookies) for dessert, accompanied by Nescafe powdered coffee, which tasted like the metal canteen cups from which they drank it.

After chow each man was given a previously hoarded chocolate D-ration bar and they all went back through the mist to their quarters to drink mao tai, belch, swap sea stories and make repeated trips to the head.

Commodore Miles arrived with his fan yi kuan, Eddie Liu. Eddie had been Miles's interpreter since 1942 and had accompanied the naval officer on all his trips throughout China. His close relationship with the commodore conferred upon him a kind of special authority, which he was careful never to misuse. Miles's intensity was immediately apparent to the men and officers who had never met him before. Yet the intensity and burning drive was tempered by a friendly manner and a warm way of communicating with his command. Wallace thought that Miles was a little fanatic and naive and that he demonstrated a marked tendency toward paranoia.

His deep-set probing eyes were seldom at rest; they radiated a vivid, passionate impression that he really believed his U.S. Naval Group could win the war and keep the Communists at least at bay. He trusted Tai Li implicitly, as he quickly told you. He believed that Tai was a liberal, democratic man who only established concentration camps that were strictly legal and that the money he used for his organization was borrowed from savings banks. And that Tai loved his mother and supported education for women. Miles argued that the pirates and turncoat puppet soldiers now armed by the Naval Group were not "rice soldiers" but were truly motivated by the same sentiments as the Loyal Patriotic Army. And how could he not feel persecuted and that many hands were against him, when his small tonnage allowance over the Hump was constantly threatened, argued over, mis-shipped or lost? And now

Wedemeyer is replacing Stilwell as theater commander and putting his nose into business that isn't his, wanting to change the SACO agreement with the Chinese, making Tai Li leery. Wedemeyer doesn't like the fact that the arms the Navy gives to the guerrillas are not under Lend-Lease, nor that Miles's outfit reports directly to the Chief of Naval Operations.

He made his feelings abundantly clear to Wallace in response to some "idle" questions Ian asked Miles as Gunnery Sergeant Wells drove them and Eddie Liu to "the front." Miles had told the camp commandant, Lieutenant Pearson, that he wanted to "see the Japanese," and Pearson had detailed Wallace and Wells to take the commodore to the end of the road to the east in the camp jeep. The roads were rutted and slippery with wet mud over frozen uneven roadbed. The day was darkly overcast and threatening more snow. The wind had its own fiendish knack for getting under collars and hats and up pant legs as the jeep slid and swayed and ground up the deserted, switch-back road to the top of Tungkow Mountain.

It was blowing a gale out of the west from behind them as they stiffly got out of the jeep at the crest of the road in the gap at the peak. The road had been destroyed ahead of them. There were no Chinese troops to be seen nor any sign that they might have been here except for the broken, ruined road.

"Can't see any Japanese, but they're out there," Miles confidently shouted in the wind, pointing to the east like a commanding hero about to be immortalized on canvas.

"Bound to be," yelled Ian, feeling more than a little exposed standing outlined on the crest. If there's anyone out there with glasses they'll get an eyeful, he thought, and if there's anyone that's a half-decent shot within range we'll see some blood.

"We'll stop them here!" hollered Miles. "And if we can't get the arms and ammunition we need, we'll stop them with rocks!"

Ian's Christmas Eve prayer from Ecclesiastes came back to him: a time to cast away stones. Wells caught Ian's eye and quickly looked away.

"Commodore," said Ian, "it's a long way back and we better make it before dark. Not safe here after the sun sets, and it sets mighty early this time of year. Shall we go?"

Miles stood with his hands in the pockets of his padded coat glowering at the horizon, his misted breath streaming before him on the wind. Eddie Liu stood beside him wrapped in a flapping blanket.

Wallace and Wells turned back to a jeep that had lost any inclination to start. After strenuous work with the hand-crank the engine finally caught, and while Wells warmed up the motor Wallace reminded the commodore it was time to go. Miles seemed in a trance, and Ian was reluctant to touch him. So he walked past him and slightly down the eastern slope.

"Belay that. Better not go any farther, Lieutenant," yelled Miles. "We have to shove off."

They returned to the jeep, struggled to turn it around on the narrow track and finally started down the mountain in four-wheel-drive, low gear.

"I've heard of you two," said Miles. "Wallace and Wells. Wells and Wallace. Been a lot of talk at Happy Valley. Upset us a little with your defiant feat at Paoching. Defied the enemy—defied orders—defied the Chinese—defied fate. But that, your performance at Shihtan and the way you brought those people out have helped us. Your success in getting the unit at Nanning trained and armed and in the field has not gone unnoticed, nor have your effective efforts in returning your unit safely through Liuchow. We've convinced the Chinese, and my friend Tai Li in particular, that Americans can deal with difficulty, can live like the Chinese guerrillas, can take their place in combat working closely with Chinese unit commanders. That's why we sent the green-light message. What do you think of it?"

"Commodore," said Ian over the growling transmission and the whistling wind, "we think it gives us a chance to really do something besides using the Chinese as surrogates. I've got a project up my sleeve that I'd like to carry out."

I guess this is an end run, Wallace said to himself, but I've already told Pearson about it so why not. *L'audace, l'audace! Toujours l'audace!*

"What is it," the commodore asked, his interest stirred.

So Wallace told him about his house-boy Nien in Nanning, Nien's cousin, the Haikou prison camp on Hainan Island and the expected prisoner train. He said he'd like to take a small highly trained group and get the prisoners off the train and he knew how to do it.

"Good for you!" said Miles with enthusiasm. "I know about that train. Tai's people are watching the matter very closely and have told us they expect to be able to report when it moves."

"I'm concerned," Wallace said, "that the Chinese might try to gain face by pulling off the stunt themselves, but I think the operation is too important for it not to be a joint effort. The action needs to take place in a carefully selected spot where the terrain favors the attackers and protects the prisoners. A place where we can spirit the prisoners over the mountains quickly to caches of food and clothing and medicine. That'll give us the best chance to save as many men as possible."

"You've given this a lot of thought," said Miles after a long pause during which he stared at his knees, "so I'll make a bargain with you. You successfully carry off the action we're planning in Hunan and I'll see that you are put on detached duty with a special unit of the Chinese Commando Army to take that train. I'll give you all the support I can. Your orders will merely say that you are to carry out the verbal orders I have given you so that we don't get a lot of counsel and advice from other quarters. And so that we keep the matter in the family, so to speak. We'll let Pearson know so he can provide support, but nobody else unless there's a need to know. Is that clear?"

Ian was excited and buzzing and snapped, "Yes, sir!"

They got back to Chenyuan in the late dusk, frozen to the bone and wracked with hunger. The commodore thanked Wells and Wallace, and he and Eddie Liu went to their quarters.

"What do you think, Asa?" asked Wallace.

"Well, sir, it's not my place to comment on flag rank officers, and it seems as if he's got two wheels in the sand, but he sure as hell cottoned up to your idea. As a matter of fact, he'd have probably been eager about any operation that got Americans in combat. But I dunno, he strikes me as a real blivet."

"What the hell is a blivet?"

"Why, where I come from it's eight pounds of shit in a six-pound bag."

Pearson told Ian that Miles mentioned the prisoner train and would cut orders for Ian to lead a party to scout the area for selection of a locale for the attack. He didn't think Ian had done an end-run but rather that Ian had seen something in the rumor that he, Pearson, had not. Pearson was impressed that Miles and Tai knew about the train. He didn't know that Ian had brought the opportunity up when he was with the commodore.

They were told that the Hunan operation, code named *T'ieh Ying Tao* (Iron Cherry), involved a diversion at Siangtan to draw troops away from the Japanese base at Ninsiang, a main command center just south of Tung Ting lake. It was from here that any drive toward Chihkiang Air Base would be directed. The command center and staff quarters were on an island in the middle of the Tzu Kiang tributary, connected to the south bank by an ancient iron bridge. The main objective of the guerrillas at Ninsiang was to capture a Japanese general officer. Tai Li had cooks and house-boys working for the Japanese who would poison the general at the evening meal and carry him unconscious to the river where SACO troops would take him away, after which the bridge and radio tower would be blown to deter pursuit.

Fix was to lead the Ninsiang party and Wallace was to lead the Siangtan group. Fix was taking Treviso and a corpsman and Wallace was to be accompanied by Wells and Pagani. The Siangtan unit was to create its diversion just at dusk, blowing up godowns and barracks but not communication facilities, so that word could be sent to Ninsiang and troops dispatched from there to assist the Siangtan garrison. This was to weaken the guards at the command center and focus attention elsewhere. Two hours later Fix's unit was to do its work to snatch the general and blow the bridge.

Separately, following the Siangtan affair, Wallace was to take a hand-picked group of six or so Chinese guerrillas and scout the railroad while the two raiding parties fled westward through Hunan.

"It sounds pretty complex to me," Ian said to Fix as they checked and packed the little gear they would be carrying.

"Ah, yes" said Fix, who didn't know of Ian's separate orders, "and maybe it's just a little bit of grandstanding to show the new theater commander how hot we are. And do you know why the operation is code named Cherry?"

"Tell me."

"The sunken, intense eyes of our fanatic leader saw a vision. First blood for the Americans!"

The two American units of six men and two interpreters traveled northeast together in a charcoal-burning truck on a grueling, cold journey of two hundred twenty miles to Changteh, northwest of Ninsiang. The city was a desolate ruin, destroyed by the Japanese in the 1930s and fought over ever since. Here they stayed in local hostels built of rubble by the American Catholic missionaries who had remained or returned despite the fighting.

They saw many irregular soldiers, perhaps bandits, in the ruins. There were a few peasants selling pitiful wares and dried fruits and vegetables in the lanes. People hunkered down and skittered away as they passed.

Ian wondered why the Japanese wouldn't know all about the presence of the Americans before they left on the next leg.

Fix and Ian visited the priests at their own hostel, named for St. Ignatius Loyola. Ian was surprised to find some Chinese priests among the group. He was told by Brother Claude, the missionary wine maker, that since the time of Matteo Rici in 1610 there had been a Catholic presence in China. A big church in Peking. Jesuits got thrown out in 1724 but came back in the 1840s after the Opium Wars. Dominicans accused the Jesuits of making too many concessions to the Chinese, but since the 1920s there had been Chinese priests and even a bishop or two.

They went to a well-attended vesper service. Wallace was amazed at the difference between the attitude here and at the Bridgeman Chapel at Pinyang. It's hard for me, a Protestant, to accept, he told himself, but the Christians at Pinyang treated the Chinese as servants. Here the Christians behave as servants.

The service ended with what Ian had always sung as an old New England hymn, "Sun of My Soul, Thou Savior Dear," and he was floored to note that the music was from the *Viennese Katholisches Gesangbuch,* circa 1774.

They took a two-day, fifty-mile hike through the mountains to a hill hamlet called Tem Pin Li where they met detachments of Chinese from General Ho's Second Column. Twenty Chinese officers and men were assigned to each American unit. I hope, thought Ian, that my next experience with Ho soldiers at Siangtan will be better than the first. I have already supped on the bread of adversity and the water of affliction with that bunch.

"Watch out for these guys," he said to Fix. "Remember the last time."

"Don't teach this fish to swim," snorted O'Reilly.

The units went their separate ways, Ian leaving first to cover the seventy-five miles to Siangtan. Fix waited a day before leaving to travel the thirty miles to Ninsiang, where they would hole up in the hills until the appointed hour.

Henry Chen was the fan yi kuan assigned to Ian as interpreter, and he, Wells and Wallace watched the detachment as it worked its way through the mountains and across the terraced paddy dikes, seeing whether they would take advantage of the terrain and generally follow the suggestions made by Ian. Henry Chen would translate Ian's "orders" to the Chinese NCO in charge, and Ian and Chen would observe how well the detachment reacted. They were pretty good, though slow to carry out the directions of the NCO. No arguing, thank God.

By the end of the first night's march Ian, Wells and Henry agreed on the six men Ian and Henry would take to scout the railroad. Wells, the NCO and the balance of the Chinese would be sent back to headquarters, wherever they were at the time.

They studied a rudimentary map of where in Siangtan the Chinese thought the Japanese had established supply godowns and where the Japanese barracks were. They assigned teams to set fires and toss grenades, pointing out that wires were not to be cut.

Privately, Wells assured Wallace that as he listened to the Chinese talk among themselves he was convinced that this was a pretty aggressive bunch; they were not likely to run away, and they understood their assignments, including where everyone was to assemble in the event they all got separated, a very likely possibility.

Then it started to snow, a wet heavy snow from a dark low sky with an increasing wind.

"Gives us more cover," said Ian, "though it will slow us down a bit. We'll start early, keep to the high ground and work our way into Siangtan just before dusk. If we can tell when that is."

Hunched over, they plodded through the deepening wet slush with poor visibility. Their guide led them on a circuitous route, avoiding the tiny villages as they descended the hills toward their objective. Outside some of the hamlets through the snow Wallace could see little boys sitting on the backs of water buffalo. The boys wore conical hats and straw capes and seemed to be doing nothing—usually the boys were leading or herding the buffalo. The beasts weren't working.

"Why are the boys sitting on the buffalo," Ian asked Henry Chen.

"To keep warm," Henry replied.

The snow and slush filled in their footprints quickly, and they felt relatively unobserved until they reached a tiny one-lane shuttered village in the early dusk, somewhat behind schedule. The point man came pelting back toward them pointing and hissing to his NCO.

"*Jih-pen chi ping lai!*" Japanese cavalry comes!

Wells, Wallace, Chen and the NCO quickly waved the Ho soldiers to cover and slid behind spirit doors, under deep eaves, and behind walls. A squad of eight Japanese horsemen appeared at the head of the narrow lane and plodded toward the men, heads lowered against the driving snow. Their horses were coated with matted snow, and ice had formed on straw and bark capes and forage caps. A *gunso* sergeant in a steel helmet had the lead, and his *gunjin* soldiers were strung out in single file behind him. They passed so close to Ian in his doorway that the reek of horse was almost overpowering. Their flanks steamed, and the breath of the soldiers blew away on the wind. Ian held his breath. The troop was no more than six feet away in the narrow lane.

And then the squad stopped, and there was much shouting and Wallace heard *kome* (rice), *yama* (mountain) with pointing to the west and *kawa* (river) with pointing to the east. Then a command came down the line, and the Japanese patrol unslung their *raifuruju* from their shoulders, checked their loads and waited.

Ian shivered and said to himself: do not faint in thy day of adversity nor drink the dregs of the cup of trembling nor be weighed in the balance and found wanting nor sneeze nor cough nor fart nor any such thing. He almost giggled at the predicament and realized he felt the need to urinate and the need to believe in God or *Shang Di* or somebody he could pray to. He was sweating profusely as he quivered, and he feared the enemy would smell him, see his breath or be told by the spirits of the middle air that an assembly of evildoers was at hand. It kept getting darker.

Then the gunso shouted and waved his arm forward, the gunjin slapped their mounts and the small squad plopped down the lane and out of sight into the darkening countryside.

Wallace waited for a count of ten after the last horseman had disappeared and then stepped into the lane. He gave a low whistle, paused, and gave another. Asa Wells poked his head around a spirit wall, looked in both directions and then joined Wallace in a crouching run.

"Where the hell are the others?" Wallace asked.

"Scared shitless probably and have tooken off through the back for our assembly point."

"Damn," said Wallace and looked at his wrist watch. "Let's haul ass into town and throw some fire around. Gotta give Fix some support. We'll raise some two-man hell and then join up with the others. With me?"

"Aye, aye, sir!"

The two Americans trotted off down the inclined path toward Siangtan, stopping just outside the western edge to survey the situation. All seemed quiet. They were shivering in the cold and in the anticipation of it all. Their feet were soaked and almost frozen.

"We'll turn to ice if we don't keep movin', Lieutenant. Colder'n an Eskimo's picnic lunch," said Wells.

"Keeps the flies down, Asa," Wallace retorted. "You got your grenades? All set? We'll meet back in that last village if we're separated. Come on."

They ran hunched over, down the slippery stone street toward the river, stopped and saw some buildings with weak flickering lights. Horses were tied up outside. They heard voices inside, stepped up to the paper-covered windows, pulled the pins on two grenades each, one per hand, spat out the pins, let the handles fly and hurled the MK IIs into the room, then stood aside against the wall as the building was rocked by almost simultaneous explosions followed by immediate fire as paper and wood burst into flame.

"Scoot!" said Ian, and started running back up the hill. Wells took down the horses with his TSMG. That hurt Ian, but he understood. He covered Wells with his Model 70 as Asa trotted up toward him. Shouts and activity could be heard in other buildings, and people appeared in the snowy street lit by the flames of the burning building. Wallace quickly dropped two men with his rifle, and Wells scattered the rest with his Thompson. They hurled a couple of grenades down the path to discourage the chase, fired a few more rounds and huffed up the hill through the swirling snow and onto the paddy path down which they had come.

They reached the little village breathless and just in time to hear the calvary patrol returning. They ducked into the lee of a lonely tile-roofed farm building standing alone outside the village and waited. The patrol came on. Rather than make tracks at the front and only door they heisted and pulled each other up under the rear eave and squeezed through the narrow space under the tiles. They found themselves on two-foot-square rough saw-pit-hewn beams running from the long front wall to the rear wall. They could smell the residue of charcoal fires.

The patrol stopped directly outside, and they could hear the Japanese dismounting. The Japanese gunso led his troop into the building with a small hand light. They shed their capes and hats and brushed the snow from their uniforms. They lit a small wick in a bowl of oil on a wooden bench and spread a wet map at which they pointed and jabbered.

Wells and Wallace shrank themselves onto the beams as their body heat began to melt the snow from their clothes. Wallace watched a rivulet of water start toward the edge of the beam directly over the map below. He felt naked. His private parts rolled up like a window shade. He heard the Japanese speak of *tasu kaigun*. Many Marines!

Ian slowly raised his eyes and looked at Wells. Asa was looking at him and slowly mouthed the words "that's us," winked, and worked at his belt. They sure as hell knew we were coming, thought Ian. They're looking for us.

Snow blew in under the tiles and settled on them. It floated down on the dimly wick-lit troop below. Ian could smell men, straw and bark capes, and he could smell horse. Cavalry. How the hell do we outrun them? The little light glinted off the wet steel helmet that the gunso had put on the makeshift table.

The Japanese sergeant brushed off some of the sifting snow and lifted his gaze to the beams, to the tiles. Wallace stopped breathing. Without moving his head he looked at Wells. Asa had his last MK II grenade in his hand with the pin out. He looked at Ian and scrunched up. Wallace did the same, making himself as small as possible on the heavy beam. Wells let the handle fly off and the Japanese immediately tensed.

"Yojin suru!" Beware!

Wells and Wallace were deafened and nearly knocked off their perches by the concussion as the grenade exploded its fifty-two serrated parts into the bunched troop, blew out the light, shattered the roof tiles and spooked the horses. As the mounts stampeded, Ian and Asa crawled back to the eave and lowered themselves to a drift, brushed off dust and tile chips, heard thrashing and groaning inside and loped off through the snow.

They came upon five of the Japanese horses at the end of the village lane, reins trailing in the snow. They clucked their way up to them, selected the two that looked the best and mounted. Asa looked at Ian, who nodded, and Wells shot the three remaining nags. Then Wallace and Wells, the first and only American Horse Marines since the Marine Guard at the Legation Quarter in Peking in 1933, turned their horses' heads and trotted off through the storm to the west.

O'Reilly saw no activity at the Japanese barracks on the island and quickly decided to carry out the operation whether or not Ian's diversion took any troops away.

At dark some of the Ho men waded upstream in the shallows, hidden by the snow, climbed into the underpinning of the old iron bridge and wedged bamboo sections filled with TNT, fitted with blasting caps and wire. They carried the wire back downstream to a hellbox and attached the leads.

Another group crossed the water on floating logs and crawled through the snow to the radio tower, which Fix thought looked like the old RKO Radio trademark. The pings wired it for blowing. They were unseen. Too much snow for the Japanese, who sensibly stayed indoors. I hope they wired it right so it will really blow, thought O'Reilly.

Then Fix's unit waited for something to happen. They were looking for a shaded light that would signal that Tai's people had the prisoner. Fix kept looking at his watch and shaking. He was hungry, he guessed.

Two hours passed. Nothing except cold and snow and shivering. Then dimly, on the far bank, a weak light moving up and down! Fix told his fan yi kuan to tell the Ho NCO to take out the Japanese bridge guards as silently as possible and bring back the prisoner.

Just then shots rang out on the island in the vicinity of the radio tower, and the excited Ho soldiers downstream turned the crank on the hellbox and the bridge blew up in a shattering explosion, showering iron fragments along the bank and turning the surface of the river to froth as the old structure crashed into the water. Hearing the explosions at the bridge the other Ho soldiers blew the radio tower, which slowly tilted and crashed into buildings, smashing through roofs, overturning blazing huo-puns and throwing the glowing coals on paper matting, tatamis and silk hangings, starting fires immediately.

Fix swore and then saw that his Ho NCO had commandeered a small, narrow shan p'an from the shore, and he and two other men were poling furiously across the river. On the far bank, in the light of burning barracks, Fix could see four civilian Chinese holding a rug rolled up like a sausage, tied at the ends and squirming. The NCO beached the shan p'an, and the sausage was dumped into it as the civilian Tai people jumped in and shoved off.

The gunwales of the overloaded shan p'an were just barely above water as the men poled for life. There was a spattering of rifle fire from the opposite bank, and Fix yelled at Treviso to hose the area with his Thompson and then move his position in anticipation of return fire. The Chief let go a couple of good long bursts, but as he scuttled to his next spot the rifle fire opened up again and the stern oarsman was hit and toppled over the side tipping the boat into the water. The brown, cold river poured in and the sausage and several of the men were carried downstream in a welter of foam and waving arms and faint piping cries.

The Japanese set up a Nambu and took the river under fire and then the far bank. Treviso and the Ho NCO who had struggled to shore pointed to the northern end of the island, where through the snow in the light of the burning encampment Fix could see Japanese pushing off from shore in little motorized boats to cut them off.

"Screw this!" said O'Reilly, and rounded up the men that were left and zig-zagged to the place where they expected the Japanese pursuit party to land. They hunkered down, spread out, concealed and waited until the Japanese were almost on shore and then Fix opened fire with his Thompson. The shore blazed as the Chinese opened fire with TSMGs, carbines and pistols. Japanese jumped from their boats and tried to wade ashore but were cut down by the hail of fire from the bank. Boats and bodies rolled as they were swept away.

The fire on the island was a raging inferno as the wind-whipped flames leapt from one inflammable barracks to the next. Fix could feel the warmth even through the storm. He looked around and counted noses. Sixteen men left.

"O.K., *wo-men tau Tem Pin Li ch'u!*" he shouted, and the unit formed up—exhausted, soaked, frozen and starved—and trotted off in single file through the storm to the west.

Wells and Wallace found their cohorts at the designated rendezvous and without rancor, in consideration of face, told the Chinese they were glad everyone was all right. Then Wallace sent Wells and his group to the west, while Wallace, Henry Chen and their six men headed south to swing around the bottom of Siangtan city, where the river headed east.

They passed out of snow and into rain and at about midnight, after posting guards, bedded down in an abandoned farm compound. Wallace ate a little cold rice from the rice balls he carried in his musette bag. No fires allowed.

In the misty morning they stayed on the high ground and worked east toward the railroad. Once, as they rested, they looked down into a valley and saw a formation of troops, maybe sixty, slowly moving north along the valley floor. Wallace looked at them through his glasses and was astonished to see Americans in full gear: steel helmets, field jackets, web belts with ammo pouches, M1s, laced leggings! They had scouts out on parallel rice paddy paths and a point man up ahead. An officer on a big horse rode just behind the lead section. Ian wondered where the hell they thought they were going. Maybe another fucked up OSS unit. Maybe they thought they were in Greece. Maybe they were one of the new U.S. Army training units assigned to a specific Chinese army, lost but doing it by the book. There was a coolie train following the Americans, carrying drums of fuel, tent floorboards, crates of supplies. Ian was sure they had their PX goodies with them.

Late in the day Ian and his men found themselves on a ridge overlooking the single railroad track where it had been cut through a narrow mountain valley to the north of their present location. Wallace glassed the cut and thought he could see uniformed figures patrolling the vulnerable parts of the line. He squatted with the Ho soldiers and the NCO and Chen, letting them use the binoculars to see what could be seen.

"At dawn we'll find out more about what's down there," he said. "There's a track mender's hut where those Nips seem to congregate. Can't be more than about six of them in all. Let's work our way down in the dark and be prepared to rush the hut at dawn. See if we can't take that crowd out and find out what they're supposed to be doing and looking for. And just maybe pick up a little food."

They pointed out their respective positions, set the time for the attack and carefully eased their way down the long precipitous slope between groves of pine and bamboo.

Ian rolled up in his poncho and watched the sky as the stars started to appear. A good omen he thought, even though he knew that the weather changed rapidly in these mountains. He dozed fitfully—too keyed up to fully surrender to sleep and too worried about the rotation of the Chinese watch-keepers. The superior man, he thought, must be taught by the scars of the past and use caution therefore.

In the morning they ran into browned and booted seasoned troops from the Indochina peninsula with Arisaka *raifuruju*—not the old Danzig '98 rifles with dust covers on the bolt and five rounds of ammunition apiece — and with Nambu light machine-guns and plenty of ammunition. They shot low like combat veterans. Not high and hurried. And they wiped the unit out. Almost. Despite his cautions, the Chinese picked by him and equipped with M1 carbines had, like Chinese, moved in late in growing daylight, almost without concealment. He was watching carefully to locate and note guard-posts when the firing started, and as he dove for cover he saw his people and

Henry Chen go down. The earth around him became a beaten zone as the machine-guns searched the ground in short bursts. He had his Model 70 rifle and scope, but his gear and musette bag were yards away where the lot had fallen as he dove for cover.

With his toes and elbows he moved himself from cover to cover until he reached the bamboo trees. He heard the Nips shout when they found his gear. He rose and ran uphill through the forest.

The Japanese pursued him. Occasional shots. Occasional shouts. A horse's whinny from the little Chinese horses they were using to follow his trail. He climbed most of the day, generally heading west, heading for the downslope that tumbled to a river far below. It started to rain in the last few gray hours before dark and then changed to sleet as the altitude increased. He could still hear pursuit.

Then the sleet turned to snow and he listened, but could only hear his own heavy breathing and the rush of wind. His ears popped and he waited. Nothing.

He spent the night in an abandoned charcoal burner's hut just below the tree line wrapped in his remaining blanket and poncho, muffled in his parka. He counted his blessings as he lay there: he was ahead of them and it was snowing harder; he still had his rifle and about thirty rounds... could he eat the leather sling if he had to? ...he still had some biscuits, some dried fruit and two rice balls... his canteen was frozen solid, but he could eat snow.

Well, he said to himself, they've brought in veterans to protect the Hankow-Canton rail line and I'm not surprised, since we've shut off the sea lanes. So we'll take that into account when we come back. We'll get the CACW to bomb and block the cut so we can ambush the train guards and the locals and get the Americans off the train and up into the mountains, hopefully without pursuit or casualty.

Here I am, he thought, alone on a mountain through my own fault; but I will goddam well get out of here, come back with another detachment, blow this train and get the men off it if it's the last thing I do.

Exhausted, he drifted off to sleep, his breath misting, hovering and becoming rime on his beard, his blanket and on the shallow timber ceiling. He was stiff and lost, but he felt compelled to do something, anything, to atone for those whom he had sacrificed, who were missing and gone.

The flakes were bigger in the morning. The snow that had been fine and wind-driven when he wrapped up in his blanket was sifting through the empty chink in the logs by his feet. Now, squinting, he could see the big flakes drifting past the slit. He thought he saw patches of clear sky. He lay unmoving—watching—listening. The thump of heavy snow from a bough quickened him, but he heard nothing else. No birds, beasts or bad guys up here, he thought. Just Ian Wallace, half a world from home, hungry, cold and wishing for help from a God about whom he wasn't so sure any more.

He wondered what the Japanese thought when they found his musette bag with the Marine emblem on the flap; with his Colt .45 that he should have been wearing; with his compass, map, dry socks, field dressings and the tincture of opium for his dysentery. His bowels cramped.

The snow stopped, and the sun lit up the crest. Stir your stumps, he said to himself... regardless of how I got into this rotten mess, I've got to get out of it. Too many lives at stake. I've already blown away too many, and there's work to be done and atonement to be made.

He eased himself out of the charcoal burner's hut into the brilliant blue-white sunlight of the snow-covered tree line. He blinked to accustom himself to the glare. This won't do, he said, and looked for a piece of bark. He stripped some off a fallen tree still green with needles. With his knife he tapered the ends of the strip, cut two eye slits and tied the bark around his head to act as a glare shield. It worked. He stood in the shelter of the last trees and surveyed his route to the top while he ate some dried fruit, one of his last two rice balls and a little snow. The sun would be moving left to right, and the snow formations would be casting shadows soon to hide any tracks he might leave. Unless an aircraft should spot him while he was in the open, or unless the Japanese had pressed on last night and had the area surrounded, he'd be able to make the crest all right, leaving his trail in the shadows which would form in an hour or two. He relieved himself, fore and aft with the help of some cold snow (with his left hand like a Hindu, he thought) and kicked over a drift to cover his spoor.

He looked about, checking all directions and, hunkered over, commenced loping through the knee-deep snow, angling toward the crest, breathing hard and beginning to sweat. He ducked under a rock outcropping and listened as his breath slowed. Nothing. He launched himself into the snow again and pushed toward the top, grunting, heaving, plowing the snow before his legs. A blind man could see this track, he said to himself, but what the fuck choice do I have? Two hundred yards to go.

He reversed direction to avail himself of a cornice-sheltered route and paused. He thought he heard an animal snort. Only fifty yards to the top. God knows what's on the other side at this location. This sure as hell wasn't where they'd come over on the way to the railroad tracks. He listened and watched his rear. A great shower of snow fell from branches two hundred yards below and to the left of him. Somebody there? He squinted and held his breath. He waited an eternity. No movement.

Well, he said, Our God is a god of salvation; and to God, the Lord, belongs escape from death. He hurled himself into the open and powered his way under the cornice, skirted around it and slid over the edge, where he braked himself and stared in awe at the hundred-mile view over the mountain ridges to the west. Every valley shall be exalted, and every hill shall be made low: and the crooked shall be made straight, and the rough places plain. "You bet," he said aloud. And he thought: *But they that wait upon the Lord shall renew their strength; they shall mount up with wings as eagles; they shall run, and not be weary; and they shall walk, and not faint.* Isaiah, I'm waiting on the Lord. Show me.

He was clinging to bare rock just below the topographical crest of the mountain, breathless and wonder-struck. No shots, no pursuit, with All That Is Under Heaven spread out before him. He looked down the long declivity toward the roaring white-foamed river thousands of feet below. Little snow on this side, the windward side of the mountain. Blown over into great cornices at the eastern lip, revealing rock and shale at the higher elevations of the exposed western flank. The mountain fell away before him, and he could not see the bottom except where great ravines led to spray from whirling gouts of twisting water.

He stepped down and found his feet sliding out from under him in the shale. He caught a rock and stopped his slide. Well now, this calls for some innovative thought. He looked at a possible route to the bottom, glissading from rock to rock, *if* he could direct his trajectory properly. Did shale react to downhill pressure the same way snow did when you skied? He didn't know. He'd done a lot of skiing at home in Massachusetts, and they used to kid about skiing on the rocks, but this was all new.

He picked out a nearby rock and gently launched himself toward it, riding on his butt and steering with his heels. He drew one leg up at a time and found that he could almost control his direction. He tended to put his hands down but soon found they were easily cut by the abrasive action of the shards. He tried using his rifle butt as a paddle and that helped. He hit his target rock with a thud that took the wind out of him. He paused and thought, I can't walk down or the rocks will take over and I'll hurtle over some parapet, broken of bone, and be dashed into that watery cauldron. Better try it from rock to rock.

He pushed off gently toward the next rock, about fifty yards away, and made it safely, though he had gathered an enormous amount of momentum before he was able to stop himself. His ankles cracked as he jarred to a stop. He looked back up the precipitous face. He was leaving a fairly discernible trail of disturbed shale. He sidled over to a nearby rock and with a breath of prayer started it on its journey to the river below. It slid at first and then, propelled by a bounce against a ledge, it catapulted into the air, landed fifty feet below and shifted a great wedge of shale that started an avalanche that followed the boulder down, down, down until the entire rock slide flew off a cliff into the chasm and threw itself into the roiling waters with an enormous plume of spray that was whipped away by the surface wind.

Well, that leaves another track, at least, but what a hell of a way to go. I better take it in short hops. He kept his rifle in his hands and navigated with his feet and his rifle butt for several thousand feet, angling toward the less steep side of the descent. The heels of his boondockers were wearing fast, and the poncho he'd hung over his belt at the rear was in tatters. His behind stung, his ankles ached and the heels of his hands were bloody—but he was making good time. He came to a stop at a boulder and looked down for the next one. There it was, perhaps thirty yards away, and a good thing it was there, for the view beyond it disappeared into the abyss. Wallace swallowed and pushed off. He steered well and came directly to the boulder, which gave way the instant he came up against it, and Wallace found himself part of a thundering, hissing cascade of rocks, slabs and gravel headed toward the rim. He back-pedaled with his feet, back-watered with his rifle butt, reached out with his bloody hands for rocks as he swept violently by, but was lost in the grip of gravity as the tons of igneous debris swept over the edge and into the gorge.

Wallace flew into space; his rifle was torn from his grip; he saw the water below foaming and boiling. He arched to avoid the great boulder in front of him. He put one hand over his groin and the other over his nose and mouth, crossed his feet and prayed. He hit the water feet first in a shower of lesser stones whose impact was cushioned by the water. The shock of the cold temperature and the depth to which he plummeted made him want to gasp. He opened his eyes and could see no light. He was boiled over and over. He felt himself falling and somersaulting through space and came to the surface in an eddying swirl below a waterfall, gasping and blowing.

He breast-stroked toward the western muddy bank in his sodden clothes, just able to keep his head above water. He pulled himself ashore with his elbows, rolled over on his back and stared at the blue sky as the water leaked from his boots, his trousers and his parka. His rifle was gone, and as he felt his pockets he knew his meager food supply was gone as well. He had no hat and couldn't find his web belt. His knife was still in its sheath attached to his trousers belt. "Well that's something anyway," he said out loud. He heard himself, and he laughed. "How about that, you jamokes? You yahoos want to catch me?" He roared with laughter and began to shiver and couldn't stop himself from shaking and laughing. Soon he was on his hands and knees, his head hanging down as he tried to bring himself under control.

He stood up unsteadily and realized that at this lower altitude the temperature was warmer, and he immediately shed his clothes and carried them up the bank and into the trees. He was covered with goose flesh and shook, but he wrung out what was left of his garments and hung them on limbs to dry. He found a rock formation out of the wind and warmed by the sun and stretched himself out. The sun warmed him, too, and he began to feel sleepy. Watch out, he told himself, and sat up hugging his knees, listening and looking.

He checked for wounds: torn hands, bruised elbows, sore ankles, lacerated rump. He checked for equipment: no rifle, no watch, just torn clothes and broken boondockers. How's your spirit, he asked. Pretty goddam good, all things considered. The bastards knocked off my men, but they didn't catch the old man of the mountains. I'll get back to Unit Two where we'll make plans to deal with the veteran troops we'll be facing. Then we'll set up supply caches with food and clothes between here and the base camp. When the train's ready, we'll be ready. We are going to save those poor goddam prisoners if it's the last thing I do!

When the sun was as straight up as it was likely to get at this time of year, Wallace dressed in his damp but warm clothes. His boots were stiff, but he finally got them on. He stood and started downstream, careful to maintain his concealment. In some places he had to wade, and he made peace with the facts that his feet and lower legs were going to stay wet and that he would blister.

Late in the afternoon the terrain he moved through dropped sharply, and the river tumbled down in steep rapids. In the distance Wallace could see a wide alluvial plain cultivated with paddies. There were also some small villages and occasional farm compounds. Better stay up here and walk the ridges. The bad guys will be down there helping themselves to what the Kuomintang or the bandits haven't already plundered. God knows how I'll eat.

He turned back uphill, toward the west, when his eye caught movement in an eddy above the rapids. He squinted at it. A body? Caught on some branch? He slid down slowly and peered into the pool. A GI, for God's sake, face down with his hair slowly spinning out from his head. It had to be one of that group they'd seen on the way out. He cut a stick, hooked it over the sling across the body's back and tugged. The body rolled but would not move toward Wallace. Ian could see equipment strapped to the man and eased himself into the water, groping for the bottom. The water was waist deep, and Wallace waded the few feet between the bank and the corpse. He tugged, and the body moved a bit and came to a halt as the sling caught on the bottom. Wallace reached around the body and felt a weapon, hooked on a tree stump. He went back to the bank, removed his shirt and parka, waded back into the pool and went underwater, groping for whatever the sling was tangled in. His hands found a weapon snagged on the sunken stump, and he tore it free, surfacing with a gasp, weapon in hand.

Ian towed the body to the shore and pulled it up on the bank. The man had two bluish puckered bullet entrance holes in his neck and one in his cheek. The blood had long since washed away. His eyes were milky and his skin wrinkled. Wallace undid the sling and pulled in a Thompson submachine gun, dripping and choked with mud. The oil and thong case was in the butt well. He'd clean the piece later. He put it gently back in the water, tying the sling to his ankle, leaving it there until he could pull it out and dry it, thus avoiding rust. He removed the man's webbing and discovered a canteen, first aid packet and two magazine pouches of .45 caliber ammo for the TSMG. He removed three wax-coated K-ration boxes from the man's blouse pockets. It was all the food the man had. Ian checked for dogtags, but they were gone.

Can't have this poor man's body floating by some Jap outpost, Ian mused, so he pulled it into the trees, covered it with leaves, twigs and earth as best he could and knelt beside it.

"For out of the ground were we taken," Wallace paraphrased, "and to the ground will we return. Ashes to ashes and dust to dust. May the sometime departed soul of this body find peace at Thy side." And thank Thee for Thy small miracles, he said to himself, as he rose and buckled on the web belt and suspenders and stowed the K-rations for emergency use. He cleaned, dried and oiled the TSMG, clicked in a magazine, slung the weapon over his shoulder and headed uphill in the gathering dusk.

Sometime before dark Wallace smelled smoke. He tested the breeze with a wet finger and followed the scent upwind. He came around the nose of a ridge and saw a little mud and tile village with small terraced paddies that seemed to march up the mountain and others that stepped down in serried ranks toward the valley. He hunkered down to observe.

These people had to do a lot of up-and-down climbing to get to their fields, he thought, but then again they don't have to pump water with those foot-powered paddle wheels, either. Gravity does their irrigation for them. Most of the houses were shuttered. On the far side of the stone street he could see the dim glow of a lantern coming from the open front of what appeared to be the inn. He could see narrow benches and rough tables. And he could smell food cooking in oil. His stomach turned over and growled. As best he could tell from his angle of vision, there were no more than five or six people in the inn, not counting the *p'eng t'iao,* proprietor-cook. No Japanese would bother these people so far up and with so little to provide, so it looked as if it was safe. Don't want to spook 'em, though. He removed his webbing and stashed it and his weapon in the brush, tugged his knife around to the small of his back, ran his hands through his hair and whiskers and stepped into the little empty street.

Wallace stopped in front of the inn and saw that it was one dark, smoke-stained room with rough narrow benches and tables and a dirt floor. There was a mud brick counter at the rear behind which a man was stirring something in a pan over glowing charcoal. Ian could hear the low buzz of conversation from the half-dozen patrons. Oh well, he said to himself, and stepped up the two stone steps and entered the room. Immediately the talking stopped as heads turned in his direction. The p'eng t'iao lifted his stick from the pan with a look of wonder and fear on his face. I must look like the yeti, Ian reflected as he walked to the rear of the room. He towered over the cook and the rest of the customers, who seemed frozen to their seats. One started to rise and Ian sent him a look and the man sat down again.

"Wo yao sh-er t'sao chi tan." I want twelve scrambled chicken eggs, Ian said. The p'eng t'iao simply stared, with his mouth open.

"Chi tan-ah, t'sao chi tan-ah, sh-er t'sao chi tan-ah," said a man on the nearest bench to the cook, using the Hunanese *"ah"* to help make the cook understand. The rest of the men gave a hissing intake of breath. Twelve eggs! For one man! They started to chatter with one another as the cook began to prepare Wallace's supper. The helpful man came up to Wallace and spoke to him in Hunanese dialect.

"Please, foreigner, tell us from where you come."

Wallace figured the man didn't give a damn if he had come down the mountain, and besides, Ian didn't want anybody here to know where he'd been or where he was going.

"I am Beautiful Country man."

"Mei kuo ren!" said the talker to the others.

Then to Ian: "What is it you want from us?"

"Only to *ch'ih mi*." To eat, Wallace replied. "And to pay."

"To pay! A wonder!" said the man.

"Let us give gracious consideration to the difficulties of the lao pan, the landlord," Wallace quoted.

"A wonder," said the cook, stirring the eggs in the pan.

"Have tea have not?" Ian asked.

"Shih te-ah! Yo cha." Yes. Have tea.

Wallace devoured the eggs. Nothing had ever tasted so good. He drank tea. He asked for a second order and the conversational buzz stopped again. "Again one time, lao pan," he said.

"Again!" shouted the p'eng t'iao, smiling.

Wallace paid with wet bills from his money belt, bowed to the talker and to the room in general, said, "Small mouth, wide eye, *hsieh-hsieh*," and stepped into the dark street. It was the best meal he had ever eaten.

The talker looked wise. "The mei kuo ren seeks to catch lice on the head of the tiger," he said sagely.

"You should join him, then," suggested a voice from a dark corner.

"When a horse produces horns!"

Wallace made a burrow for himself in the dry pine needles of the forest floor and, cradling his weapon, tried to sleep. He was spent, his belly was full and he should have drifted off. But his mind kept wandering and making him worry. He worried about not going to sleep. He wondered whether he was loosing what he was fighting for by his association with Tai Li. He worried about Diana, to whom he could rarely write, and from whom he rarely got mail. He wondered if he was judging his new world by a morality that simply did not apply to a people who lived otherwise. Live and let live. Fix had said it: stop worrying and press on regardless. But he did have one valid and immediate worry: survival and return to Camp Two.

He woke in the late watches of the night, shook the kinks and stiffness out of his frame and trudged off westward, as best he could judge by the stars. He had decided that the better part of wisdom was to travel at night as much as possible and in the daytime to cling to the high mountain ridges. Travel would be slow, and he would have to cross many valleys. Maybe in the valleys he could find food. At night.

As he trudged he disciplined his mind to conjure up a vision of the map he had lost at the railroad skirmish. He saw the contour lines and the shadings, the rivers and the mountains, and slowly came to realize that he could not retrace his steps through Tem Pin Li and Changteh to get to Camp Two. He would be traversing two sides of a triangle if he did that. Time was too important. He'd continue straight west.

At the end of three days he had walked much and slept little and eaten less. The weather was clear and mild. The temperature suited him, but he would have preferred some rain and mist. He was angling between settlements that quartered Japanese troops and from which they sent out patrols. He had been hoping to find an occasional friendly farmer from whom he could get something to eat. But the Japanese patrols had beaten him to it. The farms were deserted and destroyed.

He believed he was near the town of Lowti and remembered that the large mountain there that ran east and west was rumored to be a Japanese bastion, an anchor of their line of advance. Caves, fortified positions, barbed wire, machine-guns with cleared fields of fire. Lion Mountain it was called. *Shih kao shan*. He would have to pass through the valley beneath the mountain, avoiding patrols.

He ate the last K-ration and rested in the forest until dark, then started out along the well-worn rice paddy paths he had memorized from his observation. The farms here were still functioning, probably under Japanese duress, soldiers living in the farm compounds to see that the families did what they were told.

The night was dark. No stars. He wondered how Asa Wells would describe it. Darker'n three foot down a bear's throat. No lights at the farm compounds. No lights on Shih Kao Shan. He slipped off the path and got one foot soaked with whatever was in the paddy. It stank and squelched. He heard a dog bark at a farm ahead. Dogs? He hadn't thought about dogs. He presumed they'd been eaten long ago. As the path led him by the farm, the dog yapped incessantly. He trotted a few hundred yards to get away from the barking alarm. Before he got to the next compound, its dog started up. If you plot this on a map, he thought, you catch your man by following the barking dogs.

He passed a dozen farms, all under the shoulder of Lion Mountain, all with dogs. He had a hollow feeling between his shoulder blades, and he sweated and trembled and cursed and hoped never again to hear barking.

Apart from his fears there were no problems crossing the wide valley until he got to the western limit of the paddies and was about to head into the wooded hills. He sensed something and stopped to listen. Someone was walking toward him, carelessly. He slid into the last paddy, just keeping his eyes above the dike. The walker stopped. Ian heard equipment being shifted about. The creak of leather. The scratch of a match followed by its flare as it was brought to the cigarette in the mouth of a Japanese sentry. Wallace could see the man's eyes under his steel helmet before the match hissed out in the paddy.

The soldier sat down cross-legged on the path with his rifle in his lap facing west toward the hills and smoked.

He's going to be there all night, thought Ian, and when it's light, here I'll be and there he'll be and that's no good at all. Wallace slowly slid out of the water and slithered carefully down the path. He'll hear me if I stand and drip and slosh, he thought. So I'll have to take him on my belly, before that cigarette goes out. Silently, or they'll call out the full guard and band.

Wallace left his TSMG in the path and slipped his knife into his hand. Every time the soldier took a drag his head and shoulders were outlined by the glow. Wallace fixed the Japanese's position and slid forward. When he got as close as he dared, he eased himself to his feet. The soldier was about to take a pull but stopped and cocked his head a little, his hand holding the cigarette inches from his mouth. Satisfied that he heard nothing, the soldier took a big drag and, as he removed the butt from his mouth, Wallace sprang. Ian's left hand went over the soldier's nose and mouth and yanked back against the knee he had put in the man's back. His right hand plunged the knife in the left side of his victim's neck and sawed through veins and windpipe as he pulled the blade to the right. Blood and smoke flew out of the severed neck. Bowels and bladder let go as the body went limp.

Ian rolled the dead man to the edge of the path and searched the body for food. He opened the tunic and found the man's "thousand stitch" belt tied around his middle over a Japanese flag, signed by many. Wallace stuffed these in the man's pack, took his bloody blanket, his rice balls and dried fish, and pulled the corpse and rifle to the edge of the paddy and pushed them in. He stepped on the soldier's back to get the body fully under water and out of sight. Then, shaking, he turned and vomited the acid K-ration and was convulsed with the dry heaves.

With the Japanese pack and bloody blanket over his shoulder, Wallace retrieved his TSMG and scuttled off to the western mountains. He panted as he ran. God help me, he said to himself, for I am indeed undone. He remembered his bull session at Quantico with Fix and Lewis and Perry: this close-up killing bothers me... I'd rather pull a lanyard or serve on a battleship. How close up can you get? he asked himself.

The dead soldier's food sustained him for several days, and the bloody blanket kept him warm at night. He studied the cardboard-mounted sepia picture of the soldier's family that he found in the knapsack. A pretty little wife and two small children. What had he done to their lives? But whose fault was that, he asked himself. He got mad. The son of a bitch shouldn't have been here in the first place.

In a week's time his legs started to give out. Poor diet, he imagined. No protein. No fruit. No greens. No meat. No fucking food. Is my mind giving out too?

He decided to rest and holed up on a mountainside facing the southern sun. He camouflaged himself with boughs and branches and slept for a day in utter exhaustion. He woke only to evacuate his bowels, cramped and straining. Once he heard a solitary American plane and fantasized about the flier, comfortable in his cockpit, heading for home base and a hot meal with ketchup.

He stumbled into a mountain village and found he was among Miao people, not Han Chinese at all. These people were remote dry-rice farmers who never got to the valleys and who had their own language. They were kind to him for two days, while he gathered some strength before he left them.

He was totally out of food and a little out of his head when he came across a Chinese unit in the mountains. They were nominally under the command of the Communist Fourth Route Army, though they had little communication with Yenan headquarters. They were suspicious of him and took his weapons. They tied his hands behind him and tied his feet around a tree. He tried to talk to them, but could not be understood. They let him have some watery cabbage soup, and he could feel it in his bones. He spent a night tied to the tree with his hands underneath him behind his back, shivering, dreaming, waking, fouling himself.

In the morning an older Chinese man appeared, and Ian presumed he was an officer though he wore no rank on his padded uniform. He squatted on his heels by Ian's head and looked at him for a time before speaking. He asked, in Mandarin, why the foreigner was alone in these mountains. Ian replied that he had been fighting the monkey people in Siangtan and had lost all his men. He was anxious to get to his unit in Kweichow.

The older man called one of the young soldiers to him, and Ian's bonds were untied. The Communists had heard of the raid, the older man said, and admired the daring of it. Ian was given more soup and his weapons were returned. Then they parleyed, and Wallace decided it would not be a good idea at all to let these people know he was working with Tai Li. He simply said he was a Beautiful Country soldier on assignment, needing guidance to return to his people, and *ch'ing chieh te ku-tza,* clean pants.

Two young Chinese in peasant dress were selected to conduct him through the mountains toward Chenyuan. They would not take him all the way, they explained, because it became unhealthy too close to Nationalist troops. But they knew where the Japanese were, and were not, and would help him.

Wallace was given coolie trousers that were short in the leg but ample at the waist as are all Chinese pants, which he wrapped around his middle and folded down, Chinese fashion. He thanked the older man, and his party started off, number one man carrying a yo-yo pole with two baskets of small supplies and number two man behind Ian carrying Ian's TSMG and captured knapsack. Wallace hoped he wasn't their prisoner.

On the second day of their journey Wallace felt weak and flushed in the morning and spit some blood. He felt light-headed again in the evening, and his body felt hot. Not now, he said to himself. Can't get sick now. Gotta get back and gear up for the train. Gotta get back.

By the fourth day he was being helped to walk by the Chinese who was carrying the knapsack and TSMG. They halted at mid-afternoon, watching an ancient U.S. P-40 strafing some target in the next valley while his wing-man circled above. The plane made two passes, its guns rattling. Two passes is one too many, Wallace thought. They zero in on you. But the plane pulled up and over after its second run and screamed down the valley again. This time the gunners on the ground riddled it, and smoke and fire burst from the engine. The plane climbed trailing smoke and flame, then rolled over on its back and the pilot fell from the canopy, a tiny tumbling figure jerked upright when the parachute blossomed. The flaming plane disappeared behind a ridge and exploded. The pilot drifted down into the valley directly in front of Wallace and his two escorts.

"We get him," Wallace said to his two men and started to rise.

Number one man put his hand on Wallace's arm and said "*Pu sz*," and pointed. A squad of Japanese soldiers was running to the paddy where the downed American was trying to disengage himself from the parachute shrouds. Ian could hear far away shouting as the soldiers ran. The pilot freed himself and limped away only to be hit by a Japanese rifle butt in the back of the head as his pursuers caught up with him. The American fell spread-eagled in the water and was yanked up by the Japanese, who cuffed and kicked him and slapped his face and spat. Wallace started to rise, but was held down by the two Chinese.

The pilot's wing man buzzed the group who fired at him without effect. The plane did not return fire for fear of hitting the American. It circled and buzzed and then waggled its wings and left.

The Japanese dragged the pilot to a small farm compound and stood him against the pale tan mud wall. They shouted at him and hit him. Three peasants came out of the spirit gate to watch and were grabbed by the Japanese and made to kneel down. One of the Japanese shouted at the elder peasant and then disappeared through the gate. He returned shortly with some stakes and a maul. The soldiers stripped the pilot and were starting to drive a stake into the wall when the elder peasant made a motion to stand up. The Japanese in charge turned to him, shouted, and then drew his pistol and shot the peasant in the forehead; the body tumbled backward. Wallace could hear wailing.

The Japanese proceeded to drive stakes in the wall and tie the pilot to them, feet apart and arms outstretched. When they started to go to work on him Ian leaped to his feet and was tackled by number one man. Number two man had unslung the Thompson and pulled the bolt back. He pointed the weapon at Wallace and said, "*Mei-yo fadtze.*" No way.

Wallace covered his ears to keep out the sounds from the compound, but it didn't help much. He knew the Chinese were right not to try to rescue the pilot, outnumbered as they were. But that didn't help much either. The three men slowly crept up into the woods and over a ridge, followed by the pitiful cries from the valley below. Wallace was light-headed and weak. He spit blood. He hated the Japanese. He hated himself.

His guides stopped on a hillside overlooking a little river along which ran a dirt road. "*Chenyuan na bien,*" said number one man pointing down the valley. Wallace saw an occasional vehicle crawling on the road.

"We go now," said number two man, handing Wallace his captured knapsack and a gray, dirty ball of dough. Wallace put his hand out for his TSMG, but the soldier shook his head, cocked the weapon and, pointing it at Ian, he and his comrade backed slowly into the woods then turned and loped off. Small enough payment, Wallace thought. Though it wasn't mine to give.

Dizzy, he descended to the road below hoping a truck, a bus, a jeep, a stagecoach, a locomotive, a palanquin, a phalanx of cherubim and seraphim, Bellerophon on Pegasus his winged horse or any damn other thing would appear headed the way he wanted to go and with an available berth. He stood swaying and hatless at the road's edge, shaggy, bearded, tattered, with a blood-stained blanket around his shoulders and a Japanese pack hanging by the straps from his hand. He could smell himself.

The vehicle that arrived much later was a U.S. Army 6x6 crewed by a couple of corporals from Chihkiang Air Base on their way to Kweiyang for supplies. Wallace lifted his thumb in the classic appeal, and the truck slid to a stop in the mud.

"Who the fuck are you?" shouted the corporal in the passenger seat, nervously cradling his carbine.

"Got to get to Chenyuan," Ian hollered over the engine noise. "Been lost in the boondocks, and I'm damned near done in. How about a lift?"

The two enlisted men looked at each other and then at the unarmed, filthy figure on the roadside.

"Ain't nothin' in Chenyuan but a whorehouse," said the passenger suspiciously.

"Naval Group," said Ian. "Up on the hill."

"Oh, them! Jesus! Well, climb in the back, and we'll let you off at the steps."

"Can you give me a hand, please?" asked Wallace.

Wallace was dreaming that he had been captured by the Japanese and was being crucified against a wall under the direction of a faceless Flying Tiger pilot in a leather jacket with the Kuomintang flag and survival message on its back. Even though the figure had no face Wallace could hear it laugh.

"Take it easy, Ian," said someone, shaking him.

Wallace opened his eyes, focused slowly and recognized Doc Lou Boyd sitting on a stool next to the cot where he lay under blankets. Behind him stood Tom Pearson.

"Welcome back," said Pearson. "Thought we'd lost you for good."

"All I remember," said Ian, "is starting up the goddam steps. What happened?"

"Chief Steger found you laid out on the top step and dragged you to Doc, here."

"When was that?"

"Yesterday," said Doc.

"What the hell is the matter with me?"

"Well, after scraping off your clothes and burning them, and washing the crap off you, we decided you were basically pooped as hell. Got a bad case of the shits. Starved to death. And a little FUO."

"What's that?" asked Ian.

"Fever of Unknown Origin. What that really means is that I don't have the faintest idea what ails you in the fever department. And you've coughed a little blood. We'll try you on some paregoric, some sulfa and some APC, that's really aspirin-phenacetin-caffeine. If that doesn't do the trick we'll take you down to the barbershop and have the proprietor put a couple of leeches on you to draw out the bad blood."

Ian laughed weakly and told Pearson that he had a pretty long report to make. He said he felt rotten about losing his men but encouraged at the prospect of doing the operation in the spot he'd scouted, though it would take a bigger party than he had originally contemplated. He asked about Fix and Wells and was gratified to learn that Wells's group had all made it back and that Fix had lost only three men, but the rest returned O.K. after damn near sinking the island at Ninsiang.

"You guys are the talk of the Group. Miles is so pleased he's ready to split. Talking about medals for some of you. Yours was to have been awarded posthumously."

"Screw the medals," said Wallace, "there's too much to do. Can I get up?" He looked at Doc.

"We'll stuff some food and medicine in you for a couple of days and see how it goes," said the doctor. "Not only coughing blood, but you've been delirious. Sounded like a union organizer, talking about a five-day week!"

Ian told them about his stay with the Miaos. They were so isolated they developed their calendar based on how frequently it was market day. There were five villages in the mountains, and the market was held in a different village each day. A new week started when the market was in your town. Five-day weeks.

Ian looked at Pearson, looked at the doctor, and then asked Pearson if there was any word about the train.

"Miles knows you're back. We messaged him last night. He says get well and get back to that railroad and wait for word." He nodded his head toward the doctor and winked.

Hot damn! thought Wallace and felt better already.

"Ask Fix and Asa to come over, will you? I want to hear what happened."

Wallace's mail was all from Diana except for an absentee ballot for the previous November's election, which had swept Franklin D. Roosevelt into a fourth term without any help or hindrance from Wallace and his companions. Diana's letters were cheery and full of good news about her new job at the Navy Department working for Deputy Assistant Secretary Lucas Duval. "You remember him," she wrote. "You met him at the Occidental Restaurant the night we were there with Irene."

Wallace hoped Duval would keep his hands off Diana, but felt pretty sure she could take care of herself. She told him how much she missed him and how she longed for mail from him. But, she said, she understood something of the nature of his assignment and how difficult it was for him to stay in touch. And hurry back, oh, hurry back.

Wallace mended rapidly thanks to regular food and the Doc's ministrations. He talked with Pearson about the men he'd need for the train operation, and they settled on a core group of Americans: O'Reilly, Wells, the chief radioman Steger, the inseparable pair Samanov and Fugakis, and the corpsman Pagani. The Chinese would be under the command of Colonel Li Tao Shan, a sharp English-speaking officer who had the respect of his men. Only fifty guerrillas would be needed, but they would have to be good shots and people with demolition training. Guides would be recruited from the Commando Army, and a coolie train would be organized to carry food, medicine and clothes to caches along the return route.

"Can you get this large a group through the hills with such a long way to go?" asked Pearson.

"We stay to the heights and cross the open country only at night and we'll make it. I'm not so much worried about the Nips as I am about running into other people—Communists or the OSS or some misguided U.S. Army bunch on an exercise. My main worry is getting a good enough radio so we can get word when to act."

"Let's go to Chihkiang," said Pearson.

At the air base they were able to become involved in some tactical discussions with the Fifth Chinese American Composite Wing about the possibility of calling in targets from occupied territory. The wing commander liked the idea. The only problem, Ian told them, was the need for a reliable radio that could throw a decent signal over the required distance. The wing commander led them to his supply section where a cooperative sergeant and some creative bookkeeping enabled Pearson and Wallace to load a brand-new uncrated V-101 radio into their old jeep. As an added bonus, Wallace was able to wheedle a new Springfield Model 70 .30 caliber rifle from the sergeant, along with a Lyman telescopic sight and four bandoleers of ammunition.

Wallace's unit studied maps, checked logistics, staging points, cache sites, combat loads, demolition requirements, time allowances and code and radio schedules. They fired on the range and selected only those Chinese who were outstanding riflemen. They trained two teams to fire the two 3.5-inch rocket launchers. *Huo chien p'ao,* the Chinese called them. Onomatopoeic thought Ian. They discussed the operation only among themselves. Colonel Li Tao Shan was the only Chinese in the group who knew what they were up to. Even the fan yi kuan were not told. The interpreters tried to figure it out based on the operation code name: *Mo Shuh Fu Yu,* Magic Rescue.

The Fu Yu team departed on a night late in February without saying adieu to their mates who were staying behind, nor to the barber or his whores. The team did not descend the steps and follow the road east, but walked directly into the hills from the high Chenyuan camp. The group was healthy, the weather favored them and good time was made. Colonel Li put two peasant-clad soldiers in front as point men, and thus the unit was able to avoid confrontation with any unfriendly, or friendly, souls who might compromise their operation.

The coolie train held them up on some of the steeper ascents, but the rear point men goaded them on with their carbine butts. Ian asked Colonel Li what would happen to the coolies who would not be needed as supplies were dropped off in the caches. Would they not talk? Would not the supplies be jeopardized?

They will not talk, Ian was assured. They probably won't be able to, Ian thought, either herded into prison or dead. He hoped it would not be the latter and told Colonel Li so.

Each night they ran a radio schedule with Camp Two using the hand generator-powered V-101 transmitter. The signals got weaker the farther away from the camp they got, but it was agreed they could transmit and receive even at strength two if the weather was half-way decent. A week into the trek they received a message that caused Ian to stop Fix as he was walking into the bushes.

"*Teng i teng,*" wait one wait, Ian said, and Fix came up to him and said, "Make it quick!"

Ian quoted from the decoded message: "Subject: Promotion. In accordance with Marine Corps Reserve Selection Board procedure number so and so Second Lieut. O'Reilly, Francis Xavier, USMCR, 022820, is recommended for promotion to the grade of First Lieutenant. It is the opinion of the Board that you are professionally qualified for such promotion.

"Prior to being tendered the promotion for which recommended, it will be necessary for you to report to a Medical Officer of the Regular Navy or Naval Reserve for physical examination to see if you are qualified for promotion.

"Upon completion of the physical examination, you will return the completed forms to this Headquarters (in triplicate) for review. All questions on the forms must be answered."

Ian handed the message to Fix, who stared at it in disbelief.

Ian smiled and said, "Maybe Pagani qualifies as a competent medical authority and can attest that you are, at least, not full of shit. Congratulations. And you can congratulate me, too. Our date of rank is the same."

O'Reilly stormed off to do nuisance in the bushes.

They traveled through the late-winter mists and rains and the occasional snow flurries of March at the higher elevations. For two days they stayed on a mountain top and watched as a full division of Japanese troops moved southwest in the direction of Chihkiang. A moving brown snake of a column of infantry, machine-gun companies, pack artillery, horse carts, mules and an army of coolies toting gear of every description. This information they put on their nightly radio transmission for two nights, sending blind, since they got no acknowledgment. Ian prayed that they had not run out of radio range. On the third night, however, weather conditions were better and they received confirmation of their messages. In the morning they could see aircraft in the distant southern sky, dogfighting and strafing.

At about the time of the vernal equinox the Fu Yu team positioned itself high on the slopes above the railroad cut where Ian had lost his detachment, and studied the terrain. The eastern side of the cut was precipitous. The western side was flat near the tracks except for the rail embankment itself, and then climbed upward in worn out, unused rice paddies, like little plateaus, toward the forest. The northern end was narrow and provided an ideal place to derail the lead wagons or the engine and block the route. Ian hoped he could get the CACW to bomb the cut just there. If that was done just before the arrival of the train, Ian would not have to blow the tracks.

The southern end of the cut was two miles uphill from a water tower where the engine was expected to replenish its supply.

Of the track mender's hut and the veteran guards there was no sign.

They sat for three days and then got a signal from Tai Li via Miles via Pearson: the special train was under way carrying American pilot prisoners. Make-up of the train: flatcar with Japanese infantry, machine-gun and extra rails for replacement use; locomotive and tender; goods wagon for Japanese troops and supplies; closed wagon with prisoners; goods wagon with small troop of Japanese calvary. Train traveling some portions of track by day, especially in mountains. Anticipated arrival at Fu Yu rendezvous: two days.

Ian was excited. He, Fix, Wells and Li decided to mine the track at the northern end of the cut as a precaution and did so that night, running the wires to a hellbox at the edge of the forest. The relative lack of rail traffic made the job easy. They scouted the water tower and made a plan to watch the train there when it stopped, to get a preview of what they would be facing.

They laid out their firing positions and gave instructions about who would do what. Colonel Li had agreed to take command of the firing party with the objective of clearing Jap troops off the leading flatcar and keeping the other troop cars buttoned up. Fix, Wells, Ian and a small group of Chinese would get the prisoners out of their wagon and hustle them up into the trees.

The two days dragged by. An occasional small train passed, each one heavily guarded. They all stopped at the water tower regardless of whether they were headed north or south.

Late in the afternoon of the third day a runner came back from the lookout position at the water tower and said that what appeared to be the prisoner train was approaching. Wallace told Wells to carry out the predetermined plan, and Asa left with a small detachment of Chinese to eyeball the train and learn what they could. Wallace and O'Reilly expected the train to stay at the tower until morning. The mountain cut would be a bad place to be caught in the dark.

The men at the cut waited impatiently for Wells's return with news. Hours passed, and no one showed up. They heard no firing so presumed the scouting party had not been seen. It grew dark and it became obvious the train had stopped for the night.

No one could sleep. Ian paced and worried. Fix kept humming *"The rich girl uses Vaseline, the poor girl uses lard, my girl uses axle grease but she does it just as hard,"* and polishing his TSMG. Pagani checked his medical supplies for the hundredth time. Steger kept his ear to the radio. Fugakis and Samanov prowled the Chinese positions with Colonel Li, staying just at the edge of the forest.

At three A.M. Wells and his unit arrived. "Hao pu hao?" asked Wallace.

"Hao, hao, by God!" said Wells breathlessly. "Train's just like they said. They watered it and then strolled around some. Everybody's armed but the engineer and the fireman. The horses were let out to graze and do their business, and then when it got dark they were reloaded and the train was buttoned up for the night except for a few patrolling sentries. Then I seen somethin' and got an idea. That choo-choo's on a grade headin' uphill, so I took three guys and we crawled to the track bed and, while the three Chinese were lookouts, I put a hunk of busted tie from the track bed behind the rear wheels of the cavalry car and uncoupled the chains to the prisoner car."

Ian was aghast. "They'll see it!" he exploded.

"Naw they won't. I led some of their own chain up under the car from the chocks and secured it to the axle of the next car, then tied the chains of the cavalry car to the prisoner car with a couple of strips from my pants so the wagons still look coupled. When the whole shebang starts out in the morning the chain will pull out the chocks and the horse car'll start backwards down hill, alone."

"Christ in the foothills!" said Fix. "I hope you're friggin' right. They discover what you've done and the shit'll be in the fan for sure."

"Too late for anything but hope," said Ian. "Good work, Asa. You may have made the odds a little better.

They radioed Camp Two, which had been on constant radio watch on their frequency, and told them to have the CACW bomb and close the northern gap at these map coordinates just after dawn. Then they checked their gear again, repositioned the bazooka rocket launchers and waited.

They heard the engine before they saw the train, and they saw the smoke. The old Skoda was shooting up plumes of gray smoke, which carried off in the early morning wind from the west. The engine was not truly laboring, just making work of it with the small train coming up grade. A scout came running.

"Lookout signal! Fire cart come. *Ma ch'e* roll down hill!"

Horse cart left behind!

"Where the hell is the CACW?" Fix growled. Ian yelled at Steger to get on the horn in plain language and tell the CACW to do it now!

"Look," said Wells, pointing.

All eyes swung to the south and there a five-plane flight of P-51Ds was peeling off about two miles away.

"The bastards are after the water tower, for Chrissakes!" yelled Fix.

The engine driver must have been aware of the fighters, for the tempo of the chuffing increased as the driver adjusted the regulator and called for more speed.

"Asa, tell Colonel Li to get to the hellbox and blow the tracks. We got no help from the air. Tell him to wait until the flatcar is about twenty-five yards from the TNT. Then twist the handle, and take the flatcar, engine and troop car under fire."

"Aye, aye, sir," said Wells, and ran off.

Wallace wondered what was happening to the horse cart and was sure the bastards would catch up. Have to get the guys off the prisoner wagon before the calvary get here, he told himself.

And then they saw the train. It entered the cut and was just about the way Wallace had visualized it. Flatcar in front with the machine-gun manned and a half-dozen steel helmeted Japanese soldiers crouching behind sand bags with their Arisaka rifles at the ready; rusty, patched old Skoda 2-8-4 *huo ch'e* puffing smoke and shooting steam from the cylinders, driver leaning out the window; half-full tender, one sweating rag-head heaving coal into the fire box; wooden troop car, closed up, with rifle slits in the sides; wooden prisoner wagon, closed up with its rear coupling chains swinging free, other chains dragging the broken tie chocks.

Wells slid to a stop next to Wallace and said, "All set."

"Keep your fingers crossed," said Ian.

"I hope the hell you're gonna get more help from on High than that!" said Fix.

When the train was two thirds of the way through the cut Colonel Li's people twisted the handle on the hellbox, there were two explosions in front of the train, and track ballast and steel rails flew into the air in a hail of stones and smoke. The engine driver shut the regulator and throttle valve and reversed, the engine clanked and complained, steam flew from the cylinders and the drive wheels spun backwards as the momentum of the train carried the flatcar into the hole blown in the *t'ieh lu,* the iron road, by the TNT, brake rods and spare rails spearing into the hole in the track bed. The car dug into the hole just as two 3.5-inch rockets slammed into the Skoda's boiler and scalding water spurted and steam mushroomed. The engine rammed the flatcar and the train stopped abruptly as the following cars smashed into each other. The engine's front bogie was off the tracks.

The Japanese on the flatcar had been catapulted from it and now came under automatic weapons fire as the Chinese hosed the train except for the prisoner car. Wallace wondered that the boiler hadn't blown up at the first hit. He could see that the pressure was diminishing rapidly. The engineer was draped over the driver's side window, his blood running down the rusty black steel plates. The Japanese on the flatcar were all down, he saw, except for two who managed to run to the troop car where rifles were being poked from the gun slits.

"Keep cover!" Ian yelled. "Spray that troop car and keep 'em busy! Fix! Asa! Follow me!"

Running crouched over toward the after-end of the train, out of reach of the traversing Japanese fusillade, they reached the foot of the track embankment. Safe there because the Japanese weapons could not depress enough to take them under fire, the three men raced for the boxcar where the prisoners were locked in. Heavy fire from the Chinese was not deterring the Japanese return fire. Ian cursed as ricochets and spent rounds hissed and whined. Chinese couldn't hit a bull in the ass with a manure shovel!

There was shouting and pounding on the door of the prisoners' boxcar. Ian could hear American voices but the volume of firing made it impossible to communicate.

Wallace shouted in Fix's ear, "Shoot that hasp off the door. Asa'n' I'll open it. You lead the prisoners down the embankment and up into the bamboo and wait for us."

Fix laid his Thompson parallel to the side of the wagon and squeezed off three rounds. The shouting and pounding inside the car stopped. The hasp and part of the lock hung down swinging from a sheared bolt.

Wells and Wallace grunted and pushed, and the door rolled slowly back. Looking down at them were the most haggard, gaunt, gray-skinned, sunken-eyed, unshaven, rag covered, barefooted, stinking human beings Ian had ever seen. They were silent.

"We're Americans!" Ian shouted. "We'll help you down. Then follow that man," he said, pointing at Fix.

The men were weak from hunger, stiff from inactivity and diet-induced joint swelling, but as Asa and Ian handed them down, they began to trot behind Fix. One man said, "There are three who can't walk."

"You'll have to carry 'em for now," Ian told him.

The lame were handed down and carried off. The Japanese fire seemed to be slackening as the guerrillas maintained steady volume at the troop car. We better get those poor devils up the mountain before that bunch from the rear catches up, Ian told himself.

Still too much firing from the troop car. He motioned Wells, and they crawled under the prisoner car and looked forward. A half-dozen Japanese soldiers lay in heaps on the far side of the track, where they had been caught by rounds coming underneath the troop car as they were trying to get off the side opposite from the firing.

"That musta discouraged the rest of 'em," Wells said.

"Let's see if we can pop a couple of grenades in that open door," said Ian, and they crawled on their bellies to the bottom of the embankment in defilade from Chinese fire.

The Japanese who had tried to leave the car had left the sliding door open. Wells and Wallace made hand signals. Wallace crawled beyond the door. He and Wells each pulled the pin from a grenade, let the handles fly off, counted two and tossed. Wells's grenade sailed through the door toward the front of the car, Wallace's toward the back. The two explosions sounded as one, followed immediately by an extraordinary concussive roar that blew the roof and sides off the car and broke its back. Wallace and Wells were deafened and lay with their heads under their arms as debris of every description rained down at them. Steel, wood splinters, body parts, burning clothing.

They listened. The firing had stopped. They thought they could hear a thin, reedy, piping cheer from the bamboo grove. They crawled under the prisoner car, now also burning, and Wallace shouted, "Colonel Li! Hold your fire!"

The two men crawled from under the car as the Chinese began to stand up from their concealed positions, weapons at the ready.

"We musta got the ammo or sumpin' big," said Wells.

"Thank God for that!"

"What now?"

"You collect the Chinese and get 'em up to that grove. Those prisoners need help getting up the mountain, fast. We gotta give 'em some quick chow. Then we gotta get 'em out of here before those other Nips catch up. They must have heard the fire-fight and be pushing to get here. I'll check the prisoners' car. You get going!"

Wells ran off, making hand signals, and Wallace hoisted himself into the burning boxcar. It reeked of excrement and urine. He cast about to see if anyone didn't make it. In the light of the flames he saw a gaunt figure on its back. He crawled over and pulled the man to the door, out of the smoke. The prisoner was skin and bones, short white hair, prominent nose and Adam's apple, dressed in tattered khaki, bottoms of his feet like leather, scabs instead of fingernails, a huge, spreading bloodstain in the middle of his breast.

Ian checked for a pulse. None. The man's open eyes were unresponsive. Wallace ripped off the man's dogtags, stuffed them in his pocket and looked at the face. So near and yet so far. Can you forgive us? Can God forgive us? Can we forgive ourselves? May you now be at peace with Him whoever He is.

Wallace pushed the body back into the inferno and leaped to the track bed. Better to be cremated by your friends than desecrated by your enemy he said to the corpse, and ran up the mountain.

Uphill, in the cover of the trees, Fix and Asa had the gaunt prisoners wolfing food and gulping tepid cha from canteens. The Americans were too stunned to talk, too weak and too conditioned by years of captivity to do anything but what they were told to do.

Wallace arrived and told Asa and Fix about the dead prisoner, choked down some tea and said that the group couldn't linger. The force from the uncoupled car was worrisome; he wanted these people up and over the mountain to the first supply cache before dark.

"Move out now," he said. "You know the route. I'm going to stay here for a bit and slow down anyone who shows interest in this shindig. When you get to the cache set up the V-101 and in the clear tell Camp Two 'Make the bed and light the light.' "

"You alone ain't gonna keep those people off for long," said Wells. "It'll be hotter than seven kinds of smoke when they come after us. Don't overstay your leave."

"We'll wait for you on the downslope," said Fix.

"Sharp eye, itchy feet," Wallace said. "I'll catch up with you. I can travel a hell of a lot faster than the group. Get the Chinese to lend a hand with the three who can't walk. Carry 'em piggy-back in shifts until you're over the crest and into the trees again. Then make litters. Go on! Beat it!"

Wallace eased himself to the edge of the trees, got himself and his Springfield into position. Good *feng-shui* he told himself. Good wind-water relationship. He laid out some clips. About a thousand yards to the train. Six hundred yards to the first cover of rocks and bushes. Master Gunnery Sergeant Edward Ruditis, patron saint of boots on the Parris Island Range, I am on the slippery slope of life. Don't fail me now.

He watched for any signs. He turned and could just make out the party struggling off uphill. Fix in the lead, Wells as rear point. As he watched, Asa turned and faced Ian, raised his hand palm forward, Injun style. Ian saw Asa's mouth say, "Hao."

The Japanese rear party arrived sooner than Ian thought they could have. About twenty of them with rifles and what looked like a couple of small mortars, riding double on little Chinese ponies. He saw the Japanese look at the charred body of the prisoner left behind, and he remembered the dogtags.

Wallace pulled the tags from his pocket, and between glances at the Japanese who were gesticulating and pointing up the mountain, he read:

Avery
Charles
Cooper
Lt. J.G. P
T-8-42 B
USNR

Wallace went light-headed. He got tunnel vision. His blood pounded. His flesh went cold and damp. His sight dimmed. He almost screamed.

The bastards! They shot him down! They never said he was a prisoner of war! They tortured him! He was an old man! The white hair, protruding cheekbones, prominent nose and Adam's apple! Wallace could see Coop's features in the corpse he had found. The corpse that riddled him with guilt. Death from the carnage in the troop car. His responsibility.

He looked at the Japanese as they started to trot up the mountain in single file. He saw red. He shook his head and steadied his breathing. Take some of them with you, he said to himself. Take some for Coop and for Lewis and for Peter and for Perry and the Flying Tiger pilot and the people at Shihtan and all the poor misbegotten sonso'bitches who have been massacred by these scum!

He lined up his sights on the front man on the lead horse of the line of mounted men following the trail of the escaping prisoners. He led him a little, held his breath and paused. Don't shoot the front man. The others will see him go down. He swung to the aft horse, led him a little and squeezed off a round. The shot reverberated in the valley, and the little pony stumbled to its fore-knees, threw its riders and rolled over on them. The column stopped at the sound of the shot, looking up hill, unaware that the last horse was down.

You shot too low, he said to himself, and gave the sight a click of elevation to compensate for the distance. The column started uphill again and Wallace drew a bead on the next pony and squeezed the trigger. The shot went through the head of the front man on the animal and the chest of the man in the rear.

"That's not the four ring!" Ian hollered aloud. "How about that, you bastards!"

He heard shouting from below and brought down two more riders and a horse as the Japanese tried to disperse. He put in a new clip and slammed home the bolt. He squeezed off two more. Two more men tumbled.

"That's for you Coop!" he yelled as he fired. "That's for you Peter! That's for you Dick!"

The dismounted Japanese rushed into defilade carrying what looked like a mortar tube and baseplate. Wallace did a little rapid fire and saw one of them tumble, but couldn't tell if he was truly hit.

He was keeping their heads low, firing and shouting. His blood sang and his palms were wet. Vengeance is mine!

When he had one clip left he rolled on his back breathing hard and staring at the sky through the cathedral-like bamboo leaf patterns. He shouted, "O God, dear God, *dulce et decorum est pro patria mori!*"

When Wells heard the firing and Wallace's shouting he stopped and frowned. Then he loped back down through the trees in time to see the first mortar round burst in the tree limbs over Ian's position. More rounds came and created a haze of smoke, flying branches, leaves and steel. Asa watched as tree-burst after tree-burst spattered shrapnel to the ground. He was furious. There was nothing he could do. The firing from Wallace's position had stopped. Then the mortar quit. As Asa watched from his spot up the mountain, he saw three Japanese soldiers leapfrogging from cover to cover toward the source of the rifle fire. They entered the trees and Wells waited. He knew he should go back to the group and help lead it over the mountain. But they should be safe now. Wallace had stymied any immediate pursuit.

One of the Japanese soldiers came to the edge of the forest and signaled, and several of the men mounted their little horses and came up to the trees and disappeared into the woods.

Wells knew Wallace had to be dead but still he waited.

Soon the Japanese troop started downhill, horsemen in the lead, some men on foot, then one mounted trooper dragging a bound, stumbling, bloody-headed, shouting man at the end of a rope. Two foot soldiers followed, occasionally whacking at the stumbling man's calves and ankles with heavy sticks.

Wells could just make out the reeling captive. One of the monkey men was carrying two rifles, his own and the prisoner's. Why didn't they kill him, Asa wondered. Probably he's their only trophy from a bad morning and they need him, for now. God help him, I can't, thought Wells, furious that he couldn't. He cursed, levered himself to his feet and ran up the mountain to help the others.

A cold, damp November wind blew through the streets and *hutungs* of Shanghai, two months after the surrender of the Japanese aboard U.S.S. *Missouri* in Tokyo Bay. Shanghai's streets were again choked with pedestrian and wheeled traffic; rickshas, pedicabs, American military vehicles, coolies toting yo-yo poles of bricks, cabbages, personal gear; peasants pushing wheelbarrows or pulling heavily overloaded two-wheeled carts, goods piled high and tilting over; Chinese civilian cars and trucks perpetually blowing their horns; Nationalist soldiers rudely pushing their way through crowds; sidewalk merchants hawking anything they could get their hands on to sell, sisters, wives, daughters, black market cigarettes, American military supplies stolen from godowns or from lighters on the river, knives, carvings, jade. The throb and roar of the city went on night and day.

First Lieutenant Francis Xavier O'Reilly and Master Gunnery Sergeant Asa Wells, dressed in Marine greens, came out of the Prisoner of War Office at the Hong Kong and Shanghai Bank building, walked up the Bund past Nanking Road and Peking Road and onto Garden Bridge over Soochow Creek. They stopped and leaned on the green iron railing, looking northeast to where the Creek's foul waters met the sluggish Whangpoo River on its way to the Yangtze estuary. Anchored in midstream was a gray American warship, U.S.S. *Cleveland*, a cruiser about to return to the States with a load of returning servicemen. O'Reilly would be among them.

The crowds shoved and surged behind them, shouting and pushing.

"You sure you don't want to give all this up? You sure you don't want to get home?" O'Reilly asked Wells.

"For what?" asked the sergeant. "I ain't got no folks. Only home I got is the Corps. I'm a Regular, and I'm headed for Tsing Tao to latch up with a line outfit and see what the Corps is like now-a-days. Another ten years and I'll go out on twenty. Might as well get overseas pay while I can."

O'Reilly paused and looked at the swirling brown water. "You aren't going to go looking for him, are you?"

"Thought about it some," said Wells, "but after listenin' to what them birds at the Prisoner of War Office said, it don't seem as if they's much point."

"I don't see how he could have escaped," said O'Reilly. "I think the bastards killed him and reported that he escaped."

"Don't think so," said Wells. "Them folks at that bank building got a mountain of statements. People seen him when he was drug into that prison compound at Wuhan in April. People seen him get put in the dirt hole in the prison yard, with the log lid over it, still shouting. People seen him took out for punishment and then dumped back in. Then in May people seen the honey bucket coolie get pulled out of the hole instead of Wallace. I bet he carried a yo-yo pole of buckets right under them Jap noses, just like him and me did at Shihtan. Monk at the Jade Buddha Temple says he heard of a blue-eyed barbarian out Tsokung way, between the Salween and Mekong, in the mountains way up in back of nowhere, near Chamdo, maybe not even in China. He sure as hell got loose."

"Maybe so," said O'Reilly. "Sure as hell hope so. But why the hell hasn't he shown up? He doesn't know that we got all the prisoners out; doesn't know he got the Navy Cross. Doesn't know Miles was summarily relieved. Probably doesn't know the war's over, what with the Japs still running the railroads and most of the rest of the boondocks while the Chinks fight each other."

"He'd likely be a Section Eight," said Wells. "I think he went mad, tetched, laying there in the trees, knowin' what he'd found in the boxcar, knowin' what he had to do. He'd been building up to it for a long time."

O'Reilly reached inside his blouse and took Avery Cooper's dogtags out of his pocket and looked at them. "You were a fool to go back down there the next morning," he said, "but I'm glad you did. We'd have never known otherwise."

He put the dogtags back in his pocket and straightened up. "Well," he said, "I've got to go home and break the news to Diana Bliss, and you've got to go ship over. And standing here isn't going to settle anything. Asa," he said, "I am proud to have served with you," and put out his hand.

Wells shook the hand with some embarrassment. Then he said, "It weren't like the Old Corps, Lieutenant, but we give 'em something to think about, by t'Jesus. And I'm proud to have sojered with you, sir. And with him."

Asa Wells saluted O'Reilly. O'Reilly returned the salute, and they parted, Wells to North China to serve another hitch and O'Reilly to the United States to break Diana Bliss's heart.

Cease, every joy, to glimmer on my mind,
But leave, oh! leave the light of hope behind!
What though my winged hours of bliss have been
Like angel visits, few and far between?

—Thomas Campbell
Pleasures of Hope

Epilogue

ASIA 1950

IN 1950 CONGRESSMAN DANIEL BENSEN (D, 21st Dist., Ohio) and a small congressional delegation with their wives left Washington, D.C., on a foreign aid fact-finding mission during April spring recess. Their journey took them to India, Pakistan, Nepal and Afghanistan. Bensen had long advocated greater aid to the subcontinent to help develop ties to that noncommitted part of the world. True, India and Pakistan were members of the British Commonwealth, but they appeared to be flirting with the Soviet Union. Bensen felt that friends were needed in the area who could help blunt any Soviet or Chinese expansionary moves toward the Bay of Bengal and the Indian Ocean's warm water, ice-free ports so lacking in the Soviet Union. Free access to the oceans of the world would let the Soviets shed the restrictions placed on them by the need to transit the Dardenelles, the Baltic, the North Cape or the Sea of Japan to reach open water.

The Chinese had long contested the high frontier regions on the India-China border and were exerting strong influence on the budding governments of the Indochina peninsula. No one knew who was in charge in northern Burma and Thailand.

Congressman Bensen was a leader in the fight to strengthen foreign aid to this area of the globe. As a naval officer he had served in the Pacific and seen the loss of so many good men. He was determined to do what he could to see that lives lost to rid an area of domination and threat from one evil re-gime would not have been spent to open doors to others who would subjugate peoples only recently freed from tyrannical and colonial yokes.

The congressional delegation visited Bombay, Karachi, Calcutta, Mysore, Delhi, Lahore, Kabul and Katmandu. They saw primitive farms and factories, shoddy self-help and educational facilities, backward schools and technical training centers, sloppy military outposts and unsanitary hospitals.

Numbers of the congressional couples stayed on in the higher, cooler climates for a needed rest at the conclusion of their official and arduous trek. Congressman Daniel Bensen and his wife chose to go to Lhasa, Tibet. They traveled by truck and by foot. They stayed in primitive inns, visited monasteries and at last reached Lhasa. They were made welcome at Potala, the palace of the Dali Lama on Red Hill. They shared tea and curd with the Dali and were invited to a religious festival of atonement the following day.

In the morning Bensen and his wife, the only foreigners, stood at the side of the chill, dim ancient hall lit only by candles and redolent of burning joss sticks and incense. The huge, mournful brass horns had summoned, and the cymbals had called. The saffron-robed priestly procession chanted sutras and shuffled and swayed as it passed by witnesses and followers of the Four Noble Truths.

Congressman Bensen's wife noticed one shaven head towering above the others as it neared them. She clutched her husband's arm and stared. The sunken-cheeked monk had long scars which puckered his scalp, and had lost half of the near ear. He swung a smoky censer. His eyes were blue. Diana Bliss Bensen gasped.

The monk heard and looked. Their eyes met, Diana's wide and glittering; the monk's now filled with sublimity. The monk looked at Daniel Bensen and back at Diana whose moist eyes were closed. As she opened them she saw such a look of relief, affection and blessing from the monk that her knees weakened. Her husband's arm tightened around her. The monk continued by swinging his censer and chanting softly.

Ian Wallace had, at last, found peace.

In doing research for **HORSE-HORSE TIGER-TIGER** *the author consulted numerous sources, many of which were not only educational but entertaining as well. Readers who have a continuing interest in China or the period covered in this book may wish to refer to materials listed here.*

Bibliography

Allen, Charles. *Plain Tales From The Raj*. New York: CBS College Publications, 1985.

Bailey, Cpl. Gilbert P., USMC. *Boot!* New York: Macmillan, 1944.

Ballard, J. G. *Empire of the Sun*. New York: Simon & Schuster, 1985.

Bartholomew, J. & Son. Map of China. Edinburgh: World Travel Series, 1977.

Becker, Stephen. *The Chinese Bandit*. New York: Random House, 1975.

_____. *The Last Mandarin*. New York: Random House, 1979.

Berry, Henry. *Semper Fi, Mac*. New York: Arbor House, 1982.

Butterfield, Fox. *China: Alive In A Bitter Sea*. New York: Quadrangle/Times Books, 1982.

China Guide Series Limited. *China*. Hong Kong: 1986.

Churchill, Sir Winston Leonard Spencer. *The Second World War, Their Finest Hour*. Boston: Houghton Mifflin, 1949.

_____. *The Second World War, Closing the Ring*. Boston: Houghton Mifflin, 1950.

Danforth, K. C., ed. *Journey Into China*. Washington: National Geographic Society, 1982.

Durant, Will. *The Study of History, Our Oriental Heritage*. New York: Simon and Schuster, 1935.

Faligot, Roger, and Kauffer, Rémi. *The Chinese Secret Service*. New York: William Morrow and Co., 1987.

Hocking, William Ernest. *Types of Philosophy*. New York: Scribner's, 1939.

Hook, Brian, ed. *The Cambridge Encyclopedia of China*. Cambridge, England: Cambridge University Press, 1982.

Huntington, Madge. *A Traveller's Guide to Chinese History*. New York: Henry Holt & Co., 1986.

MacGruer, Malcolm S. China papers, unpublished. 1943-45.

Miles, Milton E., Vice Admiral, USN. *A Different Kind of War*. New York: Doubleday, 1967.

Morison, Samuel Eliot. *History of U.S. Naval Operations in World War II, vol. XIII, The Liberation of the Philippines*. Boston: Little, Brown & Co., 1959.

Nalty, Bernard. *Tigers Over Asia*. New York: E. P. Dutton, 1978.

National Geographic Society, Richard J. Darley, chief cartographer. "The Peoples Republic of China." Washington: National Geographic Society, 1980.

New, Christopher. *Shanghai*. New York: Summit Books, 1985.

Preston, Antony. *An Illustrated History of the Navies of World War II*. Feltham, Middlesex, England: The Hamlyn Publishing Group, 1976.

Quon, James C. *Concise Chinese-English Dictionary* (modified Wade-Giles transliteration). Tokyo: Charles E. Tuttle, 1955.

Rand, Benjamin, Ph.D. *The Classical Moralists*. Boston: Houghton Mifflin, 1909.

_____. *The Classical Philosophers*. Boston: Houghton Mifflin, 1936.

Rosholt, Malcolm. *Flight in the China Airspace, 1910-1950*. Rosholt, Wisconsin: Rosholt House, 1984.

Samson, Jack. *Chennault*. New York: Doubleday, 1987.

Seagrave, Sterling. *The Soong Dynasty*. New York: Harper & Row, 1985.

Schaller, Michael. *The U.S. Crusade in China. 1938-1945*. New York: Columbia University Press, 1979.

Smith, S. E., ed. and comp. *The The United States Marine Corps in World War II*. New York: Random House, 1969.

Smyth, Albert Henry. The Writings of Benjamin Franklin, vol. IX, 1783-1789, p. 207, "A letter from China." New York & London: Macmillan Co., 1906.

Snow, Helen Foster. *My China Years*. New York: William Morrow & Co., 1984.

Spector, Ronald H. *The Eagle Against the Sun*. New York: Macmillan, 1985.

Summerfield, J. *People's Republic of China*. New York: Fodor Travel Guides, 1986.

Taylor, John W. R. *Combat Aircraft of the World*. New York: G. P. Putnam's Sons, 1969.

Thomason, John W., Capt. USMC. *Fix Bayonets!* New York: Scribner's, 1926.

_____. *Salt Winds and Gobi Dust*. New York: Scribners, 1934.

Tokson, Elliot. *When Dragons Dance*. New York: Avon Books, 1982.

Tuchman, Barbara W. *Stilwell and the American Experience In China, 1911-1945*. New York: Macmillan, 1971.

Young, Brigadier Peter. *Atlas of the Second World War*. New York: G. P. Putnam's Sons, 1974.

Voisin, R. L. and J. M. Leverenz, eds. *The New International Atlas*. New York: Rand McNally & Co., 1982.

Ziegler, Philip. *Mountbatten*. New York: Knopf, 1985.

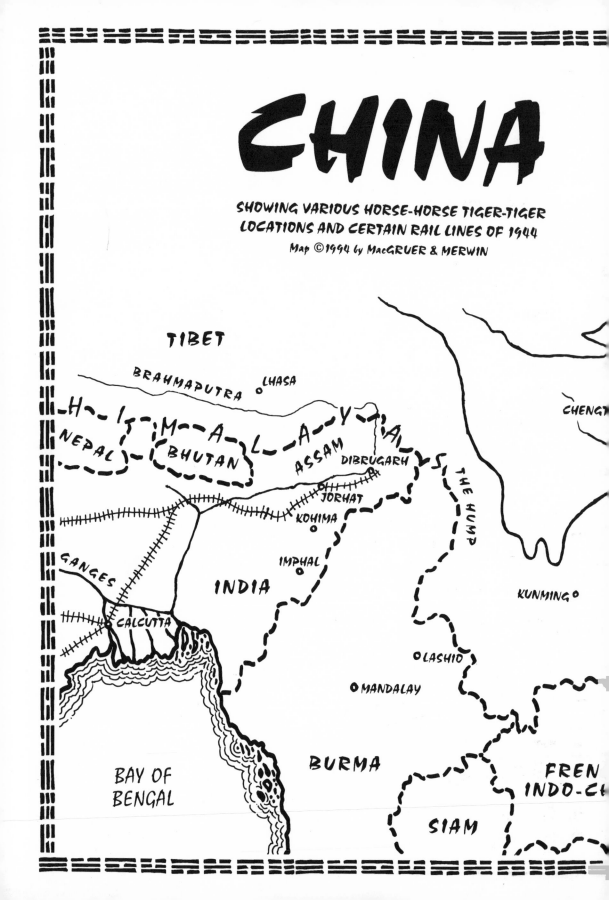